THE CLASH OF HARI HARA

ANTAR ATREYA

Om Books International

First published in 2024 by

Om Books International

Corporate & Editorial Office
A-12, Sector 64, Noida 201 301
Uttar Pradesh, India
Phone: +91 120 477 4100
Email: editorial@ombooks.com
Website: www.ombooksinternational.com

Sales Office
107, Ansari Road, Darya Ganj,
New Delhi 110 002, India
Phone: +91 11 4000 9000
Email: sales@ombooks.com
Website: www.ombooks.com

ISBN: 978-93-6395-750-3

Printed in India

10 9 8 7 6 5 4 3 2 1

THE CLASH OF HARI HARA

Antar Atreya is a bestselling and award-winning author, speaker, mythology enthusiast, and writing coach. An alumnus of Ramjas College and a graduate in economics, he has spoken at several literary fests, including invitations from the National Book Trust. As a writing coach, he has trained students, judged events, and delivered workshops for IIT Bombay, SRCC, and IIT Palakkad, among others. He is from the state of Assam but considers himself a 'Dilliwala' as well, having spent almost a decade in the capital.

Antar enjoys soulful music, long drives, true crime, and storytelling on the screen. He is also passionate about mental health and vocal about his own experiences.

Through this story, he wishes to bring out a grand but forgotten tale from ancient Assam and Hindu mythology to the world. As a mythology enthusiast, he also creates content on Hindu mythology.

This book is dedicated to my family—my mother Rupa Borah, father Jaganath Pokhrel, and younger brother Aadar Atreya —and all the other Indian families that have stood resolutely behind their members' dreams and struggles.

Contents

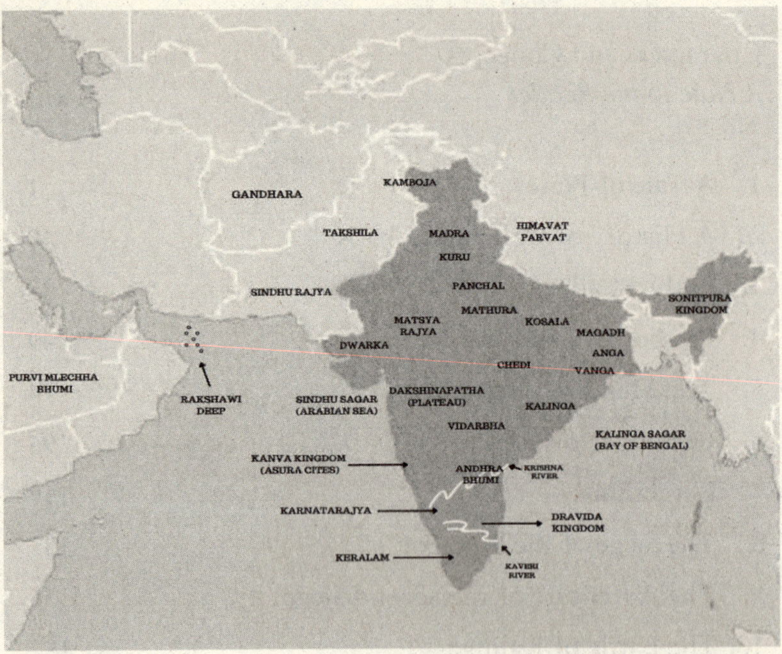

Aryavrata: Capitals after the Kurukshetra War

Characters and Concepts

The Trimurti

Brahma, Vishnu, and Mahadeva make 'The Trimurti'. They are self-manifested and the most ancient energies. After they created themselves, the concepts of time and space began. Brahma created the Universe, when any of his designs turned self-destructive, Vishnu preserved them. Mahadeva destroyed the dark matter and debris formed as a byproduct of Brahma's creation.

With time, three more creative and kinder powers—Saraswati, Lakshmi, and Shakti—emerged, also known as 'The Tridevis'. They assisted in making the creation better and more sustainable, working in cooperation with Brahma, Vishnu, and Mahadeva.

Narada

Brahma created several energies that performed various roles to aid creation. They were the 'creation-aiders'. Narada was one such energy; his chief function was to analyse the flaws in the different things born in space. He informed the Trimurtis and Tridevis of those flaws and suggested corrections.

Devas

The Devas were smaller energy fragments formed when the various 'creation-aiders' merged amongst themselves. They were the first to have stabilized powers concealed inside a visually attractive physical casing. That same physical shape (limbs, face, and torso) was adopted even by the Trimurtis and Tridevis. The realm that they formed to reside in was called Swarga.

Asuras

The Asuras were a faction of the Devas who endorsed using humans and creating other lesser powerful beings whose sole purpose would be serving the Asuras and Devas alone. They were against working for the progress, growth, and evolution of the various celestial bodies to make the universe more beautiful and organized. Their philosophy was to remain static and relaxed rather than striving to enhance existing things.

Over time, the Asuras began envying the creative prowess of the Devas and formed a group of their own, creating their realm—Patal Loka. Unfortunately, the envy soon turned into hatred.

Some Asuras desired to rule over Earth, as beings on Earth worshipped and adored the Devas. Interestingly, certain Asura descendants on Earth were benevolent, like Virochana, Prahlada, and Mahabali.

Gandharvas and Yakshas

They were beings created by the Devas who had specific powers and talents. The Gandharvas conceived the concepts of art and culture that spread peace and happiness. The Yakshas were learned in the positive utilization of negative energies (magic), and the recycling and revival of dead matter.

However, the energy inside every Yaksha and Gandharva was destructible, and without the inner power, their physical forms ceased to exist.

Krishna

Vishnu manifested in different forms whenever humans required guidance on righteousness, spiritual development, and to ensure justice, liberty, and equity in the world.

Krishna was the eighth such manifestation in the form of a human. However, before Vishnu took birth as Krishna, he had a philosophical argument with Mahadeva. According to Mahadeva, humans could never live in harmony and remain virtuous if they followed the path of development and progress. Shiva wanted to inspire humans to dwell a life in close association with nature and give up striving for materialistic improvement. He was confident that growth was an individual and selfish concept for humans, not collective and inclusive of the greater good. Vishnu disagreed with Shiva. He opined that his duty as the Preserver and Protector was to counsel humans whenever the world turned unrighteous. He believed that through such counselling in the capacity of different avatars, humans would continue progressing and uphold morality.

A NOTE TO THE REA

Now that you have started reading this book, we have a connection. I am incredibly grateful you have decided to give this book a chance.

The Hari–Hara war is the bloodiest war in Hind ythology. Such was the aftermath that the pla he war was named Sonitapura, meaning a city d. I belong to this place, and even today, my dis retained the name Sonitpur. I grew up visiting t aces believed to be associated with the war.

So, bringing out this story is my tribute to my hometown.

I would also love to connect with you beyond this book and be a friend. As a friend, I will be privileged to lp or support you however I can. Most importantly, I ld love to listen to what you wish to share. Sharing tions helps us discover our own honest thoughts

Be kind, selfless, helpful, and take care of yo ell-being.

Best wishes,

ntar Atreya
ectantar@gmail.com
uthorantaratreya

Chapter 1

A Tale of Piracy

The night was dark, and the sea was calm and quiet, barring the rise and fall of the occasional short waves. The gentle overhead wind shook the lamps hung on the four wooden posts on different parts of the long-sized boat. The rowboat moved at a decent pace, penetrating the darkness, with four young men energetically rowing it.

"We should reach our destination by tomorrow morning," Samar said, smiling contentedly.

"Yes! I reckon so. It has been so many tedious days at the sea. I guess tonight has been the calmest of all the days and nights. Otherwise, it has always been we versus the angry waves, tides, or storms or us sneaking and diverting the attention of the Aryavrata Royal Navy," Palan said. Among the four, he was always the one who was more anxious and stressed in any difficult situation.

"Well, tonight could be just the calm before tomorrow's big storm." Sanjam looked behind at Palan and winked.

"Aaah! Tomorrow either everything would work out well for us, or this entire voyage might have been a waste. Let us speak positively," Palan countered.

There was a very brief silence, but Sanjam again spoke in his usual composed demeanour. "You shouldn't worry. We have come so far, and we shall not have to retreat empty-handed."

"Absolutely!" Rudra screamed animatedly, the most vigorous and energetic of the four.

A few moments passed by in small talk before Palan hushed everyone. "I just saw something in the water," he spoke softly and continued staring at the water.

Everyone else tried to see what had stunned Palan. But they could see nothing.

"What did you see? Are you just trying to be funny or hatching a playful scheme to scare us?" Samar joked.

Palan looked into his eyes and murmured, "It seemed like something huge. But, unfortunately, I could only get a glimpse of its head, and if I am not wrong, it is a Brihamatsya."

Hearing him, everyone looked at each other, the mood immediately turning tense.

"But, do they still exist? I know those large fishes inhabited these parts of the Sindhu sea, but nobody has ever seen them in the last three decades, right?" asked Rudra, looking at Sanjam to his right.

"Yes, but that might be because, in these parts of the sea, only large trading ships ply, escorted by navy ships. Small and medium-sized boats never enter this region, fearing attacks from the pirates. And this large, carnivore fish species might not emerge or attack when many big ships are traveling together." Sanjam's rationality was hard to debate.

"And are they truly man-eaters?" Palan nervously asked.

"At least they were! Some forty-odd years ago, the Brihamatsyas that the state-sanctioned hunters killed in these parts of the sea were larger than men. They reached up to ten feet in length and weighed almost half a ton. They were undoubtedly the most potent aqua predators, at least in the Sindhu Sea, and could devour anything made of flesh and blood.

"Their frequent attacks in large groups on even big contingents of ships made the Kuru kingdom order a massive hunt to trap or kill the species four decades ago. And during those hunting endeavors, many hunters perished, before the realm could finally eliminate those carnivores."

Sanjam had read almost everything about the Sindhu Sea before making the voyage. But, the species that he thought was extinct, was in fact, not.

Everyone gathered at the afterdeck and looked around the waters, with Samar and Sanjam holding a lamp. They even made some high-pitched voices, thinking that human voices could attract the creature and it might show up. But nothing occurred.

Sanjam could sense that his companions were doubtful and tensed. They looked at him, waiting to hear what their next course of action should be. Sanjam, too felt the need to be unambiguous about the threat of the gigantic fish. They all could die if the fish made a surprise attack, in a cluster or even alone. After ruminating for some time, he turned to the others.

"I have a plan—quickly, get two of our extra oars and two spears. And hand me one of the spears." The three rushed towards the front deck and returned to him with the objects.

"What are you going to do?" Samar asked with curiosity, handing over a spear to him. Samar followed every word of Sanjam's but was also concerned for him as Sanjam never shied away from taking necessary risks.

"Trust me, and hold your weapon steady," Sanjam said, raising his left arm in the air and took a deep breath. The next moment he touched his left palm with the spear's edge and made a deep slice. Blood dripped in no time into the waters. If there were indeed any Brihamatsyas in the seawater, detecting the smell of human blood, they would emerge.

Samar, Palan, and Rudra surrounded Sanjam, gripping their weapons tight and expecting an attack anytime. Suddenly, a giant fish leaped out of the waters and opened its mammoth mouth to bite off Sanjam's hand. Fortunately, Sanjam pulled aside his hand in time, and Rudra hit the creature with his oar at that very moment.

The impact broke the oar in half, and the beast dived into the sea, causing powerful waves to sway the boat.

"I think there is only a single beast and not an entire group, right?" Palan asked.

"Well, we would know that for sure in the next few moments," Sanjam said, turning towards his companions. "Samar and I shall take a position on either side of this deck, and you two take positions on either side of the front deck. And be ready to face a raging attack! Only spears this time!"

Sanjam trickled some more blood down the boat's hull adjacent to him as the others rushed to take their stands. Then he wrapped his wound with a cloth and tightly gripped a spear with both hands, pointing its edge in midair. The Brihamatsya was fast and smooth, emerging out of the water and taking the group by surprise. It pounced at Sanjam, flapping its large front fins with several tiny pointed spines. Its eyes were intimidating with a dark bluish hue. When it opened its mouth, it revealed the sharp triangular-shaped teeth that terrified Sanjam. But he wasn't someone who would easily let fear rule over him. He hurled his spear at the creature right when it had moved towards him, its jaws widening to devour him. The spear connected to the left skull of the creature but failed to penetrate its flesh, only managing to hurt and push it away. The Brihamatsya was a strong creature. However, the group realized it was not an intelligent mammal; it had attacked again at Sanjam after sniffing the blood he'd trickled down the boat.

Everyone, therefore, stood surrounding Sanjam, awaiting the next assault.

Moments later, the creature jumped at the four again, and everyone pushed forward their weapons. Three spears hit the beast on the skull, deflecting its leap. Rudra managed to deliver a cut on its left frontal fin, and a thick trail of blood oozed out of the wound.

"This won't work. We must hit it every time, and it will only be injured. But if it manages to dodge even one attack and leap on our boat, we shall stand no chance," Rudra panted.

"We need to hit it with greater momentum," Sanjam said, hurriedly placing three drums of different heights in ascending order.

"Are you sure about this tactic?" a concerned Samar asked.

Sanjam nodded and patted his shoulder to assure him. He approached the boat's front deck and stood alert, with a spear in each hand.Sanjam could feel the eerie silence of the sea. He threw glances at his comrades, who gripped their weapons tighter and confidently nodded at Sanjam, trying to reassure him. But, he could decipher their nervousness. After what seemed like forever, suddenly, the beast surfaced from the back deck, leaped out of the water, and ferociously dived at the boat.

Sanjam made a run-up, his spears tightly gripped in his hands. Mounting on the three drums, he leaped from an elevation, thrusting both his spears straight into the open mouth of the screaming carnivore. The beast trembled with agony as the weapons penetrated its skull, and it dropped down into the waters, with Sanjam still holding onto the spears. His friends immediately rushed to the stern deck, looking for any signs of Sanjam in the waters.

"I am diving in," Palan announced.

However, Samar interjected. "Wait! Look over there. I can hear something." They quickly moved to the left side of the deck and sighed with relief. Sanjam was safe, attempting to pull himself up into the boat by holding the top of the hull. The rest of the group heaved him up and laid him on the boat deck. Sanjam took several deep breaths and coughed out the water from his lungs. He rested for some moments and stood up after his breathing became normal and the numbness in his body subsided. The four then had a group hug and cheered.

"Ahh! It was one hell of an adventure and that too, against a top-notch predator!" Rudra joked.

"Yes. But did you notice it didn't scream or roar even once? It cannot emit sound and moves silently, slipping through the water like a ghost," Sanjam remarked.

"You are always so terrific! And bad situations tend to make your brain and senses work harder," Palan said, making everyone laugh again as they hugged each other in relief.

***

It was a sunny morning at sea. Rudra and Samar were rowing, while Sanjam and Palan were sound asleep inside the small hut in the middle of the watercraft. The sea looked glitteringly blue, and a gentle breeze provided some relief from the blazing sun. However, the serenity was disturbed when Rudra's eyes suddenly saw something at a distance.

"Hey, hey! Do you think it's a ship?" he asked Samar, pointing to a spot ahead.

Samar took time and then confirmed, "Yes! And apart from that, two more vessels are sailing towards us," he gestured at the ships approaching their boat from two sides.

Rudra quickly ran inside the hut and came out with Sanjam and Palan. Sanjam looked at the approaching ships with his lens. "The ships have flags bearing the Kuru Kingdom's emblem; a golden moon surrounded by planets. But aboard the ship, there are pirates."

Rudra mildly growled. "So, these pirates disguise their ships as the capital's vessels and move in the waters. That's why they can make surprise attacks at the escorted merchant ships!"

"At last, our weeks at sea have not been in vain. Listen, get me the black bag from inside and drop every single weapon in the water. Hurry up!" Sanjam directed Palan and Rudra.

Very soon, the boat was surrounded and pirates pointed arrows at the four. Then the pirates from one of the ships threw a rope ladder at the long rowboat, and one by one, the four climbed it up.

***

The four stood on the ship's main deck, facing a structure erected towards the stern. The large sails that moved the vessel were behind them, closer to the bow. Pirates with axes, bows, swords, and spears surrounded them. None of them said anything but threw menacing looks at the four. The pirates had all worn the same attire and accessories—mud-colored dhotis covered their legs, and circular leather pieces strapped their dhotis to their waists—their uniforms. The leather pieces had sheaths designed on them for their knives. A long, thin fabric from each shoulder covered their chests in a cross pattern. They also had a silver chain on their necks, silver bracelets on their arms, and a grey rag on their foreheads.

Several moments passed by silently and after what seemed like an eternity, the door on the building noisily opened. Two pirates pushed it open, and a tall, bulky, middle-aged man approached the four. His steps were slow and poised, and he looked more privileged than the other pirates. Although he wore a dhoti and cross pattern fabric like the rest of the pirates,a shawl covered his upper body, and the chains on his neck were golden. He also had gold earrings, and instead of a band on his forehead, he had a turban on his head. It was clear to Sanjam and his companions that he was the pirate chief.

"So, what brings you to my marine territory?" the chief asked as he extended his arms, the baritone of his voice supplemented with a courteous smile.

After a glance at each other, Sanjam walked forward a few steps and bowed. He folded his hands and said, "Mukhiya Ji, we acknowledge your sovereignty in these waters. And we are merely traders who have entered your territory only with a commercial interest, beneficial to both of us."

"Commercial interest, hmm?" the pirate leader smirked. "Do you think it's a coincidence that we caught you in our waters in a mere routine inspection? I have an empire in these waters. I have my council, my soldiers, and spies! Before making this voyage, you stopped at a cheap tavern to gulp liquor, and there you animatedly spoke about possessing something priceless. My men heard you, and following you, learned of your voyage. But they didn't hear you talking about making a deal with us."

"Stopping at that tavern was a part of our plan, and so was speaking aloud about our possession. We knew there'd be your spies, and they'd soon inform you about us and you would then locate us in the waters. We could never reach out to you, for nobody knows how and where to find you. That's why we wanted you to find us."

After a brief pause, the pirate leader asked, "And how did you know that there'd be my men in that tavern?"

"It was a calculated gamble. That tavern is the closest one to the shores of the sea and the only one in the area. Moreover, it's cheap and filthy, and so the navy soldiers hardly visit it. But former convicts are often found in it. And despite the place being so low-priced and full of unruly people, it is well-managed, organized, and scandal-free. So, someone powerful must be managing it indirectly with representatives. And obviously, it had to be you!"

The chief nodded and sighed. "You seem too street-smart to be a trader. But maybe you are an intelligent trader. But what hardly convinces me of your story is the look of each one of you. You four do not look like traders who enjoy the pleasures of life but rather like those who toil hard. Moreover, your tall structures, athletic physiques, and toned bodies tell me that you can be anything but traders."

"You are right about your observations, Mukhiya Ji. But we are not those typical traders with a family business. Our fathers were partners too, and during the reign of Maharaj Dhritarashtra, they smuggled weapons and sold them secretly. It was easy to bribe officials and soldiers back then and get anything done. But when Yudhisthir became the Chakravartin Samrat of Aryavrata and Krishna became the so-called Supreme Advisor, it became impossible to bribe and smuggle anything. So, we started investing in excavations and constructions. However, we still have our fathers' genes and habits, so we cannot look like the typical fat traders, right?" Sanjam smiled, ending his answer, but it couldn't hide his concern about how the chief would react.

"So, what is the deal that you have for me? And why do you want to make a transaction with us, taking so much risk?" The pirate chief finally asked.

There was a smile of relief on Sanjam's face as he heard the question. He quickly took out a spherical metal from a bag slinging on his right arm and carefully held it in his hands. "This is the rare Lutandhatu, Mukhiya ji. It is the most robust metal found on Earth. People fashioned weapons out of this and also used them to construct towering, mammoth buildings. But it went extinct three centuries ago. And now we found it while our workers were digging at a site in the Panchal kingdom. It is unbreakable.

"We have discovered almost a ton of this metal, but there are no potential buyers except you. You can buy this metal from us and then sell it to the warring tribes of the Purvi Mlechha Bhumi, situated west of this Sindhu Sea. Those tribes have no association or exchange with the Aryas of the Aryavrata. But you don't have any constraints in negotiating a deal with them. Those tribes are perennially at war, and whichever tribe will have access to Lutandhatu can wield superior weapons and become the most prominent clan. So, in exchange for the metal, they would give you any gold, diamonds, and rubies found abundantly in their lands."

The leader of the pirates remained mum, closed his eyes, and analysed Sanjam's proposal. Then, sometime later, he opened his eyes with a smile and held the metal in his hand. He gauged the metal and found it was heavy. He dropped it on the floor with a thud; the metal remained intact despite the fall, but a spot on the ship deck cracked. "So you weren't lying, boy! Pick it up for me, please."

As Sanjam bowed to pick the metal up, he felt a sword on his neck. Nervous and surprised, he looked above at the chief. The pirate chuckled. "You know why pirates have survived for so damn long? Because we always distrust outsiders!"

In no time, Palan, Rudra, and Samar were surrounded.

"So you will all die, and then we shall look for the Lutandhatu reserves ourselves." Screaming out the last few words, the chief raised his sword. But Sanjam fell at his feet and begged, "Mercy, Mukhiya Ji. We are nothing but simple traders." Sanjam even started weeping and trembled with fear. The other three also went on their knees with folded palms and begged for their lives.

"You only have one way to live. Accept me as your master and become my slave! And for that, you must lick my spit." The pirate leader shouted in a hoarse voice and spat.

Sanjam, still trembling and sniffling, looked at his partners once, who had tears in their eyes. Then he slowly lowered his face towards the sticky spit on the deck. He pushed out the tongue with extreme disgust, closed his eyes, and almost reached the gooey spit when he heard the chief speaking. "Stop! You may rise."

Sanjam rose slowly with a confused expression. The chief apologized, "Pardon me, but it's better to be safe than sorry. And I have my ways of pushing people to ascertain the truth. I am interested in your deal. But I do have a term. You and two of your partners shall stay here with us, and the fourth can go and bring the rest of the Lutandhatu. In twenty to twenty-four days from tomorrow, he should arrive at this area with the rest of the stock, and we shall exchange four quintals of gold for the entire metal stock. And until then, you three would remain as our guests."

After a brief discussion, Sanjam, Palan, and Rudra sent Samar to bring the rest of the metal reserves. The pirates confined the rest to a prison room on the ship. The room had three beds, two small windows, a table and chair, and two attached cabins; one bathroom and one toilet. They were kept locked but unguarded.

***

"Were you going to lick the filthy spit?" Palan asked Sanjam as soon as they were left alone.

Sanjam nodded and then stared at Palan. "What is our profession?"

"We are spies," Palan whispered.

"So nothing comes in between our missions, not even our self-respect. If we value our life or self-esteem more than our mission, we are not doing our job as we ought to. We are here for an assignment and must fulfill it, no matter what. We must discover the settlement of these pirates and dismantle it completely. Piracy must become a thing of the past." Sanjam's words made his partners proud.

Sanjam, Rudra, Palan, and Samar were childhood friends and exceptional spies for the regime of Aryavrata. The four played together as kids, attended the same Gurukul as teenagers, enlisted into the Army of Aryavrata in the same year, and undertook espionage training in the same batch. On completing their training, the state commissioned them as spies, and for the last seven years, they had been working as secret agents for the Aryavrata regime. Since their recruitment, they had accomplished several missions as a team, ranging from relatively straightforward to complicated ones. However, the ongoing task of discovering the pirates' covert settlement was their most challenging assignment yet.

The three friends were trying to get some sleep but failed miserably. Their minds were immersed in thoughts about the mission, the brutality of the pirates, and their scheme.

"Is it not strange that the pirates have been a threat in the Sindhu Sea for five hundred years now?" Rudra whispered, turning his face towards Sanjam.

Palan also chimed,"For centuries, pirate ships and boats have raided merchant vessels and cargo ships, ferrying bulk items from the northern Aryavrata to the rest of the kingdom. Why have we been unable, for so long, to stop this menace?"

Sanjam took a long breath and narrated like a story. "The pirates ambush and loot the vessels at night and then retreat to the north-western part of the Sindhu Sagar to hide in an island group between Sindhu Rajya and the Mleccha lands. Despite the repeated piracy nuisances, the kingdoms in the past never took many stern measures. Although the states increased maritime security and provided naval escorts to the merchant ships, the pirates still carried out their looting."

" So, are these pirates significantly better fighters than the navy soldiers?" Rudra inquired.

"Darkness is their aid. Unlike the Aryavrata Navy, the pirates have perfected fighting in the dim of the night," Sanjam replied."They can also dive into the waters and stay undetected for long. And in cases, where the Navy foiled their raids and pursued them, the pirates found a haven in a scattered island group closer to the Purvi Mleccha Bhumi," Sanjam added.

"And as mentioned in our briefing, somewhere in those islands, where the naval soldiers can never even set foot, the pirates have their covert settlement," Palan mentioned. He paused and asked Sanjam, " Do you think that place is honestly so perilous?"

Sanjam looked at Palan and Rudra and sat up comfortably. "Yes, you have heard it right, brothers. A savage and primitive tribe of cannibals inhabits those island groups. They are ancestrally a clan of the Mlecchas, belonging to a coastal region. But during a phase of the inter-wars of the Mlecchas, when another dynasty seized their lands and drove them away, they fled and occupied the islands that we know of. They kept themselves inside the deep forests of the islands and faced stagnation without any evolution. They ate raw meat of animals and birds, remained wild and relentless hunters, could not develop their intellect, and communicated with sign language and random noises."

"How did we learn so much about them?" a curious Palan asked.

"Well because some centuries later, a proportion of that tribe crossed the Sindhu Sea and reached Aryavrata. The newer generations of the tribe craved to taste different meats, and those islands only sustained a few species. So, they decided to explore the world beyond their habitat," Sanjam answered again.

"Yes, and I have heard the rest of the story," Rudra added. "In Aryavrata, their presence first created a storm of fear and terror. Their long unkempt hair, razor-sharp nails, thick and curved teeth, hairy bodies, and attires made of animal hides made them fearsome. People called them Amanavs. The Amanavs roamed secretly in groups in the kingdoms of Takshila, Sindhu, and Gandhara. When the kings of those kingdoms came to know about them, they ordered their soldiers to capture them. Once captured, they realized that the Amanavs did not attack humans but feed on raw animal meat. Out of compassion, the three kingdoms collectively established a settlement for the Amanavs and appointed trainers and mentors to help them evolve and civilize. It took the Amanavs two centuries and three generations to grow as refined humans. When they became civilized, the kingdoms recruited them in the shipbuilding industry and marine sectors."

"But perhaps, greed is the fundamental character of the Mlecchas. Their craving for newer meat brought them out of their natural habitat and then, they desired riches," Sanjam spoke, suddenly becoming somber. "They soon saw another great opportunity in the waters and became pirates. They resorted to looting items, food, meat, and valuables from trading ships and settled in their ancestral island groups—Aryavrata calls them Rakshawi-dweep."

"But how could they fit in with the original regressive and carnivorous tribe?" Palan asked with raised eyebrows.

"Their retained ability to communicate in sign language and random nature-inspired noises helped them establish a connection with the cannibal tribes. Also, they could offer them new varieties of meat which kept them pleased," Rudra answered, also explaining that he had learned this years ago, from his teacher.

"Oh, is it? What else does scholar Rudra know?" Palan teased.

Rudra smirked, "When the Pandava-Krishna regime came into power, they wanted to dismantle the pirate settlement. That's why they had designed a massive offensive in the Rakshawi islands. The empire planned to dispatch a large fleet of ships carrying heavily armored soldiers with countless weapons and explosives. Those soldiers could penetrate the jungles, counter the guerilla defense of the pirates and cannibals, and kill or trap the pirates. However, the center, soon realizing that such an invasion would result in the loss of the cannibal tribe population, dropped the idea. Instead, Mahamahim Shri Krishna advocated utilizing the spy network and entrusted the task of discovering the pirates' dwelling to us."

"Of course. And we will not fail the great one," Sanjam said, determined.

***

Sanjam's company was close to concluding its assignment. On their third night in the pirate ship, the vessel safely anchored on the shores of Rakshawi-dweep. But the group had to remain inside the ferry ship for days until Samar arrived with the rest of

Lutandhatu. After two more restless nights dawned the night of the mission's last leg.

"There are no movements of the sentinels on the deck above. I bet they are asleep, assuming we won't try to escape even tonight," Rudra whispered gleefully.

"Well, these pirates have shown some hospitality to us. They have kept us locked but never bothered to guard this place," Palan clapped and laughed.

Sanjam finished sharpening and shaping a thin piece of wood with his teeth, which he'd taken from the table in the room. He quickly glanced around and pushed the splinter inside the lock through the bar gaps to unbolt the prison gate, pushing it open. The three tip-toed out of the room and went to different chambers, to look for weapons. After scouring the rooms, everyone quietly gathered on the main deck. Everyone had found a sword and shield, but Sanjam had picked up a metallic bow and a quiver of arrows.

"You found metallic bow and arrows here?" Palan said, incredulous.

"Thankfully. Without them I can't conjure divine weapons. Fortunately, I found these in the pirate chief's chamber. But I don't think he can invoke divine weapons. He must have grabbed these from somewhere and kept them in his chamber as a souvenir or as a trophy."

"Use it!" Rudra urged.

Sanjam sighed. He drew an arrow, looked at the sky, and closed his eyes. One must know specific phrases and murmur them in a specified tone and decibel to conjure divine weapons. Sanjam muttered a mantra. Soon, the sound waves it created amalgamated with different elements in the air. As the waves and energies in the air blended, a glow emerged on the arrowhead that turned the arrow heavier. On sensing the increased weight, Sanjam opened his eyes and released the arrow. It went high in the air, made a thundering noise, and generated a whirlwind of thick white fog. The fog soon reached the surface level and engulfed an enormous area. Thus, Sanjam successfully launched the *Sammohanastra*, and it hypnotized the guards on the deck and sent them into a trance. He, Palan, and Rudra had covered their nose and mouth with cloth pieces and soon deboarded the ship.

The three friends had reached the shallow waters of the shore when they saw countless pirates with bows and arrows rushing towards them. They had heard the thundering noise created by the divine weapon and found the guards on the ship lost in a trance. Several more became victims of the *Sammohanastra*, but others diverted the foggy layer and rushed towards the shore from alternate courses. The incoming attack forced Sanjam to launch another celestial ammunition. He invoked and fired the *Parvatastra* that caused several mid-sized rocks to drop from the midair at the marching pirates. Almost immediately, Sanjam shot another divyastra that produced fireworks in the sky. It made a tremendous incessant noise with multiple blasts in the air.

Sanjam's attacks made the pirates nervous and they retreated inside the island's forest cover. On the other hand, the three friends stayed on the shore, waiting for Samar to show up.Before Samar was sent from the pirate ship to bring the rest of Lutandhatu, they had instantly made a plan. They decided that Samar would row to the nearest Aryavrata Naval Ship, reveal his identity, and gather an army of armored soldiers. They would then hide closer to the Rakshawi island group and wait for a signal from Sanjam's team. The team's alert would notify the soldiers of the location of the pirates, and the soldiers would then attack that particular island.

Sanjam's company had to wait for a prahar before Samar arrived, who arrived with a large fleet of ships, and numerous armored soldiers flanking the deck. As the soldiers rushed inside the jungles to decimate the pirate settlement, the group embraced each other.

Ending the long-lasting embrace, Rudra laughed hysterically, confusing everyone else.

"Are you so happy that you've gone insane?" winked Samar.

Somehow controlling his laughter, Rudra replied, "A single piece of the extinct Lutandhatu available in the historical archives of Dwarka collapsed a five-century-old pirate authority. Greed can cause anyone's downfall."

Chapter 2

A History of Calm and Chaos

Ten days later, the four reached the Takshila-Sindhu border on their horses. The sun had almost set for the day, and a timid mixture of orange and yellow colors painted the sky.

"Only a week more, and we would be in our homes," Samar said, sighing with anticipation.

"Home after so long. It's been almost two years!" Palan added.

"Finally! The joy of sleeping on a good bed, eating delicious meals cooked by the family, and spending time with people. I bet my mother would feed me so much this time that I'd soon turn fat." Sanjam exclaimed.

The friends were debating whether putting on a little weight would make Sanjam look better. But the carefree mood was disturbed by several horses neighing and galloping towards them. Moments later, men on horses surrounded them. Those men were dressed in black dhotis, long black boots, and silver chest plates covering the entire torso. One of them dismounted from his horse and handed a letter to Sanjam. Sanjam quickly read it and looked at his friends. "I must accompany him, and you should go with the others into a tent in the nearby jungles. Don't worry, they are friends."

***

Rudra, Palan, and Samar were inside a tent enjoying a fine meal when Sanjam entered, his face serious.

"*Bandhuon*, I met the Dwarkadhish himself. Shri Krishna had summoned me for an imperative matter. I am sorry to inform you that we aren't going home. Instead, we shall journey towards Magadh at first light tomorrow. We have a new assignment."

Sanjam's words stunned his friends. Everyone desperately wanted to visit their homes and stay with their family for a few months. They deserved the break as they were living in disguise for the last two years, living different lives for three varied missions. But they also understood that the new project had to be crucial and urgent as otherwise, Shri Krishna would have allowed them the much-deserved break. Moreover, their sense of responsibility outweighed their family sentiment, and they unanimously volunteered for the new job.

"What is this new task? What are we infiltrating this time?" Rudra intriguingly asked.

"This is probably our final and most challenging mission. And if we succeed in this, Aryavrata would not likely even need the services of spies for the next few decades." After a brief pause, Sanjam continued, "Our task is to infiltrate a cluster of the radical rebel outfit—The Band. Once we are in it, we need to find its mysterious origins, actual goals, supporters, and leaders. The Band cluster in Magadh is recruiting new members, so we must reach there as fast as feasible."

The team retired for the night in the tent, to get some sleep and mentally prepare themselves for the mission of their lifetime. The following dawn, they were to start a new ride and cover more than a thousand miles to reach Magadh.

***

DWARKA MAHA NAGAR, KINGDOM OF DWARKA

The city of Dwarka was not just an epitome of peace, prosperity, and inclusive growth. It was also a testimony of what engineering marvels, intelligent governance, and welfare plans could achieve. Under Krishna's leadership, the engineers of Dwarka had properly planned and constructed the entire city. According to the specifications and house-tax amount paid by each household, the state engineers had built houses on either side of every major and minor road. They connected the drainage system of every home to a single system, and the waters from each household streamed into a large filtration tank in the outskirts of the city. The tank consisted of minerals and metals that completely purified the water, making it useable for irrigation.

Additionally, people kept their garbage outside their homes, and every morning garbage collectors would bring them to the Dwarka Renewable Energy Plant. In the energy plant, innovators segregated the waste. They used some for creating manure and fertilizer and some to power small mechanical tools.

Even the economic policies of the kingdom were unique. Workers like potters, artisans, cobblers, weavers, and others were encouraged to work together in state-run establishments. As they worked together, the production was buffered and exported or sold to merchants and retailers. It also enabled the state to pay them a higher wage. With such practices, the state had significantly prospered. Other kingdoms also adopted those innovative practices after Yudhisthir became the emperor. However, the Kuru Kingdom couldn't flourish as much as Dwarka.

***

Krishna was in his private chamber, preparing for an all-kingdom assembly in his palace. The ruler of every kingdom was already in the Dwarka Fort, enjoying the kingdom's hospitality. Although it was customary that the royal members were dressed and adorned by servants, Krishna never bothered his man-servants with such trivial things; he loved dressing up and grooming himself. He often took time to get ready and always looked divine. He was in his early fifties but looked no older than forty: precisely trimmed beard and mustache, tall, with a broad upper back and chest, shapely arms, and a dark shade of skin on his oval-shaped face that had a divine glow. His blue eyes were hypnotic, his brows were medium-thick and flat, his eyelashes were neat and sharp, and his lips were full.

Preparing for the council, Krishna had worn a yellow-hued dhoti with fancy embroidery and a garter belt made of glittering gold and floral design. He also adorned his chest with several dark multi-colored necklaces of different appealing metals. On his arms and wrists, armlets and bracelets made of emeralds and rubies complimented his look. A red turban crowned with diamonds, green rubies, and a colorful peacock feather completed his entire appearance. As Krishna finished dressing up, he went to the open window of his room, from where he could see the whole city. Witnessing the bustling town and thinking of the scheduled meeting, his thoughts wandered to the past.

Twenty-five years ago, the brutal and annihilating but necessary war of Kurukshetra ended with the Pandavas victory, guided by Krishna. Their opposite belligerents, the Kauravas, and their supporters and allies resisted progressive changes. They wanted to hold onto primitive systems, norms, and traditions that ensured their unaccountable power and safeguarded their self-interests. However, most of them either perished in the war or had to accept the new regime.

Post Kurukshetra, Yudhisthir claimed his right on the throne of Hastinapur, the Kuru capital, and his uncles Dhritarashtra and Vidura coronated him. Next, he declared himself an Emperor of the entire landmass of Aryavrata, and most of the kingdoms accepted it happily. The Pandavas also allowed the states that didn't honor Yudhisthir's suzerainty to remain independent, provided they altered specific laws and took up welfare schemes and policies of accountable governance. However, when they denied those terms, the Pandavas waged small wars and conquered the rebelling states. Finally, with an amalgamation of twenty-two kingdoms, the empire of Aryavrata under the Pandava-Krishna realm came into being.

After designing the blueprint for a new administration and bureaucracy system, the Pandavas appointed Shri Krishna as the empire's Supreme Advisor. Krishna's first suggestion in his new capacity was to include the Asuras as part of the empire. The Pandavas accepted the proposal and invited the Asuras, who were settled in the challenging icy environment of the Himavat region, to join Aryavrata. The Asuras acknowledged the offer, and the regime helped them to establish a kingdom. Their territory, named the Kanva Rashtra, was in the mid-western coastal area, just below the plateau region that started the southern Aryavrata. Three Asura cities- Punya, Kasara Nagar, and Kollapura, soon flourished in Kanva Rashtra as they built a strong economy by taking advantage of the coastal resources of the Sindhu sea.

The Asuras were previously a potent species that had emerged on the planet long before humankind had evolved. Their anatomy and biology were different from humans, making them taller and stronger. They even possessed the knowledge of sorcery and could conjure energies from nature. Eventually, they lost their sorcery ability but retained their physical might and often confronted and clashed with humans. But Bhisma, the grand-uncle of the Pandavas, had vanquished the Asuras, and they started dwelling in the icy terrains of

Himavat Parvat. However, the Asuras that lived in the first-ever built Asura kingdom, Sonitpura, had diplomatic relations with various states and continued to exist as a part of the Aryavrata federation.

The next focus of the Pandava-Krishna alliance was on social amendments and the prevalence of equity, justice, and welfare in the empire. The empire brought in revolutionary laws like lifting the ban on widow remarriage and making caste-based discrimination an offense. It also banned gambling, prostitution, child labor, and slavery. The command rightfully addressed domestic violence and women safety issues too. In addition, the empire established several medical facility centers that provided free health care and set up institutes to study scientific subjects, practice art forms, gain varied vocational training, and learn warfare. It merely took three years and riding on noble governance and pro-people policies, the Pandava-Krishna rule molded Aryavrata into a land of absolute peace, prosperity, and perfection.

The blissful period without chaos existed for more than a decade until a virus outbreak created turmoil in the empire. One fine day, the external minister of Dwarka Kingdom informed Shri Krishna that an unknown virus had contaminated the waters of Krishna and Kaveri rivers in southern Aryavrata. Krishna immediately decided to leave for the states affected – Keralam, Andhra Bhumi, Dravida Kingdom, and Karnatarajya. As the Supreme Advisor, it was his duty to visit the impacted kingdoms, and he also had a personal association with those states. The economic status of the southern states was pitiful when Yudhisthir had ascended the throne. That prompted Krishna to replicate the Dwarka model of growth in those states by personally staying there. He successfully made the replication, and the masses of the four southern states were delighted and grateful. In gratitude, they even renamed a prominent river with tributaries flowing in each of the four states as River Krishna.

Touring the four kingdoms, Krishna was left heartbroken at the plight of the citizens. People had used the waters of Krishna and

Kaveri for several days, unaware of its contamination, and the virus present in those waters impaired their red blood cells responsible for carrying oxygen. Consequently, the low oxygen caused damage to brain neurons and blood vessels, resulting in several deaths. Those who didn't die reported multiple organs failures. As the waters of the region's two major rivers turned useless, the nearest states to southern Aryavrata, Vidarbha, Kalinga, and Kanva, sent food, water, and medicines to the affected kingdoms.

The Kuru capital had swiftly set up effectively functioning relief camps in the affected states. However, the death toll crossed thousands within a month. By then, the empire's leading innovators also identified the particles in the virus but failed to find its origin in the waters. Fortunately, knowing the particles helped Krishna use sorcery and create a mixture of metals and minerals to filter the rivers. However, the filtration process would require two years, and the kingdoms would remain uninhabitable for those two years.

The entire predicament pained Krishna more because of the dilemmas he had as an avatar. Being a human manifestation of Vishnu, the supreme God, Krishna realized every major incident just before it happened. The virus outbreak episode was no different. But living as a mortal being forbade him from taking any step to stop the epidemic, as it would be a Godly intervention. That was his first helplessness. Secondly, Krishna could also clean the contaminated rivers by using his celestial powers in the blink of an eye. That could provide instant relief to millions of people but would be against the laws that an Avatar had to follow. So, despite possessing the ability to end the sufferings, Krishna was forced to do nothing, and that remorse was his cost of being an Avatar.

With the four kingdoms rendered unsustainable for two years, the regime undertook the bold but complex step of migrating their people and settling them in different northern states. It was the only viable solution as relief camps couldn't sustain for two long years. However, the decision was not popular. The kingdoms of the north empathized with the citizens of the south. But they were also concerned about the various problems that would arise to support the immigrated masses. Nonetheless, the empire successfully carried out the large-scale migration in countless big horse-carts.

The administration arranged the immigrants' settlements in open tracts of lands in the outskirts of major northern cities. They had built temporarily sustainable brick houses and dug ponds in those land tracts. The central command financed the entire resettlement project from its royal treasury's contingency fund, but it had to increase taxes and slash citizens' salaries for some other aspects. The immigrated people were first provided medical treatment and then hired for different jobs by the states. In parallel, the Crown also sent several Special Units of the Aryavrata Army to the four southern states, with buffer food and water stocks. Those units worked on cleansing the two rivers with the special potion created by Krishna and focused on keeping the kingdoms conducive for re-population after two years.

Almost two years had passed by, and the appreciable role of the realm prevented the virus outbreak from causing irreparable damage and chaos. But the command couldn't avert the dissatisfaction of a certain proportion of people. Some public disliked the Southerners living in their cities and instead favored them residing in the relief camps. Others were unhappy because they had to pay more taxes and received a decrement in their salaries. Eventually, the officers, traders, and professionals started accepting bribes and exploited the low-income earners to compensate for their monetary losses. At the same time, the Pandava-Krishna alliance had to divert their attention elsewhere. Some united tribes of the Purvi Mleccha Bhumi had built large ships and long rowboats and started naval attacks on Aryavrata. The targets were Gandhara, Sindhu, Takshila, Kamboja, and Dwarka that shared the Sindhu Sea coastlines. Responding, the five kingdoms, with Hastinapur's assistance, defended the waters and engaged with the

Mlechha navy for nearly a year. At the end of a year, the Mlechha navy retreated with heavy casualties, but until then, economic inequality and corruption had bred in several kingdoms of Aryavrata.

The most detrimental consequence of everything that had occurred in Aryavrata in the last three years was the sudden and secret emergence of an armed rebel outfit- The Band. And complimenting it was a mysterious cult entity, Swaha. The Band attacked the houses and establishments of merchants, traders, and nobles at night and looted their wealth. They kept parts of the loots for themselves and distributed the rest among the poorer sections of the society. The Band members were excellent fighters, and they also received support from people, making it difficult for the state forces to apprehend them. Concurrently, the occult entity, Swaha, that organized surreptitious worships and prayers for ghosts and ghouls encouraged people to join them. They propagated that Gods and God-like men, like Krishna and Pandavas, could never give people eternal peace, comfort, and luxury. The entity even blamed Krishna for the war of Kurukshetra and the realm's incompetence to predict the virus attack or the assault of the Mlecchas. While a large population remained unconvinced of the ideologies endorsed by the Band and Swaha, but many supported them too. The threat was that the number of people who supported the two organizations increased slowly with every passing year.

***

Krishna's ruminations were interrupted by a knock on the door.

"Do come in."

A sentinel, who was standing outside, bowed. "Hail Lord Krishna! Everyone has arrived in the Royal Court."

Krishna acknowledged him with a smile and started making the long walk to the Royal Court. As he reached the large doorway of the courtroom, two drummers positioned on the doorway on either side played their drums, after which everyone stood up and bowed in reverence. In response, Krishna joined his hands together, and with slow steps and a mesmerizing smile, walked the red carpet that stretched right from the doorway to his throne, which was at an elevation. Krishna sat on the gilded throne with a peacock-shaped headrest and a group of men blew trumpets from just below the dais, signifying the assembly's start.

"Who would like to speak first?" Krishna asked.

The King of Anga rose from his seat and bowed. "O' Dwarkadhish, I Anganaresh, would like to begin today's discussion. Now that the threat of the pirates is over, we must all focus on dismantling The Band. In the past decade, they have caused many financial losses, killed innumerable soldiers and patrol officers, and have been a nuisance and threat to anyone with money. The upper strata of society have been living in fear for so many years, and the lower strata people are disillusioned and consider The Band a benevolent outfit. It's time that we come together, join forces, and destroy them."

The other rulers present affirmed and endorsed the King's passionate call for action.

"My greetings to every honourable representative present here," the King of Vidarbha rose, "the center and the states have always carried out welfare schemes for the poorer people. We take responsibility for their care. Also, we have all collectively constructed plans to alleviate poverty in the next seven to ten years. Aryavrata abolished poverty entirely once, and we can do it again. But it is unacceptable that an unruly group incites people against the realm and creates disorder and chaos. Therefore, I believe we should not just focus on destroying the Band but also find out its real goals first."

Almost everyone found his proposal more rational and wise. With complete certainty, they seconded the suggestion of the Vidarbhanaresh.

Krishna raised his right hand in the air to silence the murmuring. "O revered rulers and representatives of the kingdoms, I too believe that we must learn about the Band's origins before destroying it. And for that, I have already sanctioned a special team. I assure you that we will soon learn everything about the Band and expose them in front of our subjects."

Krishna trusted the abilities of Sanjam and his team, and he reckoned that in a year or so, they would succeed in their assignment. That's why he revealed nothing about the infiltration scheme in front of the council.

***

THE MATHURA-KOSALA BORDER

After riding for days on their horses, Sanjam and his mates were on the borders of Mathura and Kosala. Upon entering Kosala, it'd take them only a few more days to reach their destination—Magadh.

Pulling his horse close to Sanjam's, Rudra asked, "Is it not hard to digest that the entire army of Aryavrata has been unable to discover and destroy the Band?"

"An army or even the patrol force is more equipped to fight opponents in the battleground or hideouts. But the Band arrives like thunder, raids like a storm, and vanishes into thin air. Moreover, the people aid them to flee or hide."

"Umm…but it is a known fact that the entire Band, divided into several groups, takes refuge in the deep and thick forests of various kingdoms. So why are our forces unable to penetrate those forests and detain or kill them?" Rudra sounded more puzzled this time.

"There are reasons for that. First of all, the regime doesn't sanction the destruction of forests to apprehend the Band. And every time our forces barge inside the jungles, they set fire to the woods. Of course, the state military can face the fires with suitable armor and resources, but to decimate the Band, if we end up destroying so much of the woods, it would be a massive scar on the regime.

"Second, the Band has to defend while the state has to attack. There the forest acts as their ally. Band members stationed on treetops and small hills can see the forces coming inside the woods even from afar. Once they are visible, the soldiers are easy targets for them. They use guerilla warfare and deliver heavy casualties. Hence, the jungles for the Band are what the Rakshawi Islands were for the pirates. A haven." Sanjam smiled.

Palan, riding just behind Rudra and Sanjam, put his fist up in the air. "But we were successful in the islands, and we'd be successful here!"

***

Traveling a week more, the four had reached the Kosala-Magadh boundary. It was a full moon night, and they lay over their rugged portable beddings, gazing at the clear and open skies. They had also lit a bonfire by the side of a pond in the semi-forested area. Although their lives were full of risks, discomforts, and unpredictable adventures, they still enjoyed the small moments of joy they could find in their missions. Lying by a pond, surrounded by the trees that arranged for a gentle cold breeze, and enjoying the scenic beauty of the moon and stars was beautiful.

Samar turned towards Sanjam and asked, "*Bandhu*, you had mentioned that this mission was personally important for you, and for me too. So what did Krishna Ji tell you exactly about it?"

Smiling, Sanjam looked at Samar. "You know how he is. He speaks in riddles. But there was an exciting giggle on his face when he told me that this mission would start professionally for us and end up being very personal. We would even forge new connections that would last for a lifetime."

Samar's eyes widened and lit up. "Seriously? A lifetime? Is it a hint that we would find our soulmates in this mission?"

"Well, as I said, he speaks in riddles. So I am not expecting anything. Also, such a situation would only complicate and jeopardize our assignment."

"Ah! But we do have a life outside our work. And if we don't fall in love at this age, we'd be wasting our youthful years."

Hearing Samar, Sanjam laughed out. "I never knew you were so anxious to fall in love. So anyway, this would be our last mission, and we can then enjoy our youth."

"But falling in love in a mission would be more exciting and cherishing. Imagine the story we can tell our grandchildren!"

Sanjam did not reply but agreed in his heart that it'd indeed be a wonderful experience to fall in love in such an unpredictable way. He did not even have a dream girl in his mind, but recalling Krishna's words, he felt that Samar's thoughts could come true!

***

Sanjam and his companions were seated at a roadside food corner in Magadh. The place had only three more customers, and an elderly man managed it alone. The four looked like amateur sword-wielders who offered simple services like being temporary personal guards to affluent travelers. They wore a dhoti and loose-fitting kurta on their bodies, upanah on their feet, and carried a sword inside a long steel sheath that was strapped to a garter belt on their waists. The feeble-looking owner of the food corner glanced at the friends several times while they were eating. And when he came to collect their plates, in a low and quivering voice asked, "*Yuvako*, are you looking for any job, or do you simply want to be of service as swordsmen?"

"Of course, jobs would be great. But it is hard to find employment, so we provide our services as sentinels and escorts mostly," Rudra replied.

The older man cleared his throat. "Where are you from?"

"We are all from the Mathura. Our fathers were foot soldiers in the Mathura army. Even we had joined the army some years back. But, sadly, the kingdom slashed our salary and also decreased our fathers' posthumous pensions. So it turned more profitable to be employed privately," Samar deliberately sounded disgruntled, sniffing out air angrily.

The man nodded and held his hands. "Do not worry, *yuvako*. I can help you get hired. Just give me some time. I shall collect payment from the other customers and get back to you."

The man quickly went behind the food corner and returned to collect the payments from the other three customers at different tables. As he finished his task and the customers left, three men arrived on horses with daggers. They swiftly jumped off their horses and stormed inside.

The tallest and meanest of the three growled and held the man by his neck, almost choking him. "You frail old stupid fellow! You have no family, and yet what is your issue to hand over your piece of farmland to the Mahajan? Whom will you bequeath it; to the state, huh?" He pushed him away, and the elderly man landed on the four friends' table.

Attempting to hold his breath, the man spoke painfully, "Please help me. I had promised to help you find employment without any selfish interest. Please save m—" Even before he could complete the sentence, another of the assaulters pulled him up and pushed him to another table.

The attacker pulled out a knife. "If you die now, the Mahajan can take over your fertile farmland with ease. After all, who'd claim it anyway?"

As the thug sauntered towards the helpless old man, Sanjam whispered to his friends, "We have to save him. But remember, we need to fight like ordinary soldiers. We don't want anyone's attention here,"

The four swiftly lifted their table and crashed it on the assaulter's back. He wailed in pain and collapsed. Seeing them intervene, the other two assailants pulled out their swords. They together charged at the four, but the friends moved out from the incoming strikes. Then, tactfully, they went near the cooking area, and as the two thugs charged again towards them, Rudra and Palan lifted the cauldron and lunged the burning oil at them. The attackers jumped away, but their bodies were still burnt in a few places. It was an opportunity for the friends to turn aggressors. In no time, they surrounded the fallen hoodlums and pulled out their swords.

"Take your buddy and leave right now!" Sanjam commanded. Palan was smart enough to grab the swords of the thugs.

The two hooligans stood up in pain, lifted their third partner, and went away.

The owner of the place joined his hands and thanked his saviors. He further extended his gratitude and said, "*Yuvako*, my house is just behind this food corner. You have traveled long, so please rest and stay tonight in my humble abode. I shall inform the patrol forces about this incident, seek protection, and fix an appointment with a Seth who would certainly employ you as guards in his banking establishment."

Rudra tapped on his shoulders. "Thank you for your offer, *mahashaya*. And we hope to find the employment you mentioned."

***

It was midnight. The four were asleep in a hut, built in the same premises of the older man's brick house. Suddenly, a group of masked men stormed inside, breaking the door. Some of them carried bows, while others had axes and swords. The friends woke up, startled. Even before they could gather their thoughts, the masked men held each of them and dragged them out. They gagged them first and kicked, punched, and moved them to a semi-forested area behind the hut. The four resisted but were overwhelmed.

Once inside the forested area, the masked group made them kneel below a giant Banyan tree. Then, they removed their gags but tied their hands.

One man from the group sat in front of them on a flat wooden seat. He dangled an ax near their faces. "Who are you? Why are you here?"

Throwing confused and scared looks, the four friends looked at each other and the surrounding masked men. Then they tried to mutter in low, broken voices that agitated the man sitting in front of them. "Speak clearly!" The man barked out and pointed his ax at Palan. "You answer me, and the rest stay silent."

"We... we are here looking to find jobs or find employment as swordsmen. And we have come from Mathura."

"The realm offers so many jobs, yet you have come here looking for one?"

"Yes, the realm has job offerings, but the pay is less. The central command came into power promising better opportunities and livelihood, but in the last few years, they have stopped paying as much as before."

"But they have the best pay scale of the last few centuries. What makes you so greedy?

This time Palan looked into the interrogator's eyes. "We are not greedy. Those men had promised that after the Kurukshetra, the empire would only see peace and prosperity. Our fathers, uncles, and elders fought for them in the war because they trusted in their abilities and promises. So their failure to continue with the higher pay scales and other monetary benefits is a shame no matter the reason! And if private employment helps us earn even a little more, how does seeking it make us greedy?"

The man remained silent for some moment. "What about those engaged in petty employment? The Aryavrata economy may not be weak, but the workers have received lesser and lesser wages for the past years. Even the empire has not been able to do much about it with the frequent famines and droughts."

"I believe even the current rulers are not the correct men for the throne. They waged a wage for power control, disguising it as a revolution. Hence, the Gods must be displeased and cursing us with natural calamities," Palan said.

"So, if you get a chance to bring down the regime, you will do that?" The man asked sternly.

Palan paused and looked at his friends. He was confused about what his answer should be.

Sanjam crawled on his knees a few strides ahead and said, "I would. I don't know about the others, but I would. I believe in the Band's opinion that there should be no central or provincial rulers but community heads. Of course, the empire discards the idea, citing it would cause division among communities, and there would be no unity and only extreme competition and struggles. But I say, the system is worth a try."

The man looked curtly at Sanjam. "So you are a Band sympathizer?"

"Not just him, even me!" Rudra clenched his teeth.

The man chuckled and suddenly stood up. "Hold this fellow up and light a fire for me." Some of his helpers quickly grabbed Rudra immobile, and a few arranged for a fire. The man strolled to the blazing fire and warmed a sword in it. Then casually, he walked towards Rudra. Rudra could see the edge of the long blade turn orange and struggled to break free from the five men pinning him against a tree.

The commander of the group brought the sword closer to Rudra's chest. "You are a traitor! You support the Band and loathe the regime. Accept that you are a traitor and seek forgiveness, or else I'll melt you down."

Rudra continued struggling but said nothing. Then, all of a sudden, the commander laughed out loud and clapped his hands. The masked men holding Rudra left him, and the ones surrounding the other three also moved back. Everyone dropped their masks as well.

"I am sorry for all the torture and trouble, my friends," the commander took off his mask and continued speaking. "We are the recruiting team for the Band cluster of Magadh. And we had to test you before offering you to join us. The owner of the food corner had promised you about this employment."

Palan, Samar, and Sanjam stood up as the Band members opened their hands. Rudra breathed heavily and sat on the ground, tired.

"It's an honor to join the Band, Sir. We would always be loyal assets," Sanjam said with a smile.

"I believe so. My name is Puniya, and you can call me Puniya Ji. We need to ride into our cluster settlement right now; we should be there by tomorrow morning."

Chapter 3

In the Band

The four, with the other Band members, had entered deep into the jungle. They were so deep into the jungle that apart from a few places, not even the morning sunlight could penetrate through the extensive and tall trees.

"Look over there. Our abode starts," Puniya pointed a finger ahead.

Several large rocks and fat sacks demarcated an area in a semi-circle shape. But essentially, the perimeter went beyond the vision of the four partners, making a complete circle with a giant diameter. On careful looking, they could see archers of both sexes, right behind the constructed barricade. On the different treetops, there were small wooden platforms where archers remained vigilant. "You must have missed, but there were many more archers camouflaged on tree canopies on our way inside," Puniya said with a smile of pride and continued, "Get off your horses. We have to walk over the rock-and-sack cordon and reach the settlement area. There are people to take care of the horses."

Sanjam's company followed Puniya. They climbed the cordon and continued walking straight. After tramping over bushes and shrubs for about a quarter-mile, they could see an expanse bustling with men and women. The zone was devoid of big trees, tall plants, and wild herbs and weeds.

"We had to clear off this stretch to build the huts and stable timber tents. Now, I am taking you straight to our Pradhan's tent," Puniya said, gesturing them to walk ahead.

The mates continued moving behind Puniya and looked all around the place. There were men and women, mostly in their twenties and some in their mid-teens. A proportion of them were practicing combat with various weapons, while others were busy running errands. Some were also training to climb trees faster, and the rest were categorizing their recent loot.

"I thought the Band people wore leaves or faded and torn-out clothes. But they are in decent attires with dhotis, kurtas, long skirts, and blouses. I bet they loot only the finest of clothes." The other three giggled at Palan's remark.

The four stood at the entrance of the Pradhan's tent, while Puniya walked towards his table. The Pradhan, who was leaning on his chair and leisurely reading a note, threw a glance at Puniya and then turned his attention to the four. "So…these are our latest recruits?"

"Yes, Pradhan Ji. They have passed our test with flying colors and are audacious, anti-establishment, and loyal endorsers of our outfit."

"Hmm… I see." The Pradhan stood up from his chair and bent forward, resting his knuckles on the table. His intense eyes scrutinized the four. "We do need more men in our cluster, Puniya, but we cannot compromise the quality of our recruits."

Finishing the sentence, he picked a long-edged knife from the table and launched it at Sanjam. Fortunately, Sanjam covered his face timely and took a cut on his arm.

The Pradhan nodded. "Nice! You have good reflexes. So, welcome to my Band cluster. You may now go out, and Puniya will send someone to help you settle down. I need to have a little discussion with him."

The friends bowed and took his leave. Once outside the tent and a few feet away, Palan sighed. "Thankfully, you just defended yourself with a cut on the arm instead of grabbing the knife in the air."

Sanjam winked. "I wasn't very quick, but I'd seen him picking up the knife."

"Hey, I guess he is our tour guide," Samar giggled.

A young boy, about 16-17 years old, walked towards them with a big smile, flashing his teeth. "Namastey, brothers. I am Mahesh. Puniya Ji had asked me to take you to a hut and inform you of the basic things and rules of our community."

One by one, each of the four introduced themselves to Mahesh and walked behind him to an empty hut. Entering the hay-house, they could only see four earthen pots on a bamboo stand and four mattresses on the clay floor. Mahesh looked at them and tried to presume whether they were discontent or decently satisfied with the residence. "You will start liking it gradually. Every hut accommodates four individuals, and they soon turn into best mates. But as you four are already friends, staying together would be comfortable, right from the start. Now listen to some instructions, my dear brothers.

"There is a well just on crossing this residence area from where you can fill the water pots. Beyond the well, a quarter-mile to the right would take you to a pond of fresh and clean water. The men bathe in it in the evening and the women in the morning. Crossing the pond, you will find a long trench to clear your stomach. We use it at night, and in an emergency during the daytime, you will have to cross that long ditch and enter the bamboo plantations. At dawn, everyone has to wake up upon hearing the beating of a drum. Within the first prahar, freshen up at the well and eat your fill of the fruits found in the nearby plants and trees. Then you will have to start your training under

Guru Mahat Ji until mealtime in the afternoon. Every day, three huts in collaboration need to cook for the entire community according to their turn. The superiors will add you to that routine only after three months of basic combat training."

After hearing Mahesh blurting out the instructions in almost a single breath, Sanjam's group came out of the hay-house. "Now, I shall take you to the tent; it's already been stockpiled with clothes. Choose 3-4 sets for yourselves according to your size and preference. And on the way, I shall also introduce you to everyone," Mahesh declared as he started walking. On their way, they often stopped as they encountered several fellow Band members. Ultimately, after a seemingly long journey, they got to choose their clothes, and Mahesh left them alone.

The friends felt welcomed and excited in the new environment. The fellow Band members they had met and talked with were amiable and lively. The lifestyle and ambiance of the community were also fascinating to them. They realized it wouldn't be difficult to adapt and mingle in the cluster, and they could soon start working on their mission.

***

The sun was beginning to set for the day. Nevertheless, unlike the rest of the forest interiors, there was still light in the settlement and adjacent area. Sanjam and Samar were somewhat away from the residence zone, collecting fruits.

"We don't know what and how much food they'd serve at dinner. The lunch was terrible. It's wise that we collect as many fruits as possible for the night," Samar said while plucking some berries.

Sanjam, however, was distracted. He had heard some giggling and footsteps nearby. He warned, "I think there's someone else here too." Samar stood behind Sanjam and tried to listen. They took silent and slow steps and reached a family of tall weed plants. Abruptly, from behind those plants, two ladies emerged with swords. Noticing their long skirts and blouses, they realized that the young women were Band members.

"Sorry, we did not want to alarm you. We just heard some noises and were curious to know if anyone was here," Sanjam apologized.

Seeing him, the girls looked at each other in shock, and stood immobile for the next few moments, staring at Sanjam. Sanjam, too, didn't know what more should he say. He wanted to ease the situation but ended up meekly looking at the girls, more focused on one than the other. Then suddenly, like being freed from a spell, the girls regained composure, blinked, looked away from Sanjam, put down their swords, and left without a word.

"You scared the poor girls," Samar joked, watching them disappear.

"They were so peculiar!"

***

Back in their huts, the two young women sat on the floor, both lost in deep thought.

"It can't be an illusion, right Chitra?"

"Of course not, Madhu. How can we both have the same illusion? But I think this is just some ridiculous coincidence."

"Until today, I was not sure if that person even existed. Now we know that he exists. So don't you feel there is some mystery about this?"

"No...he is just a random man who has joined the Band to dedicate himself to the organization's goals and motto. Anyway, how much can we trust a picture?"

"But what about the fact that I had seen him so many times? And this is precisely the same person."

"I don't know about that, dear Madhu. But I see it as nothing more than a coincidence.

After being thoughtful for some time, Madhu managed a smile. "I think you're right. Anyway, we should keep an eye on him."

Chitra smiled back and nodded.

A prahar later, Madhu and Chitra saw Sanjam with his friends at dinner. The Band comrades ate meals in batches near the cooking area. Madhu and Chitra sat opposite Sanjam and his mates. While having dinner, the two girls repeatedly peeked at Sanjam. After dinner, they stood near the four rinsing hands and mouths. Chitra was just beside Samar.

"Namastey, I am Samar, a recent recruit, along with my friends," he pointed at the others. Chitra just gave a half-hearted smile in response.

"The meal was delicious," Samar tried to make conversation. Chitra just nodded and then held Madhu's hand and quickly moved away.

Sanjam looked at Samar intensely. "What were you doing? They may be reserved in nature and don't like interacting with new people. We had already made them uncomfortable once."

"Ah! I was not trying to make them uncomfortable. Didn't you find them strange in the evening? And now again, at dinner, they were staring at you. Their behavior is making me curious."

"What are you two discussing? And who were those ladies?" Palan inquired.

"Come, let's go into our cabin, and I shall tell you," Samar said, ushering them quickly to their tent.

As the night aged, the friends discussed Madhu and Chitra's strange behavior and myriad of other things, including the happenings of their first day here. Finally, they fell asleep past midnight but woke up early morning with the sound of a beating drum.

***

The sun had barely risen when the four woke up. Once awake, they rushed to freshen up and then heartily ate fruits as the first meal of the day. Next, they assembled in an open tract for their training with innumerable other members. While waiting for the teacher, everyone was making small talk, and then abruptly, the murmurings stopped. The whole class had turned quiet as the trainer entered the field.

The combat and warfare trainer, Guru Mahat, was a well-built middle-aged man. He wore nothing but a loose and long lower garment, fitted with a string waistband. His upper body was bare, displaying a set of perfect abs. He also had triceps that extended his arms and a pumped chest. Further, his long beard and thick hair tied into a ponytail gave him a virile look. In a husky tone, he said, "All the recruits who had joined the cluster in the last ten days, step forward and stand behind me."

Thirty-odd young men and women, including Sanjam, Palan, Rudra, and Samar, stood behind the teacher. Guru Mahat did not pay them any heed and rather began with instructions to the large pool of cadets in front of him. "Everyone who has been here for more than ten days but has yet to complete the fundamental three-month exercise must stand behind the experienced ones. The senior members will perform a task after warming up. The chore is that you will go to the oak plantation and climb the trees. Then you've to jump from one tree to another and shoot targets that I have placed on the soil. Of course, on every tree, there is a rope to aid your jumps. Also, Puniya will be invigilating you."

Directing the experienced trainees with the challenging task, Guru Mahat spent some time with those who had completed more than ten days of training. He asked them to practice throwing soft wooden darts at each other while running. Ultimately, he turned his attention to the group of the thirty latest inductees.

He scanned every one of the thirty members and attentively gazed at Sanjam and his friends, as they were the newest faces. However, his eyes rested on Sanjam as he scanned his intent face; something about that boy unsettled him.

Continuing to scan Sanjam, Guru Mahat spoke to everyone, "A good warrior has strength, agility, stamina, and most importantly, the knack of taking blows and still standing tall. You all will start by showcasing your running, climbing, and jumping abilities. If you are decent at those, you will put weight on your back and then run, climb, and jump."

The four partners gradually proved their basic abilities within the next seven days and then started doing the same tasks with weights added. The exercises were tedious and consumed energy, but they had already passed even more intensive drills before being commissioned as spies. However, they were careful enough not to display their true prowess. After the tenth day, they had to start newer activities like walking on a tightrope and jousting.

Sanjam's team interacted with as many members as possible and learned about their lives. They also found out that the core team of the cluster had four men: Pradhan, Puniya, Guru Mahat, and the chief strategist, Madhav. Madhav mainly remained in his tent, and Puniya was the most active superior. The team also realized that Puniya constantly kept an eye on everyone.

***

In the first fifteen days, the group realized that there were many able warriors in the cluster. The guidance and training provided were top-notch, and they focused on versatile fighting types, from guerilla skirmishing to open-field battles. Sanjam was particularly impressed with Madhu. She was an excellent swordswoman and horse-rider. Additionally, she was talented at archery and wrestling. Despite admiration for her, he still found her enigmatic and mysterious. He rarely saw her and Chitra mingling much with other men or women, but he felt Madhu followed him and kept tabs on him. He discussed the matter with his friends, and Samar was interested in uncovering the girls' mystery. Soon one evening, Samar animatedly entered their hut with some information about the girls.

"Their names are Madhu and Chitra. The taller one is Madhu. They joined the Band some eight months ago together. Both had lost their parents at an early age and grew up in an orphanage. Then, they resided in a state-sponsored women's shelter where they had terrible experiences. Someone from the shelter's management molested one of their friends, and they failed to find justice for her. So, they hate the system and believe in the Band."

Sanjam sighed. "Orphaned at young ages and experiencing the brutality of the world at tender ages, they became tough and independent. And they have directed their anger at their warring skills."

"How did you get all this information?" a curious Rudra asked Samar.

"Mahesh has almost everyone's information here. I talk with him often, and he is now a friend of mine."

"I wish they had found some good Samaritan who'd have advised them to reach out to Emperor Yudhisthir or Shri Krishna. They are so easily accessible to the citizens, yet people don't reach out to them," Rudra remarked.

Sanjam patted Rudra's back. "You are right. The command is accessible; back then, both were little girls without family. And it is easy for one wrong person to corrupt and breed hatred for anyone in naïve minds."

***

Sanjam was exploring certain parts of the jungle for the first time. After dinner, he wandered away from the settlement zone as most of the Band members were inside their huts. He walked a few miles randomly to come across a river. The river attracted him, and Sanjam dived into it. It was a short and narrow river with considerable depth. As Sanjam swam effortlessly, the initial shock of the ice-cold water dissipated and became warmer with every stroke.He swam for quite some time, and upon reaching the middle of the river, rested against a big rock. Slowly, he closed his eyes, and time passed by. Then, unexpectedly, he opened his eyes when someone had jumped into the river. Startled, he looked in different directions and saw Madhu swimming rapidly towards him.

She had a look of horror in her eyes. "Look back," she screamed.

Sanjam turned, and his eyes widened as a giant crocodile, hardly a few feet away, opened its large jaws. He instantly began swimming away with the crocodile tailing. Madhu used her limbs vigorously to swim faster but realized she could not reach Sanjam in time. She pondered on an alternative and in a few moments screamed out. "When I say three, you must drown yourself and only emerge after some time." Sanjam was not assured and she could recognize that. "You must trust me. ONE, TWO, THREE!"

Sanjam dipped himself entirely in the waters and Madhu flung a sharp long-knife from her waistband at the creature.

Her aim was perfect and the razor stuck into the crocodile's left eye, making it wail in excruciating pain. In the next few moments, Sanjam came out of the water and followed Madhu to the riverbank.

"Thank you, Madhu. You helped me in time. And you are such a gifted archer. I still can't believe that you hit it straight in its eye."

Madhu flashed a long smile and nodded her head. "You're welcome. But thank your stars that I was strolling here."

None of the two asked how they knew the other's name. They both were already aware that they were curious about each other.

They both walked back silently, wet and cold—Madhu ahead, with Sanjam following her. They had several questions in their minds, but nervousness had bit their tongues. Then, just before reaching the settlement zone, Sanjam finally spoke. "Hey, thanks again, and I think you should go in first. I shall go after some time. You may not want people to see us together in this drenched state."

Madhu looked at him admiringly. "You are a good person, Sanjam." Sanjam blushed. After that, she turned and tip-toed into the residing vicinity. Sanjam stood without moving and watched her walk away. But, she looked behind once, and her face had the prettiest smile. It made Sanjam blush again, and when he realized it, a calm washed over him.

Chapter 4

Perspectives and Ideologies

"You shouldn't wander off like that all alone. You are unbeatable in attacks and combats, but nobody can predict accidents. It was your good stars today that the lady, Madhu, was there to save you," Samar said.

"I am still in awe of the skill that Madhu displayed. She has such precise aim and calculative mind." Sanjam closed his eyes, flashes of the incident passing through his mind.

"Well, praising her *here* won't do any good, *sakha*. Instead, you should let her know that you are indeed grateful and appreciative of her. And maybe that way, you can soon also learn why she has been curious about you since the first day." Palan winked and chuckled at his own suggestion. Rudra and Samar mischievously grinned and encouraged Sanjam to make conversation with Madhu.

Sanjam was reluctant. "*Bandhuon*, I don't know why but maybe because of my limited interaction with the opposite sex so far, I fail at expressing and communicating well with women."

"Of course, that's the reason. We had been on missions that hardly allowed us the scope to have any personal interactions with others. But this mission has given us the liberty to enjoy a bit of personal space and mingling, and it doesn't matter if you're mingling with a man or woman. A lady has saved your life, and she seems to be peculiarly curious about you;

you definitely can thank her and desire to know her more and probably initiate a friendship. Is that anyway wrong?" Palan's views were reasonable.

"And if she anyway feels uneasy or is unwilling to turn into a friend, you won't be bugging her! Being friends is not that bad, is it?" Rudra tried to make Sanjam's decision more clear.

Sanjam finally felt motivated. "Tomorrow after the training, I am going to talk to her."

***

Like Sanjam's friends, Chitra also reasoned that Madhu should have tried to know more about Sanjam. Their discussion had started before dinner and dragged on even after it.

"All I am saying, Madhu, is that we need to know his true identity. And it was an excellent opportunity for you. You had just saved his life. Had you asked things about his life, I bet he wouldn't have lied. And if he would have lied, you could guess it."

"I know, I know, dear Chitra. I don't know why I didn't speak more with him; maybe because I could see shyness on his face. Sanjam is an introvert, and that nature discouraged me from starting a conversation. But the very next chance that I get, I definitely would initiate amity with him," Madhu defended herself.

"I hope you get that chance soon," Chitra sighed.

The conversation was reaching the fag end when they heard a voice from outside their tent. "Ladies, may I please come inside? I have a message from Guruji."

Although both found it odd to receive a message from the Guru at almost midnight, they welcomed the messenger.

"Greetings, ladies. Gurudeva Mahat has asked lady Madhu to prepare herself for a new role from tomorrow. Guruji will make a declaration regarding it early morning before the training session starts. So, you must be present there tomorrow on time." The messenger delivered the master's words and left quickly.

"New role? And I have never been late any day for the training session. So why would Guruji then ask mespecifically to be on time tomorrow?" Madhu sounded perplexed.

Contrary to Madhu, Chitra's eyes instead brightened up. She giggled and cheerfully spoke, "Madhu, Madhu, my dear! It means Mahat Ji wants to promote you. You'd probably be an associate trainer to him!" She gleefully clapped at her own words, and the realization also brought a broad smile to Madhu's face.

A promotion meant measurable success for Madhu. Since joining the Band, she had toiled every day to hone her combat skills. She had sacrificed several nights of sleep perfecting the use of various weapons, and to please the master, she always carried out his every command successfully. She was ambitious and clear about her goals. She desired to rise in the Band hierarchy and finally had made the first significant leap in that direction. With optimistic anticipation, Madhu slept soundly that night.

***

The entire trainee contingent was in the open tract. Facing them stood Mahat Guru, three associate trainers, and Madhu.

"Trainees! Today is an extraordinary day. Since the inception of our cluster eight years ago, there has never been a student who found himself promoted to an associate trainer within a year. But this custom changes today, and it makes me joyful. So, I now, name before you the newest associate trainer, Madhu!" Completing his words of praise, the Guru gestured Madhu to move some steps forward. He then handed her a small knife that Madhu accepted with both hands in a kneeling posture.

Madhu touched the Guru's feet, seeking his blessing, and rose to the claps and cheering of the fellow trainees. Amidst everyone in the crowd, Madhu noticed Sanjam's unending smile and enthusiastic applauds. Momentarily, their eyes too met, and she felt that his eyes were as bright as her own.

Madhu but failed to see the expression on the faces of the three other associate trainers standing behind her. They were vividly displeased at her promotion and glared at her with repulsion. Envy, annoyance, and arrogance together made their teeth clench and cheeks puffy.

The promotion ceremony was short, and soon everyone was engaged in routine practices. Every drilling day started with the trainees working out and performing basic exercises. Then, while the recruits practiced exercises independently, Mahat Ji would train the associate trainers in advanced warfare. After that, the associate trainers had to oversee and help the other trainees in their varied activities.

Madhu enjoyed coaching the other trainees. She was dedicated and felt responsible for discharging her duty proactively. She didn't even realize the passing of time and felt the drilling session ended quickly that day. The trainees, as usual, rushed out of the training field the instant the practice time ceased.

Madhu was the last to move out. She sauntered out of the ground, engaged in her thoughts. She was pleased, not only because she found a promotion but for she could teach the other students well.

"Madhu!" She heard a voice that halted her thoughts and made her look behind. It was Sanjam, walking towards her at a rapid pace.

"Greetings, Madhu," he said with a pleasant smile. "I wanted to tell you a thing, actually a couple of things."

"Yes, Sanjam, is everything alright?" Madhu sounded anxious.

"Oh yes, I bring no disturbing news! Rather, I wanted to congratulate you on today's promotion. You are in a new and important role now, and you thoroughly deserved it. So, I thought of letting you know that my friends and I wish you great luck and are your well-wishers."

Madhu smiled. "I am grateful, Sanjam. And of course, I know you are happy for me. I could see your zealous clapping and the genuine delight on your face. It always adds to the happiness when there are well-wishers equally glad for your success."

"I do agree."

Then, there were a few silent moments as both looked into each other's eyes with their smiles persistent.

"So… may I know what's the second thing you wanted to tell me?" Madhu inquired with a nervous glee, breaking the serenity.

"Oh, yes. I had almost forgotten about it. It's about… Chitra?" Sanjam fumbled at the last phrase of his sentence and looked behind Madhu.

"Hmm? Chitra?? What about her?" Madhu's tone and look both turned surprising and interrogative.

"Oops, no, my bad. I meant to say, Chitra is probably looking for you."

Madhu quickly turned behind and saw Chitra approaching her.

"See, I told you no; it had to be your promotion. After all, you are a terrific warrior. I bet there's anyone here who is as good as you!" Chitra patted Madhu's shoulder and laughed aloud. She was proud of her friend's achievement and did not want to be a miser in expressing her happiness. Madhu, however, felt embarrassed by the big praises in front of Sanjam. She curtly looked at Chitra and was vividly inhibited. Chitra, who had thus far not noticed Sanjam standing nearby, pulled out her tongue. "Sorry, I did not see him," she whispered, looking at Madhu and then turned to Sanjam. "How are you? I am sorry. I was so happy for my *sakhi* that I did see you standing here. My apologies for that."

"No, you don't need to apologize, Chitra. You must have been wanting to talk to your friend, and I just kept her waiting. I wanted to congratulate her and was just about to leave." Sanjam glanced at Madhu, and she threw him a confused gaze remembering he was about to tell her something. But before she could say anything, Sanjam started walking away with a courteous good-bye gesture. As he walked, he could hear Chitra's animated voice, "My dear Madhu, I missed your felicitation ceremony. I had to treat some members who developed infections from wounds. I also wanted to gift you your favorite berries, but the berry plants nearby have been destroyed by some animals. Anyway, I shall cook your favorite 'kheer' in the evening."

Sanjam was glad to overhear Chitra and decided to get berries for Madhu and thank her for saving his life. He had essentially met Madhu to express his gratitude but saw Chitra walking towards them as he was about to begin that topic. Hence, he left without starting the thanking conversation. "Nevertheless, thanking her with the berries that she loves would be a better way to display my gratefulness," Sanjam consoled himself with that thought.

***

"We can't remain mum on this! Firstly, she is still new and naïve in this Band. Moreover, she is a lady. How could Guruji bestow her with the same rank as us? It's utterly bizarre!" Raghuwan fumed in anger. He and the other two associate trainers, Pourush and Sandhi, loathed Madhu's new appointment. They theorized, it was an act of their master to appease the women of the Band and was nothing more than a formal women representation scheme.

"I have talked with other trainees too. Many believe she was inducted as an associate trainer only because she is a woman. But it is an insult to us, our might and strength. Moreover, no male trainee will listen to a woman's command. So we must speak about this to Guruji," Pourush added.

"And if our views alone aren't convincing enough for him, we can request him to ask the other male trainees as well. Also, I can ensure that they speak in the same voice as us." Sandhi was confident of his influence among the recruits. He had a decent rapport with the trainees and commanded respect because of his combating skillsets and ability to mingle well.

Wasting no time, the three stormed out of their tent and reached their master's tent. It was Sandhi who first spoke. He was calculating with words and was apt at the art of convincing people.

"*Pranam*, Guruji," he bowed in front of the master seated on his bed. His two companions also made the formal bowed greeting.

The master kept aside the dry and coarse tobacco leaves that he was cleaning in a water bowl. "I know what brought you three into my hut at this hour."

The three looked at each other, dazzled and nervous. Sandhi attempted to take control of the situation and forced a smile that seemed unadulterated. He spoke in a revered tone, "Gurudeva, no praise can do justice to your aura. You're truly great. Please forgive me for my query; despite knowing our emotions and perspectives, why did you alleviate an undeserving candidate to the same status as us? It disincentivizes our valor and efforts, sire."

The Guru laughed out loud and looked at each of the three with a smirk. "And who gave the verdict that the young lady is undeserving? What if I tell you that she is better than each one of you!"

The master's statement humiliated the three. Raghuwan turned red with shame. He clenched his teeth but somehow controlled his tone while rebutting the master. "If you think so, Gurudeva, it puts a doubt on your coaching abilities as well. If we aren't good warriors, it is your defeat too."

Raghuwan's sharp words made the master look up instantly, his brows furrowed and his lips drawn into a thin line.

"If I can train a lady to become the best warrior in this cluster, within the shortest period, I am victorious in two ways. One, I have bestowed exceptional guidance to my disciple at a record time. Two, as that disciple is a lady, it validates that I do not see any difference between my pupils. Man or woman, younger and elder, my education can surpass all such petty divides."

"But sire, how can you judge her to be better than us; when we have never had any duel or competition? Of course, I wouldn't dare to question your judgment, but your decision hurts our self-confidence here. And it's not just about us. Your other disciples also feel that she is not capable enough to teach them or assist you." Sandhi spoke cleverly, being wary about sounding politically correct.

Guru Mahat gently nodded and said, "I see. I shall address everyone tomorrow, and I suppose you three won't mind if I put my today's decision up for a vote." The three responded affirmatively.

Leaving the master's room, Sandhitold the other two, "At this time of the night, most of the trainees will be scattered in smaller groups all around the space. It will be difficult to talk to every small group."

"We don't need to talk to everyone. There are four-five groups that can influence everyone else. We just need to convince them of our perspective," Raghuwan said with a smirk. "And I know how to do that," he added and looked at his mates with a smile.

The group met the first target group, and Raghuwan spoke. "In the history of Aryavrata, has ever a woman led an army in the war? he asked his fellow trainees. "The Battle in Lanka or the Kurukshetra or even the countless wars between Devas and Asuras, when did a Goddess lead an army? So, how do we accept a woman training us?"

After some moments of silence, one of the trainees spoke. "But...Guru Mahat cannot...cannot be wrong, and even Durga has shown that a woman too can fight and s-slay."

"Does Madhu look like Durga to you? And do not forget, Durga received all her weapons from the Tridev and other Devas. What would be the strength of an army that has no capable man and must need a woman to train?" Raghuwan clenched his teeth.

"I agree with you," another trainee responded, walking ahead from the cluster of the trainees. Looking behind to the rest, he said, "The women in our camp will never be the frontal troop in a battle. She would teach and train us and then stay behind our guard in battles. Women are hypocrites, not warriors." He laughed aloud hysterically, and everyone else joined in.

"So, we finally have the consensus we needed," Sandhi whispered in Raghuwan's ears.

***

"Students, there is a reason why I had ordered the assembly a bit early today. Yesterday, I made a decision. It was my independent decision, with no political or social reason. I promoted Madhu to the post of associate trainer purely based on her talents and personality." The master took a slight pause and looked at Madhu standing beside him. Then his sight glanced at the three other associate trainers standing in the same row as Madhu. He continued with a voice that echoed dignified pride and judicious assertiveness. "But I've learned that my decision has not been so popular. People feel that my decision is biased and is simply an action to appease the women of this cluster. So, my dear pupils, Raghu, Sandhi, and Pourush, suggested I put my decision up for voting." The master halted again and looked at Madhu.

"Are you okay if I agree to this election, Madhu?" the Guru asked.

She first looked into his eyes and then scanned the crowd of the other recruits. It was a swift examination, but she did not miss Sanjam, who slowly moved his head and indicated that she disapproved of the election.

Madhu turned to the master, her head held high, and a smile of confidence graced upon the face. "You are the teacher, Gurudeva. I shall abide by whatever you say! But to everyone else, I wish to convey that I know my strengths and limitations as well. Being a woman is not my limitation but my strength. And my restraint is, despite being confident that

I can perform great as an associate trainer, I wish to respect the majority decision."

The Guru was pleased with her answer, and so were many more in the crowd. The Guru walked two steps ahead. He stood with folded hands. "Here is my decision. I, Guru Mahat, declare that there won't be any voting. I being your Guru, have the authority to make decisions that I deem right. And none of you are neither experienced nor competent enough to question my decision. So the law here is- I say, and you follow. I am not running a democratic administration but training students into able warriors! So, never again dare to question my authority or else be ready to prove yourself as superior to me." Each word that the master uttered was clear and commanding. He had made a statement that silenced everyone's displeasure. Everyone understood that their master was powerful, impartial, and above political correctness.

Raghuwan, Sandhi, and Pourush, understood that their Guru had decided to promote Madhu with a clear conscience and based on merit. So, although they were displeased and infuriated that a lady deserved the same place as them and probably was even better, they stood with their heads lowered. But the Guru said something that shocked them further.

"I also have another important announcement to make. At my discretion, I decree the creation of another designation today. I name it Chief Associate Trainer. Raghu, Sandhi, Pourush, and Madhu will fight in four-person combat, and the winner will grace upon this new post! The combat is five days later." With that pronouncement, the master's eyes met Madhu's, and he could see that she was glad and grateful about the decision. Madhu knew it was a prudent decision of the Guru, for it would give her a chance to prove her worth and abolish any doubt in the minds of the other recruits. But, on the other hand, for the three male associate trainees, it was an opportunity to satisfy their egos by defeating Madhu.

***

It was late in the evening when Sanjam and his three mates found Madhu training in seclusion, with a silent Chitra sitting nearby. Seeing the four coming, Madhu pushed her spear into the ground.

"Sorry for this intrusion, but we wanted to aid you in practice," Sanjam quickly came to the point. "Since it's a four-person clash, your preparation would be better if the training sessions would involve three more people."

Madhu nodded with a grateful smile. "This is thoughtful of you four. I guess I do have some encouraging supporters in this place."

"Well, not merely well-wishers; we could be friends. Good friends." Samar said, and his eyes shifted to Chitra on the last two words.

Chitra stood up from her seating posture and reached beside Madhu. "Yes, we can be friends. Right, Madhu?"

Madhu, who was almost lost looking into Sanjam's eyes, turned her attention to Chitra but managed only to fumble, "Umm.. yeah, yes."

"So… since it's a four-pack challenge, I opt to sit out, and my friends will join Madhu," Samar, although skeptical, spoke out those words like a spontaneous natural suggestion.

Everyone had their consensus with Samar's suggestion. So Sanjam, Palan, and Rudra picked up a spear each and started practicing with Madhu. Samar sat with Chitra a bit away on two large rocks.

"You don't wield any weapon?" Samar enquired.

"If everyone wields a weapon, who will care for the ones injured in battles? I know things about herbal medicines and the human anatomy," she replied. It was her first decent response to Samar. Before that, his several attempts to talk with her were futile.

"Oh, is it? So have you studied medicine?"

"No, no. Although a few years ago, I got a chance to assist a physician for a brief period. I had an interest in medicinal herbs and plants always."

"Umm... so you can treat many diseases?"

"I can treat complicated wounds, certain infections, and the common diseases."

"By the way, what diverted your interest into medicines?"

"The nature," Chitra whispered gently and looked around herself. "Look, what every person on this earth commonly shares is nature. And the natural world is such a blessing. It has beauty for the beholders, serenity for the confused minds, companionship for the lonely, and kindness for those in trouble. Humanity over the years has devised violence like wars that cause wounds, but nature has in it only the things that heal."

"Hmmm. I believe you are partly right. But don't you think that nature also has elements in it that assist people in war? Arrows, axes, bows, and even explosives are made up of stuff effortlessly found around us. I feel nature gives us things that can heal as well as gears that can aid us during conflicts. And war, when waged to defend land, rights, or an ideology, is justified. But violence to conquer and grab is wrong."

Chitra remained quiet for some time. She had found reason in his philosophy and felt that Samar was wise, contrary to his outer look and personality. "I agree with you. That is why I am a part of this Band. However, I also advocate that people can solve any issue without violence, provided both the involved parties have righteousness in their hearts."

Samar nodded, and they talked about other things. Nevertheless, a new thought processed in his mind. Chitra's words made him feel that her personal opinions and philosophies could never endorse the activities of the Band. She was in the Band for some specific reason, or her childhood experiences and the Band's illusioned image blurred her judgment about the outfit. He was more convinced about the latter.

***

DWARKA MAHANAGAR

The city of Dwarka was vibrant with the hustle and bustle of the Mahashivratri festival, due in a couple of weeks. Every year, Dwarka celebrated a week-long fair to celebrate Mahashivratri. The royal treasury sponsored the festival, and there were a plethora of activities included in the fair. There were debates and discussions about religion and spirituality and events like quizzes and mock treasure hunts for kids. The citizens also found opportunities to display their various talents in front of everyone in multiple competitions. Sages and scholars spoke about Shiva's philosophies, and small businesses could put up stalls and make tax-free sales. Such a jubilant and noble celebration was the idea of Krishna, and it had reaped the desired results. The celebrations united people from different sections of society and promoted love for each other.

A group of sages and their disciples were in the city for the fair. Mahaguru Shalyasree, a renowned rishi, led them. Shalyasree was an exceptional scholar who specialized in medicine and could communicate with animals and birds. Almost a hundred years old, he hardly looked over sixty. Krishna himself welcomed the group from the palace's main gate.

As per custom, Krishna washed the feet of Shalyasree and the others accompanying him. Then he escorted them to a guest chamber. Everyone was seated on mats, as Shalyasree did not prefer sitting on chairs. Krishna, out of his reverence, too, sat on a mat adjacent to the group.

"Yadavsrestha, Vasudeva Shri Krishna, I am delighted at your service and hospitality. You are as honourable as you are powerful, my lord," Shalyasree spoke.

Folding his hands and bowing his head once, Krishna replied, "O Mahaguru, it is a noble opportunity for me to serve you. Your contribution towards medicines and treatments and endorsement of animal welfare is unparalleled in this era! Hence, as my duty, I must serve you, and it's your right to receive dedicated hospitality anywhere you go." Krishna's mesmerizing smile, astute words, and soothing voice further pleased the sage.

"Shri Krishna, apologies in advance, but I must tell you my chief reason for visiting you. And apologies because you may feel bad about my words." Shalyasree's face turned solemn.

Krishna gently remarked, "Mahaguru, your words can never make me feel bad. They can either teach me or make me put forward an explanation. So, please, do speak with ease."

"You do know that I am a Shivbhakt. That doesn't mean I have no faith in other devas, but I can relate most with Mahadev's sayings and showings. Mahadeva has been residing on Earth now for more than a century. His lifestyle is an ideal way of living, and to propagate that idea, he has been living by the example. Just like him, men too must cohabit with nature and other beings. His lifestyle is beyond worldly pleasure, co-existing with his most astute followers in very basic houses. There are no needs, no desires, and hence no clashes or conflicts. His community-dwelling knows nothing but peace, unity, and love for each other. Even kings and queens, princes, and princesses have left their kingdoms and royalty to find true peace in the Shivghar. Hence, I urge you to convince everyone in Aryavrata to adopt that mode of living."

Krishna heard Shalyasree with complete attention. But as soon as he had finished, Krishna was ready with an answer. "Now, I seek your apologies. But, please don't consider my reasonings as arrogance. I don't need to ponder over your suggestion because I've thought about this many times before. The kind of livelihood that Lord Shiva endorses is good, and undoubtedly it does away with many complications. But if the entire world gives up a life that evolves and grows, the world would turn stagnant. There would be no conflict, but there would be no progress at all.

"What Lord Shiva wishes to propagate in the real sense is oneness among all, selflessness in people's hearts, and everyone having feelings of equality, love, and brotherhood. Lord Shiva believes that those qualities cannot be consistent in men and women unless they accept a static and hermitage life. But what humanity needs to understand and employ are compassion, kindness, and selflessness in hearts despite working for their own and the greater good. That would make Shiva truly proud and happy."

Krishna's clarification of what accurately would please Shiva made Shalyashree ponder. He said nothing, but nodded his head, seeming to be debating Krishna's words.

Krishna understood that he had to elucidate his views better. "Sage Shalyashree, you are wise and learned. Think about the realm of Swarga and how it functions. In Swarga, some eminent Devas like Indra, Agni, and others enjoy a higher status and are more revered. It is because they perform greater and more crucial responsibilities. Hence, their status is their reward, and everyone else accepts it. Likewise, other Devas and demi-gods serve under the eminent Devas. There are also the Gandharvas, Apsaras, and souls of great humans, taking care of the Devas and demi-gods. They act according to the wishes of the Devas. So, even Swarga has a hierarchy based on who can perform what duty."

Exhaling a long breath, Krishna continued, "But what makes Swarga a blissful and divine place is that there everyone acknowledges their role and the related status with an open heart. They don't have envy, greed, and selfish motives to take over someone else's place. Everyone performs their duties with utmost dedication, respects each other, and lives with contentment. Hence, the realm constantly progresses, evolves, creates newer stuff and concepts for the welfare of the creation, and yet has compassion, kindness, and empathy. Similarly, humans need to behave and think like the beings of Swarga, and I have always strived to preach that."

Krishna's views touched and moved Shalyashree. In a single conversation with Krishna, his understanding of life turned even more profound. He accepted Krishna's philosophy and said, "Thank you, O Great Vasudeva. I now realize the true ideology of Shaivism and shall preach it far and wide." Thus, Krishna won over the heart of a person who had a diametrically opposite thought process to him.

***

BAND CLUSTER IN MATHURA

It was the day of the contest. Madhu stood in the middle of the training ground, along with her three rivals. The other recruits had encircled them and were both the spectators and the arena perimeter. Sanjam, his friends, and Chitra stood on the northern side of the arena perimeter.

The contestants had chest plates and long boots on. Each had a spear in hand and also wore headgear. The cluster's Pradhan and Guru Mahat stood upon a metallic structure on a treetop to enjoy the aerial view of the challenge. On Guru Mahat's signal, a person blew a conch, and the contest started.

On one part of the arena, Sandhi and Pourush faced each other. They started quickly combating with their spears, but both were defensive with their maneuvers. Some distance away, Raghuwan and Madhu stood against each other, with their spears raised. They looked intensely into each other's eyes. Raghuwan's eyes had fury, while Madhu's eyes were attentive and confident.

Raghuwan made the first move as Madhu hardly moved her feet. He rushed and pushed the spear towards her chest, but Madhu kneeled at the right moment and rammed the pointed end of her spear at his spear. Raghu briefly lost his balance but came back hard. Madhu blocked his vertical spear attack as she held her spear horizontally with both hands. He continued to drive the spear through her defense, but she used her strength to block his push. Suddenly she let her spear loose and moved swiftly left. Her abrupt move caused Raghu to fall onto the ground because of the momentum behind his pushing stance.

The early fall for Raghuwan stunned himself and the spectators alike. The spectators rallied behind Madhu and cheered her name. It made Madhu more enthusiastic but irked Raghuwan greatly. Feeling humiliated, he rose with a growl and rushed at Madhu again. This time Madhu too ran towards him, and as she neared the range of his spear, she rammed her spear into the ground, close to his left foot. She had not intended to penetrate it into his boots. Raghu hit his left knee on the spear on the ground and tripped. He was down for the second time and understood he could not beat Madhu.

All of a sudden, an idea surfaced in his mind. Acting accordingly, he avoided rushed and aggressive maneuvers and engaged Madhu in rudimentary spear-fighting moves. Making her relaxed and defensive, he kept moving and reached Pourush and Sandhi in some time. It was late when Madhu realized that she had been encircled by the three.

Raghuwan quickly whispered, "You two, now attack me. Simultaneously. Do not engage with her." The two did as instructed. They continued consistent attacks at Raghuwan, and he defended himself and even used his superior raw strength to shove them with his bulky framed body.

Madhu turned clueless against the new strategy of the three. She was not attacked or challenged but entirely ignored. She looked around as the spectators had begun rooting for Raghuwan. Suddenly, she felt nervous and anxious.

In the audience, Palan asked, "What are they trying to do?"

"Raghuwan is portraying himself as the hero who can easily fight off two men together. They are expecting Madhu to feel helpless, and soon, she will end up attacking everyone. Then the three would ally and counter-attack her. That way, they would defeat her first by probably injuring her gravely. After that, Raghuwan would win the contest, and the three-on-one attack would seem justifiable as he too had fought simultaneously against two and three at different stages of the contest," Sanjam deduced.

"It's cheating! The three cannot defeat Madhu fairly. We must do something about this dirty and dangerous plot!" Chitra looked at Sanjam and he sighed; he knew that the unfair strategy was not illicit or evident to all.

The three had trapped Madhu right in the center of the arena. While Sandhi launched his spear from the left, Raghuwan attacked from the right. Madhu somehow used both ends of her spear to block the attacks with strength and agility. But right then, Pourush rushed from the center, and his spear hit her chest plate. She fell to the ground and coughed. She quickly tried to pick herself up, but Raghuwan threw away her spear with a kick. Thus, she was unarmed and surrounded and staring at defeat. She, however, remembered that she had a knife in her right boot. She planned to throw sand on Raghu's eyes and pull out her knife when Sanjam unexpectedly ran into the action. He had carried a log in his hand, and with three quick blows, took out each of the three.

***

Sanjam's action forced the Pradhan and Guru Mahat to intervene. Sanjam explained how the fight was turned unfair by the three, and they could have maimed Madhu for personal enmity, thereby going against the Band ideology. The Pradhan and Guru agreed that they too realized how the three had turned the contest into a vengeance but didn't intervene as they wanted to see Madhu's limits.

"No matter what, you must have had trust in us. You did not notice, but Mahatji was ready with an arrow. Had the three attacked Madhu while she lay defenseless, he would have released the arrow and saved her," the Pradhan sternly told Sanjam.

Sanjam quickly apologized and said he was foolish not to trust Mahat Guru and intervene on his own.

The Pradhan accepted his apology and decreed that the three could no longer be a part of that cluster and must rejoin another. Mahat Guru, on the other hand, was pleased with Madhu and declared her the contest winner. The show was over, and the trainees started dispersing with many congratulating Madhu.

Sanjam, his friends, and Chitra looked at Madhu, standing some distance away.

There was another group of five men that were looking at Madhu with interest. One among them stared at her from top to bottom, particularly ogling at her curves. His look was not appreciative but lusty. He remarked, "I haven't seen a lady like her, *bandhuon*. She's bold and fiery. Look at her body, those firm melons, and that fleshy rear. Neither those chest plates can cover the magic of her bosom chest, nor the thick, tight trouser can make me not imagine that ass!" Everyone laughed and agreed with the remarks. Then, another from the group spoke to the one who had made the comments. "Brinjaldesh, I bet she would be as dominant and uninhibited in bed as she is in battle. So waste no time; go and congratulate her. Anyway, that fellow must have already started fantasizing about her on his bed after saving her."

Brinjaldesh scoffed and walked with confidence to meet her. "Congratulations, Lady Madhu. You undoubtedly deserved the win. And I am sure even if that guy had not intervened, you would have found a way to win. As you must know, most men believe that they should always protect women. But not every woman needs a man acting as her bodyguard.Anyway, it'd be a pleasure to learn things from you as the chief associate trainer." Brinjal smiled and shook her hand.

Madhu nodded meekly and thanked him. She wanted to add that Sanjam must have interfered only out of concern, but she remained mum.

After Brinjaldesh left, Raghuwan too approached Madhu. He congratulated her, and while shaking her hand, he whispered with a mean smile, "After all, you needed help; first, the intervention of a guy and then of the Pradhan and guru." She pulled her hand away, but he stood in front of her and went on with his depraved criticism. "Everyone would always rescue you because you need saving. Did you see anyone complaining about my friends trying to attack me together? Do you think if it was me on the ground unarmed and surrounded, someone would have intervened? No! They rescued you because men always want to protect women. Not because of selfless reasons but with the expectation of getting between your legs someday. And I am sure that guy would soon be inside you." He moved away after speaking those words, leaving Madhu embarrassed, vulnerable, and distressed. She froze and stood immobile as the ground cleared. His words rang in her mind, and her eyes turned moist.

Chitra, Sanjam, Rudra, Palan, and Samar walked towards her as they saw her motionless.

"Is everything okay?" Sanjam asked with concern.

Madhu didn't reply but looked at him blankly, staring into his eyes.

"What happened, dear?" Chitra asked, holding her hand.

Madhu said nothing but walked away, pulling Chitra with her. The unexpected cold behavior of hers staggered Sanjam and his friends.

***

It was dusk when Chitra met Samar and Sanjam outside their hut. She was visibly disturbed.

"Give her a couple of days maybe, and she would herself tell you why she turned so upset abruptly." Despite repeated requests, Chitra was unwilling to share what was going through Madhu's mind. Madhu had shared her distress with Chitra but took a promise that she would say nothing about it to anyone. Madhu was displeased by Sanjam and his intervention in the contest. She told Chitra that she was anyway going to re-attack them with her knife. Sanjam's intervention only caused her to face humiliation. Chitra tried to reason that Raghuwan's words were manipulating her thoughts but to no avail.

Sanjam and his friends were left further anxious after the interaction with Chitra. They knew something personal and probably related to Sanjam was troubling her. However, despite their ponderings, they could not find any such reason. At last, at his friends' suggestion, Sanjam decided to meet Madhu the next day with the berries and thank her for saving his life in the river. They were hopeful that it would be a good start to talk, and she would then voluntarily share her troubling issue.

***

The next afternoon, Sanjam saw Madhu practicing with a spear all alone. He had already managed to grab some of her favorite berries from a remote part of the jungle. Madhu sensed Sanjam coming near her, but she continued with her exercise.

"Greetings, Madhu. Can I have some of your time?" he asked.

Madhu neither turned towards him nor replied.

"Madhu?" Sanjam called her name again.

She did not stop her training but replied, "Hmm..anything important?"

She sounded irritated, yet he decided to continue with the interaction. "Yes, it's important," he started casually, "you know, since the day you saved me from the crocodile attack, I have meant to thank you decently. Unfortunately, every time I try to do so, something interrupts us. So today, I'm determined to come straight to the point. I have also got some of your beloved berries."

Hearing him, Madhu threw the spear away. She let out a sarcastic laugh and looked at the container of berries in his hands. She chuckled. "So, that was it, huh? I saved you, and you couldn't find peace unless you satisfied your male ego by saving or helping me in return; no matter whether I needed it or not. First, you decided to protect me in a contest, and then you got berries for me and tried to impress me? What do you need in return? You think I'd feel wooed by such actions and get into your arms?" Her sharp, insensitive, and accusing words deeply hurt Sanjam. He was dazed momentarily and could not process how to react and what to say. He eventually just managed to inquire softly, with a quivering voice, "Madhu? Are you in your senses? Are you accusing me of trying to chase you?"

"Of course! How did you even know that I loved berries? I never told you. You eavesdrop on my conversations with Chitra. And how could you make that contest an opportunity to impress me?"

"Madhu, I believe you are uselessly angry and irrational. Yes, I overheard Chitra telling you about berries, and I interfered in the fight only because not me but everyone was worried that those three would gravely wound you in an unfair fight."

"Battles are never fair. But I am competent enough to

tackle any predicament. I am a warrior, not a damsel in distress; I needed no help."

Sanjam exhaled a long breath and shook his head. He took a step closer to Madhu and looked into her eyes. "A true warrior doesn't feel ashamed in accepting help. Only someone doubtful of their prowess feels insulted if helped. You may be physically strong and skilled at combat, but your heart is weak and slender. Anyway, as you think, I chase you, so never again shall I come into your way. You do well and try to turn into a true warrior, someone whose heart is not feeble." Sanjam sighed as he ended his words.

He placed the berry container on the ground and stormed away without waiting for Madhu's reply or reaction. As he walked away, he felt a heaviness in his heart, and his breaths turned rapid. He did not realize that there were goosebumps on his body. He only could experience the feeling of losing something very dear to him.

Chapter 5

The Mending Attempts

"No, Madhu, you did a terrible thing. You insulted him for no reason. Even the shastras say that no matter how mighty a person is in battles, he is not a warrior if he cannot control his emotions and conquer his heart," Chitra explained to Madhu. "Sanjam intervened in your challenge only after I panicked and turned restless. We had anyway accepted them as our friends. And as a friend, he had the duty of aiding you. He only intended to help you from getting hurt."

Madhu realized that her reaction to Sanjam resulted from the unfair thoughts put in her mind by Raghuwan. However, despite the insight, Madhu sat quietly in one corner of their hut. Chitra, therefore, tried to convince her further.

Chitra went and sat near Madhu. "Initially, surprised by Sanjam's appearance, we stalked and stared at him. But, despite knowing that, did he ever try to take advantage of that fact? Did he or his friends try to be over-friendly or anything such? No! They are decent men, and so, you must apologize to Sanjam, dear," Chitra urged.

Madhu turned towards Chitra and hugged her. Her eyes were red and moist.

"It's okay to weep, *sakhi*. Weeping won't make you weak. On the contrary, you are strong as only a strong person can quickly accept her mistake and apologize. Moreover, your thoughts being astray was natural. In the last few days, people constantly belittled you for being a warrior woman. They questioned your skills, and you were put to the test only because you are a lady. Nevertheless, what matters is that now you realize you were a victim of manipulation, and you must promise yourself that never again you'd let anyone manipulate you."

Madhu allowed her tears to flow. She sniffled and wept. "I promise to be stronger and never allow my mind to get corrupted again," she vowed.

***

Sanjam's friends did not blame Madhu entirely. Instead, they said that she was not herself, and the stress of the contest and how things panned out in that contest must have caused Madhu some trauma. They reasoned how it was not easy for a lady to find acceptance as a profound warrior and that she would always have to fight not only opponents but also regressive mindsets. Hearing his friends, Sanjam regretted his criticism of Madhu. He now thought he could have walked away silently and given her more time to gather her thoughts. His rethinking made him realize that he ought to talk to her again and requested Samar to tell about that to Chitra first. Samar was happy to help, and he soon met Chitra.

***

"It was not Sanjam's fault at all. I talked to Madhu, and she now feels that she thought and reacted immaturely. She too wants to meet him to say sorry," Chitra assured Samar.

"No, no, Sanjam does not need an apology. He merely wishes to talk to her and have the same friendly rapport as before. And I should thank you for helping Madhu cope with her situation and also being unbiased."

"I had to be unbiased. You four are wonderful people, and I could not let a misunderstanding hurt our friendship."

"Our…as in yours and mine?" he winked.

She blushed and stammered, "No, I meant the friendship of the group." However, she soon changed her inhibited demeanor and added, "Of course,mine and yours is also a friendship that I value greatly."

The last sentence made Samar smile wide. There was a kind of spark in his eyes, and he nodded gleefully.

***

The next evening, Sanjam waited by the riverside for Madhu. He had a new box of berries with him and waited impatiently for Madhu to arrive. He was getting restless, thinking why she had not come in due time.

Madhu wanted to be on time. She had planned how she would apologize to Sanjam. But on her way, she was stopped by Brinjaldesh.

"Greetings, lady Madhu. I hope you are well," Brinjal said, emerging suddenly out of some trees.

Madhu forced a smile and greeted him back.

"Are you heading somewhere? If you are going towards the river, I can accompany you. Evenings by the riverside are so beautiful. And a beautiful companion would further enrich the experience."

Madhu was hesitant to tell him that she was indeed going to the riverside to meet Sanjam. She lied instead. "No, I am not that big a fan of nature. I was taking a lazy stroll. I love some me time." She hoped that Brinjal would get the hint and leave her alone to retreat to the cluster's residing zone.

Unfortunately, neither did he return, nor did he stop chatting. "Talking about being a fan, I am one huge admirer of nature and its beauty, but now I am turning into your fan too. Your beauty and boldness mesmerize me!"

Madhu smiled at the compliment, although she felt it was very early for Brinjal to compliment her. She also did not sense a good vibe from him. But she did not want to offend him for no reason.

"Thank you. Let me take your leave now?" Madhu politely asked.

"Why? Are you trying to ignore me?" Brinjal sounded arrogant, but he made a smile to suppress his displeasure.

"No, I am not ignoring you, but I cannot talk much with you now; maybe, some other time?"

"Oh yes, that is fine. We're friends, and as friends, we will get many opportunities to spend time together," Brinjal replied.

Madhu felt irritated with Brinjal's choice of words. She nodded and smiled without reverting to his proposal. Brinjal, however, continued making small talk, and she had to involve herself in those.

Sanjam, by then, had come looking for Madhu, and seeing her busy with Brinjal, he felt she was still not ready to talk with him yet. He was somewhat hurt but acknowledged that it was her choice to consider him a friend or not. With that thought, he went away without asking or telling her anything.

Meanwhile, after being able to excuse herself from Brinjal, Madhu reached the riverside and did not find Sanjam. She considered that he must have been there but did not like waiting. Also, she was hesitant to attempt again to rebuild the amity with Sanjam and left it to fate. She told herself that she was in the Band for some concrete reasons and not to make friends. Hence she decided to concentrate on her core responsibilities.

Sanjam, too, took a similar decision. He told his friends that although he was not angry with Madhu, he would not think any more about her or their friendship. Instead, he urged that the group needed to focus more on its mission.

Over the next few days, Madhu continued training herself harder and worked efficiently as the chief associate trainer. Sanjam's company also got busy with their prime task, and in between the routine Band activities, they found out more about the Pradhan, Mahat Guru, and some other senior members of the cluster. The Pradhan was a former Senanayak in the erstwhile Trigartha kingdom, now merged with Sindhu Rajya after the Kurukshetra war. Trigartha was a crucial ally of the Kauravas, but most of their royal members' deaths left the territory without any able ruler. Moreover, the war and previous bad decisions also drained their royal treasury. Therefore, later the Pandava-Krishna realm merged it with the nearby strong kingdom of Sindhu. The move was prudent and effective in reviving Trigratha's administration and economy, but several loyalists to the former Trigartha regal family disliked the decision. The Pradhan, Dhumketu, was one such loyalist, and he left the land and wandered for long, with a small army, before joining the Band.

Mahat Guru was from Keralam. He was an extraordinary Brahman warrior who taught both warfare and scriptures to the Keralam royal princes. However, he left the region when Keralam's king decided to fight for Pandavas. Mahat viewed the entire war as a family feud and did not endorse the kingdom's participation in it. Mahat protested against Keralam being a Pandav-ally, but the king decreed that Keralam would aid the Pandavas, and Mahat Guru too had to participate in the war. Mahat Guru could even conjure divine weapons, but he never in his life had used them, for he knew of their destructive nature. He was a Maharathi who propagated peace and joined the Band because he believed there should be no state or central rulers but only community-level leadership.

Sanjam and his mates had discovered much about the senior Band members. They also found out that soon, someone from the Band's central leadership would visit their cluster. In the meantime, they took part in some small ransacks and loot of warehouses storing valuable products.

***

DWARKA MAHANAGAR

The chief minister of Dwarka came running to Krishna in his office chamber. "*Pranam*, Yadavsreshtha! I need to inform you of something."

"Yes, Mahamantri Ji, what makes you so anxious?" Krishna rose from his seat and folded his hands behind his back.

"There are disturbing reports from various parts of the empire. Our soldiers have discovered symbols representing the entity, Swaha, marked on different public buildings in almost every state. And the numbers are increasing day by day. I am afraid that the masses are starting to convert into sympathizers of the rebel outfits and losing trust in the realm and religion."

Krishna heard his minister and closed his eyes for some time. "Mahamantri Ji, announce that I shall be making tours across Aryavrata and having public discussions on our citizens' issues. Inform Samrat Yudhisthir about it formally and make me an itinerary."

The minister bowed and assured him that he would get the tasks done in no time.

***

THE SINDHU RAJYA BORDERS

Krishna wasted no time in starting the journey for the public addresses. In a few weeks, his entourage was almost near the southern border villages of Sindhu. The central regime had set up those villages for the population of the areas gravely impacted by a series of earthquakes some years ago. The earthquakes had primarily affected parts of the Sindu, Gandhara, and Matsya kingdoms. The center gave those resettled masses in the border villages financial assistance as well. The central administration also started exploration projects close to those border villages. The area was rich in metals that were used to construct utensils, specific furniture, and small but essential household items, and hence it was a feasible option. Those projects employed people only from the resettled population, thereby giving them jobs.

Although those measures ensured that the settlers did not turn poor, they were far from their previous decent financial status. Krishna and Emperor Yudhisthir did acknowledge that fact, and so they initiated a policy. Accordingly, the regime provided every household with tools and raw materials to make clothes out of a delicate and expensive fabric. The center even bought the finished products at decent rates and sold them through merchants and traders. Hastinapura further encouraged the people in those villages to cultivate Vastrapuli, that offered the fiber to make those elegant fabrics.

Even with the best intentions of the regime to revive the financial status of the Sindhu border villages, the public had to be patient to experience the revival. Unfortunately, they were not patient, and they remained displeased with the regime. Their dissatisfaction was an advantage for the Band and Swaha. Influenced by Swaha, many households in the place began worshipping spirits and demons and practiced black magic. Also, youth from those villages joined the Band in great numbers. They fought for the Band pillaged affluent establishments, and shared their loot with their families.

Krishna had reached the rural border area. Witnessing him coming with a small escort party, people found the courage to gather in his path, almost surrounding the entourage. Although those onlookers said nothing they threw hateful looks. Krishna looked at the angry faces and thought about how he could initiate a conversation with them. However, before he could devise any method, an older man stood right in front of Krishna's horse.

"What brings the great sorcerer, Vasudeva Shri Krishna, to this refugee camp?" the old man asked with a mocking smile.

Krishna stayed calm, managed a smile, and in a soft voice replied, "Greetings, friend! I am here to talk with you all, listen to your grievances, and know how we can serve you better."

The man laughed aloud and looked at the other villagers around him. The others also joined him in the laughter.

"The royalty talks about serving? O Krishna, you may be God-like for other people, but we know about your cunningness and political statements."

Krishna came down from his chariot and walked towards the man. The man suddenly felt he had made a mistake by disrespecting the most powerful person on the planet. His smile ceased, and his face turned sour.

Krishna placed his left hand on the man's right shoulder and smiled again. "The fundamental task of any royalty is to serve the citizens. Maybe we have failed in some ways to serve our citizens, but please do not mistrust our intention. So, tell me, friend, what problems do you face? What are the drawbacks here in the education, medical, transportation, and economic activities?"

The older man threw a confused look and once again glanced around at his fellow villagers.

Seeing him nervous, a middle-aged man from the crowd said, "All those are good, but there is no affluence in this refugee area like we had in our erstwhile lands."

Krishna sighed. "Human's best and elementary quality is accepting change and adapting to new things." His eyes scanned every face in the crowd. "You call this place a refugee camp, even though every household here owns surplus lands. If you cannot love what you have presently and continue with the dissatisfaction of losing what you had in the past, how can you make your future better? The state has ensured your basic amenities, given you occupations, and provided the blueprint and support to revive your financial status through the cultivation of Vastrapuli. However, it is your lack of motivation and patience that has kept you dissatisfied and angry."

Krishna's words started some murmurs in the crowd. Among them, some agreed and realized how mistaken they had been all these years, while others dismissed Krishna's reasonings as futile consolation words.

The same old man who had taunted Krishna gathered courage and said again, "But since we lost our businesses, houses, savings, and properties in a natural calamity, why does not the royal houses compensate us entirely?"

"You all were affected by the earthquakes. Likewise, floods, landslides, cyclones, and epidemics have impacted others. Royal houses can't pragmatically compensate for the cumulative loss in every case. And we cannot reimburse selectively. Rather we can sponsor and aid in resettlement and redevelopment,"

Krishna and his escorts continued ahead with their journey. The Interior Minister of Dwarka had accompanied Krishna as a senior-level official required to assist a leader in such public events. Soon after restarting their journey, the minister, who shared Krishna's chariot, said, "Maybe, we should have made these public interactions sooner. You could have convinced people long ago that Band and Swaha are misleading them."

Turning his head, Krishna responded, "Mantri Ji, this is the apt time. If we had countered the Band's bogus public agendas right at the start, the people would have only felt that we were insecure about a political pressure group. Moreover, if we had concentrated on the Band instead of dealing with the aftermath of the numerous natural calamities in the last few years, we would have failed to help our citizens. Everything has its own time."

The Interior Minister nodded. "You are right, Vasudeva Ji. I had almost forgotten that the Band even propagated that because the Pandavas and we are wrongful rulers, the Gods are cursing the empire with natural calamities." Taking a pause, he laughed and said, "However, if later we discover that even the natural disasters have been acts of the Band, I would not be surprised."

***

Two weeks later, Shri Krishna was in the capital of Sindhu Rajya. His entourage was deliberately small, consisting of only Dwarka's Interior Minister, one Senanayak, and some bodyguards. The whole team stayed as guests in the royal palace of Sindhu, as the first public address was due in the next three days.

Krishna asked his Interior Minister to provide every household in the capital with a blank leaflet two days before his public address. It would allow the families to write their questions anonymously and store them in a large box near the stage.

Three days later, the event was underway. As expected, the crowd was massive, and there was a seating arrangement for them. From the stage to the crowd's sitting area, the whole place was roofed with a plastic sheet to ensure relief from the summer heat. Shri Krishna started his talks by explaining the necessity of the Kurukshetra War as an event to create a new and improved era. Next, he reminded how he, the Pandavas, and every other state's king initiated a period of peace, justice, equity, and dharma. Krishna also agreed that they were not entirely successful in permanently ensuring such a period as new challenges and crises emerged. But he promised that soon the issues troubling the countrymen would dwindle. Vasudeva even explained the reasons behind some of the regime's failed policies transparently. He sought apologies for them and elucidated how the command had shifted to newer schemes. Even without the public sharing their thoughts, Krishna himself spoke as if he was one among them.

Then, he earnestly requested the public to wait for some time so that the administration's solution-centric steps could show the desired results. Krishna also explained to them that good things take time. "To build or renovate something is time-consuming, for its foundation has to be solid. But to decimate something requires no time, for anyone can do it haphazardly," he said.

The audience was impressed with the transparency and honesty in Krishna's approach. They clapped, cheered, and hailed Krishna and his statements several times. Their trust in Krishna and the regime increased spontaneously, and the crowd was eager to question Krishna on different things directly. The most common question asked was why God allowed innocent people to go through stressful times, and why doesn't God intervene to do away with people's sufferings.

"My dear friends, brothers, and sisters, please listen to me carefully and try to comprehend my words. Sometimes, our bad days are the result of our activities. They may be some very old actions whose consequences we are bearing only late in our lives. But, also, in other cases, we face terrible times because of some external and more significant reason. For example, my uncle, Kamsa, imprisoned my parents, and they lost seven of their kids right after their births. My parents went through terrible times for years, and they, too, were innocent souls. But, even during those years, they did not lose their belief in God and fate. Maybe so; in my life, I found resources and opportunities that allowed me to slay my uncle and emancipate a kingdom from authoritarian rule. In simple words, my parents took the pain that resulted in the emancipation of countless men and women.

"Moreover, if Gods intervene in human's good and bad occasions, where is our independence? Imagine a simulation where God decides everything for us; then, will any of our actions be independent? And when there are situations where one's positivity becomes another's negativity, whom will God support? Two states are at war, and both seek God's blessing to win; for whom will God then intervene? Hence, the way God has been functioning is accurate, and let it be so. What we humans can do is understand God's nature and philosophies better."

In one public appearance, the people understood spirituality and the human-God relationship like never before.

***

MAGADH BAND CLUSTER

"It's been almost a month since the contest day, and Madhu and Sanjam have not been like before yet," Samar sadly told Chitra.

"Yes, I feel sad for both. The two talk formally when necessary during the training sessions but nothing more. Madhu tells me that she wishes to concentrate on other things, although she is not displeased with him."

"Sanjam feels forging friendships in this kind of a place are unnecessary distractions."

"So does not he discourage you from keeping a close relationship with me?"

"No way! Just like Madhu does not interfere in your amity with me, Sanjam also does not hinder our friendship."

"Honestly, I can talk with Madhu and maybe mend things between the two. However, let them realize the friendly bond that they share and miss it. And I sense that it would happen soon."

Samar and Chitra were having the conversation, close to the cluster's settlement area. Their talks were disturbed when they suddenly heard shouts and screams. Both quickly rushed into the settlement zone and learned that a fourteen-year-old member had been missing since the morning. Wasting no time, everyone started looking for him. While Samar quickly joined his friends to search for the kid, Chitra went with Madhu.

***

The search had started in the late afternoon, and now the sun was about to set. However, nobody could find the boy yet. The Band members in tiny groups were in different parts of the jungle. The forest was also enormous, and hence, its entire search would take a long time.

Sanjam separated from his friends and went towards a cliff. Thorny bushes covered the path to it. It was unlikely that the kid would have taken that route, but teenage minds are fickle and rebellious. Sanjam looked around himself and saw nobody near. He closed his eyes and swiftly conjured divine energy on his small silver knife. When the knife possessed the celestial power, he dashed it on the thorny and the force of the air moved aside the weeds and plants and cleared the route.

Sanjam then took steps towards the end of the cliff. As he neared the edge and looked below, he was horrified. A skinny and lanky fellow was lying on a flat rock that extended from the cliff surface in the midair. It somehow was attached to the cliff.The boy's eyes were closed, and there was dried blood on his feet and legs.

"Boy, hey boy!" Sanjam's screams startled the teen, and he woke up dazed. He started crying and begged Sanjam to rescue him. "I came to see the scenery below the cliff but found the road too challenging. So I retreated, but some monkeys attacked, and I ran over the thorny bushes and then fell off the edge onto this rock. I called out so much for help; none came, so I slept being tired."

Sanjam was relieved that he was alive. He was thankful that the boy was lucky and fell on that rock instead of diving down. However, his eyes caught the attention of the flat rock. It was feeble and could anytime detach from the cliff's body. He said nothing to the kid and tried looking around for any rope or rope-like stuff. Unfortunately, there was nothing, and he wasn't sure how much longer the rock would remain glued.

Unable to find a way of pulling the boy up, Sanjam felt helpless and nervous. Suddenly, a rope went past him and fell near the injured boy. Sanjam looked up and saw Madhu there, getting ready to tie the rope to a strong base.

Holding the rope in her hands and looking at it, Madhu turned introspective.

"What happened?" Sanjam asked softly.

She lifted her chin and looked at him. "Hold this, Sanjam. I won't be able to pull you up with the kid, but you can pull the both of us. And I get that there is no shame if a warrior needs help." Madhu walked to Sanjam and, handing him the rope, said "I must accept support when I truly need it. A warrior must know their strengths and also weakness"

Sanjam smiled at her and nodded. He quickly grabbed one end of the rope, and Madhu fastened herself securely with the rest of the rope. Sanjam held the rope with all his might while she carefully walked down the ridge, stepping on rocks and stones. Fortunately, the cliff was robust, and she could walk fast.

Madhu reached close to the kid in a short time. She then extended her right arm to him and told him to clutch it tightly. The boy was hesitant and fearful of holding her hand and moving up. "Listen, this rock won't last long. It is feeble and won't take your weight for long. Please trust me; I won't let anything happen to you," Madhu revealed the risk to the boy.

The kid still wept and said in a quivering voice, "I am afraid, Please pull me up, please!"

Madhu herself was turning worried and uneasy. Holding the boy was only the first part as Sanjam had to pull them up as well. Moreover, time was running out. She but managed a smile and tried to sound calm. "Dear, what's your name, boy?"

"Sudhan," he timidly replied.

"Sudhan, you have to trust me. I have a brother of your age at my home. And in you, I see him. I love him so dearly, and I won't let anything wrong happen to someone who resembles him. So, please trust me and give me your hand."

The boy breathed deeply several times and caught her arm with both his hands.

"Pull us up!" Madhu shouted.

Sanjam pulled them up with all his strength. He was sweating profusely. The nerves on his arms were visible, and his muscles stiffened. He continued pulling them up, and they almost had reached the top. Chitra, Sanjam's friends, and some more recruits arrived at the spot by then. They probably heard the boy's screams while being pulled up. Ultimately, Sanjam managed to pull them both up, and Chitra and Samar quickly helped the boy and Madhu sit on the ground.

***

The entire Band was relieved that the boy was safe and sound. The camp was happy about it, and so after dinner, everyone sat around a bonfire. The members congratulated and appreciated Sanjam and Madhu. Even the Pradhan expressed his gratitude.

Madhu and Sanjam sat near each other in the bonfire and talked while their friends were happy to see them amiably together. That day, finally, Sanjam and Madhu asked each other about their reasons for joining the Band. Sanjam told the same story that he and his friends said while entering the Band. Madhu, too, shared the story that Sanjam and his friends had already discovered.

"I want to ask you something, but I am afraid that that would offend you," Sanjam said.

"Why do you say so? Do you want to know my age?" Madhu joked.

He shook his head with laughter. "No, see, I may be wrong," he started. "During the initial days, I used to feel that you and Chitra looked at me peculiarly. So, what is the secret behind that? Or was it just my misunderstanding?"

Madhu blushed and giggled. After remaining briefly quiet, she replied,"Let me be honest; you remind me of someone. I mean, you have a resemblance with someone."

"Oh, is it so? I hope you don't have bad memories with that person."

"Well, it's complicated. I don't have any memory of that person. The fact is, I haven't even met him!"

"Ah! So you are pulling my leg." Sanjam did not believe her.

"No, I swear to you. I haven't met that person, and yet there is a connection with him. I would tell all about it, but someday later. Is that okay?" She ended her sentence with a sweet yet pleading expression.

Sanjam happily nodded. He understood that the distance of the last few weeks between himself and her only helped them come closer. He looked at the stars in the clear sky and thanked them in his heart for bestowing him with an incredible friend in Madhu.

***

The following day Sanjam's friends noticed that he was in some self-introspection and a little sad. After avoiding their interrogation initially, he eventually shared his thoughts. He said that he was unhappy about having to lie to Madhu about his identity. She was a dear friend of his and he hated lying to her. Unfortunately, his duty barred him from sharing the truth that he was a spy. His friends consoled him that once they completed their mission's objectives, he could share his identity with her and help her see the accurate picture of the Band as well. Sanjam instantly agreed to that.

***

Madhu was also in a dilemma, just like Sanjam.

"I feel so terrible lying to him about myself. Since inducting into the Band, I know we have said this same story about our lives to everyone. But lying to a friend, a true friend is not correct," Madhu confessed before Chitra.

"I concur. But Sanjam is a loyal Band member. Someone who believes and supports their ideologies. Telling him about our reason for joining the Band may make it a dilemma for him. And what would he choose in that dilemma; friendship or duty and loyalty? I suggest you should know him more, and if he is someone who can see the authentic picture of Band, you can tell him the truth about yourself."

Madhu found wisdom in her friend's logic. "You always clear things for me, my love. I should idolize you."

"Oh, wait, I have something for you," Chitra broke the embrace and walked to a trunk containing her belongings. She searched for some time and then stood in front of Madhu with a manuscript. "Now that you said about idolizing, I remembered about this. You had asked me for this manuscript when we headed to join the Band. I managed to find the book but forgot to give it to you. Look, here is the biography of your idol."

Madhu's eyes widened as she grabbed the book. Then, involuntarily, her eyes turned wet as she moved her right palm over the cover of the book and murmured its title, "My Life Tale – Banasura." Also, in her mind, Madhu decided to read portions of the book every night before sleeping.

BANASURA

I wasn't born on Earth. Instead, my birth realm was called Ashishloka. It was paradise, a true blessing of God's creative prowess. The entire landmass was full of innumerable natural caves that had sizeable holes in them for ventilation. Those caves were residences of the people in the realm. Every cave was also surrounded by trees and plants that grew independently and needed little external care. Most of those trees and plants had edible fruits and vegetables with great nutritious value. A gentle and teasing breeze blew incessantly in the realm. There were even some rivers and many ponds and streams here and there that provided clean drinking water. The place was truly magical. However, while growing up there, I had two complaints. One, there were only three more kids in the whole realm with whom I could play and have fun. Two, I missed my father because those kids had their fathers with them. My mother had told me that my father was an extraordinary ruler of someplace, but he died early. Post his death, the Gods took his soul to live with the Trimurtis and blessed us to stay in Ashishloka. I was proud that my father's greatness allowed us to live in such a blissful and comforting place.I'd have but lived happily even in some uncomfortable environment if my father was with us.

As I grew up, my interest diverted into weapons and warfare. There was an elderly learned man, Prahlad Ji, who lived near our cave. Every morning he would start practicing the wielding of primary weapons and then conjure powerful magical weapons. He was so gifted that he created temporary spaces where the miraculous artilleries would land or blast. I wanted to learn those techniques and abilities and hence requested him to teach me. He denied it several times for many years. But Prahlad Ji loved me as if I was someone of his own. On my fifteenth birthday, when he asked me what I desired as a gift, I asked for his tutelage. He finally agreed to teach me the art of warfare and combat.

Prahlad Ji praised that I was a quick learner. By the next four years, I had mastered the ability to fight using all categories of divine weapons. Like him, even I could create a duplicate space with my energies. Prahlad Ji bestowed the title of Maharathi upon me as well. However, I was not satisfied with whatever I had learned. I wanted to gain more prowess and skills. I was in particular interested in sorcery, but Prahlad Ji did not know sorcery. The person in our realm who had mastered sorcery was Yakshrajan Ji. He was a feeble, older man who kept mostly to his cave. I had been to his cave many times and served him as he was sick. Once helping him with small tasks in the cave, I stumbled upon his treasure – a box containing books on magic and some paraphernalia that helped perform enchantments. I took them with me and decided to learn things myself, no matter how long it took me. I just hoped that he never found out about my theft.

Chapter 6

Coming Closer

The Band Cluster had planned a big loot. The target was a factory that manufactured expensive artifacts using gems, rubies, and gold. As it was a high-value factory, both private guards and soldiers of the Magadh royalty guarded it. Right at the start, the factory's main entrance had a few security personnel, who were ever vigilant and competent to thwart any ambush. The second tier of security was a line of sentinels standing from some feet away after crossing the main entrance and covering the ground till the gate of the factory building. Again, inside the factory, the employed archers used poisonous darts that made their targets unconscious. It allowed them to freely shoot as even if they hit the factory workers, they would only be senseless for some prahars.

With extensive security, it was challenging to plan a heist in the factory. However, the cluster's Pradhan asked everyone to develop some scheme, no matter how bizarre it sounded. Many came up with plans, but the Band sanctioned the plan devised by Madhu-Chitra and Sanjam's company.

On the heist day, a team of fourteen Band members was ready, including Sanjam and his friends and Madhu and Chitra. All of them were great with their aims and handled spears commendably well. They put on saffron robes. The men wore long, unkempt fake beards, and even the women put on a layer of some substance on their body skin. The material made their skin appear dry and coarse. They also took several sacred paraphernalia with them. Four men carried a medium-sized idol of Ganesha on a wooden palanquin, and the other men had musical instruments like dhols and nagaras. The women held brass utensils, emitting smokes from the burning dammars in them. Singing sermons, the group walked through the streets that went to the factory location.

The team of fourteen reached near the factory land in the late afternoon. They executed the plan as soon as they were opposite the main gate. Adhering to their arrangement, one of the group's ladies, Meena, acted ill. She shortened her breaths short, trembled her body, and complained that she had a dry throat and felt unconscious. Other members of the group panicked and shouted for help. That place had no residences or commercial establishments apart from the factory in the immediate vicinity. So, as the guards at the main entrance saw the chaos, two among them came and inquired the group about their distress. The two guards felt convinced that the lady was very sick and quickly brought water for her. Sometime later, the lady appeared better, and it was time to execute the second part of the heist plan.

The group informed the gatekeepers that they wereGanesh devotees traveling from a faraway place and heading to a famous Vighnaharta Mandir. They added that they offered prasad to people on the street and tied sacred threads with tiny Ganesha-shaped bells on them. They insisted that the people in the factory also accept the prasad and bells, particularly because the guards had selflessly helped Meena. However, the gatekeepers denied it repeatedly.

One of the gate guards said, "We are here at duty. We aren't allowed to have anything from outside during working hours. Moreover, we cannot allow anyone to enter the factory premises. If we do so, we shall lose our jobs."

Madhu walked forward to talk with the guards. "*Mahashaya*, we understand your security concern. We shall first eat a bit of the prasad before you to ensure that it is safe. And you can allow just a lady to enter the factory premises, escorted by two, three, or as many guards as you want. She knows the mantras, and she would chant them quickly while giving the prasad and tying those tiny sacred threads. Please allow us to do this and express our gratefulness for your help. Without your help, Meena might have fainted, and that'd have forced us to halt in some medical unit, thereby corrupting our sacred travel. We do not rest anywhere and continue walking during the day. Such is our prayer."

The guards pondered over Madhu's logic and agreed to the group's request. Then, Madhu ate bits of a prasad, asking one of the guards to pick it randomly. Next, Sundari, one of the other ladies in the team, went inside with two guards. One of the guards carried a bag of bells, and she held a tray of prasad. It took her some time to return, and she signaled that she had completed her task successfully. It was now time to implement the penultimate step of the heist.

The team kept the palanquin over a rock on the roadside. The guards saw that and were confused. In no time, the team pulled out spears from the palanquin. Some of them also dropped several tiny metallic balls into the burning dammars. Then they first launched three of the dammar burning utensils inside the gate. Those metallic balls were inventions of the Band. They caused a vast air of smoke to emerge out, and the guards inside swiftly lost their senses. The team covered their face with clothes that had the eye portions cut out already. Then they stormed the entrance and continued the smoke attack. Once inside the factory, they used all of the smoke-emitting balls and were ready with their spears. While many of the guards were senseless, and the smoke blinded the rest. Yet, the blinded archers attempted random attacks. However, they had those tiny bells on them that made noises. Aided by those sounds, the team attacked the guards with the non-pointy end of the spears. The goal was to neutralize them and loot the factory. People supported them more when they made loot without killing and gave parts of the ransack to the general masses.

After entrapping the soldiers and sentinels inside the establishment, the group put many valuables inside sacks and walked out. They escaped the township area as devotees without raising any suspicion and soon took the forest routes. Patrolling teams within a prahar discovered the heist, but the team was in the safe zone by then.

When the group reached the cluster, the Band members welcomed them with celebration and appreciation. Soon, a festive-like mood took over them, and the next evening a fête was held. It had different meats, food items, liquor, and weed.

***

"So you, too, don't drink liquor?" Madhu asked Sanjam.

"No, although I have tried it a couple of times. I'm not too fond of the bitter taste. Have you tried it?"

"Umm…yes, a few times. But even I don't enjoy the taste or even the intoxication."

Everyone was sitting around the fire. The members sang, danced, shared jokes, and ate heartily. Even the Pradhan and Mahat Guru sat with the recruits that night and enjoyed the ambiance. Between their talks, Madhu excused herself from Sanjam. She had to clear her bladder. So she went some distance away, and while returning, Brinjaldesh stunned her. He was visibly drunk and had a cunning smile on his face. His look disgusted her, and he stood in a way that blocked her path.

"Brinjal, get out of my way before I lose my cool," Madhu responded sternly.

"Oh, my dear, why are you so rude to me? I am here to speak good things, b..b....beautiful things. You know I have something for you." He searched inside a pocket on his kurta and pulled out a diamond. "This is my collection. I found it in my last participated loot. And I got it only and only for you, my dear." He went to his knees, wobbling, and laughed at his state.

"I love you, sweetheart," professing his love, he offered the diamond to Madhu.

Madhu had no interest in him, but his romantic proposal in an intoxicated state made him even more repulsive to her. "Brinjaldesh, thank you for making this offer, but I deny the diamond and your love proposal, both. Even if you were not drunk, my answer would have been the same; but proposing in a drunken state is not amusing for me. Good luck with your life, and let's not remain even acquaintances." Madhu walked away from him and did not look back.

Brinjal, however, looked at her with rage-filled eyes, and his sight fixated on her swaying hips. Then, licking his lips, he said to himself, "Even a diamond can't get me between those globes, huh? You consider yourself so valuable, hmm? I swear I shall tear into your orifices and taste how delicious that hole between those hips is!" He touched and rubbed his penis over his dhoti, closing his eyes.Immediately the ecstasy of liquor and lust took over him, and he ejaculated in the next few moments.

***

Madhu did not share the incident with anyone; she decided to ignore and forget it. But, it was easier said than done. She noticed that he used to ogle at her body and tried to find her somewhere alone. Madhu was tolerant, but she realized it would only encourage him. So, she was determined to confront him the next time she noticed him stalking.

One twilight, as the moon surfaced in the sky and emitted its dim light, Madhu started practicing archery. She wanted to be better at hitting targets in less visibility. She was focused entirely on her task and did not hear footsteps approaching her. Abruptly, she felt a push, and she fell to the ground, hurting her forehead. Next, she felt a sharp pain in the back of her head. Someone pushed something blunt roughly against her head. She screamed through the impending dizziness and felt her eyes close when suddenly, someone violently grabbed her hips. Someone was pressing and kneading her hips and spanking them hard. Madhu willed through the pain and suddenly found some energy and struggled to move. Unfortunately, the body over her was heavier, and she found it difficult to escape. She felt fingers moving in the space between her hips, over the cloth material. Then she heard the man speak. It was Brinjaldesh as she had expected. "This is what you will get now. My penis, fingers, tongue, and nose will be inside your orifices soon, and then I shall have to cut you into small pieces. Had you accepted my proposal, you too could have enjoyed my thick and long friend." Brinjaldesh eerily laughed out and started inhaling Madhu's neck and gave bites on the neck.

Madhu somehow managed to free her left hand and looked to grab anything on the ground. Fortunately, she found something, but it was only a tiny pebble. She grasped it and hastily pinched Brinjal's neck with it. Feeling hurt slightly, Brinjal moved his left palm to caress his neck. Madhu took that opportunity and swiftly turned him over after an elbow to his abdomen. She also followed it with two more hard elbow shots in the same place. Brinjaldesh coughed and coiled in pain. Madhu experienced a sudden adrenaline rush and leaped to her feet and clutched a log lying nearby.

Brinjaldesh was stubborn and evil. Without giving up, he rose to his feet and pulled out a knife from his boots. He growled. "If not with you, then I shall have sex with your corpse, but I won't leave you!"

Madhu, despite the pain and trauma, retaliated, "You filth! You keep that knife down and surrender yourself. In that case, the Band will do your justice, and you may have a chance to live. If you raise that knife at me, I swear I shall not care even if you die."

Brinjal laughed like a madman hearing her. "This ain't a contest or a brawl. It's a street fight, ruthless and dirty." With those words, he rushed at her with the knife. She dodged a couple of his attempts, but the third attempt cut her on her lower stomach. That cut made Madhu sure that he would kill her. So, she launched her counter-attacks. Her attacks were technical and precise. Initially, she allowed him to be the aggressor. He made multiple attempts to stab her, but she moved away every time and hit him repeatedly on his back and torso with the log. Then she kicked his knees and finally broke his legs with hammerings of the tree-log.

Even with broken legs, Brinjal launched the knife at her, and she ducked. He screamed, wailed, and laughed hysterically. "I shall rape you! Even if you kill me, I shall do it as a ghost. How dare you deny my love proposal? What is your future? You girls as Band members are to find no love, no family, no pleasure. Yet you think you are a damsel? I swear; the day I can walk on my knees, I shall again find you and rape you!"

"You are a psycho," Madhu screamed out and rammed the log twice on his chest. He coughed out a pool of blood, and his breaths narrowed. His body slowly became immobile, but he yet made a sinister smile at her. During his dying moments, his friends and Chitra arrived at the spot.

Madhu had killed her attacker, but the entire episode was harrowing for her. His words echoed in her mind. His laughter lingered in her heart. His touches and fondles left imprints on her soul.

***

Sanjam and his friends and the entire Band had learned of the incident. Madhu was in her hut with Chitra and some other ladies. Sanjam or his friends had not yet met her as they thought it was better that only ladies consoled and cared her for some time. On the other hand, Brinjal's friends and allies refused to believe that Brinjal attempted to rape or kill Madhu. They stressed that Madhu must have lost her temper in some petty issue and killed him. They even propagated that the two had a rivalry, and Madhu was short-tempered. They asked for a trial to find the truth and protested against burning the corpse until the hearing was over.

The Pradhan and Mahat Guru were in a dilemma. They trusted Madhu and her words but also understood that this incident might take a different turn. In addition, a representative of the Band's supreme authority was due to visit the cluster in the next few days. If there were any protest then, even by a handful of members, the supreme command would lose faith in the Pradhan. But they wanted to ensure that Madhu could be proved innocent and acquitted before agreeing to a trial. They were busy deliberating on those matters when Sanjam sought permission to enter the Pradhan's tent. He had mentioned it was about the hearing. The Pradhan so allowed him entry.

"*Pranam*, Pradhan Ji, I wish to tell you that you need not worry about the trial. I have seen the body and can certainly say that I will prove lady Madhu innocent. Although standing trial for this justified murder is an insult to her, yet let us get done with it. I also have things to say that the ones demanding this trial must listen. However, I do have a request; once she is proved innocent, you must send the friends of Brinjal to the Band prison in the forests of Chedi."

The Pradhan, Mahat, and other seniors of the cluster looked at each other, and nobody had any issue with Sanjam's words. The Pradhan then declared, "Alright. But if you fail to prove her innocence without any doubt, it will be you who will go to Chedi."

Sanjam nodded and agreed.

"What do you think, Mahat Ji?" the Pradhan asked as soon as Sanjam had left.

"Pradhan Ji, I see that he is confident. He is a wise and intelligent fellow. So, I believe, he will get her acquitted."

***

"I am sorry, Madhu. I agreed on your behalf to your trial without even consulting you. But trust me, I shall prove your innocence. You defended yourself against a crime, and you must be strong enough to answer any question about your action. Not only you but every girl is entitled to defend herself against sexual violence, and this trial would help validate it."

Sanjam's words were comforting and motivating for Madhu. She managed a smile after a long time. "I have no issue to stand on this trial. I am happier that it's you who will be defending me. You are a good man, Sanjam." Madhu took one of Sanjam's hands into her own. The warmth of their hands was more assuring than words right now.

***

The day of the trial arrived soon. It was taking place inside the Pradhan's tent. Five of Brinjal's friends were allowed inside, and on the opposite side, there was Chitra, Sanjam, and seven others who got the chance to be present in the trial via lottery. They voluntarily supported Madhu. Presiding over the proceeding was Pradhan and another senior member. Mahat Guru had excused himself from it.

Madhu stood in the tent's center, between the judges' table and the spot where Sanjam and his opposite representative stood.

The representative opposite Sanjam was Hasthi. He had volunteered to speak on behalf of Brinjal's supporters. The two-member jury asked him to start with his viewpoints first.

"Greetings to the jury. I speak on behalf of many of us who believe that the accused murdered Brinjaldesh in cold blood. In the last few days, there have been many instances where Brinjaldesh confronted her. He thought that she received excessive praise, and since being the chief assistant trainer, her attitude towards other trainers had changed. And we believe, that evening too, during such a confrontation, she lost her temper and brutally but slowly killed him, injuring him repeatedly. I can call as many as ten witnesses who would testify about the look-down attitude of the accused upon other trainers. Some of them have also witnessed the confrontations between the accused and the dead victim."

Hasthi summoned ten recruits, one after another, who validated his accusations. Sanjam did not doubt that those ten were male chauvinists who hated and envied Madhu for her recent successes and spoke against her. Sanjam then requested the Pradhan to go out of the tent and handpick ten more random men. He made the picks, and Sanjam interrogated them about Madhu's attitude towards them and others in general. Those men spoke the truth and accepted that Madhu was kind and competent. They informed the jury that Madhu taught and aptly mentored the recruits and was always encouraging. They even added that she was humble and helpful.

"So, there can be two things. Either your witnesses lied in front of the jury or had some personal issues with Lady Madhu. The consensus, however, speaks of Madhu's humble nature. Hence, I believe the jury cannot believe the words of a few witnesses called by you. Yes, if you can randomly choose some more people and they too speak against Madhu, the jury can trust your previous witnesses." Sanjam's argument put Hasthi in a fix. He was not confident what random trainees would say, and so he remained silent.

Sanjam continued, "Right after the incident, everyone had seen Madhu's injury on the back of her head and a stabbing wound on her lower torso. On the contrary, the corpse of Brinjaldesh has no such injury mark that indicates anyone attacking him from behind. So, Brinjaldesh carried a knife with him, and he also assaulted Lady Madhu on the back of her head. The fact is, he had been stalking her for several days, and finally, he attempted to rape her. When he couldn't overpower and violate her, he went berserk and decided to kill her. Why? Because she defended herself against a rape!"

The tent was mum. There was an awkward and morbid stillness in it. Madhu's eyes were moist, but she continued to look at the jury members with strong and intense eyes.

Hasthi was nervous and yet he attempted to make some more arguments.

"Respected jury, if she was trying to defend herself, she could have killed him in a few blows. Instead, she hurt him many times with the log, broke his knees, and then rained blows on his chest to kill him. I ask, what was the necessity to kill him when he was already rendered immobile with broken knees?"

Before Sanjam could again make his counter-argument, Madhu spoke up this time. "I killed him because he promised me to rape and hurt me once he was able to walk again. His failure to rape and hurt me would fuel anger against other girls, and never a girl would be safe near him. You must understand that only in rare instances would a woman falsely mention that someone attempted to rape her. And I took part in this trial only to let everyone know that I made no such false claim." Madhu managed to hold herself back from wailing and looked at Hasthi with ghost-like eyes and screamed out, "To prove myself innocent, I am even willing to take off my clothes and show his handprint and other bruises on my private parts. No matter what, I shall prove today that he indeed tried to rape me!"

As Madhu's screams subsided, everyone inside the tent froze with blank expressions on their faces.

After allowing some moments to Madhu, Sanjam carried on with his reasoning. "Your late friend, Brinjaldesh, even told Madhu how you all claimed possessions for yourselves while making loots in the name of the Band. He also offered her a diamond from such a raid. So while you are in this tent, I firmly believe that if Pradhan Ji now sends men to look into your huts, they will find many such belongings. Now you tell me if Brinjaldesh had not made that revelation to her, how would we know of your thefts?"

"Is that true?" the Pradhan sternly asked Hasthi.

Hasthi was trapped. He couldn't lie nor speak the truth, and so he preferred to say nothing.

"Speak up, you bastard! If you confess you live, else you die!" the Pradhan bellowed and stood up from his chair.

Hasthi quickly went to his knees and started begging for mercy. "Please forgive us, Pradhan Ji. We never took anything much, but only one or two small objects. It was Brinjal's idea anyway. Everything has always been Brinjal's idea. He lusted after Lady Madhu and wanted to enjoy her in bed, and when he realized that wouldn't happen, ever, he decided to rape her." With slight pressure mounting on him, Hasthi crumbled. He could no longer stick to his lies and ended up confessing the truth.

Sanjam's gamble had worked. When Madhu had informed him about Brinjaldesh offering her a diamond from one of the raids, he guessed that even his mates must do the same. And he was right. His gamble and intellect proved that Madhu was indeed innocent.

***

Once Madhu was proven innocent, some trainees sought apologies from her because they had doubted her innocence. However, others, especially many women in the Band, praised her for her strength to stand trial. Despite those positives, it took Madhu almost a month to get back to normalcy. To help her feel better, Chitra, Sanjam, and his friends made several attempts. They went out several times into townships and roamed around among people.

Sanjam also helped her learn to shoot in dim light to divert her attention to new things. She was left astounded to know that he was able to perform archery almost blindly. She asked him how he could manage it, and Sanjam told her he would reveal it but someday in the future. "Maybe, the day you reveal who I resemble like?" he joked.

***

"And now I am entirely convinced that Sanjam is not someone ordinary. He is here for some atypical reason, just like us," Madhu shared her thoughts with Chitra.

"I won't disagree with you. I feel that everyone in Sanjam's group is not actually who they claim to be. Even Samar seems so learned, progressive in thoughts, and wise."

"Sanjam hinted that he has secrets that he would share someday with me. I am just desperately waiting for that day," Madhu paused."On the other hand, I can also sense that something significant is going to happen in the Band."

"Maybe you are right. I have noticed Mahat Ji, Pradhan, and other seniors meeting regularly and having profound discussions. I wonder what they are up to."

"Hmm... Anyway, I am thinking of gifting something to Sanjam. It would be a token of appreciation and gratefulness for standing with me during my most difficult phase." Madhu sheepishly grinned.

"Ohoo, is it? What are you going to gift?"

"I have been working with our cluster's weapon experts and making a sword. I shall gift him a nice sword, along with some words of poetry."

"He will certainly love your gifts," Chitra assured her animatedly.

***

Four days later, Madhu was ready with both her gifts. She called Sanjam to meet her where they had first seen each other. Madhu reached first and was spirited and restless. She was curious to see how Sanjam would react. She had high hopes that he would love the gifts greatly and feel emotionally involved with them. At the same time, she was anxious, thinking, what if he did not react the way she had expected?

Sanjam had finally arrived. He apologized for keeping her waiting and was curious to see her holding something behind her.

"Sanjam, the way you supported and soothed me after that incident, I have no words to thank you. I can't even imagine how terrible it'd have been for me if you weren't there. You took a huge responsibility upon yourself by determining to defend me. And I could see those days you were as worried and stressed as I was. So I wanted to thank you nicely and....," Madhu stopped without finishing the sentence.

"And?" Sanjam asked with inquisitiveness.

"Well, I have a couple of gifts for you," she blushed.

"What?" Sanjam asked with his eyes widened and excitement visible on his face.

Madhu liked the facial expression, and she confidently showed her gifts. She was holding a glittering, polished sword with a gold-colored handle. She had customized the handle in the shape of an eagle's head. "I have made this for you. Of course, I took help from our experts here, but the efforts and design were mine."

Sanjam was speechless. He took the sword from Madhu's hands, turning it over and looking at the hilt, his eyes blinking with tears of happiness."Madhu, you've crafted it so well! And I can't imagine the labors behind this. This is one of the best gifts in my life. I shall always keep the sword by my side and use it against any form of injustice."

Madhu smiled wide at his words and folded her hands together. "Thank God, you loved it. I was thinking how you'd react. Anyway, I have another thing for you." She quickly pulled out a rolled fabric piece from her trouser pocket. "It's a poem," she handed it to him.

Sanjam opened the letter and read it.

"Your might is not merely in your arms and shoulders; it's in your heart.

Your actions are not alone inspired by your mind but also your soul,

You can conquer people not with fear but by winning over their hearts.

You see and hear things concealed to the ordinary eyes and ears;

You feel emotions that cannot always be expressed!

I know there are more things in you that I am yet unaware of,

I know you are not entirely the one I know you to be thus far;

And I also know that; the day I shall know you completely

It'd only make me more happy, proud, and grateful.

The Heaven will bless you with more prowess,

The earth shall witness your more noble deeds.

And whenever you are in any trouble or feel lonely,

I promise to stand with you, resolutely!"

The poetry made Sanjam realize how much Madhu felt connected with him. He wanted to tell her a million things, but he stammered somewhat as he said, "Madhu, anyone would feel lucky to have someone who is so emotional and wishes so good for him. I do not know the correct words to say now, but I find strength in every word you wrote; and if ever I feel distressed again in life, these words will be the remedy. Thank you, thank you very much."

He wanted to embrace her, and she, too, desired to feel the comfort and warmth of his arms. But both were still hesitant to speak out their raw emotions without any inhibition. So they kept quiet, but even that silence filled their hearts and souls with passion.

***

KAMBOJA CAPITAL

UNIVERSITY OF INVENTIONS AND SOCIAL SCIENCES

Shri Krishna was in one of his final few public appearances. He wanted to speak at a few selected advanced educational institutes, particularly ones that were diverse and had students from various kingdoms. The University of Inventions and Social Sciences was one of the institutes that fit the criteria.

In his speech in front of the students, Krishna spoke about dharma, karma, well-being, positive attitude, and motivation. He also heard their issues and accepted requests for more budgets for experiments and research. In addition, Krishna also inaugurated a new research wing in the University. Furthermore, he wanted development and progress to be more eco-friendly; hence, he stressed increased research and development to make infrastructure and inventions ecological. Towards the end of his session, he took questions. Many students wished to know what the deaths of great people like Bhisma and Drona inferred.

Krishna started to elucidate his views. "Bhisma was invincible. He was virtually immortal, as you all know. He could only be defeated because he accepted his death as a penance for the misjudgments in his life. Bhisma Pitamah misinterpreted dharma. He made his vow to serve Hastinapur's throne the only dharma of his life. So, he stood by Duryodhana's evil acts every time. He failed to understand that not breaking his vow for the greater good was an act of selfishness. And when he realized that during the war of Kurukshetra, he accepted his death as a penance. He wanted his defeat and death in the war because he believed it'd be a lesson for the generations to come.

"Drona, too, realized his wrongs during the Kurukshetra. The uncertainty of one's life in war makes one more self-assured of his right and wrong acts done in the lifetime. He understood that all his good actions were on one side, but the blind love for his son made him encourage several evil deeds. Like, he knew of an attack upon Arjuna planned by his son and Kauravas. He should have taken appropriate action against that plotting even though he was confident that Arjuna could protect himself. Similarly, he did not stop Samragini Draupadi's disrobing because his son had emotionally blackmailed him. If you cannot choose to go against your family, even after knowing that they are engaging in massive wrongdoings, you are a part of their sins."

The students were so pleased and impressed with Vasudeva's visit and interaction that everyone sought his blessing by touching his feet. Some even had made gifts for Krishna that he gladly accepted.

The public appearances had undeniably increased people's trust in Krishna and the entire establishment. The realm once again began strongly supporting and rallying behind the regime.

BANASURA

It took me some years to secretly gain mastery over magic. I was twenty-five by then. After I was confident enough about using any supernatural powers, I decided to allow my soul to roam beyond the realm of Ashishloka through astral projection. I had learned astral projection from the books of Yakshrajan Ji and even performed it a few times, but allowed my soul to travel only within our realm. I desired to travel beyond our place and see the rest of the space for the first time.

The process of astral projection was complex and required precision and much focus. As step one, I had to meditate and allow only one thought in my mind and heart; I wanted to move temporarily beyond Ashishloka and witness the most populated and unique realm in the space. Then, I had to hold my breath until my soul went out of my physical form in the next step. Once the soul went out of the body and roamed with liberty, I could feel whatever the soul witnessed and sensed.

My soul went far away and transcended the boundaries of our realm. It returned at some point with new experiences and insights, and I learned several things.

Ashishloka was a tiny region geographically. Once outside it, my soul found that Ashishloka was in someplace dark and dull. Any place that existed and could sustain life must have a solar system, natural satellite, and specific energies surrounding it. But our realm had none of those things. My soul went even further and saw Swarga and Patala, sustaining within their individual solar systems. More distance away, there was the planet of Earth. My soul traveled on Earth and fortunately discovered statues and paintings of my late father, Mahabali. With all these discoveries, I knew there were many things that I hardly knew.

To know more about what I had found out, I confronted my mother and Prahlad Ji. They were astounded to learn about my mastery over sorcery, but they realized they could no longer hide things from me.

I learned about my origins and the true story of my father from them. My father, Mahabali, was an Asura king. He was the son of Virochana, and Virochana was the son of none other than Prahlad Ji. I was dumbfounded knowing that Prahlad Ji was my great-grandfather, and in all these years, I had no hint about it.

Our ancestry was regal, and we ruled over certain land territories on Earth. My father trained himself into an able and unparalleled warrior. He was also an equally proficient statesman. When he was the Crown Prince, he conquered territories habituated by barbaric tribes. He helped them civilize and turned them into subjects of his empire. Years later, when my father became the King, he launched revolutionary policies that strengthened our empire's economic and political foundations. Consequently, the Asura empire prospered, and my father discovered a new land that was as beautiful as heaven. Naming it Keralam, he established his capital there and ruled as a great leader.

The growing popularity and strength of my father envied the human rulers and nobility. Historically, Asura rulers were not benevolent, but my father, grandfather, and great-grandfather were exceptions. However, the mortal kings united against my father and warned him not to conquer any more territory. My father reasoned that he had never subjugated any land with righteous rulers, and he won't ever do so. But he also warned those kings not to command him. Enraged and feeling insecure, the human kings made several plots to overthrow and assassinate my father. To end such actions against himself and to rule better, father launched wars against the opposite kings. He proposed one-on-one duels with the kings, but they denied. So battles became imminent, and soon father defeated all the kings and became the emperor of Aryavrata and beyond.

After my father became the emperor, the Asuras of Patal Loka invited him to rule over their realm as well. They wanted him to conquer Swarga as the king of Asuras. My father, however, denied it, as he viewed the Devas' concept of creation and its sustainability as correct. But then the Asuras proposed, they would abide by his views and laws if he conquered Swarga. In that way, the Asuras would be following the decent philosophies of the Devas. All they wanted was to break the arrogance of the Devas. They even reasoned that Mahabali could end the age-old conflict between the Asuras and Devas. My father accepted those rationalities and, after a prolonged war, managed to conquer Swarga. He thus had suzerainty over Earth, Patala, and Swarga.

Indra yet ruled Swarga and the Devas continued their administration independently. Mahabali, my father, never interfered in their ways and matters. He was merely the official head of the realm.

Some years later, a dwarf Brahman arrived at the doorsteps of my father's palace in Keralam. My mother was then pregnant with me in her womb. My father welcomed him and served him sincerely with impeccable hospitality. He ended up promising the Brahman to donate anything that he requested. Little did my father then know of the Brahman's reality! Upon receiving the promise, the Brahman manifested himself into a giant shape. He kept on growing, and his expanded frame started demolishing the palace and things inside it. The Brahman then revealed himself to be an Avatar of Vishnu and said, "Rajan, I intend to grow into a colossal size. I shall continue to increase my body unless merely by three steps of my feet, I can measure the realms of Earth, Swarga, and Patala. All the three domains are yours, and once I measure them, I desire to seek them from you as my alms. You have vowed to donate me anything I ask, and I shall ask for the space of three feet of my titanic size."

My father was noble and a dedicated Vishnu devotee. Hence, his reply to the Vamana avatar was, "O Lord, I do not realize what mistake I have made, but I've understood that you wish me to give up my suzerainty over the realms I rule. O Great Vishnu, I have no greed to rule. I give up my right over each sphere, but I plead you not to turn into a super-massive size. That would hurt the creation and destroy the realms."

The Vamana Avatar had tricked my father and took back whatever territories he owned. After snatching everything from my father, the Vamana revealed that as the Preserver and Protector of the Devas, he could not refuse to help the Devas. The Devas had sought Vishnu's aid to end Mahabali's rule on the argument that even though my father was a benevolent Asura king but unbeknownst to him, the Asuras from Patal Loka carried out tyrannical acts. Further, the Devas reasoned that there was no guarantee if Mahabali's posterities, who would also have rights over Earth and Swarga, would be benevolent or not. Moreover, even though, Mahabali governed his conquered territories, including Swarga, righteously; yet he invaded territories. So, he was an invader, even though a generous one.

My father accepted Vishnu's actions against him and requested Vishnu to take him to his abode, Vaikuntha. Father also wanted mother and me to lead a comfortable and wonderful life. The Vamana Avatar of Vishnu agreed. Accordingly, he took my father to Vaikuntha and sent us to Ashishloka.

Ashishloka, a celestial region in some part of the Universe, was located in a galaxy yet entirely born. Nevertheless, it sustained and survived with the Trimurti Gods' energies and magic constantly working. When the solar system around Ashishloka would fully appear, our realm would explode. Until then, selected people who had lived extraordinary lives on earth and worked for others' welfare remarkably lived in Ashishloka for ages. My great-grandfather, Prahlad Ji, was one such remarkable man, and so was Yaksharajan Ji, the first-ever Yaksha king on earth.

Now that I had learned the truths about myself and my ancestry, I wanted to gain back whatever was rightfully mine. The Devas and Vishnu may have tricked my father to ensure the safety and betterment of the creation, but I couldn't accept the deceit and injustice against my just father. So I left a letter for my mother and landed on Earth using my sorcery ability. I had goals to accomplish on Earth.

Entering earth, I realized that the twenty-five years in Ashishloka was equivalent to several centuries on the planet.

Chapter 7

Revelations

"I have some vital information," Palan announced to his friends. "The representative from the supreme authority of Band had come to instruct about some collective sieges."

"Sieges?" Sanjam asked.

"The Band's supreme authority has planned multiple fort sieges in various kingdoms by the different Band clusters. They want to seize arms and weapons, stocks of grains, and treasures of gold. Undoubtedly, something massive is imminent."

"Do you know the target kingdoms for the sieges?" Sanjam asked again.

"I overheard a few names; Vidharbha, Panchal, Andhra. Our cluster would target Matsya and Surasena kingdoms, that's for sure."

"All right! I shall covertly send in a pigeon and call a trusted man to meet me in some days." Sanjam stated and sat on a table to write a coded letter right away.

***

On the designated day, Sanjam went out in the morning to meet his confidant in an eatery in the nearest city. But before he could move out of the woods, a Band member met him and engaged with him in a casual conversation. Eager to get away,

Sanjam, by mistake, left a bag that he was carrying with him. Coincidentally, Madhu saw Sanjam leave without the bag. The previous day, Sanjam had informed her that he was going to the nearest town and buy some necessary stuff. Madhu thought it'd be difficult for him without the bag, so she followed him to hand it over. Halfway, she thought of secretly tailing him and surprising him in the market.

It was a long walk from the interior of the woods to the township. As Madhu knew the way to the town, so she did not walk close behind Sanjam. The two walked for almost a prahar and a half and finally reached the city market. Madhu noticed Sanjam being more cautious; he kept a consistent vigilance around himself. He continued walking casually here and there, and sometime later, she saw him enter a crowded eatery.

Sanjam sat on a table that had two chairs on opposite sides. Madhu, mystified by Sanjam's atypical mannerisms, decided not to reveal herself. Instead, she sat on a packed table nearby and kept a watch on him. A few moments passed, and then she noticed a man dressed in typical city attire walking towards Sanjam. However, Sanjam quickly stood up and left the place. The man took another seat. Madhu was perplexed and immediately walked out.

She searched for Sanjam outside in the market area but could not find him. Disheartened, she lazily stood near a narrow alley when someone pulled her inside the alleyway. Madhu naturally tried to defend herself. She elbowed the attacker on his chest and swiftly turned behind, ready to deliver a punch. She abruptly paused.

"Sanjam?" she yelled.

"Are you tailing me, Madhu?" an equally stunned Sanjam inquired.

"Yes and no," she replied.

"What are you doing here?"

"I saw you leaving from our hideout and noticed that you left behind the bag that you were carrying. I wondered it might be difficult for you to bring back your stuff without the bag. So, I wanted to give it to you but then thought why don't I join you in shopping. "I wanted to surprise you and give you your bag back, but—"

"Madhu, Madhu, you shouldn't have followed me!" Sanjam interrupted as he walked away from her and leaned against a wall.

Madhu stood in front of him, and in a low and quivering voice, asked, "Sanjam, I swear I had no intention to follow you or anything. If you say, I shall go away right now and never ask you anything about today."

Sanjam removed his hands from his face and took some long breaths to calm down. "Okay, let me tell you the truth. Pradhan Ji has sent me to fulfill a crucial task. A learned Maharshi, Gyanandram, resides in the illustrious Vishnu Temple of this city. My task is to kill him secretly tonight and dump his corpse in the market."

Madhu stared at him incredulously. "What? Why?"

Sanjam sighed again, and without any remorse, spoke, "He enjoys enormous reverence from the masses. Hence, his murder would anger the people and make them distrust the administration and government. Pradhan Ji and the central Band command have planned to fuel that anger and distrust and cause severe unrest and protest against the reigning regime."

"But why? The Band claims to be the near-perfect political option for the entire subcontinent; then how can they kill an innocent sage and encourage violent uprising among the public?"

"Madhu, in great revolutions, some collateral damages are unavoidable," Sanjam curtly replied.

Madhu was not convinced at all. She hardly understood Sanjam—his reasonings dismayed her. Burdened by those emotions, she felt hopeless and helpless but then gathered the will to stand against Sanjam.

"No, Sanjam, you won't kill him. I won't let you do that. I regret considering you a good person. No compassionate person would deem that such acts are justified for any reason. Maybe your hatred against the regime and the blind faith in the Band has blinded you."

Sanjam heard her words and said nothing for some time. He calmly continued to look at her face, determined to stop him. There was also a sprouting dislike for him in her eyes.

Madhu's collective reactions satisfied Sanjam. Those reactions made him smile gently, confusing Madhu further, and then he extended his arms to hold her shoulders. "I am sorry, Madhu, but I had to say the lie to test you. I wanted to know your most genuine thoughts about the Band. And now I can say that you are a part of the Band, not for the reasons you tell people. I won't ask you many details, but I want a yes or no; do you agree that the Band is a benevolent outfit?"

Madhu was startled by his question. She was perplexed but tried not to express it.

"Yes or no? Don't think much, Madhu, but please be honest."

"No," she whispered.

Sanjam had a beaming smile on his face with her answer. He exhaled out his stress with a sigh. "I am a spy, Madhu. I work for the Aryavrata empire, and I infiltrated the Band with my group to discover its real agenda and leadership," he revealed his truth. "If we can ascertain with proof that the Band has been fooling people with their bogus public

agendas and is brewing some other sinister plot, we need to take it down!"

Madhu was again surprised, but this time it was a delightful one. "I always knew it that you are not some ordinary soldier. I also felt at times that you must be a spy or warrior. Thank God you are not a Band sympathizer."

"And what is your reality? Who are you?"

"I am no spy or warrior. But I joined the Band to learn its truth and find out who are the ones controlling it."

"And why do you want to know the truth of the Band?"

"So that innocent ones are not wrongfully accused of supporting the Band. I cannot tell you on whose behalf I wish to find the truth because first, I wish to be certain that I am not erroneous in my trust in that person. But I swear, whenever I find the truth, I shall let you know about my identity."

Sanjam thought over her promise and nodded to appreciate her wish.

"So, I should take your leave," Madhu suggested.

"No, you can stay here. I need to meet a person and give him some information. There are massive fort sieges planned by the Band. Even our cluster has to take part in some of them. I know some of the target forts, and I must ensure that their generals can defend them."

"Are you thinking of giving out the names of the forts that our cluster is targeting?"

"Why do you ask that?"

In a slightly hesitant tone, she suggested, "I think we could do another thing. Instead of giving out the fort names that our cluster would target, we must take part proactively in those sieges. If we both can prove that we are valuable assets for the Band in these sieges, we can surely get into

the core team of our cluster. Once in the core team, we can discover things quicker."

***

Madhu had told Chitra every detail about coincidently discovering Sanjam's secret.

"That's a surprise, but I am more stunned that he revealed his secret to you instead of trying to cover it up," Chitra remarked.

Madhu went into deep thought, but Chitra interrupted her, saying, "He must have a soft corner for you. Even he feels a connection with you, and that is why he shared his truth without hesitation with you."

Madhu turned around abruptly and held Chitra's hands soundly. Her eyes glittered, and her face turned delightful. "With Sanjam's truth out now, we know that he is not a blind Band follower; instead, he is a spy working against the Band. So, he is a good man and a fearless warrior. And now there is a considerable probability that he is, after all, the person who we want him to be!"

"Yeah! He could be the one. Your one," Chitra blinked her eyes playfully.

Madhu covered her face for some time with her hands feeling shy. Then moving her hands away, she said in a reassuring voice, "However, I pray that when I come to know everything about him, his identity surprises me in a good way."

***

KAMBOJA-MADRA BORDERS

Krishna's last public appearance was in a border village of Kamboja-Madra Kingdom. After the final event of his tour, his

entourage was ready to leave for Hastinapur before heading back home. Krishna was retiring for the day and prepared to sleep in his tent. As he closed his eyes, he heard a voice.

"Hare Krishna," the speaker said, and Krishna reckoned that the voice traveled from some distance away.

Krishna quickly got off his bed and went out. He signaled his men not to follow him, took a casual stroll, and walked towards a semi-forested area behind the tent.

"Is it you, Narada?" Krishna asked, witnessing a man hiding behind some long bushes.

The man emerged, dressed in a dhoti and bare-chested except for a flower garland on his neck. " My Lord, the great avatar of Narayana, you are omniscient. I am indeed Narada."

If you are here to meet me, you must be carrying some important news. What is it?"

"The Devas will soon lose their right upon Swarga. The momentum of the war has tilted against the Devas. And this is accurate to what the Devas had predicted. Hence, the subsequent prediction is likely to turn true; he will cause a war between you and Mahadeva."

"I guess it's time for me to meet Mahadeva. I shall convince my companions to leave me here tomorrow, and I shall head towards Kailasha alone."

"Yes, my Lord. This predicted war must never happen. If you two stand against each other in a war, it will be a doom for the entire creation." Narada's voice trembled upon speaking those words.

Krishna reached to Narada and patted him on his shoulder. "I am the preserver. No matter what, I shall always protect the creation," Krishna assured.

***

THE HIMAVAT REGION

Krishna had managed to convince his entourage to leave without him. He tasked the Interior Minister to halt at Hastinapur and report in detail about his tour to the Pandavas. On the other hand, Krishna disguised himself as a commoner. He wore typical non-urban clothes and a glued beard and mustache on his face. Krishna did not even take a horse but rode a mule until reaching the icy terrains near the Kailasha region. Once, he was in the last rural locality just before the Kailasha's snowy area started; he exchanged his mule and some silver coins to buy a yak.

Riding the yak and holding a flamed torch in his left hand, Krishna moved through the thin snow on the ground. He reckoned that he would only reach the Shiva settlement by the following evening. He thought about his ideological differences with Shiva and the conversation that he, as Vishnu, had with Shiva before being born as Krishna. With several thoughts engulfing his mind, Krishna was unaware that some people on their feet were following him for some time. But hearing a noise suddenly, he turned attentive and realized that there were five men behind him.

Krishna stopped his ride and dismounted. Then extending his arm that held the torch, he inquired, "Who is there?"

In no time, five young men surfaced out of the darkness. Each of them was holding an ax and covered in long furry coats.

"You are here to loot me, I suppose? Krishna asked, gazing at their faces. His sight paused on one."I have seen you. You were with the man from whom I brought this yak. If I am not wrong, you saw me carrying a pouch of gold coins, and so now you want that, right?"

The boy seemed startled but said nothing. He merely looked at the others.

Krishna pulled out a pouch tied at his waistline and offered it to the five. "If you tell me your need for money, I shall give you this pouch."

One of them walked two steps ahead and grumbled, "We don't need alms, nor do we have a sob story to share. You have money; you are richer than us. So if we eliminate you, we become somewhat richer."

"So you will kill a man for being rich and owning a pouch of gold coins? Do you perceive that I have earned money through any unfair means?"

"We don't know, nor do we care. All that we know is; that a misdeed is a crime only when you are caught. But if we kill you here, nobody is catching us."

Krishna sighed and turned around to mount back on his yak. But those unruly youth surrounded him.

Krishna softly warned, "I don't wish to hurt you."

The five men raised the axes in response. Krishna looked at each attentively and then hurled his torch at one. The targeted boy moved away as an innate response, and everyone's focus briefly shifted to the fallen torch. Quickly, another of the looters rushed at Krishna with his ax. Krishna caught his arm, picked him over his shoulder, and launched him at two others. That solitary move injured three of them simultaneously. The remaining two attempted to bring their axes together at Krishna.

Krishna swiftly pulled the woolen cloth piece placed on the yak and threw it at the two. The axes ripped the cloth, but it provided Krishna with an opportunity. He went down on his right knee and punched each with either hand. The punches were so forceful that they soared at some height from the ground and fell on the snowy earth.

With everyone down and injured, Krishna mounted his ride. "I said I don't want to hurt you. I urge you to give up on these misdeeds. Not every person who looks ordinary is fragile. So get up, gather yourself, and try to mend your ways." Krishna advised them and went away.

***

The following evening, Krishna reached the settlement that Lord Shiva had established. Nearing the place, Krishna could see what mortals called Shivghar. The residences in it were cave-like structures constructed with rocks and were snow-laden. The dwellers had set multiple torches ablaze, hung on long and thick sticks carved out of a unique tree species that grows in snow and naturally uproots in some years. People were moving around, doing errands, and dressed in several layers of thick clothes that were noticeably not woolen. The area that located the rock-houses was some miles away from the gigantic and mesmerizing Kailash mountain. Krishna hopped off the yak and reached the site of the settlement. He had by then removed his disguise.

The site hardly had visitors, and whoever came arrived to settle in the Shivghar and lead a new life. So, when they saw Krishna among them, they were dumbfounded. However, everyone staying there revered Krishna as the most pious and wise man of the era.

When Krishna reached amidst the crowd, they welcomed him with folded hands and offered whatever hospitality they could.

"Noblemen and women, I am here to meet Mahashiva Ji. Would you be kind enough to let me know how do I meet him?" Krishna asked.

One in the crowd replied, "O Vasudeva, Lord Shiva remains here during the day, and as the sun sets, he goes back into Mount Kailasha. So you can meet him only tomorrow, sire."

Krishna nodded with a smile, but right then, a voice from afar spoke, " Vasudeva Shri Krishna, I knew that you were arriving here; you don't need to wait for tomorrow to meet me."

Krishna looked over the crowd of people, and almost half a mile away, he saw Lord Shiva standing.

Shiva as a human since he had settled on Earth. He was tall, and broad-framed, and the build was not bulky yet muscular. His upper body was completely bare and looked polished, while he covered the lower part with a thick tiger hide. His face looked perfect, with his eyes, nose, lips, and ears being in ideal shape and size. Shiva tied his curly blonde hair locks into a tight and thick bun that aptly suited his face.

***

Krishna and Shiva sat on two large rocks away from the residence.

"Do you like this place?" Shiva asked.

"It is beautiful and a departure from any settlements we see elsewhere. There is indeed peace, calm, and divinity in this place. And, of course, ecological living is evident. Although there is one thing that seems cruel and non-nature-friendly."

"You and your mischievous ways of talking!" Shiva laughed. "Don't make any misjudgment; I got this tiger skin from a dead tiger."

"I thought so, though."

"So what brings you here, Madhav? I am sure you are not here to gain a first-hand experience of our lifestyle and replicate it in the rest of the empire."

"Am I not welcome here?"

"I did not mean that, and you know it."

"And you also know why I am here, is not it?"

"Hmmm...he will win over Swarga."

Shiva's confident and unworried tone somewhat surprised Krishna. But Krishna wanted to know more about Shiva's thoughts. So he asked, "Mahadeva, what do you feel? Will he always remain righteous? Will he forever stick to fair means in his invasions and conquests?"

"Every living being is independent. We don't control anyone's thought process or actions. But if he turns unfair and unjust, I believe he will face someone's resistance. And if nobody else stands against him, you will."

"If I stand against him, will you be standing against me?"

Shiva looked at Krishna intensely before answering his question. His expression was cold. "I don't know. However, if he does anything that harms the welfare of the masses, I won't be defending him."

"So, let us see what time has in store even for the Gods."

"Time is mighty. It can even test us, the Gods."

***

Early the next morning, Krishna wanted to depart, but Shiva insisted that he stay for another night and witness the routine life at Shivghar. Krishna could not turn down Mahadeva's request.

The residents, including Shiva, started the day early and reared varied types of goat-like mammals and worked to cultivate a few varieties of edible plants that could grow in frozen soil. Some would collect water from a nearby lake and store the water in a large tank made from rocks.

Small groups of people would descend several feet from their habitat to reach a river flowing miles below. They would then collect a kind of protein-rich flowers abundantly found in the riverbanks. Those flowery plants found in massive heaps took little time to grow naturally. There were plenty of trees that bore different fruits by the riverside, and the residents plucked those fruits while returning in the late afternoon. The populace cooked food using fuels from dungs of wild yaks and other animals found in and around. Shiva could interact and understand the emotions of the wild creatures and spend time playing with them.

Krishna also learned that residents from the settlement would go to the nearest village, located countless feet below, at periodic intervals. There they would do some work and buy necessary things like utensils and tools. They also had an advantage as it was easier for people from Shivghar to find jobs and get paid decently.

Krishna saw Shiva toiling the most. He worked on demanding tasks like breaking rocks and shaping them. He also climbed over mountain ranges rapidly and brought down rocks and woods from dead trees. Shiva would sit with the populace, and they ate meals together. The inhabitants undoubtedly worshiped and adored him as a God, but his relationship with them was friendly.

In Shivghar, the days ended early for everyone, and the nights were long. After Shiva would leave for Mount Kailash as the sun set, the rest would spend some time singing, dancing, reciting, and making merry.

***

"I hope you loved this short stay here, Vasudeva. Can I expect to see you here again?" Shiva asked as he interacted with Krishna while seeing him off.

"Mahadeva, I enjoyed my short vacation here. You were very kind, and the people here are very generous. There is nothing but happiness and peace here."

"But…?" Shiva smiled.

"But if the entire world adopts this lifestyle, we will remain in a stagnant position for eternity. Therefore, I would strive that people accept the incredibly essential qualities of living in unity, harmony, and peace while continuing on the path of progress and development."

"It's impossible as far as I have known humans. Growth for them is always personal, never collective. Still, I wish you my very best."

Krishna and Shiva embraced each other before Krishna left for Dwarka.

BANASURA

I reached Magadh on my journey from Hastinapur to the Pragjyotispura Kingdom. I was heading to Pragjyotishpura as a powerful, legendary, and gifted Asura king who reigned over the kingdom. He was Narakasura, and I needed to meet him.

After I had stepped on Earth, I spent almost a year traveling around the different regions of Aryavrata and learning about the empire. I realized that the mighty kingdoms were Magadh, ruled by Jarasandha, Hastinapura, reigned over by Dhritarashtra, Panchal, led by Drupada, and Pragjyotishpura headed by Narakasura. I also analysed the political and economic situation of every kingdom and studied their alliances and rivalries. Icame to know that there were not many Asura dynasties in the mainland of Aryavrata. Bhisma, Aryavrata's strongest and invincible warrior, had vanquished several Asura tribes and made them settle in the icy terrains of Himavata mountains. The only Asura kingdom that continued to exist was Narakasura's empire. His province had a cosmopolitan society, with Asuras, humans, and sages living together. In addition, the territory adhered to civilized norms, traditions, and customs.

Naraksura seemed to be my natural ally as he was also an Asura and exercised significant influence in the empire. Furthermore, his inspiring and revolutionary tale of creating an Asura empire made me confident that he would understand my aspirations. So, I was on my journey to meet him.

Narakasura was the son of Hiranyaksha, the first Asura who ruled on Earth. Vishnu's Varaha avatar had killed Hiranyaksha, and since his death, Narakasura lived in the wild with a handful of his father's loyalists. In the woods, Naraka allied with the forest-dwelling tribes and trained himself to become an unequaled warrior. He also became well-versed in the Vedas and other spiritual books.

The forest tribes were experts in herbal medicines, and Naraka learned about Ayurveda from them. During his education on Ayurveda, Naraka developed a deep interest in human health, anatomy, and bones. He experimented and created prosthetic limbs for limbless people and discovered new medicines that worked on those sicknesses that had no medication before. He further went on to invent exercises that helped people overcome several anomalies and congenital diseases.

Naraka was also an ardent Brahma devotee. From the age of twenty-two, till he turned twenty-seven, he routinely practiced meditation and worshiped Brahma to seek a boon from him. After successfully pleasing Brahma with his austerity, he sought a boon and promised to stand for weaker and disabled people. Brahma thus had to bless him with the boon of aging at a sluggish rate. Once he attained that boon, Naraka traveled across the entire Aryavrata and gathered people with various disabilities, incurable illnesses, and physical or mental weaknesses. He helped them overcome their limitations, cured them of their diseases, and thus turned them into independent individuals. Eventually, aided by the people he had helped, he created an empire in the lands of north-eastern Aryavrata and named it Pragjyotishpura.

In a short span, Pragjyotishpura evolved into an economically sound region. Using the area's abundant natural resources and making it a medical tourism hub, Naraka peaked the expanse in economic terms. After making it an economic powerhouse, Naraka also created a powerful standing army for his kingdom. With the astounding richness and strong military might, Pragjyotishpura became an enviable empire for the other Aryavrata states.

When I had made the journey to meet Naraka, he was over five hundred years old but looked hardly fifty. I first saw him outside his palace. I tried entering his residence but was not allowed by his soldiers and gatekeepers. So, I waited for Naraka to step out of his fort, and after a wait of some days, I saw him going on ahunting trip.

The very first night of his forest stay, I found an opportunity to gain his attention. He was seated in the open on a throne-like chair, enjoying a dance and song program with hookah and liquor. Although his soldiers and guards surrounded him from all directions, including archers on treetops, I could shoot an arrow at him from trees located some distance away. Of course, not everyone could hit a target from that distance, but I was confident of my skills and years of practice.

I climbed a tree with a thick covering of leaves and positioned myself with a bow and arrow. Along with the distance, darkness was the other obstacle for me. However, I took my time and precisely ascertained my target. I decided to hit the chair's right armrest and released the arrow. It zoomed and almost reached the mark, but Naraka stunned me with his talent. He caught the dart right before it hit the armrest, and in no time, he stood up and hurled back the arrow at me. I leaped off the tree and rushed away with his troops hunting me.

I jumped and ran, dodging the arrow shots and spears hurled. I kept running ahead of the ones chasing me and took advantage of the darkness. I hid behind some thick trees and swiftly climbed one of them. As the soldiers moved far ahead of my hiding spot, I quietly disembarked from the tree and crawled and walked cautiously to reach Naraka.

Several troops of soldiers were still searching the jungle far and wide. However, a large army of sentinels was still around Naraka, defending him. I raised my arms in the air and walked into everyone's sight. Soldiers immediately encircled me, pointing spears and arrows. I looked straight into Naraka's eyes and said, "Greetings, the great Asura king, Naraka. I apologize for my earlier attack on you. My target was only your chair's armrest."

"And you missed hitting it," Naraka scoffed.

"I agree. You are terrific and immensely skilled."

"I suppose you are skilled as well. My men are still looking for you unsuccessfully, and you are here in front of me. You are audacious and confident. What brings you here?"

"I tried meeting you at your palace but failed. So I wanted to grab your attention here."

"You don't yet have my attention."

I heard him and sighed. "Please ask one of your guards to blindfold me and hand me a knife."

Naraka gestured to a soldier, and he quickly blindfolded me and handed me a spear. I then heard Naraka say, "Not a knife. You get a spear."

I asked one of the soldiers to volunteer and release an arrow high in the air with a light ghungroo tied around it. However, I knew that a spear couldn't soar as high as a knife or arrow because of its longer length and higher weight. So, I broke the spear and held only the pointed end of it. In the next few moments, someone shot an arrow with a ghungroo fastened to it. I heard the tiny bells ringing and hurled my weapon above. The pointed spear end flew in the air, hit the arrow, and dislodged the ghungroo. As the ghungroo made a free fall, I jumped and grabbed it in mid-air with one hand; while using my other hand, I held the falling arrow. Opening my blindfold, I looked at Naraka, and I could see that he was pleased.

Chapter 8

The Siege of the First Fort

Some weeks had passed since Sanjam and Madhu revealed to each other their common intention of unearthing the Band's truth. They began spending more time together in seclusion. Sanjam would tell her stories of his previous missions, and she would listen with awe and admiration. At times she would also share things about her childhood and teenage years. She refrained from mentioning names of places and other specific details but conveyed the incidents and the emotions that they made her experience. She told him how she was always intrigued by warfare, and since childhood, had a profound interest in spear fighting. Her talks made Sanjam guess that she belonged to some noble family. He was amazed, knowing that she chose to walk on a tedious and uncomfortable path despite having the option of enjoying every comfort, luxury, and care.

Sanjam and Madhu had also discovered about each other's small likings and habits. Madhu learned that Sanjam enjoyed playing indoor games and dressing up in different fashion styles and attires. Sanjam came to know about her interest in dance, cooking, and horse riding. However, regardless of the growing closeness, neither asked each other about their families. Nevertheless, Sanjam got the hint that her father's memory or odd mention made Madhu sentimental. Madhu also understood

Sanjam's relationship with his family members. She realized he was closer to his grandfather than to his parents.

***

An evening after Sanjam and Madhu had returned from their routine evening stroll, they heard an announcement about a special assembly scheduled for everyone the following morning. The broadcast mentioned that the Pradhan would address the entire cluster about something that would change every member's life. Everyone could anticipate the significance of the promised announcement, but none could guess what the Pradhan would tell.

Early next morning, the entire Band cluster gathered in the training ground for the much-awaited declaration. The Pradhan, the Guru, and the Band recruitment head, Puniya, stood before the trainees to make the all-important pronouncement.

The Pradhan spoke with passion and clout in his voice. "My dear brothers and sisters, it's time that our outfit takes a significant step to realize our goals. Your training, warfare practice, and sacrifices are finally going to yield revolutionary results." He continued, " The Band has decided to undertake radical actions. We will no longer ransack and seize the abundant wealth of the rich; rather, we shall fight and directly confront the pompous people who don't care about the ones who have nothing.

Every cluster of our organization will now pick up arms and siege forts that hoard prosperity inside in different forms. Our army shall target a garrison in Mathura and another in Virat Nagar of Matsya kingdom. It's time for us to take part in battles. Sieges are battles, and we shall be facing massive armies. But I know, despite being less in numbers, it will be us who will become victorious. Cheers to the Band's success!"

The declaration and encouragement speech of the Pradhan infused vigor and zeal in the Band members. They roared in unison, cheering the Pradhan and the Band, and the entire jungle echoed those cheering.

***

"I shall miss you a lot. I wish you could have joined us, as the physician of our army," Samar told Chitra, his face animatedly wrenched into a sob.

"You and your expressions!" Chitra giggled. "If you keep missing me during the siege, you won't even know and an arrow or a sword would penetrate you."

"How rude! You shouldn't speak such inauspicious things, although I do have a long lifeline."

"Sorry, I speak insensitively at times. But yes, since now I know that you are not an ordinary soldier but a top-notch spy, I do not doubt that you would survive and succeed in the sieges. Yet, I shall pray for you."

"Thank you," Samar replied.

Chitra noticed a sudden change in his mood and expression. In the past few months, they had spent quite some time together, and they knew each other well. She could therefore sense that he was unhappy and uncertain about something.

Holding his hands, she asked, "What is it?"

"I know we have to take part in these sieges and perform noticeably well to earn the trust of our cluster's leadership. Undoubtedly it will help us discover much more about the Band. However, in the sieges, we shall have to kill soldiers that are only discharging their duties diligently."

Chitra tightened her hold on his hands. "Statistically, the Band has killed over lakh soldiers, patrol officers, and guards since its inception. So, if taking part in these sieges helps bring down and decimate the Band, you'd be saving lakhs of sentinels. You are not taking the lives of some thousand innocent soldiers but defending the lives of lakhs."

"I, too, have convinced myself with these reasons to participate in the sieges. But the thought that I shall have to kill so many soldiers disturbs me. It's a tough job."

"And because it's an unpleasant thing to do, you must do it, for if you don't, who else will?"

Samar found strength in her words. He could gain the motivation to strengthen his heart and carry out his duty which was indeed harsh and difficult. He smiled and looked into her eyes. She smiled back at him. Inherently, they desired to feel each other closer. She first inclined a little towards him, and he reacted by leaning his body forward. Next, lost in each other's eyes, they embraced as their eyes closed.

Some moments later, the tweeting sounds of a flock of birds flying overhead brought back both into their aware state. Their tight embrace then relaxed, and as they released each other from the hug, she whispered into his ears. "Missing me might be hazardous for you, but I can and will miss you a lot."

***

The Magadh Band cluster had a strength of almost three thousand members. They all were to take part in the sieges, but the undetected movement from their hideout to Mathura was a challenge. Hence, the cluster's leadership planned to move the whole army as smaller groups, disguised as ordinary villagers. Additionally, there would be a gap of some days between the movement of two subsequent groups. The troop consisting of Sanjam, his mates, and Madhu was the last one to depart.

***

The night before the siege day, the Band members were inside a forest, a few miles away from the target fort—Gadagadh. Gadagadh stored the royal treasury of the Surasena kingdom. So the idea was to break the breach of Gadagadh and take away its mammoth richness.

The Band members stayed awake that night, preparing for the siege. Everyone started getting ready for the attack when it was almost dawn. They wore metallic pads, armguards, chest plates, and helmets that they had carried inside their simple-looking baggage. Each baggage also had weapons; a sword and a bow. The groups that departed early from the hideout had stayed concealed in that jungle for many days and carved infinite sharp wooden arrows. The final aid that the Band had with them was small explosion balls.

Once everyone was geared up and ready to ambush, the Pradhan stood before them with a worried look. "Everyone, may I have your attention? There is an unexpected hurdle before us. We shall need some time to re-strategize our attack," he informed.

The Pradhan's words unnerved everyone, and murmurs started.

"Re-strategize? Why?"

"Had the soldiers discovered us?"

"Has something happened?"

"Are we not going to lay the siege today?

Madhu walked towards the Pradhan, Mahat Guru, and Puniya. They were engrossed in solemn deliberations and seemed stressed. She was wary of interrupting them but believed that Guru Mahat would be considerate and kind towards her. As she neared them, she saw a young guy, who was not even a Band member, participating in the discussions.

"*Pranam* Gurudeva, sorry for interrupting but may I, please know what obstacle we are facing?"

Mahat Guru glanced at her and then looked at the others around him. "Madhu, we are in a highly tricky predicament, but we shall overcome it. But I ask you to have faith in us and try to keep everyone motivated."

"I have my complete faith in our leadership. I only wish to share your burden. Maybe a few more brains looking for the solution can help us in finding it quicker."

Mahat Guru nodded and sighed. "Two months ago, we had positioned this boy inside the fort as a servant," he pointed at the young guy standing near Puniya. "He had informed us that there are fewer soldiers, archers, and not much overall security towards the fort's rear side. So we had planned that I'd use a divyastra to blast open a part of the rear-side wall, and our army would storm inside. However, the fortresses across Aryavrata have tightened their defenses as there have been several castle sieges in other kingdoms by other clusters. So now, this fort has not just ample infantry at the rear side but also elephants and horses."

Learning of the obstacle, Madhu shared it with Sanjam and his friends. Everyone pondered over the situation. They also saw it as a huge opportunity to prove themselves as vital assets for the Band.

"Maybe, I have a solution," Sanjam said. He quickly rushed to the seniors, with Madhu behind him.

"Forgive my enthusiasm and intrusion, but I believe we can overcome this difficult situation. Is there any way that we can reach the top of the main dome of the castle?" Sanjam inquired.

The boy who worked as a servant in the fort replied, with a confused look, "Yes. There are giant towers that surround the central dome. If you scale the closest one to the dome and place something horizontally, connecting the tower top and the dome, you can reach the cupola structure. But able archers are stationed at every tower peak, and the staircase inside leading to the top is full of soldiers."

Sanjam pondered over the boy's information briefly but acutely. "Can you now re-enter the fort and place some ladders towards the backside of the fortress? Also, once you do that, you would need to arrive here with four to five uniforms of their soldiers."

Scratching his head, the boy answered, "Umm... I shall have to wait for the sun to rise, and then I can get inside the castle. And yes, I have to lie and arrange to keep some ladders behind the citadel."

"Alright, we shall wait for some time after sunrise and then begin our attack." Sanjam looked at the senior members and continued, "The plan is; my friends and I will scale the tower closest to the central dome and enter inside the citadel by blasting the cupola. The rest of the Band can concentrate only on defending themselves and providing us cover. Next, using a rope, the five of us will descend from the dome inside the castle. Once inside, I shall merge with the rest of their soldiers, and the others will bait the soldiers to chase them. My target will be to take the General's family hostage. When we have them as hostages, we shall have no trouble in grabbing the wealth inside."

The plan was dangerous and had no space for any trivial error or improvisation. It had to pan out precisely as thought. But, unfortunately, that was the only possible scheme. The seniors, therefore, agreed and informed every one of the plan.

***

The Band army rushed out of the forest. Guru Mahat raced ahead of everyone, and he conjured an Agneyastra without halting. He quickly fired it at a portion of the fortress wall, causing a massive blast.

The Band members stormed inside the castle compound and encountered a vast troop of soldiers defending the castle. Even some elephants and horses rushed at them. The members took out tiny explosive balls from small sling bags fastened on their waists. Then, igniting the threads on those balls from the burning bricks of the blasted wall, they launched them at the incoming soldiers and animals. The elephants and horses went hysteric and panicked. They moved chaotically all around, hurting, injuring, and killing the soldiers of the fortress.

Sanjam, Rudra, Samar, and Madhu were in the uniforms of the castle soldiers. So, they began fighting against the Band members. They fought with swords and also picked up shields from the dead castle guards. The four were cautious while combating the Band members and mostly injured them slightly.

The Band army kept the soldiers engaged in the fight, but they concentrated more on defending themselves rather than showing aggression. They divided themselves into several spherical groups positioned in one consistent elongated row. Each circular group had sword-wielders as the perimeter, and on the inside, there were archers.

Keeping their formation intact, the Band slowly but progressively moved ahead. While the sword fighters fended off sword and spear attacks from the opposite side, the archers periodically released arrows at the opponents positioned far and wide. In regular intervals, the sword fighters also dumped the explosives at their adversaries.

With the battle raging on, it was time for the Band to carry out their crucial plan. Accordingly, some of the Band members started looking for the ladders that had to be somewhere around. After a brief search, they found four ladders and moved with them inside the tower, closest to the castle's dome. Sanjam, Madhu, Rudra, and Samar followed them, indicating that they were chasing the members.

Inside the tower, the handful of the Band soldiers, aided by Sanjam's company of four, clashed with the fort sentinels. Three Band soldiers, however, stayed at the tower's doorway, closed it, and ensured it remained locked. While the others engaged in sword-fighting with the sentinels, Sanjam, Madhu, Rudra, and Samar swiftly ascended the stairs by injuring the soldiers trying to stop them. Their superior skills were overwhelming for the opponents, and soon they reached the peak of the tower.

On the tower top, the four had to face a troop of archers. They were busy shooting arrows below, targeting their enemy army with great difficulty amidst the chaos.

"Turn around, archers," Sanjam screamed and caught their attention. "We have these explosives with us. If you don't stop shooting now and move down immediately, we shall cause an explosion here." The other three displayed the tiny explosive balls and legitimized the threat.

A few archers reciprocated the threat by shooting some arrows at the four. Fortunately, the four moved and saved themselves. Then they quickly retreated and locked the door of the tower-top.

Rudra had carried a pack of matchsticks, crafted from a specific wood and dipped in certain chemicals. He rubbed a stick on the rough floor surface, and once it ignited, he set fire to one of the explosives. Madhu quickly opened the door slightly, and Rudra threw it at the archers. A sudden blast occurred, followed by some terrible screams.

"We have many more explosives. So it'd be wise for you to drop your weapons below the tower and kneel," Sanjam threatened.

After a brief silence, they heard one among the archers shout, "We surrender. We have thrown away our weapons." Madhu looked through the narrow opening of the door and saw the archers on their knees.

Sanjam looked at Samar and Rudra. "Go below, detonate some explosives and force everyone fighting there to take cover. The chaos should allow you to grab two ladders and some thick ropes. Bring them here quickly."

Samar and Rudra hurried down the stairs and returned with the required objects. Thereafter, the four forced the surrendered archers to clear the tower top. Once the archers went downstairs, Sanjam and the others attached the ladders with ropes. When they finished that task, they tossed explosives into the central dome structure, causing it to explode and break. Next, they put into use the two ladders that they had soundly attached like a single long ladder. Securing one end at the guardrail of the peak with several ropes, they allowed the other end to freefall, and it leaned firmly on the broken edges of the dome.

"Madhu, make an explosion in the air and signal Mahat Ji to defend us. And you shall go first, okay?" Sanjam spoke.

Madhu nodded and detonated a ball high in the air. Guru Mahat saw it, and he was ready for his defensive role.

Madhu stepped carefully over the ladder and walked cautiously towards the dilapidated cupola. However, the archers on other towers witnessed Madhu making the walk and could realize her motive. Hence, they shot volleys of arrows

targeting her. It was Mahat Guru's responsibility to defend her from that attack.

The Maharathi, Mahat Guru, used a celestial arrangement to defend Madhu. He shot an arrow that created a transparent but potent vaporous sheet around her. That mystic sheet acted as a shield, and none of the arrowheads could penetrate inside. Madhu eventually reached the end of the ladder and stood on the edge of the broken dome.

After Madhu, Rudra and Samar too followed suit. They began fastening a rope on a rod that remained intact on the dilapidated copula structure while waiting for Sanjam. Once he joined them, Rudra sent some explosive balls down the hollow roof of the dome. Those explosions cleared the floor below, killing and injuring some soldiers, and the four reached inside the castle, climbing down a rope.

Landing on the floor, Sanjam immediately hid behind some gigantic statutes while the others sprinted through the long corridors of the fortress. They voluntarily grabbed the attention of the soldiers by discharging some explosives in empty spaces. Some moments later, when it seemed safe, Sanjam emerged out from hiding and roamed around the palace looking for the General's family. He entered various rooms, and if there were people in them, he said that he was making sure that there were no intruders inside. Searching one room after another, he much later reached a heavily guarded chamber. The protection outside it made it inevitable that it was the General or his family's room.

Sanjam dropped a few explosives behind himself and then ran screaming towards the secured chamber. Huffing and puffing, he spoke in a worried and urgent tone, "They are almost here, and they have explosives. We must get into the chamber, lock the door, and stand guard inside."

"You are right, let us get in," one of those guards promptly agreed.

The entire group went inside and locked the mammoth door. Sanjam standing between the guards, began scanning the room when suddenly he heard the guards laughing aloud. He shifted his focus to them and realized that he was trapped.

One of the soldiers walked ahead and grabbed Sanjam's chin. "As soon as you all destroyed the dome, our General had devised this plan. The most secure place doesn't always store the most valuable object. Make the valuables seem ordinary, and no one will notice." He pushed Sanjam, and the others immediately encircled him.

Sanjam knew that to find a way out of his situation, he had to make the sentries feel that he was timid and they had absolute control over him. To do so, he started weeping. The cries turned louder, and amidst his sobs and sniffles, he sought mercy. "Please don't kill me. I surrender myself. You put me in prison but don't kill me. Iam just a soldier taking all the risk for our outfit."

The sentries laughed and pulled him to his feet. Seeing him tremble and putting no resistance, the soldiers did not care to bind him.

"We shall put you in prison as of now. But once our soldiers decimate your whole army, our General shall decide what punishment would suit you," another one of the guards spoke. They escorted him and began walking to the prison.

After a long walk, they reached a staircase that went to the basement of the fortress. Sanjam continued descending, and with every step, there was more darkness. Beyond a point, flaming torches hung on the walls provided brightness in the otherwise utterly dark staircase. The instant Sanjam saw those torches; he found his escaping opportunity.

Sanjam rolled down the staircase, appearing as if he had tripped. The guards laughed and mocked him without sensing the incoming trouble for them. Sanjam stood up immediately and pulled down a torch. "I still have my little friends with me," he said, pulling out the tiny explosives from the garter belt on his waistline. He ignited one ball and bowled at the stairs above. The sudden attack made the soldiers run, yet the blast injured some of them. Sanjam followed the first blast with two more and made his way out.

He warned soldiers not to chase him, threatening otherwise to burn them and began searching for the General or his family again. This time he focused on rooms and places that had little security or none. In the meantime, Madhu, Samar, and Rudra all joined him, aiding him in the quest. However, they failed to find their targets despite all their efforts.

"We don't have much time. It's a damn huge fort. There would be so many hiding places, so many secret doors, rooms, and covert pathways. We cannot continue our search much longer and need to find some other way," Rudra said, gauging the situation.

Sanjam had to agree with Rudra's assessment. He briefly pondered and had a plan in mind but faced a dilemma because of Madhu's presence. Madhu sensed that he was in some fix.

"What's the matter, Sanjam?" she inquired.

"I have a way to bring the General out of his hiding. But my method will surprise you," he replied.

Madhu stared at him inquisitively for some moments. "Alright! I shall ask no questions right now, no matter how much your plan surprises me. Do whatever you have to do; we have not much time."

Sanjam nodded and then pulled out a bronze spear hung on a wall nearby. He gripped it soundly, closed his eyes, and murmured a chant. His companions continued to cover him with swords and threats of explosions. Moments later, Sanjam opened his eyes and intimidatingly spoke to the soldiers. "Ask your General to come out and surrender before us. I have summoned a Pralayastra, and if I fire it, it will not only kill everyone but reduce this palace into rubble and even blow out the entire city. We cannot return defeated, so we are willing to die. The question is whether your General can allow the destruction of the whole city?"

Sanjam's threat horrified the soldiers. Looking behind, Madhu too was dismayed to see the spear beaming with a ray. She couldn't believe that he was a Maharathi who could use divine weapons!

Sanjam's strategy worked. The soldiers panicked, and some of them sent a message to the General. The General, a middle-aged man, soon emerged and moved towards Sanjam, unarmed and unescorted.

He walked with authority and stood fearlessly in front ofSanjam. "You can put down the divine weapon. You wanted me, andI am here. You can do whatever you want with me!" Although he had surrendered, it was only to save his fort, city, and its citizens. But he wasn't scared of dying and so was yet bold and commanding.

"Frisk him, Samar," Sanjam responded without putting down his weapon.

The General smirked. Raising his arms in the air, he said in a sarcastic tone, "You have a divine weapon raised at me, and I don't even have a knife. Yet, it seems you are afraid, and I am not."

Nobody responded to the General's taunt. Instead, Samar frisked him carefully and said he was indeed unarmed. With that certainty, Sanjam again closed his eyes and chanted something that relaxed the divine energy on the spear. Then, he placed his sword around the General's throat, and the four walked out of the main door of the fort. The General was their hostage and safety net.

When they reached the fort's premises where the battle was waging on, the fort soldiers dropped their weapons and yielded to ensure the safety of their General. The General was least worried about his life, but he felt intimidated, thinking Sanjam may use the divine weapon and destroy the city.

The Band army had decisively won the siege attack. So, they plundered the fort, found its treasury, and put as much fortune as they needed in sacks. Their subsequent step was seizing half of the fortress's horses and chariots and chasing the rest away from the fort. Then, mounting on horses and carts with abundant wealth, the Band members left the castle and galloped out of the city. The General remained as a hostage on a chariot with Sanjam, Madhu, Samar, and Rudra. When the entire cluster reached a safe place and took a jungle route to head towards their next target, Virat Nagar, they dropped the General unconscious on the road.

***

Some days later, the cluster was only a few miles away from the capital of the Matsya kingdom, Virata Nagar. Virata Nagar had a fort called Anngadh that stored the buffer grains of the northern kingdoms. Seizing the grain stocks would do two things. First, it would embarrass the central regime, and second, the Band cluster would have abundant food grains.

The success of the first siege, despite several odds against them, kept the Band members motivated and its leadership pleased. Although they had lost nearly six hundred men, the mission was a success making the martyrdoms worthy. The headship and the soldiers applauded Sanjam and Madhu for their efforts; from making an improvised plan to bearing the immense risks. They were heroes of the siege, and the Pradhan dedicated an entire speech to them.

The Pradhan, Guru Mahat, and Puniya praised Sanjam, his friends, and Madhu privately as well. The Pradhan called them precious resources for the entire outfit. He even proposed that Sanjam and Madhu join the core team of the cluster and hinted that the Band soon would make an extremely revolutionary move. He further added that Sanjam and Madhu would have prominent roles to play in it.

Curious but relieved that they would learn about the radical move beforehand, Sanjam and Madhu were happy as their gamble had paid off well. Things fell into places as they had wished, and that elated them.

Despite everything going well, Madhu was getting restless about Sanjam and his secret. So she took him to a secluded place to know the truth about him.

"So, I think I can now know how you could summon a divine weapon? I always knew you were a terrific warrior but never thought you were a Maharathi!"

Sanjam sheepishly smiled. "Yes, I am a Maharathi, and I can invoke all divine weapons."

"How?"

"I trained for it. I spent much of my younger years in Gurukul."

"And who are you? From which noble house do you belong?"

Sanjam looked passionately into her eyes and held her shoulders. "Madhu, I swear, once we learn about what radical move the Band is planning, I shall let you know everything. You are also yet to disclose your true identity to me. I promise whether you do so or not, but I shall, once the right time arrives. You do trust me, right?"

Madhu felt assured. All her restlessness calmed down as soon as he had touched her shoulders. She nodded with a smile, and Sanjam smiled back at her.

Underneath the moonlight, Sanjam and Madhu stood together, looking at each other, momentarily forgetting everything else. They stood as if time had paused and stirred only on hearing Samar and Palan calling out their names from somewhere afar. Both blushed as they walked towards their friends.

BANASURA

I told everything about myself and my lineage to Naraka. Fortunately, he accepted my friendship as I had hoped and spoke highly about my father and ancestors. I also informed him of my motives and aspirations. I told him that I desired to establish and independently rule over an empire. And together, we both as equals and allies could establish our domination over the entire Aryavrata. He agreed with my aspirations. Probably, he considered me a powerful ally because I was not merely a mighty warrior but also a sorcerer.

Naraka acknowledged that with his army and my magical prowess, we could conquer many kingdoms of Aryavrata and eventually challenge the formidable empires like Kuru, Magadh, and Panchal. However, the issue was that the general public would never accept Asuras as emperors of Aryavrata. He felt that people would always distrust us and would be susceptible to be incited against us. The solution, therefore, was to have another influential human ruler as our supporter. Naraka had already deliberated and zeroed in on two such probable supporters; Jarasandha of Magadh and Kamsa, the young prince of Surasena. He considered Kamsa as the better bet as he was young and more aspiring and fearless. Moreover, he believed that we could manipulate Kamsa but not the experienced and seasoned leader, Jarasandha.

After careful reflection and discussion, we hatched a plan to ensure that Kamsa accepted us as friends. Kamsa often went hunting all alone deep in the forests of Surasena. On one such trip, I secretly followed him. Once we were in the interiors of the woods, I used sorcery and summoned spirits of animals who had recently died there. Those spirits on my orders attacked Kamsa. The brave young prince fought audaciously and showed no panic, but he could never defeat or counter-attack spirits. The spirits quickly surrounded him and gained control over his mind. The supernatural creatures couldn't bite or scratch him. Instead, they chased him, pushed and pulled him, and made horrific noises. Gradually Kamsa began losing his mind and was soon immobile. It was then my turn to play the role of his savior. I stepped in front of him, used my magic to control those spirits, and sent them underground. Next, I picked Kamsa up and took him to a safe place.

When Kamsa recovered, he thanked me and asked why I didn't take him to his escorts. I cunningly replied that I didn't want his soldiers to know that he was injured and beaten. Kamsa was impressed with me and asked about my identity. I told him much about my life, from my father's legacy to landing on Earth from Ashishloka. In between the truths, I inserted a lie that Narakasura had appointed me as his chief advisor, and I was traveling all across Aryavrata to learn more about the empire. I even hinted to him that we were looking for a monarch that could be our ally, and together we could one day rule over the whole sub-continent. Kamsa took the bait and agreed to support us. He trusted in Naraka's prowess and my magical abilities. Soon. Kamsa accompanied me to Pragjyotishpura, where we schemed that Kamsa could marry Jarasandha's daughters and form a matrimonial alliance with him. Magadh's support would make our coalition invincible.

Unfortunately, when Kamsa went to Magadh with the proposal of the marital union, Jarasandha disagreed. Jarasandha's response jeopardized our planning, but Kamsa decided to play a gamble. He took me and a small contingent of his army and invaded Magadh's palace. Nobody could defeat Jarasandh and his army in an open war, but the guerilla attack and my magic provided him a setback. When Jarasasandha was vulnerable, Kamsa challenged him for a dual. Confident that he could never lose, Jarasandha wrestled with the young prince to face his first-ever defeat. Kamsa, after defeating him, humbly sought the matrimonial alliance, and this time, Jarasandha delightfully agreed.

Some months after the wedding, our coalition helped Kamsa stage a coup and dethrone his father to become the new King of Mathura.

Chapter 9

The Adventure of the Second Siege

Sanjam and Madhu stood beside the Pradhan, Puniya, and Guru Mahat. The three appeared worried, but they looked at the two hopefully.

The Pradhan broke the uneasy stillness. "Madhu, Sanjam, we are again in a fix. Do you know how many members we had lost in the first siege?"

Madhu and Sanjam stayed mum and moved their head in denial.

"We lost nearly seven hundred men, and now our strength is only two thousand approx. Moreover, we had also planned a more mobile and broad attack for the second siege, possible only with around five thousand soldiers," the Pradhan informed. "The cluster from Vidharbha was to join us for this siege. But, unfortunately, somehow, the Aryavrata Army intercepted them on their way, and they had to retreat." The Pradhan paused and sighed before adding, "The people who had come here to transport the seized wealth from Gadagadh informed us of this sad development."

"Do we have any alternate scheme now, or do we have to abandon our second siege?" Madhu asked.

Puniya rammed his fist agitatedly into a tree, saying, "There is no plan in place. We can't make any secret attack on that fort. There are no vulnerabilities in Anngadh that we can take advantage of!"

"That is why we called you. Maybe your young, wise, and innovative minds can come up with some ingenious scheme," Mahat Guru said, tapping Sanjam's shoulders .

Sanjam looked at Madhu, and she appeared assuring.

"May we know the complete situation, geography, and everything else about Anngadh?" Sanjam requested.

In the next two prahars, Madhu-Sanjam studied the location and comprehensive situation of Anngadh and analysed different scenarios that could help them capture the fort. Finally, a plan seemed feasible to them as well the Pradhan, Puniya, and Guru.

"I hope everything goes as we have planned. And for that, our opponents must perceive things as we want them to," Puniya made the concluding remark.

***

A few weeks later, the cluster was outside the city premises of Virata Nagar. They had entered the Matsya kingdom by bribing a contractor. The kingdom's royalty had tasked the contractor to construct a new roadway connecting the capital with another terrain. The contractor successfully brought the Band members inside the kingdom by hiding them in carts that carried various objects required for construction activities.

Once on the brink of the city gates, the cluster camped in a large grazing field. According to Sanjam-Madhu's plan, they built over ten thousand tents in the pasture. Some cluster members had purchased the clothes needed for the excessive tents on the pretext of an affluent merchant's son's wedding.

On the first night, the cluster lit tens and thousands of flaming torches. The inflated numbers of tents and torches convinced Anngadh that the size of the invading force was enormous. The General himself watched the Band campsite with lens tools and could not imagine that his view was an illusion.

The General was bewildered at how such a massive army had covertly entered his kingdom and capital. He blasted at his men and nobles and began discussing their counter-attack options. Amid those discussions, he received a piece of good news.

"Greetings, General Madhusudhan Ji! Our soldiers have caught a person trying to break inside our fortress. We believe he is from the enemy camp," informed the Chief of the Palace Security.

"That's great! Break him and find out why he was attempting to break into our fort. We may get some vital information that can put us at an advantage," the General elatedly responded.

***

It was Sanjam whom the fort security had caught. He was imprisoned and tied to a chair while four menacing men interrogated him. They had disrobed him to his kaupina tied around the waist. The interrogators repeatedly asked his army's plan of attack and why he broke into the fort. Sanjam remained silent.

The interrogators punched, slapped, and beat Sanjam with a soaked cloth. Although he screamed, cried, and wailed, Sanjam revealed nothing. So, to break him down, the interrogators increased their torture. They first waterboarded him, then pushed needles into his torso, feet, and nipples. Sanjam begged for mercy but was stubborn not to answer their questions.

After about a prahar, the interrogators felt agitated. So they untied him as they had another scheme. They took him to a place behind the fort and dumped him on the ground. Sanjam, hurt, traumatized, and dizzy, could not even sit or stand. He only managed to raise his head with much effort and looked around himself.

His eyes caught the attention of the General staring at him from a balcony of the fort. He had a fuming look on his face, and his eyes gestured to someone or something.

Sanjam heard loud and angry barking noises. Panic-stricken, he looked here and there and saw a few soldiers at some distance with half a dozen dogs. The dogs were huge and tall and barked ferociously with their tongues drooling. Their demeanor and size sent chills down Sanjam's spine. He quickly looked at the General and knelt with folded hands.

"I am sorry, Pramukh Ji! Would you please ask your men to take away these beasts? I swear, I shall answer all your questions and do as you ask. I will remain your slave forever and eat only your leftovers; please show some mercy!"

Sanjam's wails filled the entire fort. The General, pleased to see him weak, signaled his men to stop bringing the dogs. Quickly, two soldiers pulled Sanjam to his feet and took him back to the prison.

***

The General himself interrogated Sanjam this time. "Why did you break into our fortress?"

A visibly scared Sanjam said in a quivering voice, "I had to gauge how prepared you are for our attack. Also, I had to mix a potion in as many as possible torches hung on the fort walls. The solution, when mixed with fire, creates a gentle but effective aroma that gets people intoxicated. The idea was to render many soldiers unable to fight in the morning."

The General found Sanjam's answer convincing. Yet to be more sure, he asked his second question. "Why my soldiers couldn't find that potion when they caught you?"

"I threw it away before anyone could find it. You can ask the soldiers to search it near the western walls of your fort."

"Hmmm. And what's your plan of attack?"

Sanjam remained mum for some time and then looked at the General with pleading eyes. "Do you promise not to kill me if I tell it?"

"Yes. You will remain a prisoner, and we shall even have a trial for you once we defeat your army," the General assured him.

"We have another contingent of around eight thousand soldiers hidden in the forests towards the east of your fort. We also have two Maharathis in that contingent. Tomorrow, the camped forces will keep you engaged with attacks of arrows and explosives. As you defend your central gate, the covert contingent will attack your eastern walls. So while you would use all the resources to protect the middle gate, the plan is to breach the eastern fortifications."

The General, his chief aide, and other nobles were relieved upon learning of their enemy's plans. Now they could make an efficient counter-strategy.

"Let's plan our strategies here itself, General. This man can help us if any more questions about the opponent camp come up," the chief aide suggested.

"Hmm... what's your plan?" the General asked.

"Including yourself, we have three Maharathis in this Fort. We can send the other two with around ten thousand soldiers right now to destroy the contingent hiding in the jungle."

"But that would prompt the army camped in front of us to attack us right now. Raiding us instantly and in the dark would be their best bet if they don't have the aid of the other contingent. And if we send ten thousand or even eight thousand soldiers away, we would have to defend the fort with our remaining ten thousand forces. That would make the fight even."

"So what do you suggest, Sir?" another noble humbly asked.

"We shall play the game by their rules, but with the results already rigged in our favor. Tomorrow, when the camped forces attack the central gate, we shall use around three thousand soldiers and four thousand infantry to engage with them. I shall lead our defense force and use my divine weapons to overwhelm them.

"On the other hand, twelve thousand odd soldiers will hide at different places, towards the east side, outside the fort, led by our two Maharathis. They will suddenly attack the incoming second enemy contingent, decimate them and then march to destroy the army attacking our front gate."

"That's brilliant and ingenious, sir," the chief aide remarked. The other nobles agreed as well.

"And as per the protocol, we must ensure the safety of our buffer grain stock as it is a battle time. Anyway, the Band must have attacked us to loot it," the General said, looking at Sanjam. Sanjam nodded.

"Sure thing, Sir. I shall right now send the stock for Panchal, in bull carts escorted by five hundred guards."

Before walking out of the prison cell, the General stood up and told his chief aide, "Send it from the western path, although it's longer. Don't forget; the eastern side has the enemy contingent."

Moments after the General and his nobles had left, Sanjam put into action his escaping way. He pulled out a tiny seed that he had pushed inside his right toenail. He had carried it with him as consuming that seed; one would appear dead for some time. Sanjam chewed the pip and felt a sharp pain in his chest. He held his chest and screamed aloud. Then, he collapsed on the floor and breathed with great labor. The guards outside his and other cells gathered. Someone opened his prison cell and tried to make him drink some water. However, Sanjam coughed out the water and frantically moved his arms and legs. His movements sharply declined, and he began losing his breath. Seeing him die, the guards sent for the prison physician.

By the time the physician arrived, Sanjam was motionless on the floor. He was no longer breathing. The physician checked his pulse and declared him dead due to a heart attack. The General immediately received the news, and he ordered some of the fort servants to take Sanjam's corpse to the nearest cemetery and complete his last rites.

***

Sanjam regained his senses when his heart automatically started beating after the effect of the seed had subsided. He breathed suddenly and rapidly with much labor. There was a heaviness on his heart still, and he could hear his heartbeats. His vision was also blurry, and the darkness of the night did not help either. His body felt weak and lethargic, his limbs yet somewhat numb. He remained immobile for some time more and tried to get his breath normal. Some moments later, he slowly pulled down the shroud from his face and looked around him cautiously. He could see a few people talking and debating, a bit far from him. He continued to scan all around the place and realized he was in a cemetery. He also noticed that he was lying on the ground, close to some previously burnt-down pyres.

The people in the cemetery were still engrossed in their discussion, completely unvigilant of Sanjam. For them, he was a corpse and hence, required no attention. It was the chandal, who managed the cemetery, talking with the servants who had brought Sanjam. Their conversation was about his last rites. The chandal told them that he was alone and as it was a corpse with no family members, the servants had to assist him. The servants, on the other hand, were hesitant to take part in the funeral rites.

Sanjam had sharp ears. He could overhear parts of their interaction and decided that it was a safe moment for him to flee away. He emerged out of the shroud and crawled slowly and quietly towards the boundary wall of the cemetery ground. The night's dimness aided him. He continued crawling but faster, climbed over the short boundary wall, and jumped down. Fortunately, each movement of his was soundless, and he successfully escaped away from the cemetery.

***

Fleeing the cemetery, Sanjam went out of the city premises and rested inside a forest. After some time, the cluster forces joined him in the woods with the seized grain stock. They had rendered everyone involved in the transportation of the grains unconscious. So, none could inform anything to the General.

The empty tents in the campsite outside Anngadh still kept the General and his men fooled. Moreover, the servants continued searching for Sanjam's lost corpse the entire night, thinking that some occult practitioner must have stolen it from the cemetery.

In the morning, when the General and everyone else discovered the truth, the cluster was well inside the depths of the jungles and headed back to Magadh. Somewhere in the interiors of the woods, the Band members dig the grain sacks at different spots. There would be other Band teams that would dig them out later and deliver them to the central command of the outfit.

"So, your risky plan did work," Madhu commended Sanjam for his efforts. "But they did hurt you a lot. I am so sorry for the bruises on your face," she added with concerning eyes looking at his bruise marks.

"I knew the risk, Madhu. That they tortured me is trivial, but we won and that is what matters."

Samar, who was walking right behind Sanjam and Madhu, chipped in. "Don't worry, my friend is the toughest warrior you will come across." He patted Sanjam on his back, and continued with a proud smile. "Your plan to get caught and give out false information was truly ingenious. You calculated it so right that the General, following the protocols would send the buffer grain stock to the nearest kingdom on knowing that an attack on his fort was imminent. And our forces were already on the path that led to the Panchal rajya."

"The idea to make the General believe that the attack was threatening enough to send away the buffer grain stocks was not my idea alone," Sanjam spoke. He then looked at Madhu with a little blush.

"But we won't repeat this. I was scared during your detention," Madhu said with almost moisture in her eyes.

Sanjam wanted to answer something, but he merely smiled and nodded. Some silences speak a thousand words.

***

After a long journey, the cluster forces reached their settlement in Magadh. The handful of members who had stayed back welcomed them with beating drums and flower showering. Everyone danced and rejoiced despite being too tired to celebrate their victories. Even the Pradhan and Guru Mahat, who generally remained reserved, danced with the other members.

Madhu stopped celebrating as Chitra hugged her with tears of joy and relief flowing down her cheek. It was a tight, warm, and long embrace. While allowing them their moment, Sanjam and his friends stood behind them, smiling. Chitra, who was facing them, opened her eyes after a few moments into the hug and her gaze fell on Samar. Their eyes met, and she smiled at him. Samar reciprocated with a beaming nod.

As the embrace ended, Chitra greeted Samar and the others. She congratulated everyone and asked whether they could fulfill their motive of participating in the sieges.

"Of course! Madhu and Sanjam now are not only in Pradhan's good books, but he is dependent on them," Samar replied promptly.

"Oh, that's great!" Madhu exclaimed. "Alright then, I shall get the rest of the information from Sanjam later. Now I think you should all freshen up and get rest."

***

"A large-scale battle?" Palan was astounded. Everyone else was staggered as well. Sanjam had shared with his friends some sensational information that he received from the Pradhan. The Pradhan had told him that a battle was forthcoming in which every Band cluster would participate. So, over the next few weeks, the cluster members would have to train harder, and it was up toSanjam and Madhu to rally, motivate, and convince others in the cluster if required.

"Against whom?" asked Rudra.

"He has not told me that yet. But very soon, he will," Sanjam replied.

"And what will be our course of action then?" Samar asked.

"It'd be a great chance. With every cluster gathered at one single place, we can get everyone arrested. However, I hope we don't need to fight a battle and kill many to capture some of them," Sanjam responded.

Samar held Sanjam's shoulder and smiled with pride. "You have already done great, Sanjam. In the second siege, you managed to devise such a plan that made you a hero, and at the same time, you succeeded in not letting even a single person die. You are not just a warrior; you are a savior."

***

The Pradhan had announced a special assembly in the early morning. Everyone gathered in the training field with curiosity and remained attentive as Pradhan began his talks.

"My dear soldiers, first and foremost, I congratulate each one of you for making our sieges successful. You all have been brave and strong. But, unfortunately, we also lost many of our comrades in the first siege. Therefore, let us wish peace to their departed souls and thank them for their sacrifice." After some moments of pause that had complete tranquility, the Pradhan continued. "You have sacrificed and done a lot for our organization. Each of you has devoted your past few months or years entirely to the Band and its motto. But now you all have one final task, after which you will no longer remain landless and outlaws.

"First we ransacked establishments, next we sieged forts, and now we shall fight a full-fledged battle. Very soon, every cluster and each Band member shall get together and fight a bloody battle. It'd be a battle where we would have the numbers, tactical advantage, and external support. Once we win, which we undoubtedly will, we shall have our territory, absolute liberty, and royal alliance. So, over the next few weeks, train harder and fight to kill. Also, after you win this battle, the Band's supreme leadership shall bestow you with personal wealth and affluence."

The declaration of Pradhan met with unanimous cheers and applause. Everyone was motivated and confident post their recent success. Further, the promise of owning land and liberty, along with assured richness, made the Band members even more excited and enthusiastic.

The members began clearing the training ground when Puniya approached Sanjam. "Pradhan Ji wants to speak with you and lady Madhu. Convey it to her and join us in Pradhan Ji's tent as soon as possible."

***

It was for the first time that Sanjam and Madhu sat together with the seniors of the cluster. Along with the Pradhan, Guru Mahat, Puniya, and two more middle-aged men, they sat around an oval table.

"You must be curious about these two gentlemen. They are Chandran and Hira," Guru Mahat spoke, pointing at the two middle-aged men. "They stay with a handful of elite fighters in another part of this very jungle. Their role is to keep a constant but secret vigil around this forest and find out if someone is suspiciously entering or exiting the woods in the night. Additionally, they also act as the messenger between the central leadership and us. As now you both are part of the core team of this cluster, you must know them and vice-versa," Mahat Guru explained.

Madhu-Sanjam greeted them.

"Our next step is going to be our most significant move. Once we are successful at it, things will drastically change for our organization. And this step is the combined attack of every Band cluster as one mammoth army at the capital of Kalinga." The Pradhan took some sips of water before continuing. "The kingdom of Kalinga is rich and powerful. It has immense natural resources under the soil and in its coastal areas. But, most importantly, it has an island that one can reach only via the water route through the capital city. On the other three sides, towering fort walls and dense forests with tall trees act as fortifications. The Band shall receive that island as an autonomous territory on winning the battle of Kalinga."

"If we are defeating the Kalingan king, who shall hand us the island?" Sanjam asked.

"The one who is inviting us for this battle," a smiling Pradhan replied. "The Interior Minister of the kingdom, Suketu, is ambitious. Anyway, it was his ancestor who had established the kingdom of Kalinga. But because his ancestor was not a Kshatriya, he had to hand over the reins to the dynasty of the current king.

"Now, Suketu wants us to wage this war and defeat the king and his loyal forces. Thereafter, using the dead bodies of the battle from both sides, he would declare that Kalinga has defeated the Band, and sadly, the Kalingan king too lost his life in the clash. Shatrujeet can effortlessly take over the throne and provide us with dominion over the islands with the king dead. To the outside world, we would be deceased, but we would live freely on the island in reality. And on the island, in the course of the next few years, we can raise an army secretly with necessary assistance from Kalinga. Meanwhile, Kalinga would also make specific strategic alliances. Finally, when we all are ready, we shall wage war to overthrow the Pandava-Krishna alliance!"

The Pradhan's revelations dismayed Madhu-Sanjam. They were utterly shocked to learn of the Band's long-term plan and carefully calculated moves.

Sanjam was not just stunned, but there was rage and aggression building in him. Like the Krishna-Pandava regime and other monarchs, he was always conscious of the Band having some sinister goals. They also had predicted that with time, the Band would turn more menacing and threaten the peace and order of Aryavrata. However, they never expected the Band to find regal alliances and that their ultimate agenda was a war against the Pandavas and Krishna.

Multiple thoughts and scenarios were running in Sanjam's mind. Further, he was so enraged that he felt like overturning the table on the Pradhan and others. Nevertheless, he knew it'd be foolish for him to react instantly. He had learned a lot about the Band's schemes, but he needed to discover more secrets. So, gulping down his frustration, he reacted with a pleasantly surprised smile. "That's such a great plan! Although the tasks would take time, our challenge would one day surely crumble the current regime. And you have managed a prudent collaboration with a powerful kingdom like Kalinga."

"No, no, I can't take that credit. Our supreme leader merged this alliance. In fact, during our battle, he would be present in the Kalingan palace as a guest of the Interior Minister," the Pradhan said. He further added, "It was his idea that the various Band clusters siege forts and seize weapons, food, and wealth. The arms would be necessary for the Kalingan Battle, while the food and wealth would help us recruit infinite new soldiers. The new Kalingan king would handle the recruitment and logistics of delivering the soldiers from different parts of the empire to us."

Madhu and Sanjam looked at each other with a spark in their eyes. The others felt it was because they were elated at the possibility of meeting the Band's supreme leader. However, Madhu-Sanjam was excited because finally, they would soon identify and apprehend the central leader of the malicious outfit. Thus, it would be the end of Aryavrata's current greatest threat.

Madhu responded, highlighting her happiness and joy. "I cannot believe that ultimately we would succeed in having our land and be living as subjects of our great, visionary leader," she said with a wide smile in an enthusiastic tone. "I also promise on behalf of the cluster that we shall leave no stone unturned to win this battle," she added.

"Yes, each one of you must be ready to fight with no fear of the opponents and death. And do remember that we are doing this for our mission, our revolutionary goal. After dethroning Yudhisthir, we shall establish an empire with no central or state leadership, and there would be no more competition. Petty laws would not bound people, and there would be absolute liberty." Puniya said to motivate Sanjam and Madhu. He further went on, "After our alliance defeats the existing system, we shall also take over the fortune of those who are rich now; the traders, merchants, nobles, physicians, scientists, and everyone else. We shall then redistribute that wealth among the masses."

Madhu and Sanjam nodded and acted appreciative of whatever Puniya told.

The Pradhan spoke again. He stood up and folded his arms. "Now, you both and your close friends must keep every member motivated. Of course, you cannot reveal anything now about which kingdom we shall attack, what we shall get in return, and that our leader would soon rule over us. But you can tell them that this war is a step ahead in gaining our sovereign territory, making regal alliances, and soon having a merger with other anti-regime kingdoms to dethrone the current regime. In addition, when we have our dominion, every member shall receive an equal amount of wealth as incentives."

***

Madhu, Chitra, Sanjam, and his friends had gathered by the river banks near their settlement. There were also a few more groups of other Band members enjoying the evening breeze by the riverside.

"So, we have the perfect opportunity to nab every Band member from each cluster across the entire landmass. And we can also arrest the central supreme leader simultaneously," Palan said animatedly.

"I feel they have an ideology that is flawed in some ways, and the way they are attempting to enforce their ideology, with battles, wars, and bloodbaths, is utterly wrong. They could have taken a different approach. Maybe they could have convinced Samrat Yudhisthir to test their ideas in a single province first," Chitra suggested.

"The Band talks about socialism and community-level management and leadership. They also discard social rules and norms and advocate that everyone receive equal resources and payment for any services. They even want to take over individuals' private wealth and properties and redistribute them in ways they see fit. Furthermore, they want to achieve all these through battles, wars, and plundering. All of their ideas are flawed!" Rudra vehemently grumbled after expressing his thoughts.

Sanjam sighed and grinned. "They are trying to go reverse in history without studying and knowing the actual history."

"As in?" Madhu curiously asked, raising her eyebrows.

Sanjam sat on a rock to answer her in a clarifying manner. "In human history, the first political-economy system was absolute socialism with tribe-level, micro leadership. Back then, each tribe was small, consisting of only ten or twenty people, and headed by the wisest or most dominant person of the tribe. The consequence was that every tribe viewed others as a rival, and they often clashed. There were no common laws either. Then gradually, things evolved with time, and the various tribes that shared the same territory and resources merged as a community. Hence, countless communities came up, with each community agreeing on basic standard rules and norms suitable to them and started living in a socialist setup.

"These tiny but infinite communities continued conflicting with one another over trivial issues and also because rules and laws were different for each community. The smaller and fragmented population also hindered in making progress that required more hands and minds. Also, discoveries or inventions of one community remained concealed from the others, thereby hurting the comprehensive development.Slowly, everyone began to acknowledge those problems. Hence, steadily, things evolved even more, and several communities within an extensive natural boundary merged, giving rise to the concept of provinces. However, in all these ages of socio-political evolutions, the socialist economic setup remained constant."

"So history says, provincial-level headship with socialism best suits human civilization," Chitra spoke confidently, looking at Sanjam.

Sanjam shook his head, saying, "Not exactly. Although for some long years, it did work well, later new issues emerged. Lack of competition and incentives discouraged people from performing at full potential. Everyone's productivity was minimal, and the quality of goods and services suffered. New inventions and discoveries became rare, and the masses turned lazier.

"Further, kingdoms waged wars against each other to gain more land and resources. Also, every state had its distinctive customs, traditions, and norms and wanted to force them upon other kingdoms. Eventually, to do away with all these drawbacks and challenges, Emperor Bharata inspired nationhood in this subcontinent with an economy of free and fair competition. That was a radical event, resulting in the exponential growth, development, and progress of Aryavrata. Thus, our civilization advanced while the other tribes scattered in different parts of the planet remained regressive and underdeveloped."

"But we still have socialist kingdoms like Pragjyotishpura, Keralam, and Kamboja. They are surviving," Madhu countered Sanjam's history-based arguments.

This time before Sanjam could answer, Palan spoke up, "It's mainly because they have commercial exchanges with other states that are capitalist. Hence, they have to perform at full potential. A nation that has a mixture of socialist and capitalist provinces is ideal. Moreover, in Aryavrata, there is state investment and sponsorship for people's welfare. There are social security schemes, and education and health are state-sponsored. So, there is no point in the Band trying to disrupt the ongoing decent system."

"I even doubt if the central leadership of the Band truly wants real change," Sanjam commented. "If they genuinely wanted an economic system where no private property exists, with every resource being community-owned, they would have agreed to discuss their ideas with the regime. When the Band initially started their atrocious acts and disguised them as attacks against capitalism, Emperor Yudhisthir invited them for a discussion. The emperor had vowed not to harm or detain them. The Band never accepted the invitation. Moreover, the Band members are not entirely selfless people. Maybe, therefore, upon winning the battle of Kalinga, they are being promised wealth as an incentive."

Madhu and Chitra nodded in agreement and Madhu said, "So, we must let the regime know of this plan, and they can move an enormously large army towards Kalinga; maybe an army of one aukshahini sena. Against them, the fifty thousand-odd Band forces will not dare to fight and surrender without a battle."

Sanjam sighed and stood up. He took a small stroll and then turned towards the others. "I have been thinking about it, and I feel if a massive army moves towards Kalinga, the spies of Band will come to know about it. Like Hira and Chandran here, the Band must have spies at different other places too. We can only move an army of around twenty-thousand odd soldiers covertly and position them in and around the Kalingan capital. Also, the force cannot have horses and chariots. The battle has to happen, and we have to defeat the Band in it. During the ongoing encounter, a small troop has to arrest the Interior Minister and the supreme leader. However, before the battle begins, we shall once warn the Band recruits and allow them a chance to surrender."

BANASURA

Kamsa became the most influential monarch in Aryavrata after his matrimonial alliance with Jarasandha's Magadh. After that, he, Jarasandha, Naraka, and I made a sacred pact. We knew that if only one of us became the Emperor someday, it might lead to differences between us. Hence, we conceptualized the 'CHATURSAMRATAN' idea whereby once we established the dominance of our alliance all over Aryavrata, we four would rule together as a council of four. Once that idea was in place, new, vital, and ambitious chapters began in our lives.

We decided that each of us would increase our prowess and might over the next two decades. We knew that we had to be well-prepared with our opposition having warriors like Bhisma, Pandu, Dhritarashtra, Drona, Drupada, Bahlika, and Kripacharya. Hence, each one of us undertook specific responsibilities of growing our power.

Kamsa decided to maintain diplomatic ties with other kingdoms and gradually hegemonize his power over smaller provinces through financial aid and other measures. Jarasandha chose to raise and train an army, including a contingent of Maharathi warriors. Similarly, Naraka and his elite soldiers opted to learn sorcery. Like everyone else, I, too, took a task. I was determined to use these long years to look for ways to establish my kingdom with accumulated wealth and other resources.

My journey took me to different places in Aryavrata. I spent time at different sages' hermitages and stayed with smaller tribes that dwelled in deep forests and islands. I even lived amidst a population that the civilized people considered untouchables. And everywhere I went, I saw that people had their specific issues.

Some sages lived in the woods amidst acute poverty. They were scholars in different fields, or spiritual gurus, or expert counselors of varied subjects. Still, they found no importance as people preferred the services of well-to-do sages residing in the city outskirts or villages. On the other hand, several small-sized tribes lived in islands and thick untrodden jungles. Their habitat for ages had been away from the towns and villages, and they had their own primitive culture and customs. The civilized Aryavrata did not want to welcome them and ignored their existence. They had even started penetrating their habitat by clearing their jungles and building townships in their islands.

Another terrible and insensitive practice that I noticed in Aryavrata was the prevalent caste-based discrimination. The lowest class consisted of those families that worked in cemeteries, cleaned sewage systems, cleared forests, and maintained the sanitation of streets and alleys. These people were considered untouchables and lived outside the general residence limits, without any social or political rights.

Spending time with these different sections of society, I understood and could empathize with the injustice and inequality meted out to them for generations. So I decided that these people would become the citizens of my kingdom and enjoy every right and facility. Now, as I had found out the population who'd need my empire, I pondered to gain the influence and finance to establish my territory. However, despite my determination, I could not find ways to acquire them until a sage made a suggestion.

The sage told me that it was nearly a decade since Lord Shiva had started residing on Earth; in the Mount Kailasha region. The Mahadeva endorsed a life where people stayed as one solid and united community, cohabiting with the wild in the woods. Also, Aryavrata's social norms and customs, political rules and laws, and economic concepts and systems did not apply in Shiva's abode. He informed me that many people who faced injustice in this empire had chosen to shift to Shivghar. Therefore, he suggested that I meet Lord Shiva, become his disciple, and find ways of building an empire for the oppressed.

Thanking the sage for his valuable advice, I began my journey towards Kailasha. The trip was long, tedious, and even testing at times, but I eventually reached the Mount Kailasha region. I could see the tall and wide Kailasha mountain from where I stood, but it was still some substantial miles above. Thus, I would have to ascend several feet to reach it and decided to rest before the climb.

I rested by leaning against one of the many giant rocks naturally positioned on the icy ground. The rocks had turned greyish with years of snow deposited on them and the strong winds rubbing their surface. I closed my eyes and engulfed my whole body with my shawl. I was almost asleep when I heard quivering and soft but long grunts. I quickly removed the cloak and sat attentively. Then, glancing around myself, I saw a mountain deer leaping and running and some soldiers with bows and arrows chasing it. They passed right in front of me.

Wasting no time, I stood up and rushed near the soldiers. Unfortunately, by then, some of those soldiers had entrapped the deer in a net.

"Leave that animal alone," I commanded them.

The soldiers first looked at me, probably thinking who I was. Then they saw my sword and laughed.

One of them pulled out his sword and pointed at me. "Anyone with a long sword thinks himself a hero and tries to act as a savior. Move away, and don't interfere in matters not concerning you!"

His rebuke made me instantly lose my temper. Agitated, I swiftly pulled out my sword from the scabbard, diagonally from left to right. The sudden drawing of my sword struck and deflected the blade pointed at me. In a blink, it was now me hanging my sword around his neck.

"Any little man who wields a sword considers himself a warrior," I scoffed.

Reacting to my aggression, the other soldiers drew their swords, axes, and arrows at me. In response, I thrust my sword vigorously at the snowy ground. It was a mighty shove, and in no time, cracks developed on the trembling snow land. My strength amazed the soldiers, and I could see nervousness and fear in their eyes.

Next, I whirled my sword at an extreme pace, and with utmost focus, looked nowhere but at the movements of the blade. The energy of my focused eyes and a particular mantra chanting ignited a long flaming fire on my sword. This supernatural act made those soldiers move some steps behind, and their eyes widened.

"So, now do I have your attention? Do you still want this deer to feast?" I asked them.

The soldiers looked at each other and dropped their weapons. Among them, the one who probably led the troop walked towards me and went down on his knees. Then, folding his palms, he spoke without looking into my eyes, "My Lord, we don't need this species of deer for their meat. In our kingdom of Kamboja, there is an infection that is turning contagious. Half of the citizens are on deathbeds, and the only medicine that can cure the disease requires the saliva of these mountain deer. So our royal physician had asked for a hundred such deer to develop the medicine."

Hearing out their predicament, I decided to aid them. But I could not let the soldiers take the mountain deer. Therefore, I asked two of the soldiers to hold the deer, and opening its mouth, I pulled out the gooey substance from its throat. After that, using my magical ability, I created a large quantity of tonic from that substance. The soldiers had water bags with them, and they stored the brew in them. I assured them that this medicine would work. They trusted my words, thanked me, and went away.

After the minor incident, I started my ascending once again. I had hardly walked a few meters when I saw a girl approaching me. She seemed somewhat younger than me, and she looked beautiful, dressed in a milky white saree and adorned with flower bangles and a flower necklace. There was such a mesmerizing grace in her walk as well.

Standing right in front of me, she said, "O brave one, I am here to thank you for saving that little creature. I saw how you fought for that kind, little, innocent animal. I also witnessed your valiance and power. Who are you? And where are you going?"

I told her where I was heading but not why. Fortunately, she lived in the Shivghar and offered me to show the way. I was happy to agree. We continued walking together. The lady was talkative, and her name was Brinda. She told me her parents had given up the worldly and regular life and shifted to Shiva's abode ten years ago with her. She also shared how peaceful and happy their lives in this place were. "It is like one huge family with so many members," she gleefully told. Her talks were exciting, and she never ran out of topics.

I did not even realize when we reached the Shivghar.

In the Shiva-led community abode, Brinda introduced me to almost everyone. She told them about witnessing me saving the deer and the confrontation with the Kamboja soldiers. I spent the evening and night with the community residents and interacted a lot with them. They thought that despite being a warrior with supernatural abilities, I had rejected the outside world and came to join them in Shivghar. Brinda, too, felt so. I wanted to tell them that I was only a visitor at their place and had other intentions. However, I felt there was no point in explaining to them my life and motives. That night as I slept inside a cave-like structure, I remained anxious to meet Mahadeva the following morning.

I woke up early the following day and bathed with the water stored in a large tank. Thereafter, I went out in search of some flowers and collected water in a pot. Thus, with a decent preparation to greet the Great God, Mahadeva, I waited with anticipation for him to show up.

I didn't have to wait long. Sometime later, I saw a tall and broad figure walking towards the settlement. The residents also saw Shiva coming, and they bowed with folded hands. I carried the flowers in a small clay tray that Brinda gave me. On my other hand, there was the water pot. As I neared Shiva, he looked at me. I closed my eyes, and a delightful smile surfaced on my face. Shiva stood still in front of me, and I knelt quickly. I poured the water on his feet and placed the flowers too. Next, I touched his feet with my forehead and greeted him with reverence. "Pranam, the Great Mahadeva, the God of Gods. I bow at your feet and seek your blessings."

Shiva smiled. "You may rise, son. I know who you are and why you are here. Banasura."

Hearing my name from the Mahadeva made me feel blissful. I again touched his feet before standing with folded hands.

"I am at a loss of words, Mahadeva, and I don't know how to start my talk," I somehow managed to say.

"Are you here for some boon?" the Mahadeva asked.

"No, Mahashiv! Boons are earned, not asked. I am rather here for your guidance," I replied.

Mahadeva was kind. "Speak with ease, son. Tell me your thoughts, dilemmas, and desires freely."

"Mahadeva, I desire to establish my kingdom. And in my province, many outcast and downtrodden populations from Aryavrata would find a decent lifestyle and enjoy their progress. I want to do that because I want to keep the legacy of my father alive. I wish to create a kingdom, lead it as an ideal empire, and rule on the principles of dharma, just like my father, Mahabali. However, I also wish to gain back whatever was snatched wrongfully from my father. Hence, I have planned to spread my control to the whole of Aryavrata first, and then I shall even bring Swarga under my aegis. I also promise you that despite having the intention to conquer territories and realms, I do not wish to enjoy authoritative power and endless wealth. My idea is to establish everywhere a rule where people find absolute justice, equity, and goodness." After finishing my long speech, I waited for Lord Shiva's response.

"I am a God. I can read minds and detect truths and lies. All your words are honest. I also know that you have kindness, compassion, and righteousness in your heart. However, how do I know that these qualities will always remain a part of you? And what if your collaborators, Kamsa, Naraka, and Jara, do not have intentions as pious as yours?"

Shiva's questions baffled me somewhat. I could not gather the answers instantly. But after briefly pondering, I replied, "I shall take a sacred vow that the day I think of enjoying power and fortune for my self-interest, my head shall burst into infinite pieces. And if my collaborators turn anarchic, I shall stand against them, no matter what. Now I realize that I have already made one wrong decision by overthrowing and imprisoning Kamsa's father. I promise I shall rectify it as soon as I return."

Shiva's face turned solemn. "Your honesty and grit have pleased me. You seek my aid in establishing a kingdom, and I shall think about it. However, before I decide anything, I want to ask you for something."

Lord Shiva's words stunned me. "You can ask anything from me. But what can I give you, O Mahadeva? We are beggars and have nothing to give you. But, whatever you command, I shall do. If you wish me to give up on my intentions and lay my life here, right now, I shall do that too."

"What is your greatest strength? Once you have the answer, I want you to give it up for some greater good."

The Lord's statement puzzled me. I did not know why he said so and if he wanted to help me or not. Nevertheless, his words were my command. I closed my eyes and thought, what could I give up for whose welfare? Some thoughtful moments made me find the answers.

I spread my arms fisted my palms, and took deep breaths. Then concentrating deeply, I spoke with will and power. "I, Banasura, son of Mahabali, release the magical abilities inside me. And by the grace of Mahadeva, I command my supernatural energies to spread out all over this terrain's woods and wilds. I pronounce that these energies will shield the plants and animals from any external or unnatural threat, forever."

I felt as if something had gone out of my body. I immediately turned weak and dizzy as I opened my eyes. I could see Mahadeva still in front of me, and he had a satisfied expression.

"Your selflessness has pleased me. These woods will never forget you, even long after you are gone. However, I won't be able to guide you in forming a kingdom. I can only bless and ask you to find out ways to establish your empire," Shiva said.

The Lord's words shocked me, but I was happy to meet Shiva in his physical form and gain his blessings. I could find another way to build my empire, but meeting Shiva and pleasing him made my birth worthy already, So I bowed to him again, thanked him for interacting with me, and appreciated his good wishes.

As I sought his permission to leave, Shiva surprised me again. He said, "Banasura, your intentions are indeed pious. And your perseverance is extraordinary. Take a vow that you won't ever use power for selfish reasons, and I shall give you a boon!"

I fell on Shiva's feet again and, with sincerity, took the vow. "I, Banasura, son of Mahabali, vow in the name and presence of Mahadeva that I shall always use my power and skills to rule well. I shall always ensure that the places under my jurisdiction have governance based on dharma, compassion, kindness, and public welfare. Along with these, my administration shall commit to protecting and cohabiting with nature. And if I ever think of giving up on these notions, my head shall burst into a thousand pieces."

Lord Shiva was satisfied with my commitment. He held my shoulders and helped me stand. Then he placed his right palm over my head. "I bless that you shall have the ability of a thousand hands. You can create your thousand clones, whenever required and they all will perform in synchronization with your wishes. Also, in your efforts of establishing a perfect dharma-based regime across the world and beyond, if you ever need my assistance against any hurdle, I shall stand by you!" Lord Shiva further advised me to go to a part of the Himavat region and meet Kubera. Kubera, a Yaksha, guarded an endless treasure that he shared with remarkable beings for good causes.

With the boons and advice from Shiva, I started my journey to meet Kubera. But before that, I thanked everyone in Shivghar for their hospitality. Brinda was in particular happy to know my ambitions, and she wished me good luck. She also gifted me an amulet and asked me to keep it with me always. Although I never again met her, I recall her often and still have her gift tied on my left arm.

After I met and pleased Kubera, and he gifted me an amount of wealth sufficient to help establish a kingdom, I made a long retreating trip to Aryavrata. However, coming back after nearly two decades, I was dumbfounded by several shocking developments.

I learned that Kamsa had turned into an atrocious ruler over time, and his nephew killed him. Although his nephew, Krishna, was only nineteen now, he was an influential and admired person in the politics of Aryavrata. I also came to know that Naraka and Jarasandha had also turned into vile characters. In Naraka's kingdom, disregard for women's rights had made the empire extremely patriarchal and unsafe for women. On the other hand, Jarasandha supported Kamsa's authoritarian rule and developed enmity with the other dominant noble houses of Aryavrata. In such a scenario, our alliance and concept of CHATURSAMRATAN no longer were viable.

In the next few years, I worked alone on establishing my kingdom. First, I hired an army of mercenaries from different parts of Aryavrata. Then with their assistance, I turned a massive dead forested area into a habitable territory. The terrain was close to

Naraka's Pragjyotishpura. Gradually, I constructed structures, buildings, towers, houses, and other necessities in the territory by hiring engineers and a workforce from different kingdoms.

At last, when everything was ready, I brought the diverse populations who required a new land. Sages from jungles, tribals from forests and islands, and untouchables from various states began inhabiting the kingdom.

On the day of the formal establishment of the kingdom, I led the entire population for a large-scale religious ceremony. Priests and sages from across Aryavrata blessed the ceremony. However, when our Mahaguru peeked into the future of the kingdom for a suitable name, his revelation stirred me.

"Maharaj, one day, this land will be a battleground for two Gods. A war will shape the future of this land and that war will bleed this kingdom. There will be an affiliation of this kingdom with blood and brutality. One day, Rajan, the soil of this land will consume blood not water. The rivers would be crimson not blue. The roads and lanes will be drenched in red." The Mahaguru took a pause and then looked at the skies. "And for that, I name this land Sonitpura."

I looked at the Mahaguru intently, and in an intimidating tone, I said, "Sonitpura it is then! Sonit is a synonym for blood and our realm endorses that every citizen will be bonded as if they are tied by blood relations. And this is the only reason behind the name." "I hope you understand me, Gurudeva," I stressed on the last line.

The Mahaguru nodded, and I could see the hint of fear in his eyes, and it only made me feel stronger!

As Sonitpura's king, I established formal relations with other kingdoms. With Narakasura and Jarasandha turning completely unrighteous, I made alliances with the rulers of Keralam, Vidharbha, Kalinga, Vanga, and the southern Aryavrata states. I also started a socialist economy, enacted environmental laws, and focused on ecological development.

With time many more political and apolitical developments took place in the subcontinent. Naraka's kingdom gradually became a terrible territory for women, and he also had a rivalry with Krishna. Consequently, in a war, Krishna killed him. Jarasandha also began a feud with Krishna, which finally ended with his death. Jarasandha had asked for my assistance during his feud with Krishna, but I denied it as his sins had significantly accumulated. In response, Jarasandha made our age-old alliance and erstwhile plans public. He even said that I was the son of Mahabali and sought revenge against Aryavrata for the mistreatment meted out to my father centuries ago.It created turmoil for me as mighty kingdoms like Hastinapura, Panchal, and Sindhu categorized me as a distrustful ruler. It even prompted two emerging powers, Trigartha and Chedi, to ally against Sonitpura, and they found support from the mighty kingdoms. Although the alliance waged war on us, we decisively won that, thereby sending a powerful message to our rivals.

After that war, no other kingdom dared to invade or challenge Sonitpura. We kept a grand and vast standing army but concentrated more on economic progress and human development. Thus, for an extended period, we had no conflict with any power.

Things changed when Yudhisthir became the king of Indraprastha and then the Emperor of Aryavrata for the first time. It was before Kurukshetra and before the exile of the Pandavas. Ahead of his coronation, Indraprastha, the city established by the Pandavas, asked Sonitpura to accept Yudhisthir's supremacy. However, I denied it. I told them that I was a better ruler and I had created Sonitpura single-handedly. I further argued that Sonitpura had a meager crime rate, its citizens lived in more harmony, and there was absolute equality. Hence, I indeed was the better king and could not accept Yudhisthir's suzerainty. Even Krishna urged me to become Yudhisthir's ally, declare my support to Indraprastha, and address Yudhisthir as Emperor. He told me it was merely a custom and nothing more, and I'd never be required to be dependent on the emperor for anything. Yet I denied it. My decision prompted them to consider Sonitpur geographically a part of Aryavrata, but politically we were an independent empire. We continued trading with our allied kingdoms, but they were not allowed to be politically involved with us in any way.

I had no regret in remaining aloof from the politics of Aryavrata. Sonitpura was a self-sufficient kingdom with prosperity and development. I only waited for an apt opportunity to spread my regulation across the rest of the subcontinent. I was ready to take any means to achieve the result of establishing a more righteous and welfare rule.

Some years after the Kurukshetra, I unexpectedly received an additional province to rule. The territory was the Pragjyotishpura kingdom. Following Naraka's death, his son Bhagadatta ruled Pragjyotishpura. Bhagadatta but perished in the Kurukshetra war, fighting for the Kaurava coalition. Subsequently, his son, Vajradatta, sat on the throne, and he turned into an ally of Sonitpura. When he died after fighting a lost battle to rebel against Yudhisthira, he declared Pragjyotishpura to be a vassal of Sonitpura on his deathbed. Hence, according to law, it became my kingdom, and the Pandavas couldn't demand it as now politically, it was no longer a part of Aryavrata. Soon, I merged my empire with Pragjyotishpura and retained Sonitpura as my capital province.

Chapter 10

The Battle of Kalinga

It was late in the night, and Madhu was sleepless. She sat on the doorstep of their hut, lost in thoughts. She had finished reading the biography of Banasura a prahar ago and was pondering about his life. The memoir made Madhu appreciate and admire his life even more. For her, he was a person who had positive aspirations and ambitions that were good for the masses. His selflessness, sacrifices, and perseverance inspired her greatly. Also, the philosophies he practiced and preached for righteous governance were worthy of being followed by everyone, everywhere. Madhu knew that his rule ushered in an inspiring socio-political and economic age in Sonitpura. It is well-known that almost no crime occurred in Sonitpura since its inception. The kingdom's citizens had immense love for each other, and nobody exploited anybody. Instead, people were helpful and concerned and cared for others. The public of the kingdom also respected nature and worshiped it. Moreover, there were hardly any orthodox social notions prevalent in Sonitpura, and people enjoyed immense liberty.

Madhu was happy to have completed reading the manuscript before the Kalingan mission. It would be her first battle, and no matter how wrong the Band members were, she knew it would be difficult for her to kill those people. She was, in particular, sad because she would also have to fight against the members of her cluster. Even if those members were not her friends, they were co-residents and acquaintances. She had been living with them for a long time now. So she knew it would not be easy to kill or injure them. However, reading about Banasura motivated her to find the courage to do what was right. She knew that the Battle of Kalinga would end the prolonged atrocities and violence of the Band. The public would no longer remain misguided and fooled as well. The threat of inciting mass violence and brutal civil war would also cease. With such conflicting thoughts, Madhu spent the night with uneasiness.

***

The movement strategy of the Band clusters to reach Kalinga was well-planned. Using messengers, the supreme leader of the Band and the leadership of the various Band clusters coordinated the planning and execution. Kalinga was closest to the Band settlements of Vanga, Chedi, and Vidharbha, and the Band groups of those provinces could reach Kalinga, by moving through forests. Hence, several teams transported all the weapons and armor amassed by every cluster to the Band locations of these three kingdoms. They could carry weapons and armor easily through the woods without being discovered by anyone. Without battle paraphernalia, members of the Band settlements from the other territories subsequently moved without suspicion in smaller groups. They disguised themselves as ordinary folks, religious factions, theatre troops, artist groups, and pilgrims.

On a decided day, the Magadh Band cluster, too, began its journey. However, they had no idea that a forty-thousand-strong force of the Aryavrata Army had already positioned themselves close to the battleground where the Band Army would station themselves. This time, Chitra also accompanied her friends. The scheme was that once they reached the Kalingan capital, she would sneak out, find the Aryavrata soldiers, and with its tiny faction, get to the royal palace and reveal the traitor minister to the Kalingan king.

The route for the Magadh Band cluster to reach Kalinga was completely through forested areas. So their journey was not precarious. They could also manage to cook and rest in the afternoons. It was one such afternoon, and the large unit had halted for lunch and rest. The members sat in different groups, chatting and discussing things. Madhu and Chitra were lying under a tree. Sanjam and his company were helping in the food preparation.

"After this battle, the truth about which powers are financing and maneuvering the Band would become public. Then, we can head back peacefully to our homes. But before that, I'd know the mystery of Sanjam's true identity. You know, I get so restless and anxious thinking about it," Madhu shared her thoughts with Chitra.

"You are worried; what if Sanjam's identity shocks you somehow instead of surprising you? But dear, don't think negatively. Is there any doubt that he is not a good man?" Chitra counseled.

"No, he is one of the best humans I have ever seen or met. He is almost a perfect person. That is why I fear losing his companionship. I want to know more about him and continue this connection, this friendship.But..."

"What?"

"He is not one of us. And that's the most significant fact," Madhu paused briefly. "As you know, we are so different inherently, even though we are so much alike. And in case he belongs to any noble house, you know he would probably not like my origins."

"He is not someone like that, Madhu. He won't judge a person based on genetics and genealogy. I trust in his goodness."

"I trust him too."

Madhu tilted her head slightly, looking at Sanjam stirring something in the cauldron. She loved watching his face, how his eyes darted from here and there, how quickly they reacted to the smoke but how persistent they were despite everything. Sanjam's innocence struck something in Madhu's heart; there was this beneath a fearless and stern exterior. .

Chitra also glanced at Samar working beside Sanjam. Samar, too, saw her, and they exchanged smiles.

***

The Magadh Band traveled on foot for some more days and eventually reached the jungles of the Kalingan capital. They stayed there for a few days until every Band group arrived. Once the entire Band army of fifty-five thousand and seventy soldiers had gathered, they decided to attack.

The night before the battle day, the leaders of different clusters unanimously chose three leaders to act as Captains. They also selected Mahat Guru as the Commander, as he was the most veteran and skilled warrior. After those selections, the commander and the captains discussed and explained battle strategies to the soldiers. A pep talk by Guru Mahat followed it. By the time the plannings, speeches, and discussions ended, it was midnight. Finally, the soldiers began putting on their armor, gathered their weapons, and started the march to reach the battleground, some miles ahead of the Kalingan capital city.

Sanjam, Rudra, Palan, Samar, Chitra, and Madhu, walked together at the end of the army.

"Is this your first battle?" Madhu asked Sanjam.

"I have been in a couple of battles before. Those battles were to crush unjust rebellions against the Crown by some tyrannical rulers," Sanjam replied. "I believe this your first battle, right?"

"Yes. It is," Madhu said. She gripped the sides of her armor tightly, her nervous tapping not going unnoticed by Sanjam.

"Battles are supposed to make you feel jittery. Nobody ever gets used to battles and wars, not even the veteran warriors. I don't want to make you more uncomfortable, but I think you must know what you should expect. Mostly it would be the same situation as the first siege. Work in formations and coordinate with your fellow soldiers. Be constantly aware and keep moving. Look out to every side and quickly save in your brain the enemy attire and its hue. As soon as that color nears you, you must defend yourself and hit back. Apart from these, expect to see a lot of blood. Blood spurting out of screaming bodies and splashing over you is routine in a battle. You may even have to walk over corpses, half-dead men, and amputated body parts. It's your debut battle, and so you may feel nauseated; puke whenever you feel like, never hold back, but continue fighting even while you're puking."

Madhu stopped walking and her face turned pale. Chitra, who had overheard Sanjam's talk, froze as well. The ladies looked at each other.

Sensing the sudden panic, Sanjam held her shoulders and looked straight into her eyes and said, "I could tell you that you don't need to take part in the battle and go with Chitra. But I know you. You thrive on challenges and difficult situations. You are a great fighter, and you also have the qualities of a good soldier. You can face a battle; I know that. And no matter what

I say, the first battle is always to be tough and dirty. However, I promise you; I shall not let you get hurt at all."

Finishing his words of encouragement, Sanjam moved his hands from Madhu's shoulders to her face. He held her cheeks between his hands, gently and warmly. She nodded and sighed. Along with Sanjam's comforting touch and words, she also recalled her idol, Banasura. She thought about how he, as a one-person force, did so many seemingly impossible and daunting tasks. "Like him, I, too, would not shy away from odds and discomforts. So, I shall face this battle and emerge out braver," she motivated herself.

***

It was almost dawn when the Band Army emerged out of the woods.Right outside those woods, there was a large open field where the battle would take place. The battleground was a meadow. The meadow to its left had the forest from which the Band emerged, while to the right, it had a low but long-running hill range.

As soon as the Band forces reached the ground, they were dismayed despite their readiness for the fight. They had expected to calmly organize their positions and formations and wait for the surprised opponents to reach the battleground in chaos and confusion. However, the Kalingan Royal Army stunned them by already taking a defensive stand on the field.

The Band members were staggered and contemplated how the Kalingan royal house could know of the attack. The soldiers were getting nervous and felt they were on the back foot straight away. However, before the soldiers turned dispirited, the commander of the Band Army, Guru Mahat, shared a piece of decent news.

"Soldiers, do not lose heart. This man has reached us from the Kalingan Palace," Mahat Guru said, walking to the middle of the soldiers. Another man accompanied him. Mahat continued, "He is one of our men from the palace. Our supreme leader is already in the castle. So, there is no trouble whatsoever. It's just that some Kalingan city-sentinels discovered our movement in the forests two prahars ago. Hence, they got the time to prepare a defense strategy. But don't worry as we have an ally inside the royal palace. The Interior Minister has said that his loyal forces would make a surprise attack on the Kalingan Army at any time."

The assurance of Guru Mahat rejuvenated the Band forces. They further realized that while their strength stood at fifty-five thousand soldiers, the Royal Army was hardly twenty-thousand strong. The Band soldiers quickly began preparing their aggressive and penetrative battle formation to counter the Royal Army's defensive stance.

***

It was Maha Senapati Digvijaya leading the Kalingan Force. He had divided his army into two flanks. Both the flanks consisted of two rows of soldiers. In the first row were the infantry with swords, spears, and maces. The preceding category contained the archers with long-range bows. There was also a rectangular open space between the two flanks, and towards the rear of that rectangular void stood the cavalry. Thus, when Digvijay would command, the cavalry could move straight and ahead through that space between the two flanks and clash with the opponents.

Mahat responded by asking his soldiers to make a replica of the Kalingan formation. But as they had no cavalry, they stationed a contingent of swordsmen and long-range archers at the rear end of their formation's rectangular void. Mahat named that contingent 'Pralaysena.'

The battle started with Mahat screaming, "Time to attack!" His war cry met with a unison of growls, howls, and grunts from the Band soldiers as they raced ahead. Their archers shot arrows over the heads of their infantry. The arrowheads soared low but long and hit the foot soldiers and archers of the Kalingan Army. The Kalingan army, too, started with their archers striking down the Band's infantry and archers. But the numbers were superior on the side of the Band, and so they inflicted more damages.

The opposition's next move was unpredictable and threatening for the Band.Suddenly they saw two contingents of foot soldiers surfacing from the forests and the hills. Mahat and the members of the Magadh Band cluster were the ones most impacted. They felt staggered, fooled, and betrayed to see the people leading those two divisions. Sanjam and Madhu led the army emerging from the hills, while Samar, Palan, and Rudra led the army, ambushing from the forested side. They were in the uniform of the Aryavrata National Army. Sanjam, his friends, and Madhu had moved away from the Band forces when everyone was in disarray to find the already stationed Kalingan Army. And nobody had noticed their absence.

Before pushing with the charge, Sanjam looked at the Band members. Some were aggressive, some were frightened, some were confused, and some were blank. Everyone had the desire and will to fight and win, but at the same time were gravely anxious too. Sanjam also knew that the battle's adrenaline rush, the desire to live, and the rewards of winning would prompt them to fight with full might. But no matter what the Band members would choose, Sanjam felt it was righteous to give them a warning.

"Soldiers! Listen to me. The Kalingan army is not alone. The National Army stands with them, and now the numbers are almost equal on both sides. Moreover, we also know that the supreme leader and Interior Minister have a pact." Sanjam's voice echoed loud. His revelation made the Band soldiers even more dismayed and lost. Looking at their pale faces, Sanjam continued, "As I speak, there are soldiers in the palace arresting the two. Hence, this is a lost battle and a lost cause for the Band. The Band will no longer exist. So, surrender yourselves now, and you will live."

The Band soldiers started pondering their situation. Sanjam's disclosures made them feel that the battle was pointless now. So after grumbling and cursing their fate and predicament, they began discussing what they should do. Mahat understood the mindset of his soldiers. They did not wish to surrender but were utterly dejected. He also knew that with the supreme leader caught, there was no future for the outfit. But he was not someone who would surrender.

Mahat turned to his soldiers and spoke with passion and fierceness. "Listen to me with composure. Between us and the palace stands this army. But if we can overwhelm our enemies, win this battle, and reach the castle, we might be able to rescue our leader and ally. And if we do so, nothing changes for us. The only thing we now need to do is kill each one of our enemies. So, this is not the time to mourn or surrender; it's not the time to fight but to kill. Kill for your freedom because if you submit, you might live but never see the open skies again."

Mahat waited for his soldiers' response. After a brief silence, they screamed in unison and were once again full of vigor to fight. Mahat heaved a sigh of relief and nodded with a smile. Then he turned towards Sanjam. "You betrayer, I swear you will die today!" Mahat bellowed.

Mahat reckoned that the troops approaching from the left and right had around fifteen thousand soldiers each. They were with spears, swords, and short-range bows and had already neared the Band army. Therefore, Mahat countered by engaging the archers from the Pralaysena at them. However, the armed divisions led by Sanjam and his friends used shields to defend against the arrows and continued to rush into the two main flanks of the Band. Although the Pralaysena archers hit many of the soldiers, their charge persisted. Soon they began destroying the Band's main divisions.

The battle's momentum was tilting towards the defending party when something again changed the complexion of the clash. The Kalingan cavalry, six thousand strong, charged without Maha Senapati Digvijay's command. Before the defending army could sense anything, the cavalry began attacking the Kalingan archers and foot soldiers with arrows. The horses and chariots rushed at the Kalingan defenders, killing them chaotically and brutally.

One of the soldiers on the chariots shouted with a horn-trumpet. "The cavalry is of the Interior Minister. We are his loyalists. Senapati of the Band, you have our support."

The soldier's words made Mahat smile, and he was confident that they still had a chance to win the battle. His soldiers were also elated and inspired by the newfound aid.

The cavalry was completely decimating the Kalingan army. If their attack persisted unchecked long enough, the Kalingan defense would break, and the Band forces could rush inside the city. The horse-riders and charioted soldiers were shooting arrows, hurling spears, and running down their fellow soldiers. Meanwhile, the soldiers of the Aryavrata Army were now busy fighting the bulk of the Band militia.

Two Band members surrounded every Aryavrata soldier in the middle of the battleground. The ones with swords and spears struggled to fight while the ones with bow-arrows were turning dead.

An Aryavrata soldier was fighting off three Band members together. He had a spear in his hand and was striking the rival swords fast and sound. Then, in a particular movement, the soldier pushed one swordsman away and shoved his spear at another. But before he could pull out the sharp edge of the spear, the third swordsman broke his weapon in the middle. However, fortunately, right then, a fellow spear-fighter saved him by thrusting the swordsman from behind.

On another part of the ground, five Aryavrata soldiers found themselves surrounded by thrice more Band members. Yet, they had the advantage with their long spears against the shorter swords of the opponents.The skilled spear-wielders formed a circle and made powerful but quick thrusts at the rivals. The Band fighters tried defending with three swords swished on each spear. Over the next few moments, three spear-fighters managed to escape their spears from the multiple sword moves and swiftly slit several swordsmen's throats. Contrarily, the two other spearmen couldn't save themselves. The other surrounding swordsmen broke their spears and killed them.

The situation was worst for those Aryavrata archers, who had successfully reached the hub of the battlefield. It was the thickest part of the battle, and there was no room for them to nock, draw, and release their arrows. Band members had surrounded them and turned unruly and berserk.

One climbed onto an archer's back and pushed his sword mercilessly inside the archer's skull.

Two Band soldiers gathered on either side of another archer and simultaneously shoved their swords inside his neck from opposite sides. Blood oozed out like a fountain from two gaping holes as the archer fell to the ground.

***

Sanjam and Madhu stood side by side and were fighting hard. Sanjam had a long, sharp, and thick sword in his left hand, while a thin but tough sword with a curved blade in his right hand. He used the sword in his left hand to block and take blows and moved the curved sword rapidly to kill. He also used almost every part of his body to attack. Sometimes he kicked the soldiers approaching closer to his body without coming in contact with their weapons. In other instances, even while swaying his swords, he elbowed or shoulder-pushed soldiers that surrounded him. His calculations and movements were precise every time, despite all the commotion, rapid body actions, and ever-changing positions.

Madhu moved right behind Sanjam in a consistent side-body posture. That way, she allowed the opponents only a portion of her body to target. Her choice of weapon was a double-edged spear, and she also had a shield strapped tight on her left arm. The metallic shield was small, slender, but solid.

Madhu and Sanjam cleared much ground and were on a killing spree. However, as she was moving ahead, ramming and shoving her spear into many Band members, a dozen Band soldiers suddenly entrapped her. The Band members had noticed that she and Sanjam, fighting as a unit, were causing a lot of damage, so they first attempted to take her down. Madhu looked attentively at the soldiers around her and processed the permutations and combinations of their probable moves.

"Even if you all attack me together, you can't even touch me," she taunted her enemies with a chuckle.

The provoked soldiers thrust their spears at once. Madhu was agile, and she quickly split her legs. All the spears collided just over her head, and she used the entire energy of her body to crash and push her shield at the converged spearheads. Next, she instantly got into a pouncing stance and, at a lightning pace, moved circularly with her spear held tight. The spear's long blade hit at least seven of those dozen attackers, taking them down.

Madhu wasted no time and fought with the remaining five attackers. She employed a cunning but easy strategy. Instead of trying to hit them on their face or armored upper body, she bent and attacked their knees. In a few moments, they all were injured and turned immobile.

***

Samar, Palan, and Rudra were fighting at another portion of the battleground. They were leading three sub-divided sections of the army and successfully caused much damage to one flank of the Band force. They had reached the Pralaysena and were fighting them at the rear of the Band army. As archers with long-range bows formed a good size of the Pralaysena, and in close combat, their bows turned useless, they were killed easily by the troops led by the three.

Palan, Rudra, and Samar also engaged with their erstwhile cluster's Pradhan, Puniya, and leaders of other Band clusters as well. Palan, Rudra, and Samar stayed close and fought in a three-man formation against those formidable leader-warriors. However, at a point in their fight, Rudra tripped over two dead soldiers who were lying one upon another.

The fall was heavy, and even his sword escaped his grip. Unfortunately, before he could gather himself, the Pradhan stood in front of him. The Pradhan clenched his teeth and kicked him hard on his skull. The forceful kick with his boot made a deep cut on Rudra's forehead, and he started bleeding.

"Get up, you dirty swine! You are a rat. And I shall hurt you so much before I trample you dead with my boots. I swear you would want to run back inside the cunt that you came out from," the Pradhan abused him. He then stepped on Rudra's face and touched his arm with the pointed end of his sword. He slowly pushed the blade somewhat into his right arm and asked, "Tell me, you rat, how big is that whore cunt of your mother? Do you think I can push my fist inside?" While the Pradhan laughed out at his words and Rudra's helplessness, Rudra screamed and wailed with both anger and pain.

His friends were trying to reach him, but they were kept busy by the other cluster chiefs. In between the fights, they kept shouting at Rudra to help himself somehow, for some time.

The Pradhan spat on Rudra's face and struck the back of his skull with his sword handle. With that blow, Rudra stopped his wails, and his eyes started closing. The Pradhan noticed it and kicked him again, twice.

"Hey, rat! Filthy worm, wake up. I am yet to kill you," the Pradhan screamed. Rudra didn't respond in any way. At that moment, three Aryavrata soldiers rushed at the Pradhan. The few Band soldiers guarding the Pradhan countered two of them. The third managed to kill and knock two of the guards and reached the Pradhan. The Pradhan was quicker and smarter. He brought down his sword at the soldier ferociously, and with his left hand, hurled a knife that was inside a sheath on his garter belt. The knife hit the soldier's right eye, and he fell to his knees with a loud and long cry.

The Pradhan shifted his focus back to Rudra. He was yet immobile. So, the Pradhan bowed, picked him up by his long hair, and pulled him up to his knees. Rudra sat on his knees, placing his hips on the heels of his feet. He painfully opened his eyes and looked at the Pradhan's face. Blood dribbled from his forehead and left arm. His entire face was moist and crimson. But despite the pain, he started laughing. First, it was a smirk; then, it turned into soft laughter. Not much later, he laughed hysterically like a madman.

The baffling reaction of Rudra confused the Pradhan. He was uncertain whether he had lost his mind, was being over-smart, or had some plan up his sleeve. Rudra suddenly ceased laughing and murmured something. His voice was inaudible and broken. The Pradhan heard nothing, but he was curious.

"What?" he asked with raised eyebrows and an irritated face.

Rudra murmured again, and it was yet inaudible. So, the Pradhan bent a bit and brought his face close to his. As he waited to hear Rudra, the latter suddenly threw an uppercut at the Pradhan's chin. It was a massive shot that made the Pradhan fall on his back. Rudra quickly picked a shield lying nearby and pounced with it at the Pradhan.

Rudra was over the Pradhan's chest, and in one swift and massive blow, he brought the shield down on the Pradhan's face. The Pradhan died without even managing a shout. Raising his head, Rudra saw the Band soldiers fighting nearby rush at him. He quickly pulled out the few knives kept inside Pradhan's garter belt and killed those soldiers by hurling those knives at them. Despite his terrible condition, his aim and mind were sound and sharp. With those soldiers dead, Rudra started to lose his senses and fell over Pradhan's corpse. He was lucky that by then, Palan had reached him with some soldiers. "Let's take him away." Rudra heard those words from Palan as he fell asleep.

***

"Madhu, we need to take a troop and aid the Kalingan soldiers. The cavalry has been crushing them. Also, Mahat and a contingent have been assisting them for some time now. And if we don't go there, Mahat's contingent will enter the city," Sanjam said.

Sanjam and Madhu asked soldiers to accompany them. Around seven thousand soldiers sprinted with them toward the area where the cavalry and Mahat's troops were destroying the Kalingan defense. The Sanjam-Madhu-led forces were given cover by fifteen hundred soldiers. Those fifteen hundred soldiers engaged the Band fighters and blocked them from chasing the diverting party.

On Sanjam's advice, each of the seven thousand soldiers in his troop had picked up a spear and sword.

When the battalion arrived at their destination, Sanjam commanded them, "Brothers, your target is easy, large, lucid, but highly mobile. Thrust your spears at the wheels of the chariots and on the legs of the horses. You need to maintain a safe distance and hit your targets."

Each soldier started hurling their spear on the chariot wheels and horse legs. Soon chariots began crashing, horses started tumbling, and the soldiers ended up falling. The Sanjam-Madhu-led troop proved to be a precious ally for the Kalingan army. Now together, they started turning the tide by swiftly beating down their opponents.

Sanjam eventually was against Mahat Guru. No matter what, Sanjam considered Mahat his teacher and had respect for his thinking and attitude.

Sanjam said, "Gurudeva, I plead with you to drop your weapon. I promise you won't have to go to prison ever. I..." However, the Guru cut him short and shouted, "You are nothing but a traitor to me. My allegiance and also my dharma lies with the Band."

Mahat charged at Sanjam with his ax. Sanjam defended with his thicker sword and pushed Mahat away with his shoulder. Mahat reciprocated quickly by swaying his ax, aimed at Sanjam's neck. Sanjam responded by ducking and thrusting his attacking sword to penetrate Mahat's lower abdomen. But Mahat pulled back his body timely, thereby saving himself.

The attacks and counter-attacks of Mahat and Sanjam continued without either being able to make even a single cut on the other.

***

Madhu was fighting with the defending soldiers in a chaotic and congested situation. She was in such a position and state that it had become difficult to identify which soldier belonged to which side. Soldiers were moving all around her, screaming, howling, and wailing. Two soldiers, one behind the other, rushed at her with maces. She battled them by shoving her spear into the first attacker and then pushing it through his body to penetrate the other. The second attacker managed to sidestep. Madhu attempted to pull out the spear swiftly, but it took her a brief moment. That gave the attacker a chance, and he threw his mace at her. Madhu managed to pull out the spear, but as she turned left, the mace thumped her head, and she was down.

Her head spun, and she was hurt. She moved her head sideways and was horrified. There were dead and dying men and women all around her. On her immediate right was the chopped head of a lady. The dead woman's face was pale white, and her eyes were wide open as she had died in shock and fear. Her mouth was open and her tongue a bit pushed out. Her nose was half lost and dried blood pasted on her cheeks. After witnessing the sickening scene, Madhu could not hold herself back and puked instantly, unfortunately on the chopped head. Coughing and taking short breathes, Madhu turned her face away from the frightful sight. But wherever she looked, she only saw dead and red. Somewhere, lifeless soldiers had piled up; elsewhere, soldiers were stamping and running over still-breathing individuals. Some soldiers sat or knelt in the middle, tired or lost. Few even cried and wailed even though they were unhurt.

Madhu could only hear the screams echoing in her head and closed her eyes to relax. Tears inherently escaped her eyes and ran down her cheeks. She grew oblivious to everything going on around her. She felt she had been lying on the ground for a long time now, but it was hardly some moments since she fell. Shortly some Aryavrata soldiers surrounded Madhu and helped her rise on her feet. Quickly she somewhat gathered her thoughts and realized where she was. Then, supported by a few soldiers, Madhu started walking away from the action when her eyes caught Sanjam fighting.

***

Sanjam and Mahat were still at loggerheads. Sanjam was bleeding from his right arm and nose, and Mahat was limping with a deep cut on his thigh. They both had to defend themselves from random opponent soldiers trying to kill them.

Sanjam was slowly moving, trying to predict Mahat's next attack when he felt a sharp pain in his left thigh. A dying Band member who had been immobile on the ground for a long time had grabbed a fallen spear and shoved its edge into Sanjam's thigh. Sanjam screamed in pain and wobbled.

Mahat saw his chance and went back a few steps. He picked up a spear and took a run-up. As he neared Sanjam, he leaped at him with tremendous force, attempting to push the spear through his torso. To defend himself, Sanjam raised both his swords in the air and crossed them. He put all his weight on his bent right knee.However, before Mahat could land on Sanjam, Madhu arrived on the scene. She soared above Sanjam's posture and rammed her spear through Mahat's chest. The momentum of her lunge took Mahat a few feet away in the air before landing on the ground.

Coincidently, right then, drums and trumpets blew as around five thousand soldiers accompanied by the Kalingan king himself marched towards the field from the city premises. An injured Sanjam looked at that sight with a smile and said to himself, "So, the reserved forces and the palace security have finally defeated the Interior Minister's loyal soldiers in the castle."

Chapter 11

Confessions

The death of Mahat, the Band's commander, and at the same time the arrival of the Kalingan king culminated in the Band soldiers losing heart. Some of them submitted, and the others didn't give much of a fight. They all lost. The Kalingan patrol force took the surrendered soldiers prisoners, while the injured from both sides received immediate treatment and attention in the castle.

Chitra's medicines and care helped Sanjam, Samar, and Palan heal their wounds.Rudra had to receive treatment from several physicians as he sustained significant injuries. He was safe but needed intensive care. Madhu was not injured much; however, she was still in some trauma. Nevertheless, she talked to her friends and Chitra, her trauma dissipating with every shared experience.Barring Rudra, the others turned much better in two days. Sanjam could walk, although he needed a walking stick.

Sanjam met the Kalingan king after remaining on bed rest for two days. The king thanked him earnestly and informed him that the Interior Minister, Suketu, and the leader of the Band were in their prison. Although the Band leader said nothing but Suketa had revealed everything he knew about the leader. The king shared everything with Sanjam that Suketa told.

***

Sanjam, Palan, and Madhu had surrounded the Band's leader in prison.Sanjam was asking him many questions for quite some time, and he only kept mum. The man neither showed any expression of fear, worry, or anger. Instead, he sat still, leaning against the prison wall, like a dead man.

"So, you fear nothing; not the lashes of the sentries, neither the torture of the interrogators nor the bites of the hounds," Sanjam whispered. He then sat in front of him with a gentle smile. He held the leader's head and pulled him closer. "Are little Kanu and gentle Rambha as fearless as you?" Sanjam whispered.

Sanjam's sentence finally brought expression to the prisoner's face. He looked at Sanjam with an enraged demeanor that soon turned into dread.

Sanjam stood up and sat on a chair. He exhaled before speaking. "Your friend, Suketu, told us everything. We only had to promise him to reduce his sentence from the death penalty to ten years of imprisonment. We know that your name is Namantal. You are the son of the former Commander-in-chief of the Kambojan army. Your father fought for the Kauravas and died in Kurukshetra; so did your three uncles. Your mother died at the same time as she was already ill and couldn't bear the loss of her husband. As you became an orphan at a young age, you lived with your maternal uncle. Maybe your childhood at your uncle's place was traumatic and complicated, and probably you blamed the Pandavas for your plight. Hence, when you found a chance to lead the Band, you accepted it, as it was also a way to seek vengeance against the Pandavas. We already know your story, and now we want to know who helped you raise and lead the outfit?"

Namantal yet said nothing. He looked at Sanjam intensely and then gazed at Samar and Madhu.

Namantal remained quiet. Sanjam leaned closer and whispered in his ear, "If you don't help us in all the ways we ask you to; we will have to let Suketu take your name in public—probably in your village's weekly market. Then the public would quickly learn that you had seized a lot of wealth with the assistance of Band and hidden it somewhere. After that, I believe the public will talk to your wife. First, they'd ask, then they'd interrogate, and finally, they'd attack her."

He then ran his fingers between Namantal's hair. "But don't you worry. Our men would always be nearby. They would save your wife and let her be. We won't let people kill or gravely hurt your wife, but she will live through trauma every day. And as little Kanu grows up, he too will meet the same fate."

Sanjam's psychological torment worked, and Namantal broke down. He started weeping and whining. Moments later, in a broken voice, he spoke in between his sobs, "Promise me that you will do my family no harm. I shall answer your every query but please, make a vow that nobody will learn of my identity, and even my family won't know my truth."

"Where is the bulk of the fortune that you have looted in recent times hidden?" Sanjam asked.

Namantal gave out several spots and locations, and Samar quickly noted them down on a slate.

"Are there any more secret Band clusters or groups anywhere?"

Namantal nodded. He revealed the addresses of four more tiny Band settlements that had some formidable and loyal Band warriors.

"Do you have any association with the occult entity, Swaha?"

Namantal thought before answering that question. Then, after some consideration, he replied, "Yes, I led Swaha as well.

It is an outfit to fuel hatred and anger against Krishna and natively promote the Band. All its occult practices and rituals are bogus and harmless. Their main hideout is in the Chedi kingdom, in the Singha caves. A man named Gagan oversees their overall activities by taking instructions from me."

Samar looked at Madhu and Sanjam with a surprised expression. They shook their heads in disbelief. Nobody wondered that the Band and Swaha were affiliated organizations.

Ultimately it was time for the last and most crucial question, and Madhu wanted to ask it. She knelt near Namantal. "So now the final question. Which powers supported and financed the rise of the Band? And why?"

Namantal sighed and closed his eyes. He didn't wish to reveal the names of his masters, but he realized that he had no choice. Anyway, his master's plan had failed with the fall of the Band. So he began his reply, "The current prime minister of Gandhara is one of the two powers who created the Band and Swaha. He is a younger cousin of Shakuni. He loved Shakuni immensely, and they both shared a unique bond. Therefore, he has always considered Krishna his enemy for helping the Pandavas win the Kurukshetra war. And, of course, he hates the Pandavas as they killed Shakuni."

"Who is the other person behind the creation of the outfits?" Sanjam asked, curious and restless.

"Banasura," Namantal replied.

As soon as Namantal took Banasura's name, Madhu took two steps behind. Sanjam and Samar looked at her. Her mouth opened wide, and her eyebrows frowned. Her lips moved slightly, but no words came out. Then after some time, she walked with anger at Namantal and slapped his face hard. "You are lying! Why are you lying? Whom are you trying to protect?"

Namantal disapproved of her accusation. "Why would I lie? Whom will I protect, and why?"

"Okay, then tell me, what was his reason for forming the Band?" Madhu asked, grabbing his chin tight.

"I don't know much about him. I often meet the Prime Minister of Gandhara, but I have met Banasura only once, that too, years ago. I only know that Banasura does not like the ruling regime as he believes he is more competent than them," Namantal spoke in a single breath.

Madhu left Namantal's chin and stormed out of the prison.

***

Madhu was in a room with Chitra for a long time. Sanjam and Samar waited outside, worried and confused. Chitra eventually appeared out of the room. She looked gloomy and low.

"What is wrong with her? Why did she react to the name of Banasura? Why?" Sanjam asked Chitra.

"Sanjam, this is a sensitive and confusing situation for Madhu. She wants to talk to you, but please don't overreact on hearing her. You probably would be shocked and angry, but give her a chance to explain," Chitra replied.

Sanjam was even more perplexed. He nodded to what Chitra said and then took small steps into the room.

Entering inside, he saw Madhu seated on the bed. She lifted her head to look at him. Her eyes were red, swollen, and teary. Her cheeks were pale, and she was still sobbing. Seeing her in such a state, Sanjam was touched and moved. He quickly reached the bed, sat beside her, and held her hands.

Gazing into her eyes, he asked, "What happened, Madhu? I know it's something that you believe would upset me. But trust me, I know you'd never hurt anybody intentionally. So, even if your words sadden me in any way, I'd understand it must be a situational error."

Madhu continued staring into his eyes without a blink. She held his hands tighter to find the strength to speak whatever she had in mind. She took some deep breaths and bit her lips in nervousness. Her hands also trembled somewhat.

Sanjam could comprehend her emotions and mental state. He wanted to make her comfortable, and so he grasped her hands into a firm and assuring grip. Then without any inhibition, he moved his face closer to her. Their faces almost touched. He smiled sweetly. "Tell me, dear. I would understand. And not just today; I shall always try to understand your sentiments and situations."

Madhu, too, felt much more assured and comfortable hearing those words. She blinked and then said, "My name is not Madhu. I am Usha, the daughter of Banasura, and I had infiltrated the Band to learn who created it. She paused and gauged Sanjam's reaction. Sanjam was still holding her hands, and he whispered, "Go on, Usha."

"Years ago, when the Band was a new outfit, Shri Krishna had accused my father of creating the Band. He had called my father to a council assembly in Dwarka, where he made the allegation. My father denied the charge but, in response, gave up ruling and politics. He even left the palace and family and retired to the forest. I was merely six then. Since then, I have never seen my father. It's our Minister-in-chief, Bahurajan, who has been ruling our kingdom all these years. At a certain age, I understood why my father had retired so early. I felt that my father should have tried to bring down the Band and prove his innocence. But as my father did nothing of that sort, therefore, I trained myself into an able warrior. I wanted to know about the real founder of the Band and thus prove my father's innocence.

I believed that it would make my father return to his family." "Only some months before you had joined the Band; I turned confident of my training and inducted myself in the outfit to discover its true founder."

Usha's words left Sanjam in a dilemma. Leaving her hands, he stood up but did not move. Though he continued staring into Usha's eyes and wanted to express his thoughts, he couldn't speak.

Usha stood up as well. She sensed that Sanjam was not angry or upset, but he was in some dilemma.

"Sanjam, what are you hesitating to say?" she asked.

Sanjam sighed. After some more moments of silence, he spoke. "Not Sanjam, I am Aniruddha, son of Dwaraka Supremo, Pradyumana, and the grandson of the great Vasudeva Shri Krishna, the Supreme Advisor of Aryavrata. It was because of my grandfather that your father retired early and left the family."

He was the scion of the era's greatest and most revered man, while she was the daughter of an Asura.

"Do you hate my grandfather? And now, do you hate me too?" Sanjam asked, breaking the uncomfortable silence.

"No, I don't hate you at all. I can never hate you, Aniruddha! And I don't hate Shri Krishna either. Instead, I look up to his teachings, his philosophies, and principles. He embodies so many great thoughts and a perfect way of life." "I wish he had not accused my father as there was no proof, but I also think that my father should have discovered and revealed the truth behind the Band instead of retiring."

Usha's answer brought a smile to Sanjam's face. He felt relieved that she had no hatred for his grandfather. Aniruddha loved his grandfather greatly, even more than his father. It was his grandfather who taught him about life and everything else. He also had more memories with Krishna than with his father, Pradyumana.

"Do you still believe that your father is innocent?" Aniruddha asked.

"Yes, without a doubt," Usha replied promptly. "My father has not come out of the forests even to meet mother or me once, then how can he run the Band? I believe someone else is using his name for some reason."

Aniruddha sighed. "In that case, let's meet your father and see for ourselves," he said. "I shall go with you to your motherland, and only if we both are sure that your father is in the wrong, I shall reveal his name to my grandfather."

Usha was elated on hearing Aniruddha's decision. She hugged him tight, and they enjoyed a comforting tenderness. Then, while some quiet moments passed in the embrace, she whispered, "Thank you so much, Aniruddha. I swear, if my father is indeed the culprit, I shall accompany you to meet your grandfather."

Their hug turned firmer.

***

Aniruddha was in a room with Samar, Palan, and Rudra. Rudra was resting on his bed; he still required time to heal from the injuries and wounds. Aniruddha had informed his friends about his decision to go to Sonitpura with Usha. Chitra had also shared with Samar about Usha and herself, while Aniruddha was in the room with Usha. Chitra's full name was Chitralekha, daughter of Pragjyotishpura's Minister-in-Chief. She was Usha's childhood friend, and they both had grown up together. Chitra even revealed to Samar that she possessed magical prowess. Her family belonged to a house of sorcerers who had used magic to heal people and counter nature's fury since ancient times.

"Do you trust that Banasura is innocent?" Samar asked.

"I don't know. Honestly, I see no reason as to why Namantal would lie. But since Banasura had not even visited his family in the last two decades, he must be doing something more important in the jungles. So I want to see what his post-retirement life truly is," Aniruddha answered.

"And what do we do? What do we say to Pitamah Shri Krishna?" Rudra asked, trying to lean against the headrest of the bed. Palan aided him.

Aniruddha looked outside the large open window of the room. He took a brief pause and pondered. Then, turning to Rudra, he said, "Tell grandfather about the Gandhara king. Take Namantal and Suketu with you. But be careful while traveling with those two. Don't let the news spread that we have the Band's leader with us. And when necessary, inform grandfather that I am in Sonitpura to ensure whether Banasura is guilty or not."

***

Three days later, Usha and Aniruddha started their journey to Sonitpura, the capital of the Pragjyotishpura kingdom. Chitralekha, instead of accompanying them, stayed back in Kalinga for some days at Samar's request.Chitralekha had stood with her, steadfast in her determination to always be there for her. Usha did not want her to go through any more trouble and convinced her to stay behind and rest for a few days.

Chapter 12

The Trip of the Two

Usha and Aniruddha were curious to know many things about each other after they had revealed their true identities to each other. As soon as they started their trip to Pragjyotishpura, they asked each other several questions.

Usha was inquisitive about why a prince worked as a spy. Life as a spy was complicated, brutal, and risky. She was rather shocked that the Yadavas jeopardized the life of their crowned prince. She finally decided to ask Aniruddha if it was his rebellious choice to become a spy.

"You are the Prince of Dwarka, and your friends are the sons of noblemen in Dwarka. Yet why did you choose a career in espionage? You could have learned to fight and solve administrative issues even as a bureaucrat or some officer."

"Well, in my training years, I displayed traits that made a good spy. I knew it, and even my master told me so. So, I convinced my grandfather to allow me to make a career as a spy. I further argued that during espionage, I would see and know the intricate things of the empire. I would also be closer to common people. Hence, what I see, hear, and learn as a spy would help me understand my citizens better when I become a ruler. And that's how I convinced him."

"You are very honest with yourself. Despite being a royal person, you chose a profession in espionage because your inherent skills suited it more. I am glad that I could be a part of your life," Usha appreciated Aniruddha. "And I hope I will remain a part of your life," she added with a tender smile.

Aniruddha felt good hearing the last line. A wide beam surfaced on his face as she whispered, "I don't think we can part ways, ever. We would always remain....friends."

A few weeks after beginning their journey, Usha and Aniruddha eventually reached the borders of Pragjyotishpura. It was night when they stepped into the kingdom, so they quickly camped and slept. Both Usha and Aniruddha had carried their bedding, consisting of a quilt and cotton mattress.

The following morning, Usha woke up when the sunlight disturbed her sleep. She rubbed open her eyes and yawned. Turning to her right, she noticed that Aniruddha's bedding was missing. She sat up, startled, and scanned the entire area with her sight.

There was a river, only some distance away, and she saw Aniruddha swimming in its sparkling, unblemished blue waters. He was splashing the water all over himself, diving and surfacing, swimming in various positions, and allowing the water current to carry him here and there.

A pleasing smile came across Usha's face on seeing Aniruddha enjoying himself. She realized just like anyone else, there was a carefree child in Aniruddha, too, beneath his ever-responsible, serious, and righteous warrior persona.

Usha stood up and slowly walked towards him. Aniruddha was still oblivious to her approaching him. Finally, when he saw her, he blushed. She smiled in response. He took a few more dives and then emerged out of the river to stand in front of Usha.

She looked at his bare upper chest and then at the wet dhoti that had stuck to his tight and shapely legs. She also noticed the various cut marks on his chest, arms, and lower torso at a glance. Suddenly her eyebrows frowned as she caught a glimpse of a golden chain tied on his waistline. The chain was unique because of the green peacock-shaped locket on it. She recognized it.

"What are you staring at?" Aniruddha inquired with a playful wink.

She continued to stare at the locket for some time more and then raised her chin. She smiled and softly said, "So that was you!"

Aniruddha threw a confused look at her, and Usha then shared an incident of the past with him.

***

Almost two decades ago, Krishna had requested Banasura to come to Dwarka for a critical council gathering. Although Banasura's empire was politically not a part of Aryavrata, he came because Krishna said that the matter to discuss concerned Banasura as well. Banasura also brought his daughter and wife along, as they had never been outside their kingdom.

When Banasura's family reached Dwarka, his wife and daughter stayed and looked around the royal palace of Dwarka, while Banasura himself was with Krishna and the rulers of other kingdoms.

Usha was six years old then, and a new and more extravagant palace captivated her. In her father's citadel, there were lesser rooms, and the decorations were also subtle. Also, there were only three chandeliers in the entire fort. However, the Dwarka palace had many rooms, and every room had a fancy chandelier. Moreover, each gigantic hall that Usha explored had a fountain. Young Usha was bewildered and hooked. She even recalled seeing many fountains, decent-looking resting shades, parks, and playgrounds in the new city while heading to the palace.

Usha was curious and bold as a child too. So, unlike most kids, she never worried about moving on her own and exploring new things. But, at the same time, Usha was wise enough not to touch any of the things that attracted her. Instead, she only looked and appreciated them.

Walking on her own through the different parts of the colossal palace, she eventually reached a big balcony. There she saw some preteen boys playing with wooden bows and arrows. They were the sons of the noblemen who lived in the palace. Usha looked at them from a distance and soon realized that they were trying to shoot birds from the balcony.

"That's bad and wrong," Usha screamed, storming into the balcony. There was concern and shock on her face.

The young boys turned around, looked at her, and laughed. Then they focused again on target practice, ignoring her, and attempted some shots at birds flying in the air. They missed every time.

"Stop it," Usha said with a further raised voice. She soon walked closer to the boys. "Give me your bows, or I shall tell pita," she threatened them in her innocent voice.

"As if we care," one of the boys smirked.

"But you should care. The girl is younger than you but wiser and kinder," a confident voice said.

Everyone, including Usha, looked behind. It was a twelve-year-old boy who stood like a gentleman with folded hands. Hearing him, the other boys lowered their heads and said in unison, "Sorry, brother."

"You should take care of birds and animals, not harm or kill them. Don't you know hunting has been banned in the whole of Aryavrata by Pitamah Shri Krishna and our Emperor?" the boy sternly said.

The others apologized again and quietly walked away. Usha walked to the dominant and righteous boy.

"Thank you. You are a very nice and good boy," Usha complimented him.

The boy smiled and knelt. "My name is Aniruddha. What's yours?"

"Usha," she instantly replied.

"Okay, Usha, I need to go, and you too should find your mother," young Aniruddha said as he stood up.

Usha nodded, and he started walking back when something suddenly fell off his body.

Usha picked it up and saw it was a chain with a peacock-shaped locket on it. She handed it to him.

"Oho! This thing is so loose for me that it keeps on falling off my waist," he said, taking back the chain.

"Tell your mother. Mothers know how to fit things," Usha innocently replied.

Aniruddha laughed and pulled her cheeks.

***

"Do you remember that incident, our first meeting?" Usha asked.

"Not entirely, but I can recall bits and pieces now," Aniruddha said, beaming.

"I instantly liked you at that first meeting. I knew you were kind-hearted and gentle, but also stern enough to take a stand against wrong," Usha said. "For the next two days that we had stayed in your palace, I kept looking for you. I wanted to befriend you. But, alas, I couldn't find you, as I had forgotten your name. Sadly, two days later, my father told us we had to leave. I didn't know it then that Krishna Ji had accused my father, and so he returned with us in haste."

"Hmmm.." Aniruddha sounded low. He didn't know what his reply should be.

Usha hurriedly tried to cover it up, saying, "Hey, don't get serious. I just mentioned it in the flow of the incidents. I have more to tell you. Don't you want to know why Chitra and I were intrigued by you when we saw you first in the Band?"

"That's one of the biggest mysteries that I want to know," Aniruddha promptly replied.

Usha sheepishly smiled and made a funny face. "When I was around thirteen, one fine day, I was playing a wedding game with my friends. In the game, we had to describe the prince charming that we wanted to have someday. I also explained how I wanted my prince charming to look."

"And?"

"For some reason, Chitra decided to make a painting of my description. Right from childhood, she has been a gifted artist. She could draw an accurate portrayal of anything described to her." Usha took a pause, looked deeper into Aniruddha's eyes, and said, "She sketched a handsome, lovely young man. But we never knew that face existed in real unless we saw you for the first time. It was you."

Aniruddha was in disbelief. He meekly smiled, a blush creeping on his face.

"So, maybe in my subconscious mind, I always had a connection and attachment for you since I had seen you as a pre-teen boy. And when I had to imagine my prince charming, my mind miraculously processed your grown-up face," Usha added to the conclusion.

Aniruddha wanted to ask, "So am I your prince charming? Do you feel something for me?" However, he couldn't ask that as he thought it was such a difficult time for Usha. She was worried and anxious about her father's truth. Hence, Aniruddha said something else. "That's such a phenomenal coincidence!"

Usha nodded. She had expected he would say something else, something profound. But when she heard those words, she felt that maybe Aniruddha considered her a good friend but nothing more than that. Simultaneously, another thought crossed her mind. She wondered if she had begun considering him much more than a friend. Several questions surfaced at once in her mind. Was he indeed her soulmate? Does she have a romantic inclination for him? Were they destined to be together forever? It seemed to her there was a divine connection; she met him as a child, then subconsciously, she saw him as her soulmate, and ultimately she met him as an adult.

***

Over the next few days, as Usha and Aniruddha kept moving closer to Sonitpura, they both had many thoughts and queries in their hearts. Usha was already contemplating if she had fallen in love with Aniruddha. On the other hand, she also felt remorseful thinking about how she could fall in love while her father's name embroiled in a grave accusation. At times, Usha convinced herself that love is unpredictable and can happen anytime, anywhere. She also told herself that often life simultaneously throws different things and contradicting scenarios.

Aniruddha, too, felt lost in his own set of confusions and emotions. His primary dilemma was whether Usha professed her feelings for him by telling him that she has always seen his face as her prince charming. Did it mean she considered him her soul mate? The second puzzlement was that he couldn't define 'falling in love.' He also recalled Krishna saying that the Band's mission would result in his association with someone for eternity. But the question was if that meant finding his better half.

After investing in thoughtful considerations, Aniruddha grasped that it was fundamental to realize if he loved her or not. As it was about spending a lifetime together, there was no scope for uncertainty.

***

Aniruddha lay beside Usha, although on another bedding. He was staring into the night sky that twinkled with stars and glowed with the moon. Moments later, he gently closed his eyes, and her face surfaced in his mind. It was not Usha's current appearance. He could vividly see little Usha and her puffed red cheeks and her bright smile. The image lingered in his mind for some time, and he suddenly realized that Usha still had that same childlike, warm smile. The whole incident of meeting Usha in childhood replayed in his mind. After that, their every eye contact, smile exchange, conversation, and interaction surfaced chronologically right in front of his eyes. The last episode that he could visualize was her gloomy and sobbing face while confessing that Banasura was her father. The reminiscence of that scene pained his heart, and he felt congestion and helplessness inside him. Involuntarily his face turned left, and he saw Usha sleeping like a child. The moonlight's reflection radiated her beautiful face, and that sight made him forget all his thoughts. He was engrossed looking at her, and a voice in his mind spoke. "This is the definition of 'falling in love'. You are in love with her. Aniruddha loves Usha."

***

Usha and Aniruddha were traveling through a narrow lane with forests on either side. They slowed and halted their horses upon seeing a crowd ahead. Two large uprooted trees were lying on the route, which blocked the thoroughfare. They both dismounted from their horses and reached the gathered people.

"How did this happen?" Usha asked a man in the crowd.

"Yesternight, there was a terrible cyclone this side that uprooted these trees," he informed. Then he added, "There is a patient in our village in a serious condition. We have to clear this road to take her to the advanced medical facility in the next town. But, sadly, despite our efforts, we are yet unable to clear the way," the man said with grief.

Hearing him, Aniruddha quickly went near the fallen trees. He asked the people surrounding the trees to disperse. Reluctantly, they did.

Aniruddha took his metallic bow and nocked an arrow on it. Then closing his eyes, he quickly murmured something and released it high in the air. The dart retreated shortly at a surreal pace, accompanied by heavy wind energy. As the arrow hit the trees, it caused a loud noise, and a thick layer of dust and wooden particles engulfed the spot. The layer cleared off quickly and revealed that the trees had turned into multiple tiny log fragments.

The crowd was happily amazed by Aniruddha's feat. They cheered, applauded, praised, and thanked him for his help.

"Quickly get the lady on my chariot and take her to the medical facility," one elderly man from the crowd told some young men. Then the man turned towards Aniruddha. "You are terrific, son! We all owe you for this aid. Would you mind staying a night in our village? My daughter has her wedding tonight with someone from the village itself. I insist that you be a part of the wedding. Don't worry; you would be our guests, not helping hands." The man laughed.

Aniruddha looked at Usha standing beside him. She nodded.

***

Usha and Aniruddha arrived at the village. They learned that the bride and bridegroom belonged to neighboring houses. Everyone in the small community came to know in no time about Aniruddha's might and helpful nature. The villagers treated them with the utmost respect and great hospitality. Usha remained at the bride's house, while Aniruddha decided to be at the groom's house.

The bride met Usha. Learning that Usha and her friend had helped the villagers, she hugged her. Although the bride had embraced her in gratitude, she ended up sobbing. It was because the wedding day had made her sentimental and sensitive.

"Hey, hey, Padumi, why are you crying? Don't worry; the woman will receive good treatment and soon get cured," Usha assured the bride. Usha thought that she was sobbing for the sick woman.

Padumi replied nothing and continued the embrace. Her sniffles had not yet stopped. Usha moved her hands on Padumi's back to console her.

"Sorry, *sakhi*. I can call you *sakhi*, right?" Padumi asked.

"Of course," Usha smiled.

"It's my wedding day, and girls get nervous and sentimental at little things on their wedding day. However, I am happy that I am getting married right to the next house and also with the person I have been in love with for a decade," Padumi smiled and blushed.

"Wow! So I guess the biggest desire of your life is coming true tonight," Usha winked.

Among the bride's friends in the room, one teased, "Well, tonight will only be about desires. They are going to become one in every sense. But I wonder can our dear bridegroom tame the wild cat in bed."

Everyone giggled and laughed at the joke. Padumi blushed more.

The conversations, teasing, silly talks, and emotional moments went on. There were several small customs that the bride had to go through. Usha stayed with Padumi in each of those traditions. During the various rituals, the married women reminisced their wedding days and shared stories. Some got emotional and cried with the bride, while others were explicitly happy to discuss their wedding episodes.

"Very soon, you too would be a bride," a particular friend of Padumi told Usha and pinched her slightly. Usha blushed and tried replying but could not gather the words.

Another girl joined the talk. "I saw your man outside. He is handsome, strong, and has an athletic build. And, of course, the entire village knows how helpful and capable he is! In no time, he has turned into a hero."

The bride's friends continued teasing Usha, and the giggles and laughter made her feel shy. There was a constant blush on her cheeks.

She knew that they were talking about Aniruddha. She wanted to respond to their teasing by stating that they were not lovers, but she couldn't say so.

After a prahar, the ritual of bathing the bride was underway in the back compound of the house. The ladies related to the bride; her mother, sisters, aunts, and friends had gathered around. The ceremony was inside a wide rectangular area demarcated by thick layers of fabric sheets.

The bride sat on a stool, and the ladies poured water on her. Next, every woman participating in the custom smeared turmeric powder, honey, and milk on the bride. Then everyone shared insights to make her marital life better. After the bathing custom was over, the bride returned to her room to get ready for the pivotal wedding ceremony with the groom.

***

Padumi was in her bride's gown and jewelry. She was almost ready, and her friends were only adding the final touches. Usha suddenly felt like entering a dream. She could imagine herself as a bride, and she appreciated how pretty she would look. As Padumi's friends teased about her soon-to-be-husband, Usha involuntarily blushed. She imagined herself as a bride, surrounded by her friends, and they mentioning Aniruddha's name. She almost giggled at the thought but regained herself when she saw herself in the large mirror ahead.

"Usha, could you please arrange my hair?" Padumi's request made Usha move.

As she started doing Padumi's hair,she randomly asked, "How were you sure about being in love with him?"

Padmini smiled and looked at her. Then turning back to the mirror, she answered, "When you recall your worst memories and then feel that if a particular person's presence would have helped you cope better with those incidents, that person is your strength. And when even the thought of something trivially wrong happening with him disturbs you significantly, you know he is also your weakness. The person who is your strength as well as weakness is the person you love. Also, a person with whom you can spend your worst days, share your most vulnerable secrets, expose your naked soul, and confess all your goodness and badness is the one you love. The person who would value your naked soul over your nude body is the one to whom you should give your heart."

Padumi's words moved Usha. She paused combing her hair and recalled every significant moment that she had shared with Aniruddha thus far.

Usha no longer had any confusion about whether she loved Aniruddha or not. She knew she was indeed in love with him. So she decided with a strong determination that she would propose to him soon.

***

The auspicious time to start the wedding ceremony had arrived. The groom was already in the mandap. The family, guests, and relatives of the groom stood behind him. Aniruddha was standing right beside the groom.

The bride's family and friends brought her to the mandap. Usha accompanied the bride, holding her hand.

When Aniruddha's eyes caught a glimpse of Usha, he was fascinated. He always found her beautiful, but now she looked ravishing. He couldn't take his eyes off her. The grey silk saree draped around her perfectly curved body seemed to be a part of her. The sparse glittering jewelry made her look like a goddess. Her long open hair in multiple curly locks, glossy pink lips, and perfect dark brows and eyelashes made Aniruddha forget who he was! As the nuptial ceremony went on, Aniruddha fell in even deeper love with Usha. Like Usha, he too imagined himself and her in a marriage ritual of their own.

The wedding process was long. It took nearly two prahars, and by the time it ended, it was almost morning. Usha and Aniruddha took some rest after the bride left with the groom.

Then they started riding with the first light of the sun. After traveling a long distance, they decided to halt and sleep for some time during the afternoon.

***

Aniruddha woke up with the sun blazing overhead. He placed his left palm over his forehead and looked at the sky. It was late afternoon, and he guessed he must have slept for a prahar and half. He turned aside to look at Usha, but she was not there. Her bedding was empty. Right then, Aniruddha smelled an aroma. It was the smell of cooked food.

Aniruddha stood and moved his eyesight. Some distance away, he saw Usha sitting on the ground and cooking something on a makeshift clay stove.

Hearing Aniruddha approaching, Usha turned to him with a pleasant smile on her face. "Don't come here," she politely warned. "I am making something for you, and it's a surprise."

Aniruddha was happily amazed. He nodded, smiled, and went away. While she continued her food preparation, Aniruddha freshened up in a nearby pond.

***

Aniruddha sat on the edge of his bedding as Usha served him the food on a banana leaf. There were several items.

"This is parboiled rice that the bride's family gifted us to help in our journey," Usha pointed at the flattened rice on his leaf. "Next, this is eggplant apple curry. Maybe you haven't eaten it, but it's a specialty of Pragjyotishpura. The other items are- banana flower veggie, fried potatoes, and a paste of wild taro plants. I hope you'd like them, although cooking has never been my forte."

Aniruddha eagerly tasted every item, and he loved their flavors. Those were also new tastes for him. He had only eaten the fried potatoes and flattened rice before.

"I absolutely love everything. And what makes the food more special are your efforts. You've managed to cook so many varieties without many ingredients and help. Yet everything tastes so delicious!" Aniruddha exclaimed.

Usha was delighted that he loved her efforts and praised her. She could also see in his eyes that the praises were genuine.

"But why have you served only one plate? Where is yours?" Aniruddha asked before eating any further.

"Well, I'd get mine soon. But, first, I just want to watch you eat," Usha said with a shy smile.

"Why? That's not fair. Let us eat together," Aniruddha insisted.

Usha took a long breath and blinked her eyes, blushing and biting her nails in anxiety.

"What?" Aniruddha asked, looking into her eyes.

"I am practicing. It's the husband that eats first, and the wife eats later. And I wish to be your wife someday. I love you, Anir." Usha abruptly said in one breath. The words that she chose to confess her love were peculiar, but she couldn't find any other way or words.

Aniruddha stared at Usha with surprising eyes and a still face. Seeing him react nothing, Usha became confused. She felt that probably she chose a foolish way to profess her love for him. She looked down, wondering whether she would have to explain herself. Thoughts were running wild in her head.

"Did I say something wrong?" Usha asked meekly after some more silence.

Aniruddha was startled. He felt as if he came out of a spell. He cleared his throat and then tried to speak. Words didn't come out easy, but a long and wide smile did.

"I love you, too, Usha," finally Aniruddha managed to say. He then quickly took some food in his hand and fed it to her. Tears rolled down Usha's eyes as she opened her mouth. She also reciprocated by giving him the next bite.

"And to be a good wife, it's not imperative that you must cook good, dear. You have other qualities, and they have already impressed me a lot. However, you do cook nice, that I now know," Aniruddha told her before feeding her the last bite.

Chapter 13

In Sonitpura

It was a full-moon night, and the wind was cool and crisp; the sound of crickets floating through the forest. Usha and Aniruddha slept in peace.Being lovers, they now didn't need separate beddings. However, they hadn't united physically yet.

Usha was in the comfort and warmth of Aniruddha's arms, with her head resting on his chest. His one hand caressed her curly hair, and the other gently rubbed her back. Usha moved her left palm on his face and forehead. The coziness that they both enjoyed made them forget everything else.Usha moved her lips to his, slowly parting them to kiss him. Aniruddha held her and passionately reciprocated. The kiss lasted for what seemed like an eternity, punctuated by the sounds of their heartbeats and sighs..

***

Riding for some days more, Usha and Aniruddha ultimately had reached the borders of Sonitpura city.

"I have a friend's home just outside the city entrance. We shall halt there, and I'd change into my royal attire so that the sentries don't stop us at the entrance gate," Usha informed. She scanned Aniruddha's dress. "You, too, should dress up like a nobleman, as you are with a princess," she winked.

"Oh, is it? As you command, my Highness. But I thought Sonitpura followed socialism. How come then there is a difference between nobles and non-nobles here?" Aniruddha sarcastically asked.

Usha sharply gazed at him and then made a silly face. "Look at yourself. After this long journey, you now resemble a hooligan or beggar. And there are neither thugs nor vagabonds in our kingdom."

"That's an insult to the Yadava scion," Aniruddha laughed aloud, but the very next moment, he turned somber. Usha noticed it and tapped at his shoulder to ask what he was wondering.

"Usha, there is a thought that disturbs me immensely," Aniruddha said with some hesitation.

"What?"

"I pray that your belief is correct, and your father convinces us that he had nothing to do with the Band. But what if he is guilty? If he is the culprit, I shall have to inform my grandfather. Would you then be able to love me?"

Usha kept mum for some time. Their horses continued moving ahead lazily.

"Aniruddha," Usha said in an assuring tone. "I do not doubt that father is innocent, and I urge you to believe in it. However, if my father has done wrong, I won't support it. I love you, I love my father, but love cannot make me advocate something wrong. So if between love and dharma, I have ever to make a choice, I shall choose dharma."

Aniruddha smiled at her response. He felt proud and happy that a firm, righteous, and noble person like Usha was his soulmate.

"Even I have a question now," Usha said with a curious expression, "if my father is indeed guilty will your family accept me? And even if he is innocent, will they whole-heartedly consider me a part of the family? After all, I am an Asura princess."

"Don't worry about that. My family would always respect my choice. If your father, God forbid, is guilty, even then, my parents, grandparents, or relatives won't judge a daughter by her father's deeds," Aniruddha comforted her.

"But you are a human and I am an Asura; won't that be a hindrance?" Usha inquired again.

"No, dear. Over centuries of evolution, there are now only slight biological differences between a human and an Asura. Like, your lungs and digestive system are more robust, you have another layer of membrane beneath your skin, and your muscles and bones are firmer. Barring these physical differences, we are no more dissimilar. I promise you'd gain all the rights as my wife and the daughter-in-law of the Yadava family."

Usha brought her horse close to his ride and kissed Aniruddha on his cheek by swaying her body slightly sideways.

***

DWARKA MAHANAGAR

Palan and Rudra had reached Dwarka with Namantal and Suketu as their prisoners. They handed the prisoners over to the Dwarka Palace guards, and soon, Krishna interrogated the captives. He learned everything from them, including Banasura and the Gandhara Prime Minister's involvement with the Band.

Krishna met Palan and Rudra and asked them about Samar and Aniruddha. They told Krishna that Aniruddha was already in Sonitpura with Usha to confirm if Banasura indeed had a role in creating the Band. They also informed him that Samar, too, had gone to Sonitpura with Chitralekha.

Krishna was displeased and told Palan and Rudra that they shouldn't have allowed Aniruddha to go to Sonitpura alone. However, he didn't mention the reason. Instead, he shifted his attention to the issue of the captured prisoners.

"Palan, take a team and retrieve all the hidden loot of the Band from the various locations. We shall soon announce the discovered amount and use it to finance welfare programs and policies to help the rich, poor, and the middle class. We also have to ensure that people get to see the enormous wealth that the Band had kept for themselves," Krishna said. He then looked at Rudra. "You take a team and arrest the Gandhara Prime Minister. We will have to wait till Anir returns, and then we can present all the culprits to confess before the public. Meanwhile, I shall send another team to detain the Swaha preachers. They will tell people how their entity was bogus."

***

SONITPURA, CAPITAL CITY OF PRAGJYOTISHPURA

Aniruddha walked with Usha inside the royal palace of Sonitpura. She told people in the castle that he was her friend and the son of a noble family in Keralam. Keralam and Sonitpura had a long commercial association.

Aniruddha noticed that, unlike other royal castles, the palace of Sonitpura was not extravagant. It did look beautiful, regal, and prosperous, but the decorations were non-pompous.

They both eventually reached a room guarded by four sentries. The doorkeepers knelt and bowed to Usha.

"You may rise. Would you please tell your queen that it's me?" Usha said to the guards. One of them quickly went inside the room and returned in a moment

The door was pushed open, and Usha and Aniruddha entered inside to meet her mother. Aniruddha stood just near the door while Usha walked further into the large room.

Usha ran to her mother and hugged her. It started as a warm and silent hug, but both mother and daughter sobbed as the embrace turned longer.

"My baby girl, you took so long to return," her mother said, holding her face. "You told me you'd need a little more than a year to visit different Shiv temples in Aryavrata. But it took almost two years."

"I am sorry, mother, but I had told you, I am making this trip to wish father's return. Trust me; I did all to ensure that Father can return to us," Usha replied.

Usha's mother showered her face with kisses, and they hugged several times, in between talks.

"Mother, I want you to meet someone," Usha spoke, pointing at Aniruddha. Aniruddha walked closer to the two women.

He bowed down and touched the feet of Usha's mother. "Greetings, Maharani Shree," he greeted with folded hands.

Usha's mother blessed him with a smile and then inquisitively raised her brows at Usha. "I see you have got new friends," she remarked.

Usha held her mother's hand and grinned. "He is not a friend, mother." She paused nervously. "I love him," she whispered.

Her mother didn't know how to react to the confession. She looked at Usha, still smiling, but she was vividly perplexed and at a loss for words. Finally, moving her hands on Usha's head, she said, "My little girl is so big now. She is in love."

Usha meekly giggled.

"What is your name and identity, young man?' the Queen asked Aniruddha.

Aniruddha sighed on hearing the question. He threw a tensed glance at Usha, but she tenderly blinked her eyes that assured him to answer.

"I am Aniruddha, Maharani Shree. I am a Yadava prince. Son of Pradyumana and grandson of Vasudeva Shri Krishna," Aniruddha replied with his head held high.

The smile on the queen's face fainted and then faded away. She sharply turned at Usha and moved her hands away from her daughter's head. "You are in love with a rival house?" the mother almost shouted. "Don't you know, his family humiliated your father? Your father considers his revered grandfather a rival. And they don't even consider us a part of Aryavrata!"

Usha felt embarrassed as her mother spoke rudely about Aniruddha's family, and he had to listen silently. She looked apologetically at him, but he seemed calm and composed, albeit slightly sad.

"Mother, please listen to me," Usha tried to pacify the queen, who was now rudely staring at Aniruddha. She held her mother's arm. "Mother, we have dismantled the Band. Its leader is in the custody of Shri Krishna. However, the leader confessed about Pita's association with the Band. He told us that it was my father who raised the outfit. But I know that it's a lie, and he is trying to malign Pita's name. I wonder why?" "Perhaps, years ago, when Shri Krishna had accused pita, even then someone was trying to frame him. However, thankfully now Aniruddha is with me. He is here to meet my father, and together, we will find out who is trying to frame him. Aniruddha loves me a lot, and for that love, he has crossed every political and social boundary to help me clear Pita's name."

The queen heard her daughter and became thoughtful. She didn't respond instantly but instead stared at Aniruddha.

Aniruddha knelt in front of the queen. "Maharani Shree, I love your daughter very much, and I'm ready to take any test for her. I beg for your blessing on our relationship. I swear, I shall not allow our family's political rivalry to harm her in any way."

"Get up," the queen said. Aniruddha stood up.

The queen sighed. "I don't know how your pita would react to this. But I shall soon meet him in the forests and tell him everything." "Well, I do bless your union, and I wish you both my best." She moved her hand once over Aniruddha's head and smiled.

***

Usha and Aniruddha were happy and relieved to receive her mother's approval. While Aniruddha spent the rest of the day touring the palace and the premises, Usha spent the whole day with her mother. She told her mother the truth about how she had joined the Band and why. She then elaborated on how she fell in love and described every adventure of hers. The day passed away rather quickly for her, and the night was sleepless.

She missed sleeping with Aniruddha. For the last few weeks, they had been sleeping together. Her face would disappear in his muscular and wide arms, with her ears placed against his heart, listening to its beats. She longed for his warmth and the gentle rubs on her back and head. She finally decided to sneak into his room as she found no sleep despite her honest tries.

***

In one of the many guest chambers of the castle, Aniruddha remained sleepless on his bed. Suddenly he heard a knock at his chamber door

"Usha? At this hour? Is everything alright?" Aniruddha asked.

Usha quickly stormed inside the room and locked the door. "I missed you," she whispered.

He smiled and took her into an embrace.

Shortly, they were both in the bed, snuggling in each other's arms. They kissed and played with each other's hair and caressed their different body parts. Their eyes met like never before, and both could see in them the desire to remove all their inhibitions. Usha suddenly bit Anir's lips, and he sucked hers. He steadily unfastened the strings of her blouse and pulled it away. She closed her eyes and let out a low moan. Aniruddha made Usha lay straight on her back. He looked at her breasts. Next, he moved his fingers on her breasts, circling the nipples with his fingers. Again, she released gentle and passionate moans. Teasing her a bit more, he eventually put his face on her breasts and then sucked them, one after another. Her moans turned louder and more intense as she held his hair.

Aniruddha continued sucking, licking, and kissing Usha on her neck, earlobes, face, breasts, stomach, and navel. His navel kisses made her giggle, whine, and tremble. Then, continuing his attention on her lower belly, he slowly pulled down her lower gown. "Should I continue?" he asked for explicit consent. "Yes," she moaned. Her eyes were still closed, and her hands were holding the bedsheet tight.

Aniruddha started kissing her legs, from her feet to her inner thighs. He gently nibbled at her inner thighs and then rubbed his face on her womanhood. He used his tongue and fingers, making her move and shudder with pleasure. He had not finished yet. He had no love-making experience before, but love-making turns fantastic with no timidity and the will to make the partner feel sheer pleasure. He wanted to adore and attend to her every part, and that desire made him do things that made her forget the world. He turned her on her back and showered kisses and long licks from her neck to her feet. He spent more time on her spine and the wide, round hips. The kisses and sucking on the hips made her sway them.

All of a sudden, she turned, overpowering Aniruddha. In a flash, she was over him. "Open your robe," she said in a seductive tone. He turned naked in a blink. Now she started making him moan by moving her fingers over his torso. She kissed his chest and then kissed his lips and neck wildly. Finally, she went south and attended to his manhood. His body jerked, and moans escaped his mouth. She sat in him and rode him slow and steady. They soon filled the room with their synchronized cries and the noise of bodies rubbing against each other. The night was long, and so was their union.

Usha left the chamber sometime before dawn, carefully retreating to her room unnoticed. She had planned with Anir that they would be visiting the city market later in the day.

***

Usha and Aniruddha were moving through the city in the early part of the day. She had dressed like a city girl, not a princess, and covered her head with a chunni. Aniruddha attentively noticed the market area and the general city scenario. Every shop was big and well-built, with multiple people working as salespersons. There was no market competition visible. Each commercial establishment sold unique goods. Usha also told him that each shop had to submit the monthly revenue to the royal treasury. In return, the treasury provided the employed sellers with a decent fixed amount.

In the residential part of the city, Aniruddha saw houses of only one type and design. There were also open-access godowns storing grains and other essential commodities. Whenever needed, citizens could take anything, only by mentioning the quantity and item to the officers supervising those godowns.

"Because the citizens of Sonitpura know that they have a rivalry with the Aryavrata states, they don't allow the quality of the goods and services to plummet. Their incentive is the desire to be better than Aryavrata. But in Aryavrata, such a system won't work, as, without incentives, the quality of products and services will drastically fall," Aniruddha told Madhu. She agreed with him.

Walking through the different city places, the duo of Usha and Aniruddha arrived near a temple that bustled with people. It was a tall and gigantic temple established by Banasura. Of all the structures in the city, it was the most pompous. The gate of the temple had a coating of gold. The stairs from the entrance to the main temple door were of expensive metals. Right before the temple door, there was a bull made of fine marble and adorned with rubies and emeralds. The temple door and the various pillars had gold coatings as well.

"It's known as Mahabhairabha Temple. Pita wanted the temple to symbolize the empire's prosperity, hence, all these extravaganzas. Also, Pita said that Mahadeva must stay in a more affluent place than our palace," Usha informed Aniruddha.

Usha and Aniruddha went inside the temple and prayed together before a large Shivalinga. After finishing their worship, they were surprised to see Chitralekha and Samar ascending the stairway to the temple door.

***

Usha, Aniruddha, Chitra, andSamar sat on a sandy riverside discussing many things. They were busy sharing stories of the recent past. First, Usha surprised Chitralekha and Samar by telling them about her and Aniruddha's love story. Then, Samar, too, stunned Usha and Aniruddha by saying that he had proposed to Chitra as well.

"It's so great that your mother has blessed your relationship," Chitra said with a smile. "I bet she would convince your father as well. Then we all can go together to meet your father, and he can also tell us who might be framing him."

Usha agreed.

"Isn't the weather turning gloomy?" Samar inquired, looking at the clouds gathering overhead.

"It would rain," Usha asserted.

The four were almost about to leave the riverside when they noticed thick white smoke emerging at some distance away. In no time, the volume of the smoke increased tremendously, spreading far and wide. Instead of moving out, the four stayed to learn what caused the vapor, and it quickly surrounded them. The smoke was thick and distinctively aromatic.

The inhaling of the aromatic vapor made the four lightheaded. It compromised with their vision as well. In the next few moments, each one of them felt sedated and fell on the sandy soil. They felt tired and paralytic, but their sight and hearing senses were intact.

A few men holding longswords walked towards the four who lay immobile on the beach. The men were tall and broad and walked with stretched and firm steps. Each had a full-sleeved slip-on red garment, with a black scapular suspending from their shoulders. They also had wrapped their heads with a thick fabric that covered their faces, barring the forehead and eyes.

Three of those men hastily picked Aniruddha up.

"He is the one, Krishna's grandson. He will help us in freeing our imprisoned brothers, sisters, and leaders. We are going to exchange him for our people," one among the men said aloud.

The three men started dragging Aniruddha away. The movement made Aniruddha aware of his predicament, and he struggled. He attempted to use his strength and escape the clutches of his captors. Sadly, he was still weak and anesthetized and failed to break free. His struggles only angered the men pulling him, and they made him kneel.

Each of the assailants surrounded Aniruddha. Quickly two of them held his extended arms. Another stood in front of him and lifted his head by pulling his hair. "You royal brat, you are so stubborn! You betray us and think you can go away without paying its price? The Band and Swaha may be different outfits, but we are brother organizations." The man grasped two of Aniruddha's right-hand fingers. "We can even exchange you with two broken fingers," he eerily laughed and snapped the fingers.

Aniruddha's high-pitched painful wail traveled long. His scream even inspired Usha to lift herself and stand on her wobbling legs. She walked a couple of steps ahead but then fell on her knees. She shouted and looked with ache and helplessness at Aniruddha. Suddenly it thundered in the sky, and rainfall started in the next few moments.

The raindrops washed away the vapor. The downpour also helped Samar, Chitralekha and Usha recuperate from the smoke's effect. The men dragging Aniruddha knew that the impact of the smoke would shortly cease. Hence, they hastened to take Aniruddha away.

Chitralekha, no longer sedated, stood on her feet. She closed her eyes and concentrated with her arms spread out. Shortly after, she pushed her arms ahead. Her magic caused the several stones and rocks on the beach to soar in the air and wallop the assailants. In no time, they fell, and Aniruddha was safe.

Samar, Chitra, and Usha reached Aniruddha. He, too, started feeling better, returning to his senses. Usha hugged him with tears in her eyes. "Let's get him back to the palace. You can treat his fingers, can't you, Chitra?" she asked, looking at Chitralekha.

Chitralekha nodded and also asked, "What about these thugs?"

"You two take him to the palace. I shall call our city soldiers and have them arrested," Usha said, looking at the fallen assailants. Then, suddenly, her eyes turned wide on seeing the now unconcealed face of one of them. She turned at Chitra with an aghast expression. "He is the elite guard of mother's dedicated escort party. Mother had sent them!"

***

Chitra was treating Aniruddha's fingers while Samar sat on the other side of the bed. Usha looked at Aniruddha from the foot of the bed. She was worried for Aniruddha and enraged at her mother. She couldn't yet accept the shocker; that her mother played with her emotions.

The door of the chamber was pushed open, and the queen rushed inside. There was a concern on her face, and she looked tense. She stood near Usha and looked at Aniruddha.

"I am so sorry for him. How did it happen, dear?" the queen asked her daughter.

Usha scoffed and clapped, tears flowing down her cheeks. "First, you send men to hurt the person I love, and then you stand here acting as if you love me?"

The queen sighed and looked away. She knew there was no point in telling any lie.

"Why, mother?" Usha asked softly.

The queen didn't reply.

"Mother!" Usha shook her mother by her shoulders.

The queen moved her hands away and curtly said, "I love you; you are my daughter. He is not suitable for you, and I wanted him to be out of your life."

Usha raised her arms in despair. "I can't believe it, mother. You knew that Anir would help us clear father's name. Then why all these?"

"He can't clear your father's name!" she screamed.

The queen's statement puzzled Usha even more. She stared deeply into her mother's eyes, and the queen moved her eyes away. Usha suddenly had a thought; what if her father was indeed the culprit? That thought sent a wave of shock down her spine, and she went numb for some time.

Usha looked around the room, and her sight fell on a knife on the bedside fruit tray. She ran and picked it up. She held it, and with a deep breath, placed it on her neck and turned at her mother. "Tell me the truth, mother. Or this is the last line I shall ever speak in this birth."

The queen's mouth gaped with fright, and Anir jumped off his bed, worried. Chitra and Samar, too, stood on either side of Usha.

"Don't do that!" Aniruddha exclaimed. Samar and Chitra urged her to drop the knife as well. Usha but didn't respond to anyone and only continued looking at her mother.

The queen stayed mum, and her eyes had tears in them. "Please drop that weapon. I swear I shall tell you everything," she said.

Usha dropped the knife, all her attention focused on her mother.

"I wanted to make you believe that the outfit, Swaha took Aniruddha away for securing the release of the imprisoned Band members. They would have killed him somewhere far," Usha's mother clarified.

Her mother revealed many more things. She started by accepting that Banasura had helped uplift the Band, although he didn't create it. Years ago, when Krishna had wrongfully accused him about founding the Band, Banasura saw an opportunity in it. He publically renounced his throne and went into the forests. However, in truth, he found out about the founder of the Band. It was the prime minister of Gandhara. Banasura met him, made a pact, and provided him with finances and able men to strengthen the outfit. Asking the Gandhara Minister to attack the Krishna-Pandava regime with the Band's revolution, Banasura returned to the forests. Next, with the help of an able warrior-sage named Bhaskaran, Banasura started planning to conquer Swarga. Therefore, he secretly raised an army, trained them in the jungles, and built necessary weapons. The comprehensive preparations took him several years. Finally, a year before Usha had left to join the Band, Banasura took his massive military to the realm of Swarga via a realm-to-realm portal travel mechanism created by Bhaskaran.

***

Usha was packing her clothes and some other things with which she had specific memories attached. She had decided to leave with Aniruddha for Dwarka. The truth about her father and the fact that her mother always knew that truth left Usha with no other option. Usha felt immensely hurt, deceived, and lost.

Usha saw Aniruddha entering her chamber and closing the door. His presence didn't pause her packing. Folding her robes, she spoke without looking at him. "I am okay, Anir. I shall need some time to pack everything, and then we shall go to Dwarka, never to return. Also, whatever Shri Krishna decides for my father, I won't object."

Aniruddha gently held her arms from behind. He moved close to her ears and softly said, "Don't be so hard on yourself. I know you're hurt. It will help if you express your emotions. Let yourself be without holding back your sentiments."

Usha could not hold back her sobs anymore. She leaned back and rested her body on Aniruddha. Aniruddha put his arms across her to console her.

"I am so embarrassed. I was utterly confident in front of you that my father couldn't be wrong. I made you travel so far with me only to show you how unrighteous my parents are. Even more, my mother tried killing you."

Aniruddha turned her towards him. Looking into her eyes and holding her face, he said, "My love, only because you brought me here, we could learn the truth. Also, I have no grudge against your mother. She arranged an attack on me only for the person she loves. It's a sensitive predicament for you, but this too shall pass; you only need to stop feeling embarrassed."

Usha's sniffles slowly faded away as she spent a long time in the comfort of Aniruddha's arms.

Someone knocked on the door, which made Usha and Aniruddha end the hug.

"Who's it?" Usha inquired.

"Your mother, my child."

On Aniruddha's insistence, Usha replied, "Come in."

The queen entered the room, her face sad and sullen. Her red and swollen eyes said that even she had cried much.

"Are you leaving right now?" the queen asked, looking at her clothes on the bed.

"Yes," Usha replied. "There's nothing more for me here. Now I realize every month that you always went for pilgrim trips; you actually stayed with pita. You both were so selfish and power-hungry that you didn't even think that your little girl should get to meet the father. All that mattered for you was political supremacy."

The queen heaved. "Whatever I say now won't make any difference. However, know that your father sought political supremacy only to spread the good philosophies that he endorsed. Also, whenever I used to stay with him, we talked little about politics and more about you. On the other hand, he always kept himself updated about you."

Usha moaned a sigh. "If you are here, thinking you can stop me, please don't waste your efforts and time."

"I know you won't stop. And probably you shouldn't." The queen paused and looked at Aniruddha. "Just like I have always stayed loyal to my husband, you too must be devoted to him. Whatever else, I know he is a good man and loves you dearly."
"I only want to make him a request."

"What?" Aniruddha promptly asked.

The queen stared into Anir's eyes. "Promise me that you will tell Shri Krishna to have mercy on my husband. That you will let him live, even if in prison," the queen said in a pleading tone.

Aniruddha nodded his head. "I promise, Maharani Shree."

Usha restarted stuffing things into her bag, and the queen turned to walk out of the room. She was fighting her tears. No matter what, she was a mother, and parting from a child almost kills a mother.

The gloomy ambiance abruptly turned into something else as loud noises of beating drums and blowing trumpets were all that everyone could hear. Shortly, shouts and screams of tens of thousands of men followed. Then, gradually, the cries became audible.

"Hail Emperor Banasura!"

Banasura had arrived from Swarga, conquering it. Like his father, Mahabali, he too had managed to subdue the Devas. History repeated itself.

Chapter 14

The Return of the Asura King

Usha's mother promised that she wouldn't tell Banasura anything until Usha and Aniruddha went away from the city. Usha knew that she and Aniruddha would need to escape at night as with Banasura's arrival, the town sentinels would be more vigilant. Moreover, if Banasura wouldn't find Usha in the castle as soon as he entered, he would alert everyone to find her.

Usha stood with her mother and other members of the royal family at the doorstep of the palace. She had convinced herself to act excited, emotional, and happy in front of her father. She had a smile on her face, concealing the heavy emotional turmoil and the mountain of sorrow and stress.

Banasura walked ahead of his troop of bodyguards. Behind the bodyguards was the elite force of his soldiers. The soldiers that belonged to the capital went through the city roads to their homes. There were also innumerable soldiers from various parts of Pragjyotishpura, and they headed collectively towards a ground that had permanent tents for soldiers.

Banasura, his guards, and the elite force entered the castle gate. The palace sages standing in two opposite lines blew conches to welcome their victorious king. The palace maids showered flowers and aromatic waters on the king. The king and his men continued walking to the stairs of the palace door.

Banasura seemed like a lion walking with remarkable calmness and poise. His steps were bold and firm. The light brown dhoti on his lower body had several prints of dried crimson, designed with the blood of his rivals. The grey metal armor on his torso also had similar print marks. The armor perfectly fit his trunk. His upper body was broader than his waist and legs in an apt proportion. His appearance was such that the entire frame was a combination of slim waist and hips, long legs, and wider shoulders. His face had no beard but a handlebar-shaped mustache. The long hair complimented his mustache well.

Ascending the staircase, Banasura stood in front of his wife. She welcomed him back by performing an aarti with a tray consisting of a lamp, aromatic sticks, and flowers. As soon as she finished, Banasura held her arms. "You look good. Where is our daughter? She must resemble you greatly now."

"I am here, pita," Usha said with a pleasant smile. She was behind two women and quickly walked to her father. Banasura looked at her face, holding her head in between his palms. Tears ran down his eyes as his gaze fixated on her face. Usha couldn't stop her tears as well. For a moment, she forgot everything else; there was no thought or memory in her mind. She only experienced the joy, content, and relief of seeing her father after two decades. They hugged.

Her father's touch and warmth made Usha experience a unique comfort. But as she opened her eyes and saw the soldiers standing below the staircase, she abruptly returned to the present. She let out a sharp sigh, and her body trembled. Banasura released the hug.

"Are you okay, my child?" he asked.

Usha looked away from her father's eyes and nodded. He felt strange but then thought it might be very confusing for her to see him reappear suddenly with a massive army.

Banasura wanted to make her daughter feel at ease and remove her queries. "I know there must be many questions in your mind. You must be even angry with me for never visiting you once in the last twenty odd years," Banasura told her. "I shall describe and explain to you everything. Of course, now that you're a grown-up girl, you would understand my perspectives. Anyway, how well did you learn your warfare training?"

Usha looked at him, surprised.

"Yes, I know you wanted to train yourself at war and weapons. I had therefore asked our minister to arrange the best trainer for you," Banasura satiated her curiosity. "I may have been away from you, but I always kept a tab on what you needed," Banasura said with a smile.

"I needed you the most, pita," Usha naïvely said.

Banasura's smile faded away, and he moaned a low groan of sadness. "Dear, I promise I shall make it up to you. And I shall tell you everything soon. You will then understand why I couldn't be with you." He kissed his daughter on her forehead.

Banasura went inside the palace with his wife and daughter. Usha, walking side by side with her father, looked at his face several times. It pained her to think that she would have to stand against him. The night was not long away, and she would be forever gone from the palace, the city, the country, and the returning father. The recollection that he hardly was ever a part of her life pained her more.

***

Usha had sneaked out of the main entrance gate of the palace. Aniruddha was already waiting for her. Chitra and Samar stood near him. Chitra had come to bid goodbye to her friend.

Chitra hugged Usha, and they both wept quietly. In between the sniffles, Chitra said, "Aniruddha has told me that he would see to it that your father gets a chance to confess his wrongdoings. He would try to ensure that Maharaj Banasura is house arrested, not sent to prison. If that happens and your father indeed apologizes for his mistakes, you definitely can come here anytime."

Usha replied nothing as her tears continued to flow.

Out of the blue, a spear jammed into the soil near the four friends. It caught their attention, and they saw a small troop of soldiers walking towards them. Leading the pack was Banasura himself.

Banasura stood in front of Usha with folded arms and stared at her with anger. The soldiers around Banasura pointed their weapons at Aniruddha and Samar. Some also held torches that brightened the dimness of night.

"How could you fall in love with someone from the Vasudeva family? Don't you know the history between them and our family?" Banasura thundered.

Usha lowered her head out of fear, not regret.

Banasura sighed. He shifted his gaze at Aniruddha. "You think you can run away after trying to manipulate my daughter? You think you are shrewd and audacious; you stay in my castle and plan my doom in it?"

"Oh! So mother broke her vow," Usha scoffed. "I can't believe she fooled and lied to me again and told you everything."

"Shut up!" Banasura rebuked. "It wasn't your mother. I have loyal soldiers inside the palace. Someone heard conversations between your mother and you." He then held her daughter's arms and asked, "How could you think of going against your father? You want to get me detained and end up in prison?"

"You have been doing vile things, pita!" Usha screamed. "The Band killed tens of thousands of soldiers and sentries in all these years. Moreover, you had planned even more wars and battles that would have resulted in the death of countless more. You have been fueling unrest in a smooth-running empire to gain political power."

Banasura left his daughter's arms and lifted a finger at her. "I agree; the Pandava-Krishna alliance smoothly ran the empire. But there is much scope for improvement. But, sadly, they can't comprehend the scopes because they are not that competent!"

Aniruddha intervened at the question of Krishna's competency. "Maharaja, being the father of the girl I love, you can tell me anything, and I won't answer back.However, I won't appreciate it if you inaccurately speak against my grandfather."

"Inaccurately?" Banasura laughed aloud. "The annual valuation of Pragjyotishpura's finished goods and services has been consistently more than any single Aryavrata state. And we are still a young empire. The crime rate here is almost nil; there is also greater harmony and unity among people, and we even have a better administrative system. So tell me, the scion of Yadava, how is Krishna more competent than me?"

Aniruddha was ready to debate. He understood economics and civics well enough. "The economy in Aryavrata is more complicated. Its states, as well as the center, have greater economic responsibilities. On the one hand, the regimes focus on commercial growth, and on the other, they sponsor welfare activities and ensure the development of public goods and services." Aniruddha took a deep breath before continuing. "The crime rate in Aryavrata was sharply plummeting until the Band and Swaha incited people. There was also increased unity amidst people, although, unlike Pragjyotishpura, the diversity is massive in Aryavrata. It was again the rebel outfits that damaged the harmony among people."

Aniruddha's counter-arguments irked Banasura. He reached out his right hand to hold Aniruddha's chin. Samar almost moved a step to confront Banasura but stood still when Aniruddha gestured him to stop.

"I don't need to argue with you, boy!" Banasura grumbled. "Yet listen, had I been the ruler of Aryavrata, I'd have undertaken alternate policies. Like, the division of kingdoms based on common ethnicities and dialects, for a start. I would have also initiated community-level leadership instead of state rulers for a more effective administration. Apart from these, focus on ecological development would have been paramount; Sonitpura is strict about environmental protection, and Aryavrata is not!

"Moreover, a socialist economy would have ensured equal and inclusive growth and more remarkable development. And above all, an iron-fisted but benevolent leader like me can inspire people to deliver their duties diligently, not a liberal one like Yudhisthir." Finishing his reasonings, Banasura pushed Aniruddha away.

"Father! You cannot hurt Anir; I love him. And you have got everything wrong." She took long breaths as the father and daughter briefly stared at each other. "Aryavrata is a vast empire, and community-based leadership would only result in frequent clashes between the various groups. Secondly, socialism in Aryavrata would drop the quality of goods and products produced. It works in our empire because the citizens here were outcasts in Aryavrata; they feel inherently inspired to do better than Aryavrata. That's their incentive. And, your biggest misconception is that an iron-fisted ruler can reign better. A stern ruler cannot always continue a good and long rule."

"You speak their voice. I trust you are no longer ours; you have turned into one of them," Banasura softly but sternly said. Then gesturing his guards to hold Usha, Samar, and Chitra, he choked Aniruddha's neck.

Usha, Samar, and Chitra struggled to break free from the soldiers' clutches, but they couldn't. They were too many of them.

"I shall give your boy a chance," Banasura said, looking at Usha. "If he can beat me in a duel now, I shall allow him to go."

"No, father!" Usha shrieked and pulled her arms, attempting with more vigor to break free. "Please don't hurt him. Please!"

Banasura turned deaf to his daughter's pleas. However, he soon left the chokehold on Aniruddha's throat but pushed him away. "Attack me, boy! And don't hesitate, for if you lose, not only you but even Usha will be confined," Banasura threatened.

Aniruddha looked at Usha and saw her crying. He then looked at Banasura, who had a mean expression on his face. Aniruddha could tell from the facial expression that he would indeed imprison Usha as well.

"Come on, boy," Banasura challenged.

Aniruddha raced and speared his shoulder into Banasura's gut. They both fell to the ground, with Aniruddha on top of Banasura. However, Banasura swiftly reversed the posture with his immense strength. He immediately sat on Aniruddha's torso with his legs across the chest. Further, his knees held Aniruddha's forearms, thus pinning him immobile to the ground.

Banasura wasted no time in turning brutal. He howled and brought a ferocious punch on Aniruddha's face that broke and bled his nose. Some shouts escaped Aniruddha's mouth, but he had not accepted defeat. Although Aniruddha took two more hard punches on his face, he retaliated next. Using his raw and brute strength, he lifted his head from the ground in a single jerk and successfully delivered a headbutt on Banasura's lowered face. The unexpected blow stunned Banasura momentarily, and Aniruddha rescued his forearms. Aniruddha's following move was a swift combination of two precise punches below Banasura's ears and a mighty push on his chest with open palms. Banasura landed on his back with a growl.

Aniruddha didn't allow Banasura any respite. He took advantage of Banasura reeling in pain and immediately brought his right knee to Banasura's temple from a height. He almost brought down a kick at Banasura's chest next, but Banasura caught and pushed the foot away. Aniruddha fell.

Banasura got back to his feet first and raced at Aniruddha fiercely. He quickly grasped Aniruddha's chest, picked him up, and gripped him into a bear-hugged. Despite the repeated struggles of Aniruddha, he couldn't escape from Banasura's grip. Finally, after making him struggle for breath, Banasura dropped Aniruddha with a suplex. Aniruddha flattened on the mud with a thud on his back. He whined in pain. Banasura rolled over Aniruddha's body and, as the last move, caught his hair and dribbled his face on the mud repeatedly. Aniruddha turned motionless as he suffered those nasty dribbles. Dirt stuffed in his nostrils, eyes, and mouth. When convinced that Aniruddha was senseless, Banasura signaled his men to drag him away.

***

Banasura imprisoned Aniruddha and confined Usha to a fort. The basement where Banasura locked Aniruddha had cells there were airtight. Only a small-sized hole at the ceiling of each cell allowed the incoming of little air. Guards on the roof of the cells passed food to prisoners through that hole as well. Outside, in the basement, venomous snakes of various kinds roamed free.

Usha's father had imprisoned her in a fort—Agnigarh, which was on a highland that had a circular perimeter of fuming fire. Guards ensured that the fire never ceased; hence, no one could get inside or come out of the fort in any way. A group of servants stayed inside with Usha as well.

Samar and Chitra remained unharmed and free. Chitra, because she was Banasura's trusted Prime Minister's daughter, and Samar had to tell Krishna about the imprisonment of his grandson.

***

It was the fifth consecutive day that Banasura was engrossed in his Yagya-worship of Lord Shiva. He was performing the Yagya in the middle of a small natural garden. He sat adjacent to a giant Shivalinga around which he had lit thousands of lamps.

"I am here, Banasura," a voice said. Banasura opened his eyes and saw Lord Shiva standing ahead, just beyond the Shivalinga. He stood firmly, with his left hand on the waist and the right-hand clutching at the Trishul.

Banasura bowed with folded hands and remained on his knees. "*Pranam*, Mahashiva, Hara-Hara Mahadeva."

"What do you seek?" Shiva responded.

"You are omniscient, Mahadeva! As you must know, I have imprisoned Krishna's grandson. I mean him no harm. All I want is that Krishna arrives for a war to rescue his scion, and I defeat and entrap him. I plan to use Krishna as a hostage and enforce Yudhisthira to renounce his throne for me." Banasura paused and raised his folded palms over his head. "O Mahadeva,

Krishna is a powerful sorcerer, and I don't have my magical powers. Therefore, I beg you to stand by me and help me win this war. I would like to invoke your boon of standing with me whenever necessary."

"I promised to stand by you whenever necessary, but only for the spread of dharma-based rule. But you're asking me to be a part of a war that you desire. Moreover, you have hindered the union of two lovers by imprisoning them, despite one of them being your daughter. So tell me, how can I assist you in this wrongful act of yours?

"Destruction is imperative for a new creation. The holy books and scriptures say that. Krishna told the same thing before and after the Kurukshetra to the masses, and everyone agreed; the sages, scholars, and demi-gods and goddesses. Similarly, even this war will bring in a new and better regime, which would initiate absolute socialism, ensure a crime-free society, and push for non-materialistic, spiritual growth among people. And for that, I am willing to sacrifice even my daughter's happiness."

Shiva stayed silent for some time after hearing Banasura's point of view. "That you will rule better than Krishna, and Pandavas is your self-belief. I don't doubt your intentions, yet I'd ask, how are you confident that you'd be the better ruler?" Shiva asked.

"Mahadeva, by your grace, I have been able to turn Pragjyotishpura into an empire of dharma. As a result, there is total peace, abundant prosperity, and kind and compassionate citizens here. I intend to replicate the same things in the whole of Aryavrata," Banasura replied.

"What of the Band, Swaha, and their activities? You supported those entities, and for years they plundered, seized, and killed. So why should I not consider you a culprit?" Shiva persisted.

"The Band and Swaha were the creation of the Gandhara Prime Minister. Of course, I financed and helped it grow, but I didn't endorse every activity of theirs. Nevertheless, I reckon that the actions of Band and Swaha have had profound and varied consequences. One, the long-term success of Band and Swaha implies that the regime of Aryavrata is incompetent to deal with such threats. Two, because of those groups, the Aryavrata administration remained under constant pressure to take up welfare schemes and appease the have-nots. Yes, the Band killed many soldiers, but innocents died even in Kurukshetra. In great wars and revolutions, collateral damages are sad but practical."

Shiva neither nodded nor dismissed Banasura's arguments. "I have my final question now. What about your invasion of Swarga? What better changes would you implement in the realm of Swarga?"

Banasura calmly answered, "Even in Swarga, the Devas enjoy more comforts and luxuries based on their powers and responsibilities. Now, no longer, that would exist. Instead, everyone would experience the same level of comfort and luxury. Had I not done that, humans inspired by Swarga would continue wanting hierarchical privileges and never accept the idea of the same status and similar treatment for everyone.

"In any community, some people would lead, and others would serve. Even I have my servants and maids, but they stay in good homes, wear fine clothes, and enjoy luxuries. Moreover, I allow my palace maids and servants to dine and eat at the same dining table where my family and I eat. Such practices but are unheard of in Aryavrata or even Swarga."

Shiva nodded on Banasura's answer. He realized that although Banasura took the wrong means, he envisioned an appropriate end- ruling Aryavrata and turning it into an even better and righteous land. There was no selfless intention of unabridged power and endless richness in his desire to rule.

"I shall fight for the defense of your city in the Hari-Hara War!" Shiva promised.

***

DWARKA MAHANAGAR

When Samar reached Dwarka and told Krishna about Aniruddha's imprisonment and Banasura's challenge for war, Krishna immediately gathered Dwarka's greatest warriors. Soon, Samar stood in a room with Krishna, Krishna's son, Pradyumana, Krishna's elder brother, Balarama, and the commander of the Dwarka army, Airawat.

"How dare he?" roared Balarama, "He attacked us all these years with the Band and Swaha, and now he traps our son and to-be-daughter-in-law and calls us for a war!"

"We should leave right now for Sonitpura and rescue Aniruddha and Usha. Only a handful of us can make a secret attack and release the two; there is no need for a war. Anyway, we shouldn't wage such a massive war that would result in the death of countless. Kurukshetra is still fresh in people's minds," Pradyumana suggested.

Krishna was silent. He was standing in front of an open window, staring into the moon.

"Father?" Pradyumana tried to grab Krishna's attention.

Krishna turned behind and looked at the others in the room. There was a blank expression on his face, the kind that none had ever seen before. His face was stiff, and his eyes stern. "I don't think Banasura is unprepared for such an attack. What do you think, Samar?" Krishna asked.

"Pitamah, Aniruddha is kept in the basement of a small castle, located closer to the city market. The elite soldiers of Banasura's royal forces and a team of Atirathi warriors vigilantly guard the castle. Contrarily, the fort in which lady Usha is trapped has a fire perimeter around," Samar shared the details.

"Hmmm," Krishna turned thoughtful, "so even if we manage to rescue Usha, we won't be able to recover Anir without fighting in the middle of the city market. That means, to save our boy, we would end up killing and injuring thousands of men. Further, the city and its hustle-bustle would constrain the use of divine weapons. So, no, we cannot go with a small team for rescuing missions. We have to fight a war!"

The others in the room also agreed with Krishna's well-calculated decision.

"I shall ready our army, Yadavasrestha," Airawat spoke. Our one aukshahini Narayani Sena will offer Banasura a resounding blow." He bowed and left hurriedly.

***

It was very early in the morning. Krishna was in some interior part of a jungle close to his palace. Nobody accompanied him, and he sat alone on a stone.

Suddenly he heard a voice from behind. "Madhava, you remembered me in your thoughts, and I am here."

Krishna made an abrupt about-turn to see Shiva standing behind. He greeted Shiva, "*Pranam*, Mahadeva. I thank you for respecting my wish and appearing in front of me."

Shiva smiled. "I know what is in your mind, O Avatar of Mahavishnu."

"You are omniscient, and I am in a mortal avatar," Krishna responded with a half-smile. "The prediction of the Devas has turned right perhaps. As the great sages serving in Swarga had predicted, Mahabali's son has become the cause of a war between you and me. That was the reason why the Devas had urged my superior manifestation, Vishnu, not to allow the birth of Banasura. But, of course, Vishnu couldn't take any action based on a prediction alone, and Banasura lived on."

"We are helpless, Madhav. There are times when principles, ideologies, and situations entrap even the Gods in a terrible fate. Like you, I, too, couldn't refrain from bestowing Banasura the boons while he sought them years ago. And even now, I have to stand with you for specific reasons," Shiva said, his voice betraying the sadness he felt. "Banasura's every action has the will and desire to establish a perfect and righteous empire. He is selfless about his yearning to rule, wanting only the betterment of people. Above all, his extraordinary and long-lasting administration of Sonitpura is a testimony of his outstanding governance and leadership skills. Please forgive me; I will have to take part in this and fight for Banasura."

Krishna nodded. He took some time to ponder before speaking again. "There is nothing to forgive, Mahashiv. Years ago, my Vishnu form couldn't deny helping the Devas, despite knowing that Mahabali had never done any wrong. However, Vishnu was helpless, owing to his vow of protecting and shielding the Devas from any ongoing or probable trouble. Mahabali could have been a reason for concern for the Devas in the future. Today you are in a similar predicament."

Shiva nodded. "If Banasura's intentions were corrupt, his head would have exploded into a thousand pieces. But his head and his good intentions both are intact. I know he is not right, but he is neither wrong."

Krishna turned thoughtful again. He then said with curiosity in his eyes, "Could you ask Banasura to challenge Yudhisthira or me on a one-on-one duel? "If he wins, he leads Aryavrata. At least that way, lakhs won't perish in the war."

"I can't say so, and I've reasons for that. Firstly, you are an Avatar, although only a handful of mortals know it. So an Asura fighting one-on-one with a Vishnu avatar would be an injustice for the Asura. And if Yudhisthira fights in a duel with him, any rebel in the future would throw a similar challenge at Yudhisthira, and he won't be able to turn it down. So that would be an injustice upon Yudhisthira."

Krishna couldn't argue more. He only wondered that how being honourable has its price and cons. Shiva's honor stopped the bias against Banasura and Yudhisthira, but it wouldn't stop the war.

***

The Hari-Hara war was going to begin. Krishna, Balarama, Pradyumana, and Airawat led the Narayani Sena and traveled via several kingdoms towards Sonitpura.

The one aukshahini army of Krishna consisted of almost twenty-two thousand-odd chariots, sixty-five thousand horses, one lakh infantry. However, the number of elephants they took was only five hundred as a vast elephant troop would slow the journey. The elephants dragged massive catapult mechanisms that hurled large explosives. Their overall strength stood at nearly two lakhs soldiers.

On the other hand, Banasura initially faced trouble while preparing his army. As his forces had fought a prolonged war in Swarga, many soldiers had died, and several others were injured. Fortunately, Banasura's advisor, Bhaskaran, came up with a solution. With the Swarga now under Banasura's suzerainty, Bhaskaran asked for the services of Swarga's supernatural healers. Those healers immediately healed the yet recovering soldiers of Banasura. In addition, Banasura's Army Chief recruited new soldiers. Banasura invited Shukhracharya, the Guru of the Asuras in Patal Loka, to train the new recruits in a short period. Shukharacharya accepted the invitation.

In the next one and half months, the Narayani Sena completed their journey to reach Sonitpura. Banasura was ready with his army in the same period. His army was nearly the same size as the Narayani Sena. Meanwhile, Usha and Aniruddha had been imprisoned for nearly two months now.

***

"Did father allow you to come and meet me?" Usha asked.

"No, but my father allowed. Maharaj is engrossed in the war preparations. Shri Krishna's Narayani Sena reached our capital borders, yesternight. Today they made their camp in the open fields of Shoolmara. Tomorrow the war shall begin, and Mahashiv will be fighting for your father," Chitra said whatever she knew about the war.

Usha's eyes widened, and her mouth gaped, hearing that Shiva would participate in the war. "Father is a fool! With Lord Shiva participating in the war, the war would turn manifold destructive. I can't fathom the catastrophe if Shiva's Trishul and Shri Krishna's Sudarshana Chakra would collide! The Vasudeva may not be a God, but all the miracles he has performed over the years illustrate his mysterious divine superpowers." "Chitra, we cannot let this war drag on."

Chitralekha was equally concerned about the aftermath of the war. "Maharaj doesn't realize that he has brought such a cataclysmic war to his doorstep. Our whole empire might decimate in the course of this war."

"We have to do something, Chitra," Usha said with urgency and fright on her face.

Chitra grasped Usha's hands. "What can we do, *sakhi*?" She sounded hopeless.

Usha stared into the ground thoughtfully from the bed where they both were seated. Some serene moments flew. "Chitra!" she suddenly exclaimed, "you can use your magic and rescue me, right? Get me to him anyhow, and I shall free him. We both have to reach the battleground and perhaps can stop the war."

Chitra immediately denied it. "No, Usha. The soldiers and your servants keep checking your presence at regular intervals. So, even before you reach Aniruddha and rescue him, the soldiers would notice your absence here and straightaway reach Aniruddha."

"In that case, can you bring Aniruddha here?" Usha asked with firm hope. "I think, before the soldiers policing Anir's prison find out that he has escaped, he could be here. Then, later, Anir and I shall leave Agnigarh, and the soldiers can't attack when he and I are together."

Chitra pondered on Usha's words. She reckoned if she was up to the task. Finally, she exhaled a long breath and said, "Perhaps, I can do that. However, we can execute this rescue and escape plan only after the war starts. Your father, the soldiers, and everyone else's attention would remain diverted then."

Usha nodded, and there was gratitude in her eyes. "I'd always owe you, Chitra. You are doing brave. The empire will never forget your effort if we can stop the war."

Usha grabbed Chitralekha into a tight hug.

Chapter 15

"Hari-Hara Yuddha" – The Start

It was the first day of the war. Barely decades after the annihilating but liberating Kurukshetra war, unfortunately, a more catastrophic war was taking place in Aryavrata. The whole of Aryavrata, the Devas in the Swarga, and the Gods and demi-gods in other realms braced themselves for a Krishna versus Shiva clash. Both were all-powerful Gods. Although people only knew Shiva as God and considered Krishna a powerful divine mortal.

On the Banasura camp, there were massive columns of infantry, elephants, and cavalry in different rows. Ahead of those troops stood Banasura and the Commander General of the army-Veidh, and three of Banasura's veteran ministers. The mighty warriors were on their respective raths, while a contingent of elephants and horse riders guarded them. Shiva, his two sons, Ganesha and Kartikeya, and Shiva's most trusted warrior, Nandi, stood at the end of the various columns of the Sonitpura Army. They were in metal armors, ready to intervene when needed.

Krishna's Narayani Sena formed an offensive formation as they had to penetrate through the opposite army. Krishna had asked his Commander, Airawat, to execute a scheme. They sent their five hundred elephants in a short row but several long vertical columns. Krishna himself mounted an elephant that moved ahead of the rest.

Witnessing the Krishna-led elephant contingent marching at them, Banasura sent the bulk of his fifteen-hundred elephants to counter-attack. His General, Maharathi Viedh, led them.

The two elephant troops marched at each other from opposite ends. The trumpets of the tuskers echoed the entire battlefield and beyond. The massive noise of their movements further subsided any more sound. The march of Banasura's elephants was, however, more rapid.

General Viedh released a divine arrow at Krishna from his howdah. The arrowhead, while traveling through the air, created a sizeable round fireball. To counter Viedh's Suryaastra, Krishna launched an arrow that formed a thick and broad ice wall in its pathway in the midair. The Suryaastra collided with the wall and broke it into infinite tiny fragments that fell on the Narayani Sena's tuskers below. However, those fragments caused no harm or halt.

Krishna quickly sent another celestial arrow at Viedh's incoming forces. It created an engulfing of dense fog that gradually condensed into boiling water. The elephants and the mahouts on them screamed and wailed, experiencing the burning sensation. Viedh neutralized the attack by shooting an arrow overhead that resulted in the shower of cold waters. However, while Viedh concentrated on protecting his force, Krishna began playing flute sitting on his elephant. Viedh was perplexed by Krishna's peculiarity.

The sound of the flute was a piece of unique music. In no time, hearing the flute sound, the tuskers behind Krishna stopped. They stayed immobile and calm. Soon, from behind the columns of the elephants, the Narayani Sena used the concealed giant catapult machines to hurl midsize bombs on the opposition army. The bombs landed some meters ahead of the opponent's elephant forces. Upon landing, they exploded with ear-shattering noises and made fearsome sparks. Those noises and sparks made the elephants in Viedh's forces afraid and hysteric, and they retreated in chaos. The retreat was devasting as they stampeded the lines of Sonitpura's infantry that were following the elephants.

Krishna took a long sword and a shield and leaped from his elephant howdah, somersaulting through the air and making a perfect land below. "Smallsword infantry, with me now!" Krishna screamed and raced ahead at an unnaturally fast pace. A sizeable troop of ten thousand infantry, holding smallswords and shields, followed him with roars and grunts. The Krishna-led infantry force reached the mess of the opposite elephants shortly and circumvented the tuskers. They pushed further ahead and were approaching Banasura and the massive troops behind him.

Banasura realized his predicament.

"We should invite Lord Shiva," one of Banasura's ministers suggested.

Banasura replied curtly, "No! We cannot involve him so early in the war." He then picked up his metallic bow and nocked a silver arrow on it. Next, he pulled the bowstring, pointing the arrowhead at the rushing in Krishna's infantry, and closed his eyes to murmur a chant. The beaming arrow soared through the air when he released the bowstring and dived down at Krishna's infantry. Some meters overhead the infantry soldiers, the arrow manifested a black mist that continued to expand. Shortly, the dark smog covered the infantry and even swallowed up Banasura's own chaotic elephants and soldiers. Everyone covered by the black fog turned sedated in some time, including the elephants. However, Krishna and many of his accompanied foot soldiers covered their mouths and noses with fabric torn from their dhotis. They waited for the fog to clear.

Meanwhile, until the coal-colored mist cleared, Banasura sent soldiers to take away their hypnotized tuskers. They were successful in moving out the mammoths, moments before the fog entirely subsided. However, when the mist subsided, Banasura was surprised by Krishna and his unhypnotized soldiers. Banasura immediately marched forward an army of ten thousand dual-armed swordsmen.

The dual-armed swordsmen clashed against the men with smallswords, and both parties combatted equally well. Banasura's double-handed swordsmen were the aggressors, chopping and beheading their opponents. The smallsword wielders defended themselves with their shield and made fast and quick cuts at the opponents.

The dual-armed swordsmen attempted to hurt and kill Krishna by attacking him in groups. Krishna, however, was too overwhelming for them. He defended, cut, and stabbed the soldiers for almost two prahars. He alone killed over two thousand soldiers in that period and injured many others.

Finally, the war of the first day ended when the sun had almost set, and both sides blew conch shells.

***

The reserved force of both sides took away the corpses for their last rites. They also carried not yet dead but dying men to their respective camps. Infinite injured and maimed soldiers received treatment from physicians. Their painful wails and traumatized shouts often shook both the cantonments. Even the soldiers that were not injured reeled with the aftershock of the day-long battle. The scenes where they had somehow escaped certain death and memories of their fellow soldiers dying in front of their eyes made them cry and tremble. Many soldiers puked, and others caught a fever. They had to take strong medicines to relax.

Banasura's side had lost more men on the first day. His army was humbled by Krishna's tactics twice. First, Krishna demolished their elephant troop, and secondly, he used a simple and effective way to save his infantry from the effects of the hypnotic mist.

"How is General Viedh?" Banasura asked his ministers.

"Your Majesty, he is recovering. It is a miracle that he did not sustain grave injuries despite being hit by elephant tusks twice," a minister responded.

Banasura, his three veteran ministers, Ganesha, Kartikeya, Nandi, and Shiva, were seated in a tent, discussing the first day of the war.

"Krishna is a master war-strategist," Shiva spoke, "who won the Kurukshetra without lifting a weapon. So if you plan to defeat him, you will lose this war!"

A disheartened Banasura looked at Shiva and asked with hope, "Then what should our approach be?"

Shiva, rising from his seat, stood in the center of the circle formed by the arrangement of the seats. The others, too, rose in respect, but Shiva gestured them to relax. He then shared his plan to baffle and beat Krishna.

***

"We shouldn't be over-confident of today's performance. Two good moves can change the course of a war. Moreover, today's victory would have no impact on tomorrow's battle," Krishna shared his wisdom. Balarama, sitting opposite him, gave the nod to Krishna's insight.

Pradyumana and Airawat, standing between Krishna and Balarama, realized that the second day could be completely different.

"Father, will Lord Shiva enter the battlefield tomorrow?" Pradyumana wanted to know his father's opinion.

"No, I don't think so. Mahadeva probably would participate in the war only after Banasura faces humiliation in battle. But perhaps, Shri Ganesha, Devata Kartikeya, and the devout Nandi will take part in the fight tomorrow."

"We must have an aggressive strategy for tomorrow. What is your suggestion, Airawat?" Balarama inquired.

"I suggest something innovative, a triangular choke formation. Vasudeva Krishna will lead a troop of chariots forming the top angle of the triangle. Maharathi Pradyumana will lead a force of horse riders creating the left base angle, and Mahabali Balarama will lead a squad of mace warriors making the right base angle. The middle area of the triangle would remain open, and the opponents would try to enter it. We shall allow that, and once they are in, I shall decimate them with an army of spearmen." Airawat also illustrated the formation on a blackboard hung between two poles inside the tent.

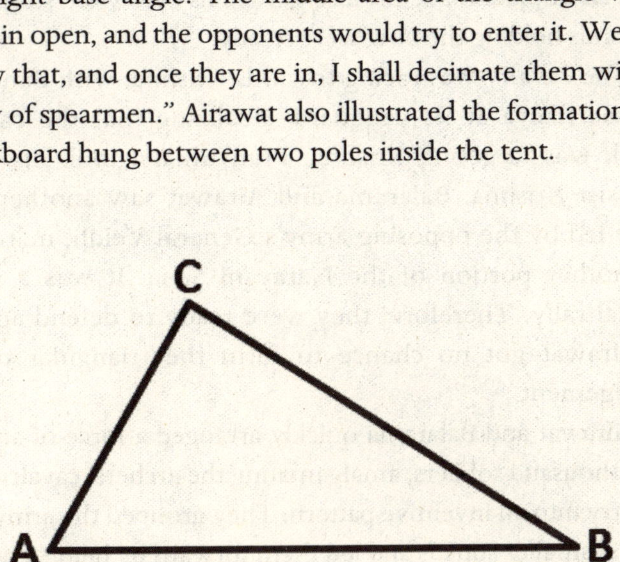

SYMBOL C – POSITION OF SHRI KRISHNA'S TEAM

SYMBOL A – POSITION OF MAHARATHI PRADYUMANA'S TEAM

SYMBOL B – POSITION OF MAHABALI BALARAMA'S TEAM

***

The second day of the war had begun. Airawat was arranging the Narayani Sena into his innovative triangle choke formation. Banasura was implementing the plan that Lord Shiva had shared with him.

Banasura himself led the charge of cavalry with archers, assisted by Kartikeya. Kartikeya was a terrific warrior but looked calm and sweet. His face was much like Shiva's, but he was leaner and shorter. The sunray reflecting on his golden-hued chest plate made his face glow. His eyes were stern, and his hands holding the bow were steady.

The cavalry was racing towards Krishna, with Banasura and Kartikeya at its vanguard. Realizing that the cavalry attack was targeting Krishna, Pradyumana took his force to assist Krishna. Balarama and Airawat saw another vast party led by the opposing army's General Veidh, marching at another portion of the Narayani Sena. It was a more frontal rally. Therefore, they were ready to defend against it. Airawat got no chance to form the triangular choke arrangement.

Airawat and Balarama quickly arranged a force of around sixty thousand soldiers, amalgamating the archers, cavalry, and infantry into an inventive pattern. They grouped the army into several smaller squads and led them forward by being a part of one such squad. As they increasingly neared the opposition, the teams started expanding, creating a semi-circular pattern, and intending to envelop the opponents.

General Viedh had schemed out a brilliant strategy that could counter any war-formation. The first elongated line of his soldiers were armored horse-riding spearmen. Behind them was an infantry of swordsmen in a square arrangement. "Swordsmen's Square, decimate the enemies!" Veidh's fierce command traveled far and wide. The swordsmen's square at once broke free and rushed from the left and right of the line ahead as the riding spearmen slowed their pace. They swiftly reached the edges of the Narayani Sena's semi-circular arrangement and started combat. The riding spearmen smashed against the soldiers in the center.

***

Krishna and his son were fighting valiantly for a long time against the archers on the chariots and horses. There were heavy exchanges of arrows between the cavalries of Banasura and Krishna. There was the utilization of divine arrows as well.

Banasura released an Agneyastra, and balls of fire fell in the vicinity where Krishna's chariot stood. Krishna neutralized it with Varunastra, which caused a heavy downpour. Krishna retaliated by shooting a Pravatastra that made large rocks fall near and around Banasura from a mystic hole that had opened up above Banasura's head. Many soldiers perished, but Banasura saved himself by shooting an arrow that swallowed all the rocks aiming at his head. Several more such rounds of exchanging divine weapons continued between the two.

Pradyumana and Kartikeya were fighting each other with maces on the ground. Kartikeya, at one point, struck Pradyumana's chest with a tremendous blow. Pradyumana coughed out blood, but he soon stood up again. The duel went on. Pradyumana couldn't muster much offensive, but he defended himself well. His primary duty was to keep Kartikeya engaged so that Krishna could slay Banasura and end the war.

***

A volley of Agneyastras brought down infinite fireballs at Banasura. Krishna could conjure divine weapons swifter than any asura or human.

Banasura created a heavy downpour with a Varunastra, yet not all the fireballs were promptly extinguished. So, sensing the danger, Banasura leaped off his chariot to the ground, a fraction before his chariot exploded. He was wise to jump with a long and wide shield, clutched tight, and that saved him from Krishna's multiple arrows. When the arrow shots ceased, he peeked and saw that some ordinary archers were attacking Krishna. While Krishna was defending himself against them, Banasura thrust his bulky shield at Krishna's immobile chariot. The momentum broke the chariot's left wheel, and Krishna landed on the ground. However, he immediately pulled out the sword from his sheath and chopped the heads of the enemy soldiers gathered around.

Krishna and Banasura stood face to face. Banasura scrutinized Krishna and silently admired how divine and calm he looked even as a warrior. The gold-painted brass headgear with two green peacock feathers seated like a crown on his head. The silver-hued plate armor covering his front torso had the sigil of two crossed peacock feathers with an arrow between them. The two armguards seemed like an inherent part of his arms. Banasura particularly noticed how Krishna's face displayed no stress or worry despite being in the middle of a raging battle.

Krishna moved in different postures with his sword drawn while Banasura stood still.

"Pick up a weapon, Banasura, and let's fight. Let the war culminate with the victory of one of us right now," Krishna challenged.

Banasura smirked. "If I fight your way, you will win. I am no fool to act brave when I can instead be smart." Banasura gestured some of his soldiers, fighting in the vicinity to come closer. "My soldiers, your king commands you to kill this man," he ordered.

The soldiers commenced a coordinated attack at Krishna. Krishna being a resourceful person, quickly held his steel scabbard on his non-sword hand. Thenceforth, while he defended himself with his sword, he used the pointed end of the solid sheath to penetrate the soldiers.

Banasura knew that Krishna would overwhelm the combined attack of his twenty swordsmen. However, his actual motive was to buy some time to execute his next move.

He had reckoned it was the most suitable opportunity to utilize his boon earned from Lord Shiva. So, guarded by a troop of his elite bodyguards, Banasura closed his eyes, spread his arms wide, and concentrated on conjuring clones of himself. As the conjuring worked, a sudden whirling white cloud appeared over his head that swiftly engulfed the area around him. Moments later, the blur disappeared to reveal nine-hundred-ninety-nine clones of Banasura.

"Krishna, let's fight in my way now!" Banasura roared with laughter. Krishna witnessed the astonishing scene of a thousand Banasuras racing at him, and even his eyes widened in awe. Everyone else on the field was distracted and looked at the wonder with gaping mouths.

Those clones encircled Krishna in no time and started a barrage of blows, kicks, and pushes on him. Krishna swished his sword and sheath at the army of Banasuras, but no matter how many he killed, there were always enough to assault him.

Three sudden and forceful punches landed on Krishna's face and skull, pushing him down to the soil. He could hardly catch his breath when seven or eight of the clones started hurling kicks at his body. Taking the abuse of countless boots, Krishna coiled and let out moans of pain. He was also bleeding from his nose and forehead, and his headgear had fallen off during the assault. There was yet no respite for him. The clones pulled him to his knees. Four of them held Krishna's arms, and one choked his throat from behind. Those five clones had rendered Krishna immobile.

The actual Banasura made his walk towards Krishna, taking short and confident steps.

***

The Narayani Sena and its Maharathis saw Krishna's plight. Balarama asked Airawat to continue fighting against the forces of Veidh, and he attempted to reach Krishna for aid. However, Banasura asked his elite bodyguards to stop Balarama. They responded to the command by attacking Balarama with arrows. Riding a horse and with a shield, Balarama continued charging ahead, but an arrow hit his right arm, causing him to fall. Balarama pulled out the dart, spluttering a fountain of blood, and pulled out his sword. He furiously swung it at the elite bodyguards, killing them in rapid moves.

Krishna's son Pradyumana also attempted to come to his father's rescue, but Kartikeya kept him busy. They kept on exchanging celestial arrows at each other, with none gaining a decisive victory.

However, the common soldiers of the Narayani Sena could reach near Krishna, destroying the general soldiers of Banasura's army on their way. Seeing their leader, their revered Lord, in a terrible plight infused inspiration in them to fight like top-notch warriors.

***

Banasura knelt in front of Krishna and stared into his eyes. "Vasudeva, you are a good leader and a great warrior. I am but better. I don't want to kill you. You can surrender right now and promise me to hand over Aryavrata's reins, and I swear, I shall turn the empire into the greatest realm that ever was or ever will be!"

Krishna scoffed. "If you were indeed a benevolent person, you would not have started this war. You could have instead tried to convince us of your principles or could have even challenged Yudhisthira or me for a duel."

"You would have never listened to my views. And neither you nor Yudhisthira would have accepted the challenge for a duel."

"That's your notion and preconceived judgment. Flawed."

"Enough with the talks," Banasura grumbled and started to rip apart the chest plate on Krishna. He growled like an angry beast as he used his immense power to tear it away. Krishna, too, howled and employed his might to throw out the four clones holding his arms. Upon freeing himself, Krishna brought his open palms with a high velocity across Banasura's ears. It was a potent blow that made Banasura's ears vibrate, and he covered his ears in pain.

Krishna stood up. He stared at Banasura and the clones still surrounding him. Krishna also noticed Balarama and his general soldiers near him. Following the examination, he looked at the sky and lifted a finger in the air, and twirled it. He had turned dangerous now, with an angry expression and fiery eyes. Shortly, incessant thunders and bolts of lightning flashed in the sky that trembled everyone on the field. Extraordinarily heavy winds accompanied the turmoil in the sky. These developments made the soldiers and warriors pause their fighting and look above with fear and nervousness.

On Banasura's camp, Shiva realized what was happening. "Nandi, get me my Trishul," he commanded.

Nandi handed Shiva his ancient-looking bulky iron-hued Trishul. Then, in a breastplate with Banasura's roaring lion sigil and a yellow tiger-print dhoti, Shiva raced to the battlefield. As he moved at a tremendous speed, soldiers from either side dropped their weapons and made his way.

***

Sparks ignited inches over Krishna's finger, which soon took the shape of a discus, blazing with fire and having pointed edges. It was Krishna's best weapon- the Sudarshana Chakra. With a slight gesture of his finger, he launched it, and the Sudarshana spun fast and angry, chopping off the heads of Banasura's every clone. The clones screamed and ran, but the Chakra chased and decapitated them. Blood flowed down like a fountain from their headless necks and drenched their body. The severed heads flew everywhere, soaring in the air. In a short span, the soil turned crimson and moist.

Banasura couldn't utter a word or cry, witnessing the destruction and horror. He stood still on his feet, and his face turned pale. In not much time, all the clones were dead, and the discus finally wheeled at him. Banasura was in shock, and his mind could not collect any thoughts. His eyes saw nothing but the radiating Chakra that neared him every other moment. Banasura closed his eyes.

Shiva was some feet behind Banasura. He was still running, determined to keep his vow of aiding his devotee. With a high and long leap, Shiva reached ahead of Banasura. He made a stable landing and pushed his Trishul powerfully at the Chakra. The Trishul and the Chakra collided. Although the Chakra continued to rotate and thrust itself forward, the Trishul did not allow it to advance. The scratching of the Chakra on the Trishul emitted sparks that splattered. It even made a sound that made soldiers cover their ears. The escaping spark pieces were violent and scorching. After holding the Chakra with his might for some time, Shiva finally shoved it hard. The shoving sent the Chakra some feet away, and its rotation slowed. Krishna witnessed Shiva's involvement and called back the Chakra. It hurriedly went high in the air and vanished after a gradual contraction in size.

Conch shells blew, and the battle ended for the day. Shiva had saved Banasura.

***

"We had almost won today! If Mahadeva had been even a little late, Banasura would have perished," Airawat said. He wanted to show the brighter picture as Krishna, Balarama, and Pradyumana were sad over losing tens of thousands of soldiers in the day's battle.

" 'Almost' is a word that hurts the most," Krishna said in a somber voice. "How many men did we lose today?"

"More than fifty thousand," Airawat softly replied.

Krishna sighed, closing his eyes.

"I am starting to fear for my son. Is our Aniruddha still alright?" Pradyumana spoke with a moan of despair.

Balarama walked to Pradyumana's chair and rubbed his shoulder. "Yes, he has to be alright. No matter, Mahadeva is standing against us, but he won't support Banasura if he does such an act of killing a hostage for no reason," he assured.

"But will we be able to defeat Mahadeva and get a win to rescue him?" Pradyumana asked, looking at Balarama with moist eyes.

"Don't lose heart. You lose a war when you lose heart, not soldiers," Balarama shared his wisdom and looked into Krishna's eyes.

Krishna sighed again. "Tomorrow Nandi, Shri Ganesha, Kartikeya, and Shiva, everyone would definitely intervene in the war. So, to beat them, we have to forget that they are Gods and fight against them as rivals," he said with passion. "We must be ready to fool, hurt, and embarrass them."

***

"Mahadeva, I don't know how to thank you for saving my life today," Banasura kneeled in front of Shiva with folded hands.

"I merely fulfilled my promise," Shiva responded. "You may take your seat."

Banasura rose from his posture and walked back to his seat.

"How many soldiers did either side lose today, Viedh?" one of Banasura's ministers asked.

Veidh stood from his seat to answer. "My king, today we lost less than thirty thousand men, and they lost nearly double of that." He turned his head towards Shiva. "We acted as the great Mahashiv had planned and reaped the desired results. Today, according to yesternight's scheme, King Banasura and Devata Kartikeya kept Krishna engaged and did not allow him to strategize anything. That gave me a great chance to attack the bulk of the Narayani forces, and we prevailed over them."

"But I don't want to see all the soldiers dying on either side. So, I, my sons, and my attendant Nandi will take part in the battle tomorrow and focus on defeating their forces," Shiva announced.

Everyone agreed with Shiva as none wanted death. But the path to success in war is built on countless dead bodies.

***

SONITPURA CITY

The soldiers outside the castle where Aniruddha was held captive were strolling carefree. With the war taking place, right outside the capital, they did not worry that anyone would try to rescue Aniruddha. Moreover, they remained convinced that nobody could flee from the prison inside the castle. They were also confident of the Pragjyotishpura army winning the war as Shiva stood with them.

A seductive girl walked towards the castle in the night's darkness amidst the moon's dim light and burning torches. The soldiers saw her and looked with awe. She wore a loose-fitting dress made of thin fabric that clung tight to her body, revealing her curves. The dress ended just above her knees. The soldiers watched her coming, noticing her firm and large breasts and slender waist. She looked like a fairy walking in the serenity of the night, fair and with sharp facial features. Her face glowed in the moonlight, and her eyes seemed humanly blue. She stopped right in front of the entrance of the castle gate.

"Who are you?" one of the entrance guards inquired.

The girl replied nothing but smiled and winked. She then turned back, lifted her dress, and twerked her naked hips. Next, she swayed her waist and moved her belly. She continued such sexy moves, and all the guards left their positions. They were mesmerized by her skin and grace. Her slow and revealing movements displayed parts of her body. The soldiers gathered around her, forgetting everything, and looked at her body.

With the guards' attention focused on the dancing girl, another lady climbed over the castle boundary wall and dropped inside. She straightaway entered the castle and went to the basement. She had a jug with her, and upon opening it, smoke emerged out. The volume of the smoke increased in no time, and it spread everywhere. The smoke was to make the snakes that covered the whole basement floor lose their senses. And the smoke did its work.

The lady walked carefully, sidestepping the immobile snakes, and reached Aniruddha's cell. The other cells were empty. She silently opened the lock by using a curved tool and entered inside.

She stirred Aniruddha, who was sleeping with his back towards her. Aniruddha hastily turned and held the lady's throat. But he quickly left his grasp as soon as he could see her face.

"Chitralekha! What are you doing here?" he asked with a surprise.

"Thank God, you can move. I see you are much better. Yet you didn't think of escaping?"

"I can't, and it's not only because there are snakes outside. The day they had brought me here, injured and unconscious, I woke up to find bandages on my wounds and a paste covering my legs. Once the paste dried away, I stopped feeling my legs."

death. Their hands trembled, and their legs turned unsteady. They neither moved nor stirred. They stole glances at Krishna with their heads lowered. They wanted to tell him that they couldn't fight Shiva or even his troop members. However, they felt awkward expressing their mindset before Krishna, as they were his loyal soldiers and held him in high regard, almost like a God.

Shiva understood the thoughts of the Narayani Sena and was in a quandary. If they didn't fight with complete determination and zeal, it would be unfair on Krishna. And he would be the cause of that unfairness.

"Narayani Sena!" Shiva got their attention. "I know you are hesitating to fight against me. But I want you to do your duty. You must fight for your leader, the Vasudeva Krishna, and you must not falter at it. It doesn't matter who is against you. I am here as a warrior, not a God. Moreover, what Gods dislike the most is when any of their creations does not perform its duty. Work is worship, and by conducting your karma, you can please God."

Shiva's words motivated the soldiers of Krishna. They understood that they must perform their duty without any other thought. As Shiva himself had advised them to fight, they no longer were skeptical.

Krishna looked at Shiva and smiled with appreciation. "You are always honourable and righteous, my Lord," he said in his mind.

The war resumed. The Narayani Sena moved around, trying to look for any opening to escape the oval-shaped trap. They found no vulnerable points.

Krishna, Airawat, Pradyumana, and Balarama shot celestial arrows at the forces forming the boundary. But the almighty warriors on Banasura's side neutralized their mystic arrowheads.

After that, Banasura's archers started to knock off the soldiers of Krishna's army. With multitudes of arrows released without pause, the Narayani soldiers could not remove their shields and muster any offense. When no more arrows remained, Shiva commanded the spearmen to attack from each of the four directions. Thousands of Narayani soldiers succumbed in no time to the brutal offensive of the spearmen.

Krishna and Pradyumana finally came up with a solution to save the massive demolition of their army. They took cover and hid between their general soldiers and shot Sammohanastras. Their arrows went high in the air and created a fog engulfing everyone in the field. The fog hypnotized everyone except the ones who had released them. Shiva, Ganesha, and Kartikeya were also unimpacted because they were Gods. Shiva took some time to grab a metallic bow and arrow to fire a celestial weapon and subside the effect of the two Sammohanastras. However, the time that he took allowed Krishna and Pradyumana to fire two arrows that created multiple more arrowheads, and each targeted only the spearmen of Banasura. So, as those soldiers emerged from their hypnotic state, they were struck down by diving arrowheads, even before they could move an inch.

***

The battle had turned into close combats. Soldiers of either side clashed with swords, spears, and maces.

Krishna whispered something in Balarama's ears. He and his selected Atirathis then went to take on Shiva's contingent, trying to open the eastern blockade of the oval. Airawat, Balarama, and Pradyumana fought in the middle along with the general soldiers of Narayani Sena.

Ganesha, Kartikeya, and Banasura continued to hold their positions and didn't allow the destruction of the oval entrapment.

The fighting in the middle was thickest and most atrocious. There was no room for soldiers even to execute their moves aptly. A soldier swung his sword hard at an opponent. The opponent ducked, and his sword instead split a severed head that was rotating fast in the air. Blood sprayed out and sprinkled on the sword-wielder.Some distance away, two soldiers pulled and detached the arms of another soldier. They flung the disconnected arms away, which fell on an archer and a horse rider. The archer, therefore, missed his mark, and the arrow penetrated someone's eye. The soldier who lost an eye screamed and went down on his knees. Consequently, a javelin aimed at him went through someone else's belly, carrying him over a distance until he landed on two soldiers fighting with maces. One of the maces flew high in the air and struck the chest of a fellow soldier, making him cough out blood.

***

Krishna and Shiva, both holding a sword each, stood opposite each other.

"Finally, fate has forced us to be in combat with each other," Shiva said.

"As you said, time is superior to even the Gods," Krishna smiled.

Krishna pounced at Shiva, holding his sword with both hands. Shiva quickly took a forward stance. He bent his front leg low, kept the back leg straight and elongated, and stopped Krishna's sword by raising his sword.

The two swords clashed. Krishna pushed Shiva behind. Shiva continued to block the push and thrust his body ahead. Krishna realized with the thrust that Shiva had greater strength. So he ducked and moved his sword to hurt Shiva's legs. Shiva reacted swiftly by jumping over Krishna's head. Shiva landed and promptly turned behind with a swish of his longsword. Krishna had anticipated that move. Therefore, rather than standing and rotating,he laid with his back on the ground. His upper body thus was closer to Shiva, and he shoved his longsword at Shiva's left upper thigh. It hit Shiva, piercing his muscles. Shiva groaned and walked some steps behind, wobbling.

Krishna arose and attempted several rapid moves at Shiva with his sword. Shiva, however, defended himself with some difficulty. But as the duel continued, he gradually stopped wobbling and cared nothing about the blood dripping from his wound. He defended himself well and well although he couldn't turn the aggressor.

***

"Lord Shiva is busy. We should execute Krishna's idea of the pyramid," Balarama said to Airawat. Airawat examined the brawl between Krishna and Shiva and then nodded at Balarama.

"Maharathis, release your arrows of illusion. Now!" Airawat screamed. Balarama, Pradyumana, and he fired an arrow each that created three dark-blue clouds in the skies. The Narayani Sena knew what the clouds were, and they never looked above. But the clouds had an appealing aroma, and the Pragjyotishpura soldiers couldn't help but look at them. As they stared into the blueness, they were enchanted. Each soldier saw in them the thing that he feared the most. Most saw themselves dying in the war, some saw their families begging in the streets, and others saw their souls burning in hell.

"These are *Mahamayaastras*. Only *Vayuastras* can neutralize them," Ganesha shouted. He wanted his brother and Nandi to hear him, and they did. Ganesha, Nandi, and Kartikeya fired a Vayuastra simultaneously. Forceful wind energies then disarrayed the clouds and melted them.

However, by then, the bulk of the Narayani Sena had executed the central plan. The soldiers standing on one another formed a tall human pyramid right at the center of the oval. At the peak were the three Maharathis, Pradyumana, Airawat, Balarama, and two Atirathis. The five formidable warriors jumped from the zenith, and they landed outside the lines of soldiers forming the oval's perimeter. They could now attack from beyond the oval-shaped army formation.

Balarama and Atirathi used their bows and arrows to attack the forces of Ganesha and Veidh. Airawat and the other Atirathi engaged with Kartikeya and Banasura by using divine arrows. Pradyumana employed his knowledge of divyastra at Nandi's troops. On the other hand, the Narayani soldiers pestered the five extraordinary opposition warriors with constant arrow shots from inside the oval.

The attack from the front and behind troubled the five excellent warriors. Although they could defend themselves, they could not safeguard their forces. A large portion of the Banasura army hence succumbed at the end part of the day's battle. It made Banasura lose an almost equal number of soldiers as the Narayani Sena.

Chapter 16

"Hari-Hara Yuddha" – The Beginning

Krishna, Balarama, Airawat, and Pradyumana were planning for the next day's battle when a sentry walked to the tent.

"*Pranam*, great Yadavas! There is a piece of happy news, sirs. Prince Aniruddha and the new Yadava daughter-in-law, Usha Ji is here," the guard said with a wide smile.

Everyone looked at him, happily surprised.

Balarama walked to the sentry and gave him a chain that he was wearing. "Send them in. Right now!"

The sentry bowed and went out. Soon, Aniruddha and Usha entered the tent.

Pradyumana hugged his son right at the entrance. They exchanged no words or tears, but the hug was long and warm.

Balarama, who was standing nearby, embraced both Pradyumana and Aniruddha with his broad arms. Aniruddha looked at Krishna and saw him smiling. He rushed to his grandfather immediately. They hugged. Krishna closed his eyes and felt the gentle warmth of his scion against his heart. He felt blissful.

Aniruddha pointed at Usha standing at the tent's entrance. "Pitamah Shri Krishna, Pitamah Balarama, and father, please meet my wife and your daughter-in-law, Usha."

Usha took gentle steps and reached the three senior men of her in-law family. She first bowed and touched Balarama's feet.

"May you find all the happiness and have a blissful marital life. I bless you with the energy of my all-pious deeds." Balarama helped her rise with a smile.

Next, Usha touched Krishna's feet and placed her forehead on them as well. Krishna quickly helped her arise. "You are as lovely as you are cultured. You are prettier than the moon, and I believe your heart is as pure as a newborn baby." Krishna moved his hand over her head and kissed her forehead. "I bless you that you find all the happiness in the world. I also promise that with your in-laws, you will experience nothing but joy and love." Krishna then gave her his ring which had a fine diamond on it. Usha accepted it and folded her hands. "I promise that I shall always try to be a daughter to everyone in my new family. May the Gods forbid, but every problem, sorrow, and challenge, that may ever befall anyone in the family shall be equally mine."

After Balarama and Krishna, Usha touched Pradyumana's feet. "Bless me, dear father," she said with a blushing smile. Pradyumana blessed her with immense joy. "Welcome to the family, dearest daughter. I wish you a long and healthy life, happiness in your marital space, and the strength to overcome any odds in life. May you bring glory to our house and clan." He, too, gifted her two gold chains.

Usha then moved to touch Airawat's feet, but he stopped her.

"You are my lady. I am merely a humble servant to you," he said. "Yes, I wish you all the happiness and even the joy that comes my way. But you don't need to touch my feet."

"But my husband told me that you are a relative, a Yadava. Moreover, as you are older to me, I have the right to seek your blessings. So I beg you not to take that right away," Usha said with a smile.

Airawat smiled and held her face gently. A little stream of tears escaped the middle-aged warrior's eyes and rolled down his stubbled cheeks. He moved his hands over her head after Usha touched his feet.

After Usha, Aniruddha sought blessings from everyone, and they both stayed in the tent for the next day's battle plan.

***

"May I say something?" Usha asked humbly to the senior men sitting around her at the round table.

"Of course, dear," Krishna replied.

"Well, we had planned to say this right on entering the tent, Vasudeva Ji. But it was a pleasant surprise that none of you asked even once why we married in such a rush."

"You both love each other. Hence, it is completely your and your husband's prerogative to get married in any manner and time you both see fit. We are more than happy to see you both as one," Krishna responded with a comforting smile.

Usha beamed at Krishna's words. She then took a pause and said, "The idea was that I too would take part in the war. Perhaps seeing me already wed and standing against him, my father would no longer persist with the war."

"It's a wise thought. Now that you both are with us, we can return to Dwarka. However, only if the opposing army doesn't chase us. If they do so, our soldiers will become easy targets for them," Krishna said and paused. "Let's start tomorrow with you speaking to your father and requesting him to allow us to go. If he allows that, no more men will die on either side."

The others nodded to Krishna's opinion.

***

The soldiers of the Narayani Sena had arranged for a new tent for Usha and Aniruddha. They were lying together atop a thick but soft mattress. The tent was dark, barring the brightness from three small earthen lamps lit on the bedside. They were lying naked under sheets, but neither desired to make love with their minds occupied with the war and its consequences so far. Over two and a half lakh soldiers were dead, counting both sides. Each side remained only with seventy-five thousand-odd men.

Aniruddha sensed Usha was more perturbed.

"What happened, love?" Aniruddha asked as he heard Usha let out a sigh for the third time.

"Your family is so amazing. They accepted me as if they had always known me. They are so warm, welcoming, and generous...."

"So that should make you happy. Why are you gloomy instead?" Aniruddha asked, running his hand over her naked back.

She looked into his eyes, emerging her head out of his chest. "I don't think that my father would be kind and compassionate enough to end the war without a win, even though we are married. I just want to try convincing him once, anyway." "Your family loves you and wants your happiness the most. In contrast, my parents care nothing about me. They humiliated and hurt you; I won't ever forget that." She sniffled, finishing her words.

"Hey," Aniruddha moved a bit to hold her tighter. Then, he moved his hand on her curls and kissed her forehead. "I don't have any sadness that they humiliated and hurt me. I am simply indifferent. And the Yadava family is not just mine; it's yours as well. Moreover, do remember that every family has great and not-so-great people. See, your grandfather, Mahabali, is still revered by people, and my great-granduncle, Kamsa, is still hated."

Usha nodded and moved her palm to his face. She had a meek smile as well. "You explain things so well. You should become a Gurudev after this war."

Both giggled and then kissed each other passionately.

***

Banasura, Shiva, Ganesha, Nandi, and General Veidh had walked ahead of the lines of their soldiers. Krishna, Balarama, Pradyumana, and Airawat stopped opposite them. Both parties faced each other in the center of the battleground.

"Yes, Vasudeva Shri Krishna, what do you want to discuss, terms of surrendering?" Banasura mocked with a laugh.

Krishna said nothing but smiled. He and Pradyumana moved away slightly to allow Usha and Aniruddha to stand in front of Banasura.

Banasura's smirk turned into a shocking expression. He fumbled, "He...he escaped that prison? And what's this? Do you have a sindoor on your forehead, Usha?"

Usha folded her hands. "Forgive me, father; we had to get married. We love each other immensely. Your daughter is happy in this alliance, and my in-laws are loving people. They adore me. For my sake, please, Father, stop this war."

Aniruddha, too, folded his hands. "Pita, I shall always keep Usha happy. She will know only joy and happiness in our home. Please, bless us and be kind. I ...."

"Bless you? You are an imbecile! You elope and marry my daughter, and now you beg for my blessing? Dare not call me pita!" Banasura looked at Aniruddha with angry red eyes.

Shiva held Banasura's arm. Banasura turned instantly to face Shiva.

"Your daughter truly loves this young man. And he, too, loves her. I can see that. I assure you that his love for her is real. And their love story would remain immortal till the end of time," Shiva reasoned.

Usha and Aniruddha stepped forward and knelt to touch Shiva's feet. "We married with you as the witness, O great Lord Shiva," Aniruddha said softly.

Shiva smiled at them. "I know,my children. Parvati and I have already blessed that your love will inspire generations to learn about real love." He placed his hands on both of their heads. They arose with folded hands.

"Banasura," Shiva turned to his left and said, "your daughter and Krishna's scion are already married. So bless them and end this war."

Banasura sighed. He stayed silent for some time and then said with cojoined palms, "Mahashiv, if that's your command, I shall do so. I shall accept this union; I shall also accept this boy as my son-in-law. However, if I end this war, what will Krishna do with me next?"

Shiva looked at Krishna curiously.

Krishna stared at Banasura's face. "You caused a lot of deaths with the actions of the Band. Your acts also harmed the peace and security of Aryavrata. Therefore, every ruler in the empire would want you hanged for your crimes. However, if you pay an indemnity for all the losses you've caused and step down as the king of Sonitpura, I can do something. Perhaps, because of your matrimonial alliance with us, the other rulers of Aryavrata may agree to reduce your punishment and keep you under house arrest. I also promise that I shall try implementing your socio-economic philosophies and principles. But, first, I shall try it in the smallest kingdom, and we will move forward in ascending order."

Banasura shook his head. He even scoffed. "So, despite ruling as the better leader for so many years and practicing and preaching enhanced philosophies for inclusive growth and development, I would remain house-arrested and lose my kingdom? Why are you humans and even the Devas always prejudiced against the Asuras? First, for no reason, my father was deceived by none other than Vishnu, and now I should surrender myself to satisfy the ego of humans. I won't! And my rule will only ensure better days for the realm." Banasura spoke with conviction, sincerity, and zeal. He lowered his head and asked Shiva, "Do you command me to surrender, even though I want to continue with the war and win it?" He waited for Shiva's response.

Shiva said in a soft but firm tone, "No." He couldn't force or command Banasura to surrender without his will, for that would be a biased act.

***

The battle was about to start. Usha wanted to take part, but Krishna advised her against it. "My dear, your father's soldiers would not attack you, and that would be an unfair move. Mahadeva has fought honourably, and so has your father. So, we also must not do anything that would be unrighteous or unreasonable."

Usha realized the merit in Krishna's words, and she agreed not to involve herself in the war. However, she stood with the five-thousand reserve force at the very end of their army to watch the battle unfold.

***

Shiva led the defense of the Pragjyotishpura army another day. He wanted the opposition army to charge at them and didn't form any fancy formation. He stood at the center of the positioned army with Banasura to his immediate left and Veidh to the right. Behind him were archers with long-range bows. On the other hand, the left flank consisted of horse riders for short-range archery. Nandi and Kartikeya led them, holding a dagger each. The right flank had swordsmen and mace fighters, and Ganesha stood at its forefront with his ax.

Krishna preferred a heavy attack as he wanted to break through the solid defensive line of the opponents. He but decided against elephants as the enemy soldiers might fend them off with explosions and fires. After some deliberation, Krishna sent a large force consisting of chariot archers and horse-riding spearmen as the first division. He followed it with a troop of mace fighters and soldiers with axes and swords. The final division consisted of the five Maharathis- Pradyumana, Aniruddha, Balarama, Airawat, and Krishna, on five different raths.

The long-range archers of Banasura's force shot arrows at the first division of Krishna's charging army. However, the five Maharathis in the Narayani Sena launched mystic arrows to swallow them up in mid-air. The five leading warriors on Banasura's side also aided their archers with celestial darts. But again, the Maharathis in the opposition neutralized them.

At a point, Shiva discarded the bow and arrow for his Trishul. He held the Trishul firmly and waited. Moments later, as the first row of the incoming chariots neared, he shoved the three-pointed blades into the soil ahead of him. The vigorous push trembled the ground heavily and carved a horizontal trench, some feet ahead of Shiva. Consequently, the chariots that moved in the primary line got stuck in the ditch. The immediate next row of chariots collided with the stuck wagons harshly. The chariots that followed in the ranks behind also bumped against one another. It was a chaotic scenario.

The short-range archers on horses behind Nandi and Kartikeya galloped to reach the chaotic area and shot arrows at the disarrayed chariot archers.

Unable to breach Shiva's defensive formation, Krishna asked all his warriors to divide themselves into groups of four men. Three of them had to guard the fourth in each group, and the fourth would consistently push inward into the opposition.

"Today, we shall either die or win!" Krishna screamed. "We aren't here to conquer or invade; we are here to tell everyone that nobody can escape punishment if they commit a crime. And Banasura committed two crimes. One, he created the Band and caused many deaths and destruction; two, he imprisoned your prince and stopped the union of two lovers. So this war is also for love!" "If you want to go back to your homes and see your family again, you'll have to survive and win. So, do what you ought to do."

Inspired and stirred with new vigor, the Narayani Sena shouted and screamed. Then, cheering the name of Krishna, they slowly and steadily marched ahead in the four-men formations.

Krishna quickly gathered the other four Maharathis of his side. "We shall employ a critical but simple change in our plan of attack," he told them. "Previously, in one-on-one combat, each one of us fought against someone superior to us. Like, Pradyumana fought against Kartikeya or Nandi, both somewhat better than him. But, instead, if he had fought against General Veidh, he could have defeated him. So, now our strategy would be...."

***

Krishna started taking on Shiva. Both fought with maces. On the other hand, the other four Maharathis executed Krishna's new tactic. Aniruddha took on Veidh, Airawat fought with Nandi, Pradyumana with Kartikeya, and Balarama with Ganesha. The two Atirathis and a few Rathis of the Narayani Sena kept Banasura engaged on Balarama's orders.

Aniruddha overwhelmed Veidh attacking him with two swords simultaneously. Although Veidh performed his best, Aniruddha killed him after a furious but short fight. He then joined Airawat, and both attacked Nandi together. Unfortunately, Nandi fell at one point on the ground, and Aniruddha placed a sword around his neck. That meant Nandi suffered defeat, and he had to go off the field.

Kartikeya had almost killed a fallen Pradyumana, but Airawat and Aniruddha arrived in time. Soon, it was a three-on-one attack against Kartikeya, and even he faced defeat.

Ganesha was far superior in his fighting skills. Despite Balarama receiving the assistance of Pradyumana, Aniruddha, and Airawat, Ganesha mounted offenses and managed to injure Airawat by making a deep cut on his shoulder.

Injured gravely, Airawat had to leave the battlefield.

In another part of the battle, Banasura fought vigorously against the Atirathis and Rathis. He had injured three of the four Rathis and killed one Atirathi.

***

"Aniruddha, your father and I shall keep Shri Ganesha busy. We must accept that even the three of us can't defeat him. So, it's prudent that you go and attack Banasura. We shall win the war if you can beat him with the help of the Rathi and Atirathi arriors. And don't worry about us." Balarama reasoned.

Aniruddha knew that Balarama was right. "Take care, Pitamah," he said and sprinted away towards Banasura. He noticed a chance to reach Banasura from behind, yet he decided to attack from the front. He ran at Banasura and, on his way, stepped on a bulky spherical shield. The shield rotated and rose, and he picked it up without halting.

Banasura was already combatting with the Atirathi and the Rathi. He was overpowering them when Aniruddha came closer to him. He slid, placing his knees on the round shield, and made a furious swish at Banasura's sword. That saved the Atirathi warrior from a nasty strike of Banasura's sword. The intervention enraged Banasura severely.

Banasura and Aniruddha stood facing each other. The Atirathi and Rathi also surrounded Banasura.

"So, now you'll take the help of two more warriors and still lose?" Banasura laughed, mocking Aniruddha.

Aniruddha thought briefly and decided against fighting with allies. "You two, kindly go and assist our soldiers. Leave this battle to me."

The two warriors were skeptical, but Aniruddha stared at them sternly, and they moved away.

From the previous duel, Aniruddha knew that Banasura had more physical power than him. His chance, therefore, was if Banasura remained the aggressor and he could use his speed and agility to defend himself and frustrate Banasura.

"Maharaj Banasura, I know, I can't overwhelm you. All I have to do is to keep you engaged," Aniruddha said with a smile of satisfaction. "Mahadeva's Nandi, Devata Kartikeya, and your commander, Veidh, are already dead. It won't take long for Pitamah Balarama and my father to defeat Shri Ganesha as well. Thereafter, they would come here, and then we won't shy away from making this a three-on-or contest. I am giving you a chance now; kill me and aid Shri Ganesha."

Banasura turned furious at Aniruddha's words. He looked around the field and couldn't see Nandi and Kartikeya. He only saw the corpse of Viedh on the top of a pile of more dead men. Banasura clenched his teeth and howled. He rushed at Aniruddha and leaped to strike him down with the sword. Aniruddha quickly sidestepped. Banasura turned and made wild attempts to hit Aniruddha. However, Aniruddha ducked, moved right and left, and even somersaulted twice. He didn't attack back but only defended himself. He knew that Banasura could be turned angrier, and that would make him more irritated. So, Aniruddha kept on smiling and laughing while saving himself from every attack.

Banasura picked up another sword, and he used two swords to harass Aniruddha. Aniruddha responded by putting his sword in the sheath and picking up two shields. Putting them to good use, Aniruddha blocked blow after blow. Then, suddenly, with no predetermination, he threw one of the shields at Banasura. Although Banasura ducked, Aniruddha had expected it, and so he managed a flying kick on his skull. Banasura fell hard and screamed.

Banasura jumped back to his vertical base, but he was visibly tired, agitated, and imprecise. However, Banasura believed he could kill Aniruddha, as it was a matter of only one perfect move. Banasura restarted his offenses.

Aniruddha continued to move with agility and escaped some close shaves. Evading those close shaves, he realized that he had to make Banasura even more distressed. So he started damaging his psychology by telling him that he would lose.

"You should have accepted the proposal of giving up your rule and remaining under house arrest. Now you are going to die instead. Shortly my father and Pitamah Balarama would reach here," Aniruddha smirked.

Banasura charged at him with a spear, but Aniruddha picked up two longswords and obstructed the spear attacks.

"Changing weapons won't change your fate. You are already doomed, Maharaj." Aniruddha chuckled.

Banasura grunted and grumbled. His attacks turned less vigorous and slower. Yet, he continued his offenses.

***

Shiva had noticed the defeat of Kartikeya and Nandi and the death of Veidh. Also, fighting for almost three prahars, he understood that neither he could overpower Krishna nor Krishna could overcome him. He had made cuts on Krishna's right arm and right leg, but the wounds did not hamper Krishna much.

Both were frustrated with the lengthy combat and stood without moving or attacking.

Shiva scanned the whole battlefield, and he saw dead bodies everywhere. Corpses were piling in different places, forming mountains of the deceased. Wherever his eyesight went, he saw severed heads and limbs, eyes detached from faces, and bodies split in half. He also found the soil drenched in red, and at various spots, blood had accumulated as water accumulates in tiny pits after heavy rain.

The barbarity all around ached him, and he closed his eyes, sighing with melancholy.

Shiva did not express his emotions. Neither his facial expression nor his body language. Yet Krishna knew that Shiva, too, felt a heartache.

Shiva had no more interest in the fight or war. He merely strolled with small steps and closely watched the dead and gravely injured soldiers. He then turned to face Krishna, and Krishna could see Shiva's face turning angry. His face turned crimson quickly; his forehead frowned, his eyes opened wide, staring hard, and he pressed his lips tight together. His teeth were too clenched, and his head began to tremble.

The nature of the intrinsic energies that created Shiva was highly volatile. Those energies were the powers to facilitate the destruction of unnecessary powerful matters and potent debris created in the process of Universe creation. So, the characteristic of the energies inside Shiva was fickle. Hence, when Shiva turns distressed and heated, he cannot pacify himself. Further, his fury was unpredictable.

The destruction and deaths of the war had suddenly made Shiva lose hope in humanity and every other form of creation.

Shiva extended his right arm forward with an open fist. Next, he closed his eyes. Soon, from thin air, a shape formed, and his Trishul was in his grip. He opened his eyes after feeling the hold of the weapon and lifted it above the ground. He promptly pointed the Trishul towards the sky and waited.

Sparks crackled at the blades of the Trishul. Shortly, the Trishul head raged with blue fire. The flames were long and ferocious.

Krishna realized what Shiva was trying to do. "No, Mahadeva!" he exclaimed, "The weapon of mass destruction will do no good. Don't annihilate the whole planet. Please repress the *Mahapralayanshakti*!" Krishna's eyes widened as he found no reaction or response from Shiva. "Mahadeva, I beg you, please don't wipe out the creation. You will undo the evolution of tens of thousands of years. Please stop."

Shiva looked into Krishna's eyes. "Madhav, the mortal beings would never think of others. Kindness, compassion, and selflessness are not their traits. Now, I feel, even though

Banasura intends to create a better empire, he has no compassion. Nothing can be more important than saving innocent lives; not even the creation of a perfect realm." "I continued to support him, hoping that at some point in the war, he would understand that more than a perfect political economy, a safe and secured environment is more crucial." Shiva paused and looked once again all around him. "Let everything perish, O Avatar of Mahavishnu." As soon as he finished his statement, Shiva launched the Trishul in the air. Krishna screamed aloud, "NO!"

***

Everyone paused in their respective spots and looked at the blue electrifying Trishul soaring high in the air. Not just the soldiers, but even the Maharathis were shocked, and they froze with the fear of complete obliteration. Each man on the ground stared at the fiery Trishul, zooming at a tremendous pace, soaring higher and higher in the endless sky. They hoped and prayed that it would stop and retreat to Mahadeva. However, the Trishul that had turned scintillating blue hid in the clouds, and lightning flashed in the sky. With repeated flashes of lightning and the constant rumble of thunders, recurring blasts occurred in the sky.

With the terror of the Trishul overhead, the soldiers feared the destruction of the whole creation. No matter which side they owed their allegiance, the soldiers screamed and dropped their weapons. They went to their knees facing Mahadeva and pleaded with him to call back his Trishul, but remained unmoved.

From Aniruddha and Balarama to Ganesha and Banasura, every great warrior also went on their knees. They, too, begged Mahadeva to have some mercy. But, sadly, even they received no response. Even from the tents, Nandi and Kartikeya, and Usha rushed to the center of the ground. However, no matter who said whatever, Shiva paid no heed.

Ganesha walked near Shiva and stood in front of him. "Pitashree, please, I beg you to restrain yourself. Please calm down kindly, and let your anger subside. Even Mata Parvati would not want this devastation," he urged.

Kartikeya and Krishna stood by Ganesha's side and pleaded and reasoned as well. Everyone said different things, all that should have made Mahadeva stop. However, when Shiva loses his temper, there is nothing but destruction.

Shiva scanned every person around him, from his sons and Krishna to Banasura and the ordinary soldiers. He then spoke, looking at different individuals one by one. "Even if today, I suppress this weapon of mass destruction, the mortals and the Asuras would again soon cause another act of war or event of extinction. So let the planet that has no compassion and kindness meet its end today."

Krishna walked over to Shiva and looked into his red and unblinking wide eyes. Next, shocking everyone, Krishna placed his hands on Shiva's shoulders. "Mahadeva, where are your kindness and compassion? I believe, you too, must show your mercy and heart to the creation. How many innocents will die if you don't stop your Trishul? The various mammals, the flying birds, the different reptiles, and the men and women who have been living in your abode, the Shivghar, all would perish. They would die a terrible and brutal death for no mistake. Please recall your Trishul."

Shiva finally could calm down somewhat. His red eyes and puffed cheeks began to turn normal. He slowly lifted his chin and glanced overhead. His eyes widened again, but not with anger but shock. "I can't stop it now, Madhav; it's too late."

Krishna lifted his head and saw the Trishul diving down with thick, fiery blue flames and a roaring noise. Shiva was right; even he couldn't stop it now. The Trishul would only pacify itself when it hits something and causes an explosion.

Krishna glanced all around himself. He could see the frightened soldiers, his anxious family members, the trees and mountains afar, and the panicking birds noisily making flights downwards. He couldn't let everything turn into ashes. Creation was a massive, time-consuming process, and evolution was even more complicated. He was the Preserver, and it was time to act. He had to protect and preserve the creation.

Krishna closed his eyes and spread his arms far and wide. A cycling layer of milky white fog emerged over his head that quickly enveloped him. The foggy layer increased in height and did not stop growing. Instead, it continued developing taller and wider and touched the clouds. The Trishul was just some feet above the summit of the gigantic cylindrical smog when the mist started to clear itself.

A little later, the entire fog wiped itself out, and the sight on display stunned everyone. A colossal-sized Vishnu was standing, reaching from the earth to the clouds. He had four massive arms. One arm had a large conch while another held a titanic Chakra. The third hand gripped a gigantic mace, and the fourth hand held a lotus flower. And he opened his mouth, big and wide.

On the ground, everyone but Shiva and Balarama were shocked. Even Aniruddha and Pradyumana never knew that Krishna was the avatar of Mahavishnu. Usha looked at Aniruddha, and he shook his head in disbelief. Everyone attentively concentrated above.

The fiery Trishul seemed tiny in comparison to the mammoth Vishnu manifestation. It dropped into the open mouth of Vishnu, and that made a series of rapid explosions in the air. The flashes and sounds of the blasts were so damaging that nobody could continue gazing at them. Every mortal covered their faces and eyes with their hands and looked away.

Aniruddha slightly opened his eyes and saw that there was no Vishnu anymore. However, he instead witnessed midsize fragments and debris from the explosions scattering and flying down. "Run!" he screamed out. Others, too, then opened their eyes and saw the flaming fragments soaring down. Everyone ran and rushed. Aniruddha held Usha's hand, and they both tried to move away from harm's way. As they ran by Banasura's side, they saw him stationed immobile.

Banasura stood still where he was. He gazed at the sky with wide eyes, and tears ran down his cheeks. His face had no fear but guilt and remorse.

Aniruddha observed two fuming round blast fragments almost touching Banasura. He left Usha's hand. "You run and go; I need to save your father."

"No, Aniruddha, it's too dangerous. It is my responsibility," Usha replied and started to sprint. Aniruddha held her arm and pulled her towards him.

"Your responsibilities are mine as well. If you don't wish me dead, you won't go and allow me to save your father." Aniruddha left Usha with no choice.

He didn't wait any longer and raced like a cheetah at Banasura. Then, just the two balls of fire, each the size of a human skull were inches away from Banasura's face, Aniruddha leaped. His frame hit Banasura with high velocity, and they both rolled on the ground.

The two balls collided on the spot where Banasura was standing moments ago. There were two big blasts.

***

Things had calmed down steadily. The soldiers surrounded the important leaders and the two Gods. Soldiers from both sides stood together. In the center of the field stood Shiva, Ganesha, Nandi, and Kartikeya opposite Usha, Aniruddha, Pradyumana, Balarama, and Krishna. Banasura knelt in the space between the two lines of the great souls and Gods.

He wept and cried as he spoke with fumbles and broken words. "My Lord Vishnu, all my life, I had hated you. I believed that you deceived my father in the name of protecting the Universe. Yes, my father had done no wrong, but you sometimes have to act based on probability as you're the Preserver. Witnessing you gulping down a weapon of mass devastation, I now know you only desire to preserve the creation."

Krishna helped Banasura rise. He gripped Banasura's arms and spoke with a smile. "I have always acted in the role of a Protector. What happened to your father was a sad fate, but trust me, he has been living in peace and bliss in Vaikuntha. He was pleased with how you had formed an empire and ruled it with great principles and philosophies." "Your flaw was believing that any route taken to achieve a goal of some greater good is righteous. I don't remember you attempting to propagate and spread your views and beliefs through peaceful and procedural ways. Before taking up violence and aggressive steps like using the Band and this war, you should have tried better and cleaner methods."

Banasura nodded with regret evident in his eyes. "I misunderstood and misinterpreted things, my Lord."

"I know. You must have thought about Kurukshetra and felt that even the Pandavas and I encouraged war to usher in a better era. However, you never pondered how much we had tried to avoid the conflict! The Pandavas had challenged the Kauravas for duels, but the Kauravas denied it repeatedly. The

Pandavas were also ready to forgive the insult and humiliation of Draupadi, but the Kauravas declined to express regret and seek forgiveness. I even asked for only five villages for the Pandavas to rule, as they were the better and rightful rulers. But Duryodhana again declined. After such constant efforts, we finally had to wage war when we realized that the Kauravas would neither act righteously nor rule generously," Krishna further enlightened Banasura.

"I accept all my mistakes, Bhagwan. I am also ready for any punishment that you see fit. And I also seek forgiveness from my daughter and son-in-law," Banasura spoke in between his sobs. "Dear Usha, I have been the worst father, but will you be the best child and forgive my misdoings?"

Usha held Banasura's conjoined palms and pulled them gently apart. "Pita, you don't need to seek my forgiveness. Let bygones be bygones. All I crave is your and mother's genuine blessings for my marital life." She smiled amidst her sniffles and tears.

Aniruddha, too, came forward. "Pita, even I want nothing but your love and blessings. I would never remember what had happened between us thus far. I'd only consider and remember the relationship that we share from today onwards."

Banasura embraced Aniruddha with a broad smile on his face. Everyone else smiled too. The soldiers in both armies cheered and clapped. They also chanted the names of Vishnu and Shiva in unison. The whole battleground echoed with cheerful claps and the names of the two Gods.

Shiva placed a hand on Krishna's shoulder. "I am sorry, Avatar of Vishnu. My temper forced you to reveal your true self. You had vowed never to reveal your real identity while you lived on earth, yet you did it to save the creation. You are indeed great and the one true Protector."

Krishna smiled. "Breaking one's vows for the greater good supersedes my vow. And I was against making my real identity public because I wanted to protect my family and keep them away from turning egoistic and arrogant. But now that I had to manifest my proper form, I left my family's future to their fates. If they continue to believe in my teachings and principles, they'd only turn more pious. And if they gradually forget what I stand for, they will meet their end."

"Dear Madhav, even though you are an Avatar, but you are still a mortal. And even you were always susceptible to getting carried away with worldly pleasures and concepts. Your mindset could have turned corrupt had you not been so virtuous and honorable. Time will end, and people may even forget the names of Vishnu and Shiva, but the deeds and thoughts of Krishna will stay on. So, even when the creation ends, your positive aura will remain somewhere safe in the space."

Shiva and Krishna shared an elongated embrace. The Hari-Hara war was over.

***

TWO DECADES LATER

After the Hari-Hara war, peace and prosperity returned to Aryavrata. A few more kingdoms followed a socialist economy and developed and progressed further. The capitalist states, too, ensured even more inclusive growth and free and fair competition. Usha and Aniruddha were married, and they had a son named Vajra. The kings of Aryavrata forgave Banasura at Shiva's behest. Banasura's Pragjyotishpura also became a part of Aryavrata.

Amidst all the positives, there was one significant negative consequence of the Hari-Hara war. Krishna's fear of his family turning wicked came true. The Yadava clan had turned proud and rowdy. They stopped listening to Krishna and his wisdom as Krishna grew older. They gradually turned atrocious, beaming with pride that they were the scions of Vishnu. It was not long before they even had inner conflicts. The conflicts ended when all the Yadavas perished in a drunken brawl. Everyone was dead, and only Vajra survived. Aniruddha, too, was killed as he tried to contain the violence. The dying Aniruddha sought a promise from his son that he would help ensure that good times continued in the empire. Vajra made the promise to his father.

While the brawl went on at one place, Krishna met his death at another site. Dejected and sad that most of his sons, grandsons, and great-grandsons had turned corrupt, he was spending time in solitude in the jungles. One day, as he was lying beneath a tree and resting, a hunter shot at his leg, mistaking it to be some animal. The poisonous dart penetrated Krishna.

As Krishna's eyes closed and it was time for the Avatar to leave the planet and emerge in the Mahavishnu form, he recalled his entire life as the eighth incarnation of Vishnu.

Acknowledgements

Writing a book is a beautiful journey when you find warm and kind people on the way. So, I take this opportunity to express my gratitude to some of the most amazing people I have met in the process of writing and publishing this book.

My mother, Rupa Borah, has been my biggest source of strength, lifting me up on my worst days, picking me up whenever I have been down. She has passed progressive ideologies to me, and a value system I trust will always be my guiding light.

My father, Jaganath Pokhrel, has taught me invaluable lessons about expressing emotions and the true characteristics of being a man. His teachings have shaped my understanding of kindness and sensitivity.

My younger brother, Aadar Atreya, kept his faith in me when I had none of it. I take pride in a brother like you!

Thank you, Suhail Mathur (of The Book Bakers), my amazing literary agent, for finding a wonderful publisher for this book. In you, I found a guide, a friend, and a creative partner. You always put your authors ahead, and your work ethics are inspiring. To countless projects together, brother! Much love to a wonderful individual. Also, a special mention to The Book Bakers team for the wonderful cover design!

Thank you, Shantanu-da (editor-in-chief, Om Books), for showing your immense faith and support in this book. I consider myself fortunate to have your association, and no word can express how grateful I am for being extremely accommodating with my requests.

Thank you, Rhea (editor, Om Books), for being an amazing editor, and making the entire editing process so easy for me. I cherish our creative collaboration.

Thank you, to the entire team of Om Books, led by Ajay Mago and Sanjay Mago. Your faith in this book brought a dream alive! Will be always grateful.

Thank you, Bhargab Jyoti Sahariah (Dean of Studies, Nemcare Group of Institutions). Bhargab-da, you have constantly inspired and supported my writing journey. Right from my debut novel, your help in my life and writing journey has kept me strong. Your life values urge me to be a better person, and I have learned what true kindness looks like. Seeking your blessings, brother!

Thank you, Khanjan Kalita (Category Manager – Books, April Moon Pvt. Ltd. by Adani). Khanjan-da, I cannot thank you enough for sharing your insights on the nuances of book promotions and always being only a call away. You are generous, dada. A big hug!

Thank you, Jyoti Khataniar (leading art critic and writer from Assam). Jyoti-da, thank you for mentoring and helping me engage with countless booklovers. I will always remember those fun days spent together and your life insights. Seeking your blessings!

Thank you, Aruni Kashyap (eminent Indian author). Aruni-da, how fortunate I am to have you in my life! Your timely suggestions on writing and life have been constant since I started writing this book. It is wonderful to have you like an elder brother. You are kind and lovely.

Also, I am immensely grateful for the teachings of Shri Krishna, the Bhagawad Gita, and my family—the family I wish to have in all my rebirths!

How to Get a Book Deal from Major Publishers in India?

Featuring:

Shantanu Ray Chaudhari,
Editor-in-chief, Om Books International

Suhail Mathur,
Literary Agent and Founder,
The Book Bakers

Antar Atreya,
Author of *The Clash of Hari Hara*

You can visit the Instagram bio of @authorantaratreya to get free access to the video.